THE BOND

or

LAST MAN STANDING

All the best
Nick Corble

Nick Corble

THE BOND or LAST MAN STANDING
By Nick Corble
© Nick Corble 2018
Published by The Independent Publishing Network
ISBN: 978-1-78926-800-3
Published in Great Britain 2018
Cover by More Visual Ltd
Printed and bound at TJ International, Padstow.

The moral right of the author has been asserted.
The author can be contacted by
email: nick@nickcorble.co.uk

*Thanks to Mike, who unwittingly
gave me the idea, many suppers ago.*

CONTENTS

There's noise, smoke, confusion, and more than a smattering of panic in the raised voices; a sense of having stepped from a highly-organized world into one ruled by anarchy.

Even our bodies are rebelling. Some have spewed their guts up and, judging by the stink, more than one has gone a step further. Our ears have been numbed by the explosion and, through a watery shield of tears, our eyes are telling us we're in some kind of cloud, even though we're certain we never even took off. Nothing makes sense. A robotic voice is telling us to leave, telling us over and over again to follow the floor lights to the nearest exit. But our limbs aren't ready to obey orders – there's little room for reason while we're still processing the unreasonable.

As the initial shock subsides, along with the smoke now gathering and condensing on the ceiling, a deep primeval instinct for self-preservation kicks in. We look around and it hits us: we've survived. We're still standing, or at least we will be once we can find the buckles for our seatbelts.

You see these things on TV, but they're not real, are they? If it's a particularly visceral drama, or even news footage of something that's actually happened, it's still TV. Abstract, removed; not real in the sense of life experienced day-to-day with smells, sensation, movement, adrenaline and fear. It's flat, two-dimensional; something involving other people.

In a nanosecond of spectacular violence we have become international news, everyone's property. We'd always seen ourselves as somehow special, different from the crowd, but not like this. Our uniqueness was something only we were conscious of – a special bond, a shared secret; not something to be pored over, analysed and judged by others as they prepare for one last flick through the channels before going to bed.

Maybe when we're ready to look back we'll see this moment as the logical culmination of a spiralling cycle. Perhaps things had been building up to this for years, but who can say why anything happens? If this hadn't happened, if these words hadn't been said, if this person hadn't bumped into that person … It's a thought, but one for another day.

And human nature dictates we will look back some day to try to trace the root causes of this current mayhem, to rationalize it; and when we finally do we'll start with school, where it all began.

The Best Years of
Their Lives

1970

First day at big school. It's a beginning, but also an ending.

Having spent so long being passed gently from one teacher to the next, each year applying another protective layer, you suddenly realize it's all going to be snatched away from you before you get the chance to enjoy it. One short year of top form, of being milk and dinner monitors and the best at sports day, before it hits you: this was just the warm-up. You've scrambled to the top of the board only to land on a snake – from square ninety-nine to square one in the blink of an eye.

But first, there's a summer of uncertainty to be got through. It starts in blissful sunlit ignorance, but clouds of doubt soon gather. Will everything be all right? Will the teachers be kind? What will the school bus be like? How much homework will there be? Summer's freedom is slowly consumed by fear.

Then the subtle changes begin. The bike that's previously been your passport to independence is cruelly snatched away and placed out of reach on a cobwebbed rack in the dark recesses of the garage. Allowed to rest at last, its tyres exhale, exhausted. The pustular multi-coloured bricks of the giant Lego towers, laboured over for hours on the few wet days that punctuated the summer, are broken up and stored away in old shoeboxes. You think this is only temporary, until Christmas maybe; but the real sadness is, you have no idea how naïve this supposition is.

Your short-sleeved shirts, the ones with plastic pictures of one or other of the Tracy brothers from *Thunderbirds* on the pocket, are washed, ironed and folded. Too late, you realize your mother's suggestion that the nice man at Oxfam knows a little boy in Africa who might get better use out of them was a statement of fact; not the floating of a possibility.

Then there's that moment when it clicks what the half-forgotten hours spent with a stranger learning clever answers to questions, and the subsequent uncomfortable half hour spent in the headmaster's office with another stranger, answering different versions of those questions, were all about. It was that which has led to this.

1

In the days and weeks before the big day, parents, aunts, neighbours and even casual acquaintances at the sweet shop put on *that* smile and try to paint a picture of some rosy, soft-focus idyll to convince you there's nothing to worry about. These constant attempts at reassurance have the contrary effect, summoning up visions more Flashman than Jennings.

The truth they're all trying to protect you from is that the years ahead will be less like some dreamy amble through a world of catapults and tuck, and more like a seven-year long-distance race. The starting gun will bring about a chaotic scramble as each contestant finds their stride. As the pack begins to stretch out, some will learn to pace themselves around the oval path, while others will peak too soon. Each year, the pattern will be repeated, although one lane further out. The distance will be further and harder, now with hurdles in the way of exams for added interest towards the end of the lap. The whole process will build an unstoppable momentum until everyone finds themselves flung out into the real world through centrifugal forces beyond their control.

Some will execute the perfect lane change every year. Others, in defiance of their good intentions, will always stumble clumsily before regaining their composure, leaving themselves the impossible challenge of catching the front runners who, rather irritatingly, always seem to be the same people. Few manage the whole process without at least one tumble on to the harsh, unforgiving surface beneath; moments which act as rites of passage, providing scars they will unwittingly carry with them for the rest of their lives.

First day at big school, the last day of innocence.

---------------------------- ✳ ----------------------------

Too soon, the day itself arrived; and for Sam Davidson – Samuel to his family – it began with that rare treat, a cooked breakfast prepared by his mother, although he hadn't really got the appetite for it. Not only was he alive with nerves, but his mother had tightened the knot in his tie so high he could barely breathe. It felt like a noose. At the other extremity, brown open-toed sandals had been exchanged for brand new shiny black tie-ups, polished to a point where, in a low sun, the glare they gave off represented a hazard to motorists. In the first of two contributions to the morning's events, Sam's dad had tied the laces to within an inch of their straining life, as if even his son's toes, so free and unchallenged all summer, now had to be corralled. His second contribution had been to take a picture of this strange new person standing nonplussed in the driveway, packaged up in his brand new uniform which smelt of new and was, despite the name of the school, light grey in colour, with red piping around the sleeves and along the jacket collar.

For Sam, the challenges presented by the first day at big school had been compounded by the fact he was entirely alone. His family's sudden upheaval meant he hadn't even had to share the others' experience of the dreaded entrance exam, hence the interview. As such, there'd been no half-familiar faces to share his discomfort with, no friends from junior school to cluster around, and no big brother or cousin to keep an eye out for him. In the absence of an anchor, or even a rudder, he'd taken refuge in the sheer homogeneity of the group of eighty or so new boys he found himself among; another single dark spot in a harmless sea of moving frogspawn.

To a boy they clutched a dun-coloured satchel, shiny with a faint whiff of leather, with bright brass buckles holding down a flap. The satchels themselves were empty, except for a pencil case nestling against a Helix Universal maths set comprising a pair of compasses and a brittle plastic trio of ruler, protractor and set square, all of which would need constant replacing (although none of the boys had known that at the time). Otherwise, like the boys clutching them so fiercely, the satchels were hollow vessels waiting to be filled with knowledge.

Sporting brand new haircuts, from above the boys bore a passing resemblance to a flock of recently shorn sheep destined for the abattoir. As they were herded towards the gymnasium, the unlucky minority on the periphery found themselves uncomfortably close to the lines of older boys perched on top of the bright red-brick walls channelling them towards their destination. These other-worldly creatures lined the route towards the newly completed sports hall: the result of a generous benefaction from a recently knighted old boy, his name discreetly acknowledged on a shiny new plaque next to the door.

An undulating, rumbling chorus from the sidelines accompanied the boys on their way: the constant repetition of a single word, 'newbug', muttered in a *basso profondo* the fresh intake could only aspire to. The shrewder among their number kept their eyes fixed to the ground, unwilling to catch the eye of a single one of their tormentors for fear of some unknown retribution.

Should they have dared to look up, the sight greeting them would have seemed improbable: a collection of freaks from the circus, with long dangling arms and unconscionable amounts of hair, some so tall they'd probably qualify to play for the Harlem Globetrotters. Like the crowds at the wrestling on *World of Sport*, they booed and yelled as the mood took them, enjoying the entertainment; their behaviour unchecked by teachers watching over the whole scene with a weary, disinterested air.

Despite the veneer of anonymity offered by the crowd, Sam suspected he still stood out, as if some kind of giant arrow visible to all but him was bobbing up and down above his head, probably with sequenced neon lights dancing around its edges. There was no particular reason why this might be the case. Average height, average build, with cropped black hair, his main distinguishing feature was probably the arbitrary collection of light brown freckles over his nose and the upper part of each cheek, but these remained hidden by his bowed head; which was more than could be said for the white band of untanned skin on the back of his neck, exposed by the clippers only a couple of days before.

The chequerboard of paving slabs, which until then had dominated each of the boys' view, mutated without warning into a slippery wooden floor, a new potential hazard for unbroken-in shoes, accompanied by a fresh smell to mingle with that of fear. Except it wasn't that fresh. Despite being brand new, the sports hall somehow managed to exude an odour of raw testosterone masquerading as accumulated sweat. There'd been speculation among the senior staff that the floor and walls had been sprayed with a specially formulated perfume before the building was handed over; a stopgap, perhaps, before an accretion of the smells of liniment, dirty kit and jockstraps could ingrain itself into the woodwork.

Despite the uniforms' intended effect of erasing any hint of individuality, once the seemingly condemned had been corralled it became possible to make out differences among them. A tall boy in front of Sam seemed to have somehow successfully avoided the barber, his hair dangerously close to the white collar of his new shirt in contravention of the letter sent out to all new parents beforehand. To his right, a squat and barrel-like boy looked like he could have blended in with the crowd outside without too much trouble, hints of dark strands already decorating his top lip. There was the usual collection of fat and thin and physical distortions, like the boy Sam had spotted earlier in the playground with laughably big ears: a rare moment of amusement during the tough, lonely opening minutes. Some stood erect, awaiting instructions as if used to obeying orders from on high, while others looked like they were about to soil themselves. An objective assessment would conclude that the assembled boys offered a fairly even cross section of white Anglo-Saxon middle-class apples of their mothers' eyes, although Sam had spotted one Chinese and a lone Asian boy. He was glad his own racial distinction was less visible.

The new boys were shadowed by their shepherds, the sixth-formers, the alpha males of the taunting pack, who on entering the hall proceeded to line up with the efficiency of riot police, as if to erase any lingering considerations of escape among their charges, their backs rested against the impressively shiny climbing bars lining the two long walls of the hall. Once inside, the mumbled chorus outside became more muted, while remaining menacing, as it echoed around the wood-lined box of the gym. Meanwhile, the yet-to-be-scuffed soles of the new boys' shoes, as shiny as fresh conkers, shuffled on the polished floor, inching their way towards the end wall: prisoners awaiting their fate. Long, tightly braided ropes hanging from the high ceiling swayed in an insubstantial breeze from outside, offering the possibility of a summary hanging for any potential rebel.

Sam's own feelings of dread, meanwhile, deepened. The fear of being picked out by the grotesques either side of him had suddenly been multiplied by the realization that one of the three pens in his inside jacket pocket, one black, one blue and one red, had begun to leak. A quick glance down had confirmed it as the red one, a blood-like stain spreading out from his heart on to his brand new shirt, as if he'd taken a .38 to the chest. His biggest fear at that point was not so much the inevitable trouble this was going to mean from his mother: although bad enough, that had lain in a future which at that moment had seemed only a possibility. It hadn't even been the thought of having to get through the rest of the day with an attention-demanding streak across his brand new, previously paper-white shirt. No, surmounting both of these had been the fear that his predicament would brand him with a nickname.

Sam knew all about nicknames from his dad, who was known by his old school friends as Stumpy. As his father wasn't a short man and had no obvious liking for cricket, Sam was pretty sure his nickname had been conferred in the communal showers at school: a direct result of the small operation his religion had decreed necessary when he was still an infant, an operation Sam had also been subjected to. As a result, Sam had a justified fear of nicknames and their capacity to reduce an entire personality into a single attribute or a one-off incident. Beyond simply surviving, his biggest ambition when setting out that morning had been to avoid acquiring such a mark of Cain.

While these disturbing thoughts whirled around Sam's head, the new boys had formed a pair of orderly queues: one for boys whose surname began with letters from A to K, and another for L to Z. The head of each queue was presided over by a black-robed master looking like a tired crow, whose job it was to issue bundles of papers from the table next to him and allocate classes, before summoning up the next available sixth-former to escort each new boy to the appropriate room.

As Sam crept ever closer to the table he inched his satchel round, hoping the strap would hide some of the stain spreading inexorably across his chest.

On reaching the front of the line, Sam squeaked his name, but the master in front of him barely looked up before handing him a pack consisting of a term timetable, a house tie and a hymnal, along with a laminated copy of the school prayer. Somehow it hadn't seemed the moment to point out that he wouldn't be needing the latter two items.

'One P,' the master announced, and realizing just in time that this wasn't a demand for a urine sample or one of the new decimal coins, but rather the name of his new class, Sam turned to go. The first stumbling block had been successfully cleared, but it was only a momentary relief. A sonorous baritone had risen above the general murmur hovering around the hall, proclaiming the moment Sam had been dreading.

'Oi, Inky, follow me.'

The voice belonged to a big brute of a man, at least six feet tall, who it seemed barely credible to think was only seventeen – a mere six years older than himself. The voice's owner was pointing a finger in Sam's direction. Mutton-chop sideburns hung down the sides of his face as if he was a yet-to-be-designated new breed of dog. His hairstyle was probably best described as late Summer of Love, falling from his head to mingle with a mass of dark curly matter struggling to escape from within via his collar, providing a human Elizabethan ruff. He also had the air of someone who'd been hanging back, waiting for his chance, and the remaining sixth-formers parted like the Red Sea to allow him through.

Inky. It could have been worse, Sam considered, as he grew ever more aware of the sticky dampness spreading across his chest. Almost bookish; intellectual, even – he liked writing: stories, adventures, diaries.

As he made his way towards his temporary guardian, Sam's hopes of passing through the day unscathed suddenly stalled as he arrived alongside the bestower of his nickname at exactly the same time as the thin Indian boy he'd noticed earlier, most of whose coal-black hair was hidden in a perfectly tied, and undeniably neat, dark grey turban. Sam noted that he, too, was carrying a presumably superfluous copy of the hymnal and school prayer.

For a brief moment the senior boy looked confused to have two of the newly arrived minnows at his feet, unsure whether the situation represented a problem or an opportunity. A quiet smile grew across his face while he looked each boy up and down, as if he couldn't believe his luck. After a brief study of the papers both were carrying, his smile broadened even further.

'Well, well ... it looks like you're going to the same place. I'll take both of you, then. That's you, Inky,' he offered, although Sam couldn't help noticing the finger was pointing at his new companion, 'and your mate here.'

A slight pause, no more than a second in reality, but a lifetime in anticipation, and then it had come: the finger now directed clearly at Sam's chest.

'Period.'

And so, Sam's nickname had been born.

1971–75

Being branded with a label hadn't fazed Mushtaq Dhillon. He'd got used to being called all sorts of names which, in his experience, tended to fall into one of three broad camps. The first of these didn't really fall into the category of nicknames, being more just simple racism, while the other two drew upon his surname. One variant was based on the guitar-playing hippy rabbit in *The Magic Roundabout*, and the other, the original guitar-playing hippy, Bob Dylan, which in turn provided a bottomless pit of jokes based on *Blowin' in the Wind*.

What Mushtaq had been less used to was having a friend, a mucker, a soulmate. As an only child, he'd had to learn to cope on his own, and over time had developed a spectrum of strategies to get himself through life. Although he was sure his mum and dad loved him and was equally certain they were inordinately proud of his achievements, it was probably fair to say that they were also slightly in awe of him. It was almost as if he was from a slightly different sub-species, or at the very least there'd been an unlikely mistake at the maternity hospital. Mushtaq was what was known by educationalists as 'gifted', which meant he was very bright but they couldn't readily explain it, as if he had gained his intelligence as a result of some rogue gene.

A cold consideration of his parents reinforced this theory. Parminder, his dad, had somehow found his way into the country towards the end of the war, and had worked as a hospital porter. On one of his rare visits to Britain, Mushtaq's *baba*, his grandpa, had once confided to him that even as a boy it had been clear his son was never going to amount to anything. He never tired of telling the story of how Parminder had fallen asleep in some cargo nets on the docks in Bombay in '44, when he was only fifteen, and been swept up and dumped in the hold of a tramp steamer bound for Southampton. Oddly, in all the times he'd told the tale, Mushtaq's *baba* had never seemed that bothered at losing one of his eight children.

Falling asleep, it turned out, was Parminder's greatest skill – time and place no barrier – although on this particular occasion it had served him well, as his voyage west to the land of rain and chips had begun two days before a massive explosion in the docks, which ended up killing hundreds of people. Parminder had always referred to this as the second greatest slice of good fortune he'd ever had – the greatest being finding his wife – and on this he wasn't far wrong.

Mushtaq's mum, Mandira, had met her husband when she tripped over him taking a nap in the stairwell of the building where she lived with her parents. After a lethargic courtship, they finally married six years later, and after a further pause Mushtaq eventually appeared, the first and last young Dhillon to emerge from this pairing. When he started to go to school, Mandira turned to supplementing the meagre family income by cleaning other people's houses as well as her own.

Mushtaq's parents seemed to rub along okay, although his mum did have a fine line in cutting remarks, especially when it came to her husband's mild narcolepsy, often remarking that the only reason her husband liked being a hospital porter was because it allowed constant access to a convenient bed. Money had always been tight in the Dhillon household, so it was a good job that towards the end of primary school Mushtaq won a free place to the academically demanding, or stuck-up, depending on your standpoint, Red Coat School in the heart of the town.

Once there, Mushtaq had at first found it difficult to comprehend, let alone accommodate, the obvious longing Sam Davidson had displayed to befriend him. Sam seemed to feel as if some kind of common kinship had been forged between them on their first day, but to Mushtaq the whole episode had been about as memorable as the Etch A Sketch his aunt Sunita had given him for his tenth birthday.

Mushtaq's pragmatism enabled him to see the advantages in having a close friend, however, and before long he and Sam, Inky and Period, had become a sort of adolescent Cannon and Ball, but with even fewer laughs, determinedly progressing their way through school almost back to back, protecting each other from every angle. By the third form, Mushtaq, ever wiry and with strong angular cheekbones and bushy eyebrows, had cultivated the black down on his upper lip into something more discernible, if not yet quite shaveable. Meanwhile,

Sam had bulked out considerably; a combination of incipient puberty and surreptitious sessions on the Bullworker his father had bought but only used once. Together, they became the classic brains and brawn, chalk and cheese self-sufficient organism.

As time went on, the fact that Sam and Mushtaq's relationship was important to them and did no harm to others didn't seem to satisfy the unseen hand of 'the system', and efforts were made to prise them apart. Their comradeship being nurtured in an all-boys school, inferences had inevitably been drawn and given dubious currency through pregnant phrases left hanging in the air, typically employing words such as 'unfortunate' and 'unnatural', whenever the boys became the subject of gossip in the staff room; the added dimension of an inter-racial element providing an additional word to describe the situation: 'unthinkable'.

By the fourth form, the Colditz-inspired strategy of keeping the two oddballs in the same place so they could be watched more easily was ditched, to be replaced by one of separating them whenever possible 'for their own good'. It had helped that Mushtaq's far greater academic ability sent him into the faster academic streams, leaving Sam to paddle around the slower tributaries; and that Mushtaq was pushed towards the sciences on the assumption, never actually tested, that he wanted to become a doctor. As such, while for Mushtaq, a Van de Graaff generator became synonymous with static electricity, for Sam they remained simply a rock band.

As the academic race shifted lanes once again, this separation was maintained by the masters dividing, and their shock troops, the prefects, conquering the pair through a combination of lunchtime clubs (Mushtaq) and detentions (Sam). Despite these efforts, there was one absolute given at the Red Coat that couldn't be avoided; the trump card that beat any other imperative, however important – even sport. This was the khaki-coloured shadow that hung over the fifth form: the Combined Cadet Force, known by its initials, even if the C, C and F stood for something different among the boys.

The CCF was, by design, a leveller; a place where academic brilliance was not only irrelevant, but positively disdained. The good thing about the CCF was that it was voluntary for those that wanted to do it. The bad thing about the CCF was that it was compulsory for those that didn't. And so, along with nearly everyone else (some oddballs opted for Navy and Air Cadet sections), Sam and Mushtaq had found themselves getting changed every Wednesday lunchtime, pulling itchy dark-green jumpers over crisply starched olive-green shirts, and squeezing their feet into ridiculously dubbined boots to march out on to the unforgiving asphalt of the upper yard. Sam and Mushtaq's friendship, never dead, but by then in intensive care, was revived in the face of a common enemy.

They were to become intimate with the black tarred stones of the playground over the coming months, with their feet, but also disconcertingly often with their noses, as the sergeant major, who was also the school's bursar, took delight in finding any fault he could with their uniform, marching style or simply all-round general attitude, regularly imposing sets of press-ups to 'give them something to think about'. He, too, it seemed, was in on the general conspiracy to keep Sam and Mushtaq in their box.

By some unwritten rule, the year's best sportsmen were made lance corporals, an insignificant rank but just enough to give them power over their peers. One in particular stood out: Ray Meadows. Captain of the Colts XV, Meadows was talked about in some circles as a prospective head boy, regardless of the fact he was endowed with the intelligence of the average stick insect. Ray Meadows's biggest advantage was that he possessed hormones that had switched on to fast track at age eleven and had forgotten how to switch back to normal once puberty was over, bringing him into the realms of extra large when most of his peer group were still stuck in medium. His sheer bulk seemed to accord him a sense of presence he took for granted, but which was undoubtedly intimidating for others. His arrival into a room, or on to a sports field, filled some with fear, others with awe. He knew no other way of interacting with the world, caring very little about any impression he left on others, simply because it didn't matter to him.

Endowed with a head slightly too large for his stock square torso, which in turn seemed just too big for his dumpy legs, Ray looked like he'd been drawn in crayon by a five-year-old: all simple lines and bad proportion. Nevertheless, Ray gloried in his bulk, which he saw as his equalizer against other peoples' brains. His short-cut ginger mop was fronted with a St Bernard's fringe that came down over a pair of sunken eyes, the sockets of which cast a permanent shadow, making him look as if he was wearing mascara – not that anyone ever dared to suggest this to him.

Whether there'd ever been any formal discussion about it in the corridors of power was impossible to say, but Ray Meadows swiftly took it upon himself to pay particular attention to Sam and Mushtaq's friendship, almost as if he was the army's, and by proxy the school's, official attack dog. His techniques were crude but effective, and ranged from humiliation through to unreconstructed bullying without the need to taint either with subtlety at any point, even if he had known the meaning, or indeed the spelling, of the word. Orders, which to others would simply be barked out, were yelled into their faces with a mix of decibels and spit, and if there were any particularly nasty tasks to be done – preferably in rain or wind, or ideally in hail or snow – then the pool of possible candidates to do them never really grew beyond two.

The culmination – or highlight, depending on your perspective – of the first two terms of CCF was a week-long exercise at a real-life army barracks in Catterick, Yorkshire; a county known to most only through cricket. As such the razor-sharp qualities of the Yorkshire wind and nose-numbing cold of the March air was, for most, beyond all previous experience. The barracks seemed to be designed to let the wind and the weather through deliberately, while the food, although filling, proved to be equally efficient in passing through in its own way.

Six days of hell were but preparation for the promise of absolute bloody purgatory during the final twenty-four hours; a period when it was promised that sleep would become a distant memory. The object of the exercise was unclear, but that was normal for the army. It started after supper on the final day with an overnight hike carrying a full pack across the moors, punctuated with spells of 'at the double'. As dawn broke over the still-dormant heather, and after a brief stop for a sludge-derived breakfast, the ranks were broken into teams with the brief to create makeshift bridges to carry each member over a stream. A series of similar exercises followed of varying degrees of complexity, the only saving grace of which was that the completion of each brought them that bit closer to the going down of the sun and the opportunity to reassess the comfort offered by their camp beds in the barracks.

Discipline and momentum were maintained through regular use of the threat of the 'tin bath' for anyone deemed to be slacking, an object of fear whose presence had been hinted at all week but whose actual details remained unknown. Given the empty hours of marching, this inevitably led to speculation; a favourite view being that it was code and had, for some unknown reason, originally been given its name by a Cockney, a group for whom rhyming was less an affectation than an affliction.

'Scarf?' one of the boys, not quite men, Terry Mungus – known affectionately as Hugh due to his surname and his size – had suggested. 'You get tied up with a scarf, out on the perimeter fence perhaps?' Although admitted as a possibility, the general consensus had been that this didn't quite seem the army's style. Brownies, maybe, but army, no.

Another of their clan, Jeff Stone, the boy whose extraordinary ears had provided light relief on their first day all those years ago, piped up: 'Hearth?' Half a dozen weary faces turned towards him. 'You know, you get toasted in front of a fire, like in *Tom Brown's Schooldays*.' While the idea of a fire had been welcome, this hadn't seemed plausible either.

'Path?' Andy Thompson suggested, his mind still reeling with different possibilities, although none of them matched Toby Connor's contribution, when he suggested 'Giraffe?' When challenged with quizzical looks, Toby clarified by twisting his neck to one side and sticking his tongue out of the side of his mouth to general amusement, after which discussion was replaced by the sound of several pairs of heavy army boots squelching rhythmically in the soft Yorkshire turf.

In the end it remained a mystery, so every time sheer fatigue caused someone to fall out of step, or a flailing rope flying across a stream failed to be caught, and the question 'Do you want the tin bath?' had echoed shrilly across the training ground, it was followed by a swift and automatic 'Sir. No, sir!' as some kind of reflex action.

For many of the group, this was to be a seminal week. Ties and friendships forged over the previous four-plus years were crystallizing and finding an expression against the common enemy of authority. Maybe it was during this week that some of the seeds for the tragedies that followed were sown, although perhaps a stronger case could be made for events later in the year. More likely, it was a process over time rather than a specific moment.

As for the tin bath, when the truth was finally revealed it became clear that the cadets had made a rookie's error of assuming the army 'did' complex. It transpired a tin bath was … just that, although with a twist. The promised treat involved having your bed, a piece of furniture many had begun to hallucinate about as the day wore on, replaced by a tin bath full of ice-cold water.

The day that had seemed as if it would never end concluded, as it had begun, after supper and in the dark. Finally dismissed, the different troops wearily trudged their way back to their barracks, but when the first one through the door flicked the brown Bakelite switch just inside the wall, nothing happened.

'Light's not working, lance corporal, sir!', the desperately tired lead boy sighed, half in desperation, half in disbelief.

'Shut up, you effin' pansy,' came the riposte from Meadows, as he stormed past on his way to his own section at the end of the hut, shielded from the rest of the beds by a makeshift curtain, put there as a sign of his greater status and to disguise the fact that, unlike the others, he actually had a mattress. 'You know where your beds are by now, don't you? Just effin' get on with it!'

Silence descended as the boys, by then exhausted remnants of their former selves, got undressed and waited for the nightly ritual of Meadows yodelling as he jumped on to his bed and tested its inadequate springs to the limit – his way of signalling the formal end of the day, and at the same time making others aware of his superior resting place.

Everyone in the room had heard him unbuckle his belt and the familiar clank it made as it fell to the floor. They also heard the gentler rustle of his trousers collapsing as they joined the belt on the floor. An intake of breath from behind the curtain acted as a prelude to a short run-up and the by-now-familiar silence before the yell and the leap.

This occasion was different, though. Rather than the sound of complaining coil springs, the unmistakable noise made by a large human being entering a metal bath full of liquid was heard; first, a deep plunging sound like a divebomb, followed by the sound of a wave rising from the deep, and, finally, frantic splashing, all stitched together into a brief couple of seconds. All other sound ceased immediately after, as everyone tried to comprehend what it was they'd just heard. After the briefest of delicious pauses, a roar filled the small hut, echoing off the wooden walls and filling the space. Miraculously, the light came back on just at the point when Meadows, grappling with anything he could reach, tore down the curtain separating him from his charges, and revealed himself in all his glory.

Not just wet, but covered in a thick black ink; not your run-of-the-mill Quink blue/black, but something with an almost bituminous quality; a printer's ink, probably, that didn't drip so much as coagulate, falling reluctantly from his body and leaving deep dark stains on the concrete floor beneath.

He'd become a creature from a horror film, his eyes bright pools of white among a swamp of black, the ink clinging to his hairy chest and arms, covering every inch of his flesh. Despite this, it was still possible to make out absolute astonishment and bewilderment on his face. Although everyone in the room knew there'd be an inquest-cum-inquisition, at that instant it sat in a remote future. Just for that moment it was worth paying any price, sustaining any punishment the army could dream up, just to have been there to witness it.

1975 – SUMMER

It was the hottest summer anyone could remember. A summer when every day, the simple act of throwing back the curtains was rewarded with skies so blue you wanted to dive into them. To those with time on their hands it seemed as if Mother Nature had tired of clouds and decided to do without them. Weather forecasters kept a watchful eye out for their P45s, and local water boards began to polish up their standpipes. Portable transistor radios across the country were broadcasting the news that Typically Tropical were looking forward to going to Barbados, adding their intention to swim in the sunny Caribbean Sea; but to most of the fifth form of the Red Coat School, landlocked in the middle of England, it felt as if they were already there.

Perhaps inevitably, Red Coat pupils were known as 'Billy's Boys', a backhanded homage to the jackets worn by entertainers at Butlin's holiday camps. In normal circumstances, any pupil equating school with a holiday camp would have been sent to Matron, but that summer pretty much the whole of the fifth form was the exception. The magnifying glass of concentration that had been revising for, and then sitting, their O-levels, was safely behind them, leaving previously unheralded amounts of leisure time to fill while the teaching staff focused on the mountain of year-end exams, mocks and A-levels still before them. So long as they kept out of trouble and on school property, the fifth form was left to its own devices. In these circumstances, most of them, given the Sahara-like temperatures, quite rationally decided to congregate at the swimming pool on the edge of the school's playing fields.

Unburdened by teachers and timetables, and in glorious ignorance of just how significant these times were to be for them, the fifth form had the pool to themselves. At first it had started with just a few of them spreading towels out on the grass banks that led up to the pool, listening to Led Zep and the Floyd on portable cassette players, but as word got around their numbers swelled.

Most of the boys had shared classes with each other at some point and, as such, they formed a tight, congenial group. Yes, there were factions, cliques even – friends/enemies, scientists/artists, brainy/average/challenged – but this variety had become, if anything, a strength, with teachers often remarking upon the particularly strong bonds that seemed to have been formed among their particular year group.

The boys had endured adolescence, exams, the CCF and the occasional mad teacher together, and probably knew each other better than most knew their own kin. They'd grown up together and were beginning to approach a point where the scary prospect of adulthood had begun to loom. Transformations in their bodies and voices had given a physical reality to the deeper stuff going on in their heads and hearts, and this maelstrom of change had forged a familiarity and a sense of shared destiny. In this, they were like other years that had gone before them, but what marked them out was the unique opportunity that nature and the exam system had provided to cement these connections.

Part of their sense of togetherness was expressed in how they addressed each other: with respect, but also with a willingness to push piss-taking to the limit. For the first couple of years, they'd echoed their teachers and stuck with surnames, but over time the use of given names had crept in, often sparked by having to ring a school friend on the phone, or by calling on them at home, and recognizing the absurdity of using the family name when asking for their friend.

Like characters in a Russian novel, most also had acquired a patronymic over time, in the form of a nickname. Sometimes conferred early on, as had been the case with Sam and Mushtaq, more usually these came about as a result of a particular characteristic or incident. Used with affection, these nicknames offered a sort of Masonic connection, whatever their origin. Those allowed to use the nicknames were part of 'us', with everyone else part of 'them'. As such, the nicknames were precious and used sparingly; even then, only when the audience was appropriate. That's not to deny that occasionally a name might be dropped out of context, like an accidental belch in polite company and causing much the same degree of embarrassment, and while using nicknames became slightly infra dig over time, they were still there, bubbling underneath the surface, even during the hot summer of 1975.

For some, their nickname seemed particularly apposite, with the boy concerned sometimes silently revelling in it. One such was Ben Bradshaw who, during that halcyon summer, seemed determined to keep his moniker alive by constantly ploughing up and down the length of the pool, barely stopping to eat, drink or even take a leak; although given the time he spent in the pool, everyone preferred not to think about the last of these.

Known as Tadpole, Ben was a county-level swimmer with aspirations to perform on the national stage. Almost unnaturally small for his age, with a hairless body, a closely cropped scalp and pudgy sausage-like fingers, Ben didn't look like a sportsman, his prowess more down to perseverance than natural ability. Ben was the reason they were all able to use the pool, making him an important person; not that Ben ever felt this was sufficiently acknowledged. Always keen to attract the reflected glory that came from any sporting success, the school had given him special dispensation to practise at the pool and had even entrusted him with a key to the gate, thereby opening the floodgates to the whole year.

For most, their nickname rested in the shadows, a sort of reserve salutation to be deployed in appropriate moments, like a spare two-pence coin kept for calling home in emergencies. Eddie Perks, for example, a ginger nut with unfortunate Pez-shaped buck teeth, had never been able to shake off the epithet Bugs, after the bunny. Likewise, Jeff Stone's extraordinary ears had marked him out from an early age as Dumbo; a nickname exacerbated by the fact that not even his own parents would have described him as particularly bright. Round-faced, with cheeks prone to flush at the slightest exertion, puberty had come late to Jeff, resulting in a subsequent confusion in his body as to which bits were supposed to grow in which order, making him not just awkward but also downright clumsy. No one ever asked Dumbo to open the ring pull on their Coke, or stood near him if he was opening his own.

For others, it was their name or initials that provided the necessary inspiration. Stevie Sanders, for example, a quiet maths genius with short hair, a faraway look in his eyes and an unfortunately high-pitched voice, had been dubbed Colonel, while Toby Connor, who despite the gift his middle name presented (it was Ulysses), was often referred to as Crackers, after the biscuit which also bore his initials. It was perhaps unfortunate that his skin turned a wonderful honey-brown in the sunshine that summer. For a while he'd been known as Pepsi as he could still recite the whole of the 'Lipsmackingthirstquencingmotivatinggood' advert for the soft drink, but it hadn't stuck. Other names, such as Mark Spencer, just had to be given the treatment, and for all of lower school he was known as St Michael; although later this was abbreviated – somewhat ironically, given some of his antics – to The Saint, even if his stocky frame meant he was never in danger of being mistaken for Roger Moore.

Many years later, when all the obituaries had been published, the journalists had written their stories and the police had closed their files, those days by the swimming pool were identified by many as the time when they'd begun to realize the special nature of what they had as a group. As sunning themselves became routine, souls as well as bodies began to be bared, and hopes and fears for the future were shared against a backdrop of the smell of newly mown grass mingling with chlorine, perspiration and factor-fifteen.

The swimming pool weeks (although, in reality, probably only days) were undoubtedly a pivot point: a time just before the loss of innocence; an idyll each knew could never be returned to; the gap of silence when changing the sides of an LP. But this is to run ahead, to use hindsight to search for and perhaps justify what could have possibly led to the tragedies that were to follow. Cohesive they may have been, but they were also individuals – some, lead actors in their subsequent story; others, bit-part players – and, as such, it's perhaps worth introducing a few more of the ensemble, both better to understand some of the constituent parts of the whole, and to provide conduits through whom their collective story can be told.

Mark Boothroyd, for example, who usually laid out his towel on the left-hand side of the bank leading up to the pool and was better known as Addy, due to a single incident when reciting some Shakespeare during an English lesson in the second form. A well-built, blunt and no-nonsense kind of a boy, a natural prop forward, Addy had once signed off a speech with 'Addio' rather than 'Adieu' when reciting the part of Falstaff in his booming baritone; a slip that had promptly earned him a detention, as well as a nickname.

Or take the case of Stuart 'Fingers' Dalgliesh, usually found sitting on his own. A tall and wiry Scot, Stuart had a ribcage that protruded from his torso like something designed to house a budgerigar. Fingers had not earned his name from his digital dexterity, or even his safe-breaking skills, but rather his fixation with all matters horticultural; the 'Green' half of his nickname having been lost back in the mists of time. As it happened, fixations came as part of the territory with Fingers, who had an obsession with things being neat and tidy. Not knowing the phrase 'Obsessive Compulsive Disorder', his school friends simply had him down as a bit of a nutter.

Fingers would regularly trim the overflowing grass next to the paving stones around the pool before most people arrived, using a pair of his own scissors. When the assembled crowd collectively decided it was time for a swim, he went around straightening their towels, making sure they were at a strict right angle to the pool's edge. His was no secret pleasure, however, the returning swimmers always making it their business to kick each other's towels out of whack on their way back to their own.

Adam Smart had the consolation of possessing a nickname derived not from the world of cartoons, his surname, a personality trait, or even an unfortunate slip of the tongue, but rather a film, enjoying the alias Emcee after the Master of Ceremonies from the Kit Kat Club in the film *Cabaret*. The fact that his middle two initials were MC also helped, of course. Dark-haired and effete, with a slim-to-emaciated build, Emcee had earned his nickname from the fact that he wouldn't stop going on about the film.

The nickname had been forged during an incident in a history lesson covering the causes of the Second World War, when George Rowlands had stood up and started singing *Tomorrow Belongs to Me*. He was followed in close succession by the others, in what was clearly a pre-planned move, until the whole class, with the single exception of Derek Henderson, had been in full voice, before slowly raising their arms into a Nazi salute and turning towards the flustered and confused Adam, each tucking two fingers lengthways under their noses. Derek Henderson had refused to join in on account of his political leanings, which were so far to the left they were nearly left behind; an attribute that had earned him his sobriquet of Stalin. Derek also had the distinction of enduring terrible acne, with craters over his face, neck and shoulders so extensive it was rumoured that astronomers were fighting over the rights to name them. In ordinary circumstances, this might have acted as the basis of a nickname, but a sort of *Pax Tunica Rubrum*, or Red Coat peace, prevailed, on the basis that there but for the grace of God went any of them.

The history lesson stunt had been classic George Rowlands. Tall and athletic, with a barrel chest and almost Slavic features, George was just coming to the height of his powers, as if he'd been treating the first five laps of the academic race as a warm-up for the main event. One of the oldest among their number, and definitely one of the most self-confident, George had one of those faces that was undeniably handsome, with a bone structure that meant he was likely to stay that way. The problem was, he knew it. He also had his own moped, 50cc of freedom, complete with learner plates. Never the first to arrive at the pool, he preferred instead to let an audience gather for a noisy entrance as he completed the final fifty yards along the bank to the changing rooms, powered by his Honda engine, a sound that offered more racket than rocket.

George didn't have a nickname. It would never have occurred to any of the boys to give him one; it would have been like desecrating an idol. Others remained similarly unanointed, although more through insipidness than reverence. Reggie Richardson, for example, an intelligent enough but really rather bland round-faced boy who seemed to be able to eat for England and never put a pound on, or Simon Grant. Simon had spent five years keeping himself to himself, seemingly existing in his own world, a place so far removed from everyone else's existence it had been impossible to find a hook to hang a nickname on.

Despite all George's Rowland's qualities, back in those halcyon days by the pool if anyone had been asked to name the most likely candidate for being their year's standard bearer going forward, perhaps surprisingly they wouldn't have nominated him, but Jake Peterson. While most knew that George's physicality and self-confidence were impressive, they also knew it was shallow. Jake, on the other hand, had a sort of silent charisma. On the tall side, Jake had sharp features, almost feminine, and carried himself in an easy, relaxed manner. He was self-effacing; not a natural leader of men, but rather someone who, if sufficiently motivated, would emerge from his shell and say and do the right things instinctively, decently and without fanfare, and over time this had earned him respect. Whether he was challenging an outmoded rule, arguing a philosophical point or standing up for someone who he felt had been done an injustice (he'd once done an afternoon detention for someone he knew to be innocent), it was Jake who said what had to be said. He seemed to have a magnetic quality, one that was just there rather than being anything he actively cultivated. It was a gift, and one he used wisely.

George Rowlands's gifts, on the other hand, were more obvious and less subtly deployed. It was he, for example, who brought about the earth-shattering shift in the idyll the boys had created around the pool.

George brought girls to the scene.

Girls were not a totally new phenomenon, but for most of the boys they existed more in theory rather than practice. With the arrival of the fairer sex on the scene, the use of nicknames suddenly became severely constrained. While the immediate comedic potential of referring to someone in front of a girl as Officer Dribble, just because he'd once left an unfortunate lemon-coloured stain down the front of his white

PE shorts, was tangible, it left perpetrators open to retaliatory action; a particularly dangerous position if, for example, all their peers knew them as Baldy due to the late onset of pubic hair, or indeed Doormat because of the opposite condition.

The gradual increase in the numbers of girls at the pool also invoked steady rises elsewhere, with the amount of feminine flesh on the scene necessitating a frequent rolling over on to their fronts for many boys. Hardly any of them had ever been so close to near-naked female flesh not from their own gene pool. The occasional shouts for everyone to jump in the pool were always followed by at least a few mumbled baritones suggesting they may hold on for a bit, all the owners of which, curiously, would be lying on their stomachs.

Different shapes and sizes of the female form were on display, but mostly these were young women just leaving the puppy fat stage and before the inevitable hormonal ravages that were to come. Some stayed all day, others just appeared for parts of the day. All were welcomed, but a handful were awaited with anticipation.

Prime among the latter was one in particular: the daughter of the school's matron. Matron lived on the main site of the school, and the boys had effectively grown up with her daughter, who was sighted coming home from her own school in town. A blonde girl of average height with high cheekbones and vacant blue-grey eyes, she'd previously kept her distance from the boys, and her occasional cameos by the pool seemed symbolic; a sort of debutante's coming-out, a symbol of the new era both she and the boys had reached in their lives.

Her pert nose and smooth skin gave her a certain doll-like appearance, an impression confirmed by an improbable chest modelled on Barbie, which her bikini finally revealed as being all-real rather than enhanced through clever use of lingerie, as many had, until that point, suspected. A latecomer to the crowd, she had skin already the colour of late-summer barley by the time she started appearing at the pool, leaving others of her sex to speculate whether she'd been tanning surreptitiously before launching herself into the developing swimming-pool scene. Although one of the undoubted stars of the pool, her appearances were more like a new comet: bright while they lasted, but unpredictable, over too soon and lamented when she disappeared. She was beyond available, out of their league, a prize no one could have, or would even dare to contest.

For most, it had taken a few days for their flesh to evolve from its initial cod-like resemblance, in both colour and texture, through a stage when it resembled more the hardened pink of a crustacean, and on to the nut-brown light leathered crust of smoked haddock. Along the way there were moments of soreness and discomfort, eased slightly by liberal use of Timothy Whites' best sun oil, but in time all the habitués of the pool looked as if they'd spent a long, hard summer toiling in the fields.

To the casual observer, the scene on the turf bank leading up to the pool might have looked like an Impressionist painting, with young people enjoying the perfect life in pastel hues, reading books, listening to music and frolicking innocently in the sunshine among dappled shade, but beneath the surface, deeper matters were the order of the day. These were young lives as blank pieces of paper about to be written upon, a generation readying itself for the world. What sort of world might they create, to pass on to those that followed? They had their agendas, none more so than Derek 'Stalin' Henderson, and they were confident they had the energy and vision to pursue them.

They weren't an entirely homogeneous group. The boffins were largely absent, as were the loners such as Mushtaq Dhillon and his wingman Sam Davidson, while Nigel Bennett seemed to prefer to spend the summer plane-spotting at the airport. Even those by the pool had their own groups. Some preferred to sit to one side and cluster around a radio, listening to the honeyed tones of John Arlott patiently guiding them through the Ashes matches on long wave. Others clustered around Mike McQueen, their year's music supremo, someone who worshipped John Peel as opposed to John Arlott.

It was Mike who stayed up through the night putting together mix tapes on C90s for everyone to listen to, and he had his own dedicated following. He'd been growing his hair through the term and it was now long enough to need an elastic band at the back to keep it together, making him the first ever ponytailed Red Coater in the school's history, his way of readying himself for the challenges of sixth form. Mike's favourite day was Thursday, when the *NME* came out (he had an instinctive dislike of anyone who read *Melody Maker*), which he would spread out on the grass and read from cover to cover, sitting to the side of the bank, where he was protected from the wind.

No one called him Mike; despite the gradual withering away of nicknames, Mike McQueen seemed destined to remain known simply as Freddie. The name was ironic. Asked to identify the one person from the music world he most despised, he would unhesitatingly have said Freddie Mercury. This hatred, along with his surname, made his handle inevitable. One day, a radio at the opposite end of the pool was offering competing sounds to his carefully compiled selections, and the inimitable staccato notes of *Killer Queen* had drifted over. Freddie stormed over in a blaze of fury, mumbling about how Queen represented all that was wrong about the music industry, and tossed the radio into the air where it performed an elegant parabola, pausing briefly at the top of its arc and then curving towards the water where it achieved an equally elegant Barnes Wallis skim across the surface, narrowly missing Ben Bradshaw halfway through one of his endless lengths of the pool. Throughout this journey, the volume emanating from the single speaker had ebbed and flowed as the radio twisted and turned, and as it finally began its inevitable slow-motion descent towards the bottom of the pool, the more famous Freddie became increasingly muffled, until he finally expired.

Later that afternoon, after Freddie had promised to buy a replacement radio, order returned. The sun that day seemed to be taking an especially languid path towards the horizon, with shadows seemingly reluctant to lengthen across the scorched brown playing fields below the pool. Australia were already one test up in the cricket and were chasing two hundred-plus in their second innings to go two up at Headingley. They'd lost some important men, though, and with one day to go the match was on a knife-edge. In the gathering shade at the opposite end of the bank, Freddie's group were listening to Genesis, while a pack of crossbenchers sat between the two, discussing politics.

Out of nowhere a sound resembling a whale blowing up a giant Li-lo rent the air, and before anyone had a chance to register its cause a large orange capsule, the shape and size of an Apollo command module, took wing from behind the changing rooms and smacked on to the still surface of the pool with a loud crack.

The shout of 'Oi!' from Ben Bradshaw was quite literally drowned out by an invasion of trunk-wearing boys, mostly bulky and unusually white, rushing from each side of the wooden changing huts that lined the back of the pool. They were led by the unmistakable sight, sound and size of Ray Meadows, his chest the shape and texture of a giant Shredded Wheat, with his sidekick The Saint and several others beside him. They dived into the pool simultaneously, sending up a ferocious, foaming tidal wave of water, and began to clamber into what rapidly became clear was a Navy rescue bell they'd liberated from the naval section of the CCF hut.

Until then, the regular habitués of the pool had been spared the harsher edge of the rugby crowd, but this was quite clearly a declaration of war. Testosterone had been injected into the scene and there were girls to impress. Taking their cue, the regular crowd accepted the challenge and leapt up in an uncoordinated mass, hoping to swamp their opponents with numbers, a collective shout of 'Ruck! Ruck! Ruck!' countering the battle cries from the invaders. Meanwhile, the girls who'd been lying on their fronts re-fastened their tops and joined the others standing by the side of the pool, adding their screams to the general cacophony and cheering on their favourites.

At once, the pool – moments before, a tranquil turquoise pond reflecting the low rays of the sun, attracting the attention of a handful of diving swallows – became a writhing mass of spume and noise.

Before long there was blood; not much, but spreading easily in the water to look like more, bringing a cloudy fuchsia-pink tint to the pool. Clinging to the side in the shallow end, Ben Bradshaw stared in disbelief. His territory, which only his generous blind eye had made accessible, was in the process of being annexed.

The fluid chaos lasted for no more than ten minutes and ended with a sudden shout of 'Pax!' from Addy Boothroyd, after which the pool emptied quickly, leaving the orange carcass of the rescue bell lying prone upon the water like an enormous used prophylactic, abandoned by those who'd brought it there, a gaping wound in its side exposing the black rubber within, rendering it useless. The rugby boys had disappeared as suddenly as they'd arrived, leaving the others to drag the dead vessel out of the water and beach it upon the paving slabs surrounding the pool. The excitement over, the crowd dispersed, shadows disappearing into the early evening, back to their homes and their teas, leaving Ben to continue his endless lengths of the pool and, it was apparently presumed, to tidy up.

The following morning the sun was shining again but metaphorical dark clouds were gathering on the horizon. Those arriving at the pool early, their towels rolled up into a neat Swiss roll and tucked under their arms or trapped under the spring of the carrier on the back of their bike, found that the gate to the pool had been secured with a new padlock. A small crowd slowly accumulated around the six-foot-high metal bars that kept them from the changing huts and the water, staring into the grounds like visitors at an empty zoo. Ben Bradshaw and his magic key were nowhere to be seen.

The school, it seemed, had decided to declare the pool a safety hazard. The member of staff whose job it had been to scatter the necessary chemicals into the pool ceased his rounds, and within days the beautiful blue water began to develop its own ecosystem, rapidly taking on the appearance of a third-year biology experiment gone wrong. Islands of algae gathered on the surface, looking and smelling like pats delivered by a cow with severe intestinal problems. When it was discovered that a giant snake had taken up residence and was swallowing the frogs that had also begun to inhabit the pool, the decision was taken to drain it.

By common agreement, the rugby pitch – the unfortunate recipient of most of the resulting water – was unplayable for all of the following season.

1975–76

O-levels became A-levels, as the academic race began its denouement. The frontrunners may have been out of sight, but for the rest of the field the emphasis was less on positions and more on finishing – ideally in one piece.

With sixth form, uniforms gave way to suits, and separate classrooms became a thing of the past as the whole year found itself sharing the converted three-storey house that was the sixth form centre. As far as was practicable, the centre operated as an autonomous unit within the school in an attempt to inculcate a sense of responsibility and, it was to be hoped, mutual respect, under the tutelage of the head boy and a small committee of elected officials.

For the first time in five years, these soon-to-be men found themselves the junior partners in a new social system; something they tolerated because they knew that positions at the top of the hierarchy would fall to them in time. There was much to do while they waited; not least, for those who were able, cultivating their facial hair.

The prize for the most audacious challenge to the school rules went to 'Freddie' McQueen, who insisted on shaving only his chin, arguing that what remained merely represented particularly large sideburns pasted either side of his face. The fact that his increasingly luxuriant growth outdid anything most of the masters could have mustered might have worked against him, but his six-foot-three height made him an invaluable asset in the lineouts when playing for the First XV, and on this, as in many other matters, members of that élite seemed to be given extra latitude. It helped, of course, that the authorities knew he was hardly likely to set a trend.

The sixth form centre was at the end of a terrace of four houses the school had bought in order to acquire the land their long gardens offered. The plan had been to extend the current quad, which incongruously only occupied two sides, and make it ... well ... a quad. Financial constraints had prevented that plan ever coming to fruition, but the houses themselves had proved useful, with one set aside as temporary accommodation for teaching staff new to the area, while another was a grace-and-favour dwelling for the school's matron. The house next to this, at the end of the row, had been converted into the headmaster's offices. The room where good lower-middle-class folk had once prepared their modest repasts now stored archives, and where they had once slept, the headmaster now ruled from his study, the holy of holies, visited only by those in deep, deep trouble, or those favoured few who formed the school's upper echelon.

Almost imperceptibly, some of the year began to find respectability conferred upon them through formal roles and titles awarded by the headmaster from that study, Harold Mitchell. He was a big believer in a school being much more than its pupils, who, after all, just passed through the system. It was the system itself that really defined what the school was about; that, and its less visible soul, what people had taken to calling its ethos, that stood the school out from the crowd.

Like many with his level of experience, Harold knew the importance of blooding a new lower sixth, of bringing them into the fold and vesting them with an interest in preserving the wider system, rather than becoming irritants within it. Harold also knew the importance of using his own power sparingly. His role was to remain above the fray and leave day-to-day rule to his deputy, Clive Porter, who was also head of sixth form. In this way, he could act as a last court of appeal or, as when he conferred appointments, a sort of benign sovereign.

It was an approach that had worked well over the years and, as the new school year began, he was confident it would continue to work with the new lower sixth, despite their reputation as an independent-minded bunch.

Nothing dampened independence quite as much as responsibility.

As it happened, fate played into his hands within a few weeks of the new term starting. Matron had made him aware of an issue that needed immediate action, one tailor-made for his getting the lower sixth on board.

----------------------------- ✳ -----------------------------

Matron had been with the school for as long as any boy, and many members of staff, could remember, but that didn't mean she'd been there a long time; just that they hadn't. Attractive when she wanted to be, Matron was identifiable more by her starched white uniform than her short-cropped hair, misty brown eyes and medium height. Like the headmaster, she'd arrived in the late 1960s and, also like him, she was single; although, controversially, she had brought an eight-year-old daughter with her. Her connections to the headmaster didn't end there, as from very shortly after her arrival the pair had known each other in a way the board of governors almost certainly wouldn't have approved of, had they ever found out.

Marion Whittle, to use the name on her birth certificate, was nothing if not discreet. She wouldn't have described her relationship with the headmaster as being one of lovers; more as sexual partners. They were both free, so in Marion's eyes no one got hurt – although that wasn't strictly true, given the headmaster's proclivities. Sometimes Marion wondered whether the thrill and danger implicit in their relationship, the tension it supplied to an otherwise ordinary life, was why she allowed it to continue, but really she knew it was something more concrete. Leaving aside the fact it would be difficult to end, the relationship provided her with some security by giving her a hold over the headmaster, and in her position as a single mother security was a commodity worth having. It wasn't an ideal situation, of course, but Matron was biding her time. Before long, her daughter would be fleeing the nest; she just needed to tolerate the situation a little bit longer to protect her fledgling.

That, at least, had been the theory, but something dreadful had happened that had caused her to rethink everything. A huge attraction of the job at the Red Coat had been its emphasis on tradition, the predictable rhythm of the school year, its reputation for decency. Now, she wasn't so sure. She'd become trapped in a world where people used rubber gloves in a way that would put you off washing-up for life, and a world which had exposed her precious, lovely, fragile daughter to … well, she couldn't bring herself to imagine it.

It had been the early days of the previous summer, school hadn't even broken up, when her daughter had burst through the front door in tears, shouting for her mummy and rolling back the years to a time when she used to wake in the middle of the night dreaming of monsters. This time, the nightmare was Marion's as much as her daughter's: the watery blood on her little girl's arms, the long blonde hair all tangled, the dishevelled sundress still damp, the sheer look of terror in her beautiful eyes.

Marion had known instinctively that, in the worst possible way, she'd failed in her mission to absorb all the filth the world could generate so that her daughter could remain unsullied. She knew she'd been down at the pool, of course, but she'd been part of a crowd and Marion had assumed, reasonably enough, there'd be safety in numbers. It seemed she'd been wrong.

Her lovely daughter was convulsed with deep primeval sobs erupting from the pit of her stomach, repeated over and over again like an animal in pain. The Red Coat boys were supposed to be the élite, the cream, future leaders; but at the end of the day, it seemed they were just men. Not even that: proto-men. Base in their instincts and desires, brutal, violent if they wanted to be. Marion Whittle understood all about men and their passions.

She'd cleaned her daughter up and calmed her down, but after that she was powerless. If she'd gone to the police the school would have got involved, and she couldn't risk her arrangement with the headmaster coming out. Besides, one silly girl against a hundred boys' futures – who would listen? The rest of the summer gave time for the bruising to surface and then go down again, and in the meantime Marion nursed her increasingly silent and distant offspring. Together, they awaited the new school term and the return of the status quo to help them forget.

Quite reasonably, Marion had shied away from asking for details to dredge up the actual events; what was the point in making her daughter go through all that again? Even if she had, she would never have found out how, in the moments before those events had unfolded, a pair of eyes and ears had, hippo-like, broken the surface of the pool and, in the failing light of the gathering dusk, scanned the scene before them.

--------------------------------- * ---------------------------------

It was true that Matron's position brought a lot of metaphorical shit with it, but very soon in the new school year this turned out to be true on a literal level, too.

The whole of the sixth form had been asked to convene in the bottom floor of their centre, a wide, open-plan area created by knocking the old kitchen, front and dining rooms together into one space. Usually taken up with various forms of indoor games and the occasional table, these had been folded up and pushed against the walls. That this meeting was almost unprecedented was indisputable. Rather like the monarch attending the House of Commons, masters only ever entered the centre when explicitly invited; not that many would have voluntarily entered areas normally only the cleaners dared to tread. This applied even to the deputy headmaster/head of sixth form, who had asked for, and been granted, permission to address the sixth form by the then head boy, Frank Robinson.

The current holder of the post of deputy headmaster, better known by the initials DHM to differentiate him from his superior, who was known simply as HM, was Clive Porter, an old retainer, with the emphasis, as the boys saw it, on the 'old'. Even though he was still probably only in his forties, he was one of those schoolmasters who seemed to embrace the affectations and clothes of someone much more senior in years than they actually were. An ORC, or Old Red Coater, he'd become part of the staff at the school in the early sixties after a shortened career in the forces, having joined up in the period after the war when the army's attention turned to propping up the Empire rather than fighting world wars. Through one reason or another, mostly health-related, he'd missed out on serving in any of the various fracas in Malaysia, Kenya, Cyprus and Suez, and finally left towards the end of the 1950s once he'd finally achieved his dream of actual combat: a total of thirty-six hours spent as part of the British forces helping the Sultan of Oman quell an uprising in the mountains of his recently united country; an experience that seemed to have scarred him, as well as contributing to his premature ageing.

Like a methane spring in a village pond, the DHM gave off the occasional whiff of something hidden and unpleasant, prone to surfacing at unexpected moments, against an otherwise calm exterior. When this happened, his temper would erupt and flare, as if an inner demon had taken him over for a few seconds, before subsiding. These incidents, which would have earned him a written warning in any other school, were tolerated at the Red Coat as an act of sympathy for the travails of an old boy, and a decorated hero to boot. Besides, along with the bursar, he was a cornerstone of the CCF.

On reflection, it should have come as no surprise that over the years a favourite target for these outbursts had been Mushtaq Dhillon. Mushtaq proved to be remarkably impervious to these attacks, which he seemed to accept as almost normal, and of course no one else ever complained or did anything about them. If life at the Red Coat had taught the boys anything, it was the heinousness of the sin of snitching.

Nothing was done, either, about the *khanjar*, another of the DHM's little 'eccentricities'. A souvenir from his days in Oman, this was a J-shaped, curved dagger about ten inches long, with another four inches that stuck out at a right angle at the tip. Encrusted with what looked like jewels in the handle, the dagger slept in a leather scabbard from which it had to be extracted at an angle. These unveilings would take place on occasional Wednesday afternoons, when the DHM would thrust the blade into a sandbag with an upward movement, producing two punctures: one at the point of entry and the other a few inches above it, as if from nowhere. The only practical response on these occasions was for someone to fetch a bucket from the caretaker to collect the sand.

As he breezed into the centre, the DHM was flanked by the school chaplain, who through some higher authority didn't require permission to enter. Known simply as the Rev, this role was usually filled by a faceless young curate who typically stayed a year or two, serving his time before moving on to a more significant role. Once or twice in the past there had been Revs who'd been older, and in these cases they were less serving time than serving a sentence, the result of unknown misdemeanours elsewhere.

Either way, given the usual brevity of their tenure, few bothered to learn the name of the Revs as they passed through, authority being vested more in the title than the individual, which was passed on from incumbent to incumbent. This particular Rev was one of the younger versions, short in stature and fresh-faced. He was also Nigerian, which had the effect of making his dog collar more prominent, as well as rendering him something of an object of curiosity at the Red Coat. By nature a quiet man, the Rev seemed to love parading around the school in his plain black vestments, which didn't quite reach the ground, revealing a pair of squeaky leather sandals.

Probably not that much older than those in the sixth form, he was fully togged-up as he entered their building, although the fact he was having to take two steps to the DHM's one as they made their way into the centre diminished any sense of solemnity he might have hoped for. The DHM was focused on the task in hand and wanted to get it over with, his other flank protected by the head boy as they lined up in front of the assembled sixth-formers.

As the triumvirate stood still in front of a full house, a funereal silence descended as if a mute button had been pressed. Their collective air was brisk and to the point, as if none of them wanted the session to last any longer than necessary; possibly because two of the three were on alien turf, but more likely because of the subject matter involved.

It had been a squeeze to fit everyone in, and Mark 'Michael' Spencer, a squat, pudgy boy with permanently greasy hair, found himself pushed back against the darts scoreboard in the corner by the massed suits in front of him, some leaning backwards a little too deliberately, leaving chalk dust against the ill-fitting back of his new Burton suit jacket. Mushtaq Dhillon, meanwhile, was keeping a judiciously low profile perched on the sill of the bowed window that looked out on to the street. Outside, the first wild winds of autumn were rattling the room's old leaded windows, tossing twigs and leaves up against the loose glass, while inside, 'Fingers' Dalgliesh was having a problem keeping the curtains someone had drawn earlier perfectly straight.

The DHM started by setting some ground rules, demanding that everything talked about in the room went no further, and appealing, as much in hope as expectation, to the boys' still-developing sense of maturity and discretion. He then immediately moved on to the main purpose of the meeting. A buzz of tension filled the room, not only because of the mystery reason behind the gathering, but also because bets had been taken on the chances of the DHM 'going off on one'. When he spoke, however, his voice was controlled and normal, making no allowances for the room he had to fill. As he went on, this reinforced the feeling among some of his audience that they couldn't quite believe what they were hearing, partly because a fair proportion were having a problem hearing him properly at all.

'Gentlemen,' he began, pausing to allow the hubbub in the room to calm down, 'to borrow a phrase from the Apollo 13 astronauts, we have a problem.' Few of the boys present recognized the reference but they retained their reverential silence all the same, keen to find out why they were there. 'And that problem is ...' He paused again, but only briefly, '... ordure.'

A palpable sense of disappointment infused half the room, principally those towards the back, who'd misheard and assumed they'd been summoned to hear yet another lecture about school discipline. In contrast, the other half of the room who could hear had had their interest piqued.

'There's no easy way to say this, so I'm just going to come out and say it: we are facing an outbreak of defecation.' A murmur rumbled from the back of the gathering, summed up neatly by the deep baritone of Mark Boothroyd, who asked, 'Who's been slagging us off now?', causing more than a few puzzled faces from nearer the front to turn towards him, before someone piped up, 'Defecation, you tosser, Addy; not defamation,' leading the heckler to raise a hand in acknowledgement of his mistake.

'Precisely,' the DHM confirmed before continuing. 'We have been having a problem with … er … motions cropping up unexpectedly.' Having introduced the main point of his message, the DHM clearly decided to land the rest without further ado. 'In the gym, in the lower hall, on the tennis courts and even on the steps outside the staff room.'

'Emotions?' came another voice from the back, the unmistakable squeak of tiny Stevie Sanders. This second interruption was clearly too much for the head boy, a large prop forward whose nose could most charitably be described as 'squashed', who decided to help the DHM out by employing the same booming voice he used to frighten first-formers.

'Turds.'

The single word echoed around the large open space like a rear-end malfunction in the middle of school prayers, delivering much the same effect of stifled laughter and exaggerated silence. 'Some toerag is leaving turds scattered around the school,' the head boy explained in the simplest way possible.

'Turds? What, real ones?' asked a fresh voice hidden at the back, with not a little incredulity.

'No, pretend ones, you idiot,' the head boy replied, annoyance creeping into his voice as he maintained a parade-ground stance with his eyes forward and his hands gripped behind his back. 'Of course, real ones.'

The attention of the room regained, the head boy looked towards the DHM to continue. 'Thank you, Robinson. You may be asking, as indeed we did, how we can be sure it is human in origin.' This question hadn't been the first that had come to mind, but the boys were prepared to run with it. 'On each occasion it has been Matron's unenviable task to make a diagnosis, as it were, and she can confirm that we are not dealing with a stray dog or anything similar.'

'How do we know, sir?' the reasoned tones of Jake Peterson enquired, injecting a sense of seriousness and maturity into the exchange. 'If I may ask?'

'You may, Peterson, thank you for the question. It seems that the final resting place of the, er, deposits, is not where they are initially, er …'

'Delivered, sir?' Peterson suggested.

'Precisely.'

'So, they get there how, exactly?' enquired Peterson, who by this point seemed to be having a private conversation with the DHM.

'Well,' the DHM went on, 'it seems there are marks; scrape marks, as it were.'

'Skidmarks?' came yet another disbelieving voice from the back, only to be corrected by one of his fellows nearer the front.

'Sir?' Jake Peterson probed, with a single word encouraging the DHM to reveal more than perhaps he had anticipated before entering the room.

'It has become clear to Matron, and we are minded to take her word for it …'

'I bet they are,' an anonymous voice mumbled.

'… that the perpetrator of these acts has been in the habit of, er, doing his business, scraping it up and then leaving it in strategic locations about the school.'

'And we're absolutely sure about this, are we, sir?' Jake Peterson asked, as if there could be any doubt.

'Look,' interrupted the head boy again, clearly exasperated with the way the conversation was going, 'there was one left on the spiral staircase leading up to the library, and not even a bloody contortionist could have had a' – and here he paused to select the right word – 'business there!'

Judging by the silence that followed, this seemed to offer pretty conclusive proof that they were either dealing with some spade-wielding circus freak or else a plain and simple nutter with an incontinence problem. It seemed the DHM leaned towards the latter theory.

'Obviously, we need to find out who is behind' – a single suppressed guffaw broke to the side of the room at this word, which the DHM opted to ignore – 'these outbreaks, not only to stop them, but to give the person …' At this point the DHM paused, struggling to come up with an alternative to 'behind'.

'Some paper?' someone suggested.

'… responsible,' the DHM continued, 'some help.'

An eruption of nodding broke out across the room, suggesting to the DHM that at last the issue was being taken seriously, and emboldening him to utter the two fatal words: 'Any questions?' As he did so, the head boy's hands came out from behind his back and lay poised by his side, as if he was ready to grab the throat of anyone who took advantage of the opportunity the DHM was offering.

'How long's this been going on, sir?' Jake Peterson asked, unperturbed.

'A few days. Senior staff and members of the student management team have been carrying out patrols, but to no avail.'

'Getting warmer, sir?', enquired someone near the curtains who sounded like Toby Connor.

'Um?' the DHM replied. 'No, they have all been stone cold by the time we've found them.'

'They?' enquired Terry Mungus, incredulously. 'You mean there's more than one of them?'

At this point the head boy had clearly had enough and intervened to bring the meeting to a close. His message was sharp and clear. The decision had been made to involve the whole senior school – in other words, the sixth form – in the search for the boy responsible, to appeal to their sense of maturity so that a swift end could be brought to the whole affair before word of it got out and, he added as an afterthought, of course so that help could be provided to the individual involved. With that, he allowed the DHM to wrap up and invoke a code of absolute silence and discretion, the breaking of which would bring about the most severe punishment. 'This is,' he concluded, 'a time for the sixth form to step up.'

'Rather than step in,' a voice offered, probably Toby Connor again, after which the meeting rapidly dispersed. In a time frame so short it would have been impossible to measure it, a codename was given to the sick individual involved: the Double S, or Sneaky Shitter.

----------------------------- ✳ -----------------------------

The Sneaky Shitter was never caught, although the whole episode provided a welcome diversion from the burgeoning realities of sixth form life, offering as it did perfect opportunities to float off-limits during break time, whether it be for a sly fag or to meet one of the girls from the previous summer at the pool in town, safe in the knowledge that if caught by a master or prefect you could always say you were following up a lead on the whereabouts of the Double S. After a couple more 'deposits' a hiatus ensued, which in time became a ceasefire and eventually evolved into a permanent truce. Having the full force of the sixth form on his tail had, quite literally it seemed, scared the Double S shitless.

Before too long the buzz the search had generated fell away and the incipient end of the first term was heralded by Christmas decorations appearing around the school. When Ray Meadows, with characteristically bad timing, bought two dozen 'Dirty Fidos' by mail order from a joke shop and scattered them in strategic spots around the school, it was clear that the whole episode had passed its sell-by date.

When they returned in early January, the upper sixth became focused on their forthcoming mock exams, and the osmotic process began whereby the lower sixth assumed the mantle of alpha males, dominating the games room and getting their choice of music on to the record deck. They had become the de facto sixth form, a process confirmed with the appointment of fresh prefects and speculation as to who was to go down in school history as their year's head boy.

The Sneaky Shitter became history. The fact that his exploits were able to mutate from being the number one threat facing the school into a joke, was possibly because their antics were seen as a victimless crime

– although Matron may have begged to differ. The whole episode had been a distraction, a warm-up before the serious business of the final circuits of the track of academe were tackled.

Before then, however, there was to be a new, much more significant menace facing the school's authorities; only this time it was almost entirely of their own making.

1977

Harold Mitchell felt good as he stared into the mirror at his lathered face, a safety razor poised in his right hand over the cracked handbasin below. The white foam beard staring back at him formed a thick U-shape from ear to ear and provided a temporary mask for the unfortunate deep cleft in his chin. Unfortunate, because to the unbiased observer this cleft looked like a miniature rear end, and doubly unfortunate because its depth usually meant that bits of whisker got stuck there, and getting them out meant pulling the two sides apart with one hand and using the razor with the other, a manoeuvre which often resulted in him nicking himself, causing a doubly distressing look.

Harold continued with his routine regardless; nothing was going to spoil his good mood. This day was going to be a good one and he wanted to look his best. This was the day he was going to set his meticulously prepared plan into action. Payback time for years of slog at the coalface of the British educational system.

The timing was perfect. Harold Mitchell had come to the Red Coat fourteen years before, then the school's youngest-ever headmaster at the age of forty-two. Back then he'd been an embodiment of an age when there was a feeling that youth should be given its head, that it was time for a new generation to pick up the baton and to let the tired old faces, most of them worn down by years of war and austerity, slip away into a deserved retirement. He didn't think it too much of an exaggeration to say that he was seen at the time as the Red Coat's equivalent to JFK, even if the reality had turned out to be more Harold Wilson than John F. Kennedy.

The beginning of his incumbency had been challenging. It had coincided with the first moves to iron out any hint of selection in the system under the then Labour government, although thankfully the local county had been at best equivocal about the whole project, and progress had been gratifyingly slow. The prevailing mood at County Hall seemed to be that Labour governments weren't part of the natural order, as if fish and chips had replaced Sunday roast, and that before too long things would most likely go back to how they were before. The local education authority had taken the view that the sounds coming from Westminster were like those of the naughty children who were their bread and butter, and that the traditional policy of just ignoring them would probably work, too. Then there had been a long road to negotiate, raising the school leaving age to sixteen, although in reality this had been less of a burden for the Red Coat, which saw its remit as producing young men more likely to work in the City than in cities.

The school, founded two centuries before, owed its name to the fact that its first pupils had been kitted out in a distinctive red jacket. Funded initially by the local guilds, the school's early intake had been drawn from the children of craftsmen who showed promise, but whose parents lacked the funds to provide them with a formal education. It had, not to put too fine a point on it, been founded as a charity school.

This status proved to be financially efficient all through the nineteenth century and for the first half of the succeeding one, although any pretence of the school existing for the benefit of the disadvantaged evaporated in the face of the rise of the middle classes. The one defining characteristic that remained was a focus on providing education for the more gifted in the community, and a selection exam had been a feature of the school for over a century, including after the war, when the Red Coat had finally been drawn into the bosom of the state system on the promise of being given grammar school status.

Along with this promise was an implicit understanding – never actually written down anywhere – that it was, of course, not just any old grammar, but more a kind of grammar-plus. This was a perception the school worked hard to retain, not least in the image it projected into its local community and the continued adherence to many of the accoutrements more usually associated with public schools, such as a link to the local cathedral; the insistence that masters (and they were mostly masters) wore their university gowns when teaching; and a place on the rugby fixture lists featuring the remaining private schools.

As a result, the Red Coat became that anomaly, a direct grant grammar school, a status that balanced expediency and aspiration in equal measure. Under this system the school could be part of the state system yet also retain a distance from it, and keep its entrance exam while having up to half its places funded by the state, with the other half subject to fees; and since a voluntary means-test determined whether parents paid, it became a mark of pride among some parents to refuse to subject themselves to such a formula.

For those who continued to aspire to send their boys to the school, this represented the best of all worlds. Those who could afford the fees were able to convince themselves they were buying a level of exclusivity, while the more aspiring but less well-off families had a school where their boys could 'better themselves', without having to take out a second mortgage on the family home. For those who took a broader view, such schools also acted as a useful social safety valve, a means of spotting the brighter children among the lower middle classes and assimilating them into the establishment fold before they got the chance to become trade union leaders, or something equally ghastly.

The return to power of the Conservatives in 1970 was received with a sigh of relief by all those connected with the Red Coat. Their faith was rewarded when an otherwise unpromising female education secretary stopped free school milk but provided extra funding for the direct-grant sector. The respite was to be temporary, however, and in 1974, less than a year after the Labour Party had been returned to government, albeit precariously, they had passed the Direct Grant Grammar Schools (Cessation of Grant) Regulations. These required all such schools to come totally under the remit of their local education authority or else to become entirely independent. Given there was already a separate boys grammar school in the town, the first option wasn't really an option at all; so independence it had to be.

This was where Harold Mitchell's big plan came in. He'd studied the pay levels for headmasters within the private system and spotted an opportunity. If he could steer the school through the process of gaining independence without too much fuss, then the governors would surely show their appreciation by raising his salary in line with the market. Two, maybe three years in, he would be able to take early retirement on a final salary pension far greater than the amount offered by the state scheme. It would be a just reward for all that he'd done and the start of a new life for him, or rather a chance to start his life anew.

Of course, he would never have dreamed of expressing any of this out loud. No, the story for public consumption was quite different. The need to retain academic standards, blah blah; retaining the school's unique heritage, blah blah; guardians for the next generation, blah blah – he could go on like this for hours. More practically, there was also the small matter of increased income. The school was in desperate need of fresh investment, the heating system looked and sounded like something Heath Robinson would have come up with after half a bottle of Scotch, and the labs were decidedly pre-war: First War, that was.

Harold Mitchell had had an idea, and that idea was not only going to speed up the whole process but give it a veneer of democratic legitimacy that would make everyone involved feel not only grateful to him, but actually rather smug about themselves. He was going to put it to the vote. Rather than independence, he was going to make it a choice, and a personal triumph along the way, finally gaining some level of appreciation from those among the board of governors who'd always regarded him as somehow too *nouveau*, not their kind of man.

Harold was nothing if not a belt-and-braces man, though, and he had something else up his sleeve to sway the waverers. It hadn't been easy, but what had started as an idle conversation at his local Masonic lodge had escalated, and he now all but had it in writing that none other than Princess Margaret would be prepared to become a figurehead rector of the newly private school; although this remained, of course, strictly on a hush-hush, need-to-know, finger-to-the-side-of-the-nose level for now. It was the ultimate trump card – no one would be able to resist the magic dust a little bit of royalty could bring.

He could almost taste his comfortable retirement. Often described as a confirmed bachelor, in Harold Mitchell's case this was not a euphemism; far from it, in fact: it was just that he'd never really seen the point of marriage. His was not to be a cosy retirement cultivating roses and playing golf. He knew precisely how he wanted to spend the twilight years of his life, and he was eager to get started. He was already planning a tour of some of the best specialist establishments catering for his particular tastes that both the western and, more particularly, the eastern world could offer.

As he washed off the last of the shaving foam and checked for any stray chin hairs, Harold Mitchell felt unusually calm. His plan was foolproof: nothing could go wrong.

------------------------------ ✳ ------------------------------

Ray Meadows had forgone the satisfaction of a good shave. He tended to put his razor away from Thursday to Sunday, having found that a couple of days' worth of ginger scouring-pad growth was capable of leaving a red rasp down the cheek of opponents in the scrum.

Ray loved his rugby. He loved the blood, the rawness, the sheer undiluted brutality of it all, expressing everything he enjoyed about being a bloke. He also enjoyed the success and, he happily admitted, the recognition it brought him. Before he'd been made captain of the First XV, Ray had always had a sneaking suspicion that behind his back his character was much maligned. Not that this was a word he would have used to describe how he felt, tending instead more towards 'rubbished', but the general drift was much the same. It wasn't his fault he was so physically intimidating. Neither was it his fault that his background gave off a lower-middle-class aura as powerful as four-day-old fish. As such, he enjoyed having something he could feel proud of that was entirely of his own making.

The imminent end of his final season with the school team had generated bittersweet feelings for Ray. Bitter, because it was his final season, but sweet, because of what he'd achieved as captain. As far back as records began, the First XV had never finished an entire season undefeated, and Ray was determined to consign that record to the dustbin.

The final match of the season was away against Halstead Grammar, a school that was strong historically, but had frankly gone on the slide after the 'Grammar' in its title had become purely nominal. To all intents and purposes, they'd become nothing but a jumped-up comprehensive, and it showed in their rugby, as some of their best sportsmen had been diverted into other namby-pamby sports such as swimming or athletics. As such, they were not really serious contenders to stand between Ray and his dream of leading the Red Coat to glory – but he didn't intend to take any chances. This was to be the team's moment of triumph, and he was going to enjoy every second.

The morning had started with the ritual of packing his sports bag, lifting the freshly ironed kit and a clean towel out of the airing cupboard and placing them on top of the pristine boots already in there, having been cleaned after mid-week practice. Mouthguard and jockstrap sat side by side at one end of the bag, while his shin guards lay at the other. Ray had tapped them all for luck, as he always did, but in his heart he knew that luck had very little to do with his and his team's success, which was built more on raw aggression and a loose interpretation of some of the less well-defined rules of the game.

Along the top he placed a toiletries bag, the key constituent of which, beyond soap and deodorant, was his liniment. After the coach journey to the ground, conducted largely in silence, they'd been met and shown to their changing room by a Halstead flunky. It was here that the ritual entered its concluding stage, and within minutes schoolboys were transformed into knights, their upper lips disfigured by a layer of hardened plastic as if they were some undiscovered genus of primate, their torsos covered with crimson tracksuits. Warm-up exercises were conducted to an arrhythmic tap dance on the concrete floor, while the smell of Deep Heat slowly overwhelmed the gentler scent of Vaseline, forming an invisible and, to those unused to it, astringent miasma in the crowded space. Ray had emitted his usual primeval yell of encouragement, prompting the whole team to join in, creating a cauldron of toneless and uncoordinated noise underscored by the occasional grunt which pumped up the adrenaline; an undetonated testosterone time bomb, ticking down the seconds.

As was their way, the Red Coat team took the field in single file, only breaking out into a trot on reaching their designated pitch. Halstead's fly half had been a handful in the home game, and in the team talk beforehand Les Andrew and his trusty sidekick Philip Christopher had taken on the responsibility to be the ones to swat him. Although sometimes aloof, some would suggest arrogant, when it came to the crunch – and this match was as crunchy as it got – Les could be relied upon to be a team player. Built with the solid physique of a second row forward, Les's outward demeanour was in fact a defence against an acute shyness that only team sports and, he'd recently discovered, alcohol, were able to breach. Philip's key attribute was a baby face that carried a permanent look of innocence, one that had been known to win over referees on more than one occasion in the past. As things turned out, all the scheming had been unnecessary as, in a bizarre twist of fate, the prat had managed to run straight into an upright and knock himself out before the game was even ten minutes old. It had been like watching an old slapstick film where someone walks into a lamp post: everyone could see what was going to happen except the poor sod destined to keep an appointment with the St John's Ambulance first-aiders.

By the time Ray had reached him, the lad was out for the count and strangely inert. Although there wasn't any blood, when his closed eyelids were raised by the ref there was a cold, lifeless look in his pupils that reminded Ray of the day the family cat was run over by a Volvo. It was unlikely the fly half heard the applause that accompanied his being stretchered off the field; in Ray's case, it was offered less in the name of sportsmanship and more by way of thanks for the supreme act of self-sacrifice he'd made.

The Halstead sub had been running the line and didn't look too chuffed about joining the fray, a feeling that had been given some credence when he'd somehow received a dead leg a few minutes after coming on, after which he never seemed to get back up to speed. The Red Coat team played as a unit that day. After a season of intense training and action they were fitter than they'd ever been before, with most at a level of fitness they'd never reach again. They ran, tackled and mauled as if it was something they'd all been born to do, giving every one of them a sense of perfect synchronicity, of being at the very peak of their game, operating in perfect harmony and using the human body as it was meant to be used.

The result was a 48–0 whitewash and, as such, a thoroughly satisfactory end to the season. The atmosphere on the coach back to school was marked by a heady mix of Brut and embrocation, underscored by musical enquiries on the status of the driver's bladder. In between songs it was agreed that some form of celebration was in order, and so it was that they all arranged to meet up later at the newly reopened and renamed Lamb and Mint Sauce on the edge of town.

Ray's original idea had been for the evening to be a team-only affair, but somewhere between the coach arriving back at the school and the pub, it grew. The word was, there was a joint eighteenth birthday bash on that night at the Lamb for Eddie Perks and Jeff Stone, or Bugs and Dumbo as Ray still thought of them, and it seemed natural for the rest of the team to crash that. Ray's initial reaction had been completely the reverse – it seemed a completely unnatural thing to do, making it less of a team celebration and diminishing its exclusivity – but somewhere on the two-mile walk to the pub he'd revised his opinion.

What Ray lacked in academic flair he made up with broader nous. He knew he wasn't going to get the grades for university and had already started to make plans for life outside school. During the walk, Ray indulged himself with a little thinking. His old man was always banging on about contacts and the importance of having them. 'It's not so much what you know as who you know, old man,' he always said, and maybe he had a point.

Here he was, part of a group of privileged, bright young men, most of whom stood a reasonable chance of making a decent way in the world. Who knew where some of them could end up? Policemen, maybe: a useful phone number to get you off a breathalyser rap. Masons, members of the council ... who knew, maybe even MPs, in time. Their world might not be his world, but simply knowing them would allow him entry.

By the time Ray got to The Lamb he'd reconciled himself to embracing his fellows, regardless of whether they were part of the straight up and down inner circle of the rugby team, or one of the weird bunch of brainboxes or punks he usually avoided. It was time to look to the future.

Quite a lot was drunk that night, and Ray was of the opinion that his involvement, along with the way the First XV had livened things up a bit, had made it a night to remember. Not that he did remember that much of it the morning after, but as his Sunday wore on, parts of the previous evening managed to bubble to the surface of his consciousness. He remembered a cake covered in a strange, deep red icing with white writing on the top, which someone at some point in the evening had altered to read 'Hippy Barfday'. No one had really wanted the cake, so later on the light sponge with strawberry jam filling had been used as ammunition in a food fight.

Ray also remembered the old glass yard of ale, part of the gentrification of the pub, being taken down and dusted off with someone's dirty handkerchief before being pressed into service, and how not long afterwards the wooden floor below was so sticky with spilt beer that it was almost impossible to walk on. Just as his mum was getting the Sunday lunch out of the oven, Ray recalled how, after the bulb of the yard had been smashed against one of the mock oak beams, he'd started a mammoth game of 'Off The Floor' that had taken over the whole of the public bar, with anyone touching the floor being forced to down a pint in one.

It was later on, after his dad had a nap on the couch and his mum came into the living room to watch Cliff Michelmore on *Holiday 76*, that Ray remembered how the evening had ended. It was probably merely bad luck that the door to the gents was next to the blazing log fire in the lounge bar. It was also possible that he might have had a sherbet or two too many. Whatever the reasons, it was probably fair enough that the landlord's patience had finally snapped when Les Andrew had mistaken the hearth for a urinal and relieved his straining bladder on to the flames, sending up a plume of amber-coloured steam that rose up to the ceiling before spreading across and condensing as droplets on to the heads, and into the drinks, of those unfortunate enough to be sitting there.

As that memory hit him, Ray dredged up another. A buzz about how special the night had been, how there'd been talk of repeating it and how friendships shouldn't be allowed to wither. Ray knew, of course, that a lot of this had been the beer talking, combined with some desperate clinging to the familiar in the face of an uncertain future. He knew all that, and yet he had also spotted an opportunity. He even had a vague recollection that he'd offered to help get involved in making sure something happened, although the details remained stubbornly sketchy.

------------------------------ ✳ ------------------------------

The First XV's exploits were to go down in Red Coat history, even if officially the powers-that-be had shown a tactful deafness to the subsequent celebration. Before anyone knew it, the final terms of what was about to become the Class of '77 were upon them, and they, in turn, were surprised to find their authority being slowly usurped by the year below them. As tradition dictated, their juniors were universally regarded as 'wet' and therefore unworthy bearers of the mantle of seniority sixth-form status brought, but their presence was undeniable and as such they were tolerated. The home straight of the final lap was coming into sight.

Sixth form had been a particularly tough time for Sam Davidson, running alone, with no team mates to cheer him on. A year before, his rock and only friend, Mushtaq Dhillon, had disappeared, failing to turn up on the opening day of Lent term. His phone simply rang and rang when he tried to find out what was up, but this was nothing to the shock of finding his house empty with an estate agent's 'For Sale' sign outside when he went round. He'd gone, disappeared, vamoosed, vaporised. Just at the moment he'd needed it most, Sam's energy deserted him. Just as a gear change was required, he'd suffered a clutch failure. He coasted, his lack of momentum noted and criticized, but he was but one of a pack who needed cajoling, and seeing as he wasn't exactly someone any teachers had ever taken under their wing, he was allowed to limp away at the back, the phantom limb of his lost friend dragging behind him.

While time hung heavy on Sam's hands, for everyone else it seemed to take on a fresh quality. Once a limitless resource, it suddenly became impossibly rationed. It was as if someone had decided to press 'fast forward' instead of 'play' on the cassette deck of life, and it seemed that the end of the tape marked 'schooldays' was imminent.

Adulthood loomed, although for most there was a Get Out of Jail Free card. Luckily for them, securing and then playing this card happened to be one of the main purposes of the Red Coat School. In fact, it was the reason a large proportion of the boys had been sent there in the first place. University, academia, the dreaming spires of Oxbridge, or the plain red bricks of the newer institutions; university offered three more years without responsibility or the need to earn money. In fact, the government gave you money. The completion of UCCA forms had cast their long shadows over Michaelmas term, although the experience had been leavened by the opportunity to go on open days and visits for interviews, followed by offers and the stark reality of what had to be achieved in terms of A-levels.

For some, this option was a mirage, achieving three passes, let alone the As, Bs and Cs most universities were asking for, being about as likely as the DHM suddenly admitting he'd been the Sneaky Shitter all along. For others, university had never really been part of the game plan, with the entry schemes of the banks and insurance companies seen, at least by the fathers of the boys involved, as offering an education every bit as good, if not better than that offered by the muesli-munching, sandal-wearing liberals who called themselves university lecturers.

The arrival of warming spring sunshine marked the end of the phoney war, as the whole year group scrummed down in one last push for the line. The masters, of course, had seen it all before: how a healthy combination of pressure and pragmatism had the power to emasculate even the most rebellious of boys. It was remarkable how they all managed to blank out all other distractions – all except one, that is: the unfortunate Stevie Sanders.

One afternoon, in the middle of a revision seminar on binomial theorem, Sanders had stood up, screamed and, without a further word to anyone, simply walked out, calm as you like, never to be seen again. The talk of the sixth form centre for a couple of days, his departure turned out to be a momentary distraction destined to become, if anything, a reminder of the importance of staying the course, of blotting out all diversions and ignoring the injunctions to rebel from the screaming Mohicans of punk now dominating the radio and *Top of the Pops*.

Different exam timetables combined with study leave meant that most classes went out with a whimper rather than a bang. After all the build-up the dip at the finishing line was staggered, and somehow its full impact got lost, as if those holding the tape had decided to nip off for a quick fag. The Class of '77 wasn't like all those that had come before, though. With hindsight, perhaps the fact that they still had enough spark left in them for a valedictory surprise shouldn't have come as a shock.

1982

School, university and assorted others had done all they could for them; there were no excuses left. They were primed, ready to go, and had finally been cast out into the big wide world. What were they all doing now, five years after school? Had those tipped for success made a start? Who among them were the surprises, doing better than predicted, or worse than their teachers and peers had foreseen?

Just as interesting as what they were doing was how they were doing it. How were they making their choices, and to what degree was luck playing a part? With the removal of the protective environment they'd lived in, grown up and been nurtured in gone, the once ever-present was now the past. The question now being posed was: for how many would that past define them, and how many would defy it?

Most had fulfilled the expectations of the school and of their parents by going to university. For some, this had proved a useful transition; for others, less so. Whereas during school, time had seemed malleable, with the prospect of there always being another year to get things right, university had seemed less willing to offer second chances. If school had been a long-distance relay race, university had been more of a hundred-yard dash.

Taking into account gap years, overseas study, years in industry and postgraduate certificates in education, by 1982 all available avenues for postponing the inevitable had been taken and used up. By Christmas that year, the vast majority of the Class of '77 were in gainful employment; whether they'd just entered it, joined straight after university, or been in it since leaving school. They'd become part of the tax-paying classes.

------------------------------ ✱ ------------------------------

Ray Meadows's old man, Trevor, had spent most of his working life travelling the country in baby prams. Ray had never revealed this information to anyone; certainly not during his time at school. The way he saw it, he'd worked bloody hard to create some kind of standing among his classmates and some things were best kept under wraps. Besides, no one had ever asked.

While Ray's dad may have been an object of little curiosity among Ray's classmates, the man himself was a person of convictions, and not in the criminal sense. He was the sort of man who believed you had to pull yourself up by your own bootstraps, even if this meant falling backwards. If he'd had his way, his son would have left school at sixteen and earned the money to buy his own bootstraps to pull himself up by. It had only been the glory flowing from Ray's captaincy of the First XV that had kept him in the sixth form (his dad wasn't immune to a little social snobbery), and it had never been remotely on the cards that Ray would go to university.

Fortunately, as it turned out, this had never been an ambition Ray had harboured. He'd never seen the point of all the ridiculous rituals, only to end up wearing a Dracula cloak and a hat that looked like it might be put to better use by a plasterer. The drinking had held some attractions, it was true, as had the possibility of high-class tottie looking for a bit of rough; but not the drugs or the drawing of dole money during the holidays. Ray's dad would have booted him out of the house if he'd ever gone 'on the social'.

It was Ray's dad's firm belief, and you only had to cast your eyes eastwards for proof, that mankind's greatest invention was capitalism. To Meadows Senior, the world was made up of two types of people, those who sold and those who were sold to, and he was firmly in the former camp. So, it was little surprise that, like his dad, Ray had become a salesman; although not of the travelling variety, his ambitions being directed towards the less tangible and knackering.

The way Ray had seen it, while everyone else was busy flushing three years down the khazi, he had an opportunity to get a jump-start on the serious task of making some proper dosh. What would people always need? Security. What provided security? Money. Ray was going to make something of himself in the changing world of personal finance.

------------------------------ ✷ ------------------------------

David Lu had followed the path put in front of him and achieved first-class honours in medicine from Edinburgh. So far, so predictable. What no one could have foreseen was that the same self-effacing, largely anonymous member of the Class of '77 would be the first to get himself a wife.

And not just any wife. Mary Langley had been one of the girls from the very top of any set of drawers, someone any impartial observer would have judged to be way out of David's league. One of the coterie of girls who'd first come to everyone's attention during the swimming pool days, along with Susie Hamilton, Fiona Stott, Shirley Tweedie and, of course, Matron's daughter, Mary Langley was blessed with a sensuous mouth, deep emerald eyes and sandy blonde hair that fell in waves around her face like a Greek statue. She seemed to float among her contemporaries with the air of someone born to ascendancy in the pack; not in an arrogant way, more as someone whose good looks and natural grace were part of her birthright.

David had admired her from a distance, but that was all. She'd seemed more interested in horses, a passion her parents had indulged all through her teenage years, leaving precious little room for boys. Her lack of availability had only seemed to add to her allure, however. She seemed to positively exude confidence in the same way a thoroughbred horse poured out sweat after a long gallop, the sort of confidence that only came with good breeding and a good education, and it had been this very confidence that had made her seem so elusive, yet so attractive at the same time.

In short, Mary Langley was impossibly beautiful and sexy. David Lu, on the other hand, was short and Chinese, with not a lot in his favour in the looks department. He was also terminally shy, and his eyes had a habit of blinking rapidly, as if they were sending out

Morse code messages, whenever he felt out of his depth. David Lu had kept his profile so low during school it had been shadow-flat, so it had come as an amazing surprise when Mary had invited him to her twenty-first birthday party. She'd just become a veterinary nurse, joining a practice owned by a friend of her father's, and was loving the sense of freedom and making her own decisions. He, meanwhile, was still only in the foothills of his long climb up the seven-year mountain to doctorhood.

The party had been a predictably lavish affair held in a marquee on the lawns of the family's Georgian pile, presided over by Mary's mother, Sally. Sally Langley was one of those women whose natural countenance appeared to be perpetually on the edge of disapproval, only lighting up occasionally into what David called automatic smiles. Her perfectly groomed hair hinted either at daily visits to her salon or, more likely, a wig.

Long trestle tables with white tablecloths had been set out on the lawn, with hired catering, chairs lining each side and waiting staff serving the guests, as if they were fully fledged adults, which he supposed they now were. Unfortunately, the chairs only had thin metal legs which lacked stoppers on their ends, and David had been placed on an especially soggy patch of grass that had failed to dry out after recent rain.

As a result, his chair had begun to sink; a slow but inexorable process involving a gradual tilt, as if he was a barometer experiencing low pressure. This being a formal black-tie affair, David had been reluctant to stand and resite the chair for fear that others would expect a speech from him, so he'd suffered quietly in silence as the table's edge got steadily nearer to his chin, digging his heels into the grass in an effort to impede his progress; an effort thwarted by his heels constantly slipping as his balance altered. The seafood cocktail starter passed without incident, but by the time the waiters came by with the red wine, ready for the main course of beef Wellington, his eyeline was level with the tops of the freesias in the vases placed down the centre of the table.

A trip to the loo had been an option, during which he could have sought out some coasters or folded up some toilet paper – anything to put under the bottom of the chair legs – but this option had been denied him when one of the legs met a hidden stone, pausing it in its progress, but not the other three, which, if anything, seemed to speed up. As a consequence, he'd begun to tip. A few minutes later, David found himself sliding gracefully off the plastic seat and on to the damp grass below.

Anyone else might have been able to laugh it off, but anyone else probably wouldn't have been so unlucky in the first place, and anyone else would almost certainly not have hit a patch of mud the colour of lightly-milked coffee. The result had been a perfect brown line down one half of his hired suit and one side of his face.

Any laughter had been stifled by Mary's well-bred concern for her guest. Sat at the opposite end of the table, she'd watched the whole scene unfold and with every drooping inch her concern and admiration for his stoicism, which came across to her as really quite sweet, had blossomed. Almost as soon as David had hit the deck she was up and running elegantly towards him, reaching him first and scooping him up in her surprisingly strong arms, leading him into the house with no concern, it seemed, for the possibility of mud transferring itself on to her own florid Laura Ashley ensemble.

Mary hadn't had to take personal control of the mopping up – she could have just shown him the bathroom and supplied him with towels – but she did so nevertheless. The simple act of dabbing his face with a wet facecloth had felt strangely intimate, and an unexpected surge of excitement passed through her as she cleaned him up, her face only inches from his – a sensation she didn't think was down to the Old Spice he was wearing. She'd found a replacement dinner suit from her dad's dressing room, which, although not a perfect fit, was fine so long as he used a belt, rolled up the trouser bottoms and left the jacket on the back of his chair. When they returned to the table everyone else had finished their beef Wellington, the waiters having been assured that they could serve by Mary's mother, who was certain that Mary would surely be back shortly after tending to the Chinese boy, whose name she could never remember.

Within weeks, she was to become a lot more familiar with David's name: both his Christian name, if indeed he was a Christian – something she had yet to find out – and his surname. The prospect of Mary Langley becoming Mary Lu was, to her mind at least, unthinkable – she wasn't a country and western singer – but over the course of the following year the unthinkable became merely ridiculous, then evolved through degrees ranging from silly to impracticable, until finally becoming a very real possibility. After that, Sally Langley began to form back-up plans. Having ditched the option of a double-barrelled Langley-Lu, or indeed Lu-Langley, she wondered aloud about the chances of changing the name by deed poll. All this before she'd even allowed herself to contemplate what any children might look like.

Sally Langley's concern was not without foundation. Within a year, the marquee hirers were back, this time armed, at the groom's suggestion, with wooden staging, and Mary Langley gained the simpler name her mother had feared. The small consolation that her daughter hadn't had to change the monogram on the front of her case of veterinary instruments didn't even begin to make up for her disappointment.

-------------------------------- ✳ --------------------------------

Not everyone had narrowed their options to the binary paths of jobs or university. True to form, Jake Peterson had opted for something else altogether, and almost as much as a surprise had been the fate of their year's head boy, Tom Joules. Tom never had any expectation of becoming head boy, and it had come as a complete surprise when he received a message summoning him to the headmaster's study. He'd assumed there was a query over his UCCA reference and therefore had been fairly relaxed about the appointment; although, of course, a meeting with the headmaster was never something to take lightly.

Up until that landmark day, Tom had been the kind of boy

who no one really noticed, and certainly not the sort who received requests for meetings with the headmaster. Six years into school, he knew no one would ever regard him as a bloke; he found swearing unnecessary, for example, as well as extremely uncomfortable. Instead, when exasperated he always used alternatives which hinted at an actual expletive, without actually saying it. This gave him the satisfaction of letting off steam without the embarrassment, although for some unknown reason his alternatives always tended to revolve around foodstuffs, such as fudge or sherbet.

Tall, with a classic runner's physique, Tom had been focused on getting a university place at Durham, or maybe Bristol, to study physics. Once he'd got over the shock of the offer to become head boy (although in truth it was more of a royal command than a suggestion), Tom had seen the logic of it. The position typically went to the captain of the First XV, but even Tom could see why the Head had wanted to defy convention for their year. Sport had to feature somewhere – it just did – and the orienteering team's recent successes at the national championships had raised Tom's profile in that area. So what if there'd been only four people in the team: he'd still been their captain, and had demonstrated leadership qualities in a demanding environment.

Tom had also understood that from the Head's point of view, his peer group may have been seen as, well, tricky. More charitable members of the teaching staff might have described them as spirited or challenging, but these phrases were really euphemisms for 'awkward buggers'. Equally, Tom had realized he was probably getting the job because he was regarded as a 'safe pair of hands'.

His parents' reaction had been to see it as an opportunity to enhance his university prospects. Oxford had been mentioned, and as his application proceeded Tom began to understand that this was part of an unspoken deal, as an extremely positive testimonial from the headmaster, accompanied by optimistic grade predictions from his subject heads, led to a fairly innocuous interview at the Head's old college, followed by a low-grade offer.

The actual reality of becoming accepted as head boy had been less smooth. While those lower down the school had paid him some respect, relations among his peers had stayed much the same. If anything, they'd probably deteriorated. Those who might possibly have spoken to him before his appointment showed less inclination to do so once he sported the head boy pin in his lapel, and as a consequence he spent much of his time cooped up in the small lockable office he'd been provided with on the second floor of the centre, originally a bathroom, listening to the muffled sounds of others enjoying themselves. To make matters even worse, he had that barbarian Ray Meadows foisted on him as his deputy, which meant they had to spend a fair bit of time together on admin and other chores such as arranging prefect rounds.

To be fair, Ray had been all right, taking his failure to get the top job rather stoically and knuckling down to the demands of the role of deputy with surprising alacrity. They evolved into a reasonable double act, their different styles complementing each other, with Tom supplying the calm decision-making and Ray's sheer physical presence, along with a hand-picked selection of acolyte prefects, acting as useful enforcers when required.

If walking this tightrope hadn't been enough, there was the excessive number of incidents that seemed to converge in his year, which sometimes made him feel like he was trying to control a pack of deaf dogs. In the end, this unholy combination of factors had an inevitable impact on his final grades. In the end it was just as well he was sitting on a low offer, as Oxford took him despite the fact that he failed to make even that; a process greased, he suspected, by a further intervention from the Head.

If maintaining his balance while standing at the pinnacle of his school had been a challenge, tip-toeing around the summit of the university system proved to him that there was only one way for him to go: down. He felt completely lost. The people, the work, the whole system, and how everyone except him seemed to know instinctively how it all worked, all seemed too much to a simple boy from a very ordinary home. He tried to find solace at the University Athletic Club but discovered that even there, compared to others, his abilities were, at best, mediocre.

By Easter of the first year, he'd dropped out. Although the initial emotion had been disappointment, both his own and that he'd absorbed from his parents, relief – almost euphoria – followed. For a few weeks he felt energized like he hadn't felt in ages; if ever. Released from responsibilities imposed by others and free to do as he wanted, he discovered pubs big-time, and ran. And ran, and ran.

Evenings were spent creating circuits of increasing difficulty and the days spent mastering them. Five miles became seven, which turned into ten and then fifteen. Hills became steeper and more frequent, terrain more difficult and demanding. The next logical step was combining the running with his newest obsession, so he bought a copy of the *Good Beer Guide* and created pub runs: like pub crawls, but much more energetic. The running seemed to vent off both the alcohol and the calories, allowing him to remain whippet-thin. In reality, though, in between all the running and drinking he wasn't finding enough time to eat, and his features began to sink into his head, giving him a skull-like appearance; and beneath his vest, his ribs became more and more prominent, such that anyone with a couple of small rubber hammers could have banged out a decent rendition of *The Lion Sleeps Tonight*.

When the emergency services had found him on the top of Munston Moor in a state of physical exhaustion, vomit down the front of his running vest, urine down the front of his shorts and blood trickling out of his ears, it was generally agreed that something had to be done.

------------------------------ ✸ ------------------------------

Tom and Jake were very much the exceptions, however. Reggie Richardson was more the sort of young gentleman the Red Coat liked to put forward as an example of what it aspired to produce, the sort of ORC they featured in the school magazine, or tap up for money at some point in the future.

Reggie had spent school always slightly on the edge of other peoples' groupings: the sports set, the swimming pool crowd, the prefects. Despite all this, he still counted the friends he'd made at school as those he felt closest to. He'd come to the conclusion that if the friendships formed at school were held together with Evo-Stik, those from university had all the permanence of the adhesive on an old envelope. The most tangible thing Reggie had taken away from university, other than his degree, had been a thicker waistline: a feature not totally unconnected with his expanded capacity to drink. This came as something of a shock, as never before had he needed to watch his weight; but, then again, he was never really part of the underage pub crowd – his mum would have had a fit if she ever smelt booze on his breath.

All that said, there was no doubt that without university he wouldn't have been scooped up as part of the 1980 graduate intake at a major retail bank, the recipient of a reasonable salary of £8,500 a year plus annual bonus. Life instantly became pretty good, and, as he reflected on it, Reggie was happy to concede that a lot of this was down to the grounding he'd received at the old alma mater, as he guided the extended bonnet of his dad's Ford Capri through the gates of that institution and looked for a place to park in the upper playground. Access to free parking in the centre of town outside school hours was a perk accorded to OCRs, although more through convention than anything actually written down.

Extricating himself from the low seat, and having made sure all the interior locks were down, he thanked God he'd taken a decent subject; unlike some of the arty-farties from his year who'd struggled to get on the employment ladder. The opening year of the decade wasn't a good time to approach the job market if your degree was as meaningful as a prossie's kiss, and Reggie understood, but couldn't necessarily agree with, the anger many of his ex-school friends directed towards the new government. Maybe they were unlucky their graduation year had coincided with the precise moment the economy had imploded, forcing many businesses to conduct that employee spring clean they'd been putting off since forever. On the other hand,

Reggie was a signed-up member of the club that said you made your own luck in life.

It had felt odd to be back in the upper playground, the place where the masters used to park their cars, swerving their Minis and 2CVs through the gates at a quarter to nine in the morning with a healthy disregard for the safety of any boys playing tennis ball football, and where they'd put in countless miles of square-bashing on Wednesday afternoons. Some things never changed though, Reggie told himself, as he was hit by the smell of disinfectant oozing out from the outdoor toilets separating the playground from the quad. A glance up at the meagre sodium glare from the streetlamp near the main entrance suggested there was snow in the air, so Reggie pulled the hood of his duffel coat up and strode determinedly towards its guiding light.

As he neared the gate he was almost struck, quite literally, by the past, as two round headlamps mounted the shallow kerbstone and aimed straight for him, like a gunner with his sights firmly set. Reggie took a sudden step back just as the driver of the car, which he now recognized as an old MG, belatedly blew his horn. Even in this the poor light, Reggie could see the car was scarred with the customary rust. There'd never been any real danger, although there might have been if the whole incident had taken place a second or two later. The MG screeched to a halt and the driver leapt out, a large man wearing a Barbour waxed jacket with the corduroy collar turned up and a matching flat cap.

'Nearly got you there, you old bugger!' the owner of the cap and driver of the car yelled, and Reggie immediately connected the voice to Ray Meadows, erstwhile school bully and knuckle-dragger, but these days, it seemed, eager to be everyone's pal, judging by the number of letters he'd been getting from him. Ray advanced towards him and stretched out his arm as if challenging Reggie to a round of rock paper scissors, and it took Reggie a while to realize Ray was offering his hand.

He took it, receiving a steam- engine handshake in return. Reggie couldn't remember ever shaking the hand of a school friend before.

'Ray, good to see you,' Reggie lied, aware that he was now condemned to walk with this man to the restaurant where that year's reunion meal was due to take place, and, as they did so, he began to formulate strategies for making sure they didn't end up sitting together.

------------------------------ ✻ ------------------------------

The annual school reunion had fallen into a regular pattern without anyone really noticing. The first meal took place in Easter '78, following on from the infamous night at the Lamb and Mint Sauce, and was put together by the nucleus of schoolmates who were still around town; either because they'd stayed on for an extra term to prepare for and sit the Oxbridge exams, or because they were on a gap year. A handful, like Ray, had gone straight into jobs, one or two into a family business, and practically everyone still counted their parents' house as home.

For the majority who'd gone to university, the Easter holidays represented something of a hole in their diaries. Most still lived in halls and were obliged to come home, but the short holiday didn't really justify getting a job – even if there had been any available, or the will to take one. They did have an option to read around their subject, it was true, but there were only so many books you could pack around your washing and still lift your bag on to a train. So a meal out with a few old chums was worth extending the overdraft for, if only to relieve some of the boredom. When it came to tracking people down, the one thing they hadn't done was contact the school. There was little doubt they'd still be *personae non gratae* there after what had happened.

Ray had taken it upon himself to fix up the initial reunion meal at a local hotel and attracted nearly half the entire year, including 'Fingers' Dalgliesh who, unbeknownst to anyone else, had turned up an hour beforehand to make sure all the cutlery was set straight. Sitting at a single long table with starched white linen, they'd been served by nervous waitresses wearing black dresses with tiny white aprons; jumpy not so much through lack of experience, but because the guests kept making feints at their backsides. In Reggie Richardson's opinion, the food had been distinctly average, but most had come for the company and comfort of old familiarity, not the food; a view confirmed when a group at one end of the table set about eating the daffodils the restaurant had thoughtfully provided in small vases along the table's length.

The meal was a success. The waitresses left unscathed, physically at least, and old acquaintance had been not been forgotten. Most notably, perhaps, copious amounts of alcohol had also been consumed, some of which was returned later, with interest, in the restaurant's facilities. It was just after someone suggested port that the hubbub of conversation was rent by the grating sound of a chair scraping back on the wooden floor in a manner that conveyed both purpose and intent. Slowly, and with deliberate care, a decidedly inebriated Les Andrew rose to his feet, the top of his head almost disappearing into the cumulous cloud of smoke being constantly refreshed by Messrs Benson and Hedges, enhanced by the occasional Hamlet slim panatela.

'Gentlemen,' Les half-shouted, in an effort to gain everyone's attention. His sheer presence usually being enough to command attention, it came as something of a surprise to him to realize that half the room were still ignoring him. Luckily, at that moment his chair, knocked off-balance when he got up, and now wobbling, decided to stop prevaricating and finally fell on to the floor, causing one of the nervous waitresses to drop a pile of dirty plates. Les seized his moment.

'Gentlemen,' he repeated, winding himself up to some kind of crescendo. 'I'm sure you'll all agree we've had a brilliant evening.' He paused, waiting for a parliamentary descant of *hear hears,* and hiding his disappointment well when none came. Seemingly unfazed by this development, he continued, a distinct hint of Winston Churchill beginning to creep into his delivery.

'Gentlemen! Never has such a band of brothers been known in the history of the Red Coat School …' This, to his surprise, was greeted with the chorus of *hear hears* he'd expected earlier. He accepted them with a nod and continued: '... and it is fitting that we have come together to mark it.'

At this point the kitchen doors swung open and banged against the walls either side of them, revealing the sight of an angry restaurant manager, his whole demeanour sending out the single message that he was ready to engage in battle. Taken aback by the formality of the scene before him, he retreated into the kitchen; a decision driven to a large extent by the sight of fifty pairs of eyes slowly turning towards him. Les simply raised an eyebrow and resumed his flow.

'For me, tonight goes to show ...' he paused for effect, before continuing, 'that the bonds of friendship, forged in the fire of adolescence, experience and challenge against authority, will resist the corroding effects of time.'

'Watch a hells he bang, banging on 'bout?' a decidedly drunk Simon Grant struggled to ask, as if his small mouth was having trouble forming the words, before he'd been shushed by an attentive Ben Bradshaw, who seemed to be clinging on to every word Les was trying to get out.

The silence that followed could have been a good or bad thing: it was difficult to tell. In an attempt to gauge how well he was going down, he threw a glance towards his best friend, Philip Christopher, who smiled benignly back at him as if in some kind of happy trance. Les concluded his audience was stunned by his eloquence and continued, blissfully unaware of the mouths around him silently, and quizzically, forming the words 'bonds of friendship' through grimaces and cigar smoke.

'Gentlemen, at this time of year people come together to recognize our Lord's Last Supper.' By this point, many had started to wonder where he was going with this: was he going to lead them in prayer?

'I say to you that this should not be *our* last supper!' The emphasis on 'our' had the desired effect and produced a murmur of approval. 'My suggestion to all those gathered here is that we make this a regular event. Let us meet once a year in perpetuity and keep the flame of our comradeship alive ...' but by this point a round of applause had started up, leaving Les to shout out a final 'forever!' over the growing sounds of approval.

Cheers, claps and the rare daffodil still left uneaten were by then filling the air, and with very little further discussion it was agreed that a central list of addresses and phone numbers be compiled and an informal society be established: the Seventy-Seven Society, open to all who'd completed their formal sixth-form education at the Red Coat School in the year in question.

It was further agreed that the names of those not able to make that evening's meal would be gathered and added to the list, and that a follow-up session should happen some time between Christmas and New Year, although it was generally accepted that they would have to find a new venue. Glasses were raised and, even though most were empty by then, toasts were made to friendship.

The next morning, it was unlikely many had a precise recollection of what it was they'd agreed to, and most of those who did remember probably suspected that nothing would ever become of it – but they were wrong.

The Seventy-Seven Society meals took root as easily and as effortlessly (although Ray may had begged to differ) as they had begun, and gradually became a fixture on the calendar of many of those qualified to attend. The formula was kept simple: an invitation – in the early days, taking the mickey out of one of the members of the society – setting out a time, date and place, with all monies sorted out on the night.

If the fact that the reunions gained the status they did so quickly came as a pleasant surprise to some, how they would evolve, and their impact on the lives of everyone involved, would have seemed inconceivable. Les Andrew was right in supposing that the Class of '77 would succeed in rising above mediocrity. What no one could have predicted was the Armageddon they would unleash in doing so.

---------------------------- �֍ ----------------------------

If one was to analyse it (and can there be a group of schoolboys whose lives have been examined more microscopically?), perhaps Tom Joules and Jake Peterson shared as many similarities that united them as differences that divided them. On the principle that opposites attract but likes repel, this may explain why Jake was such a complete pain in the neck during Tom's tenure as head boy. Like Tom, Jake wasn't part of any particular crowd, he was in a set of one. Like Tom, he was tall for his age, although he seemed to eschew any opportunity to turn this to any sporting advantage, and again, like Tom, Jake preferred to plough his own furrow. One of the ironies of the events that followed, therefore, was how, within a few short years, Tom would find himself in the position of having to eulogize him.

It is impossible to be definitive on how much of what followed would have happened without Jake Peterson's contribution. That he did certain things and they had ramifications is indisputable, but perhaps as much of his impact lay in the ripples he set off as the acts themselves.

Jake never actively sought the support of others; his actions were always spurred by a personal sense of perceived wrong or injustice. If others agreed, that was fine, but he didn't actively solicit their support. His driver was passion, although how this was directed, or where it came from, could often be a mystery. He was, in many ways, the classic rebel looking for a cause. Another irony in this story therefore, is that it was the school, or rather the headmaster, who provided Jake's biggest, and most notorious, cause.

Everyone knew that the Red Coat was being assailed from all sides in the great education debate and that its destiny was probably to become an independent private institution. This was something most interested parties accepted as unfortunate, but the overriding sense was not just that the state-run party was over, but the glasses and paper plates had all been binned, and the Hoover was about to be fired up.

For someone like Jake, the whole education debate represented something of a dilemma. Part of his inner philosophy told him that he should revile all private schools simply on principle, and that the comprehensive system was the way forward. On the other hand, he couldn't deny that the unique mix the Red Coat's funding system allowed to come together was something to be placed in the positive column. The school brought together boys whose backgrounds ranged from high privilege to council estates and everything in between, generating a social experiment along the way that created a special atmosphere, a genuine lack of pretentiousness and a quality of discussion that was hard to beat. He enjoyed being at the Red Coat and didn't want to see it change. At the same time, the Labour government he had himself campaigned so hard to help get into power were set four-square against direct grant schools. It was a tough one.

No one was surprised when it was announced that the school's governors had declared themselves in favour of going totally independent, with the caveat that they would establish a trust fund, aiming to ensure that five per cent of the intake could attend the school regardless of their parents' ability to pay. What did come as a surprise was the rabbit the HM pulled out of the hat with his plan to hold a referendum on the matter.

At the time referendums were all the rage, with the Great British public having been asked to state their view 'once and for all' the year before on being part of the EEC. While this experiment in direct democracy had enjoyed mixed reviews, there was a general feeling in the air that such mechanisms represented the future, and being a hip and trendy leader, the dear old HM had adopted it with relish.

His motives, to most, seemed clear enough. With the expected endorsement of those actually going through the school, a sense of urgency would be injected into the process, putting a rocket up the backsides of the usually sluggish officials at the local education authority. The head's plan was perfect, except for one little detail: it hadn't taken into account Jake Peterson's fervour for natural justice. On hearing plans for the referendum, Jake compared the exercise less to the direct democracy of Harold Wilson, and more to the plebiscites of Adolf Hitler. Calling the whole exercise a ruse rather than a referendum, he declared that the boys weren't so much being asked to state a view, but rather being asked to endorse a decision that effectively had already been made. He argued for, and to be fair to the school, was given, a platform to argue against the motion.

At this point Jake's perennial problem resurfaced. As with many rebels, he was absolutely clear on what he didn't want, but he didn't really know what he did want. For Jake, however, this was but a minor inconvenience, and he disappeared for a couple of days to devise his response. When it came, it was both deceptively simple on the surface and fiendishly clever at how striking another of the school's shibboleths: its worship of sport.

The school owned acres of real estate in the heart of the town that was probably worth tens of millions of pounds at least, according to the valuations Jake had obtained from one of the local estate agents. Jake argued that these could be sold to endow a foundation ensuring that not five, but the current 50 per cent of boys could still attend without paying fees. In short, the school could effectively be preserved as it was; all it had to do was sacrifice a few measly rugger pitches.

His position outlined, Jake set to his campaigning with gusto, putting the demands of his A-levels to one side in favour of the greater good. Many were prepared to back him out of sheer devilment; others were convinced by his rhetoric as, every lunchtime, come rain or shine, he adopted a corner of the quad as his own personal Speaker's Corner to outline his ideas. He also harnessed the power of the Xerox machine in the local copy shop to produce, at his own expense, a number of A4-sized 'No!' posters that he started to pin up around the school.

Although he was by nature a lone campaigner, such was the scale of his task that Jake found it hard to refuse the support of his occasional sparring partner, and sometime ally, Stalin Henderson. Stalin had been Stalin for so long that most of his fellow pupils had to stop to remember his first name, the rather disappointing Derek.

Red Coat's very own Stalin was a young man of strong but predictable views, mostly harvested from the pages of the *Militant* newspaper. Although he was regarded as a pain in the backside by most teachers, they were used to handling his type, one or two examples of which most years seemed to produce. Typically they spouted well-rehearsed arguments using few ideas of their own, which made them relatively easy to manage. In other words, they were the absolute opposite to Jake Paterson.

The campaign for a 'No' vote remained very much Jake's baby, with Stalin acting as his agent or, if one was being less charitable, his enforcer, replacing torn-down posters, finding the funds for the Xeroxing and proselytizing among the more impressionable lower forms. Having unleashed the democratic beast, it was difficult for the governing body to suppress their efforts, but as the campaign went on, they showed increasing signs of being rattled and began to fight back with their own rallies, held in the school hall and led by members of staff it was thought the boys might respect. Quite suddenly the school was engulfed in an exercise of genuine democracy, with the added complication of some real debate.

In the absence of opinion polls, it was difficult to see how successful Jake and Stalin were being, so in a spirit of intellectual curiosity mingled with a dose of devilry, George Rowlands decided to conduct one. Soon, the collective spirit that had been nurtured over the years, crystallized through the CCF, tempered at the swimming pool, nursed through the transition to the lower sixth, and finally cemented in the search for the Sneaky Shitter, came to fruition. All the creativity, camaraderie and sense of challenge that had characterized the year as it had worked its way through the school came to the surface. Jake seemed to symbolize the year and the individuality they stood for, so it seemed reasonable that he should have their support.

Jake's campaign gained momentum, and whatever new tricks the staff could think of to stop it only had the effect of providing new converts to the cause. On the eve of the referendum itself, George Rowlands' opinion polls, now taken every other day at the school gate and analysed overnight for publication on more posters the next day, indicated a majority of 65 per cent in favour of a 'No' vote. It came as something of a shock, therefore, when the actual results, given the next day, showed 56 per cent in favour of the governors' plan, with 10 per cent spoiled papers.

What had seemed an epoch-defining decision suddenly popped like a birthday balloon once the result was announced. A welcome diversion; a funfair that had come into town for a while and then moved on. There seemed little point in challenging the figures; Jake had made the fundamental mistake of those relying on passion: assuming his opponent would fight fair; and he hadn't asked to be present at the count.

The fun over, it quickly became time to knuckle down. Jake and all his causes faded into memory and, again like Tom, it came as no surprise down the line when his extra-curricular activities were seen as contributory factors to his paltry two D A-level grades: not enough for university. Jake being Jake, a reaction was expected, and he duly delivered.

Asked to state Jake's least likely destination, to a man his friends would have said the army, so perhaps no one should have been shocked when that was exactly where he went. It could have been that he had a grand plan of reform from within. Equally, he may have seen it as a stepping stone to something more worthy, or maybe in the end he simply wanted to travel the world and learn a trade. All anyone knew was that he completely disappeared off the radar after school, and that he would probably reappear at some point in the future.

What no one anticipated was how quickly, or the circumstances in which he would do so.

1984

While the first of the school reunion dinners had coincided with Tom Joules's nadir (he'd been far too unwell to attend), the dinner two years later marked the beginning of his rehabilitation. His psychiatrist had suggested it might be a good idea to go along, believing that by doing so he might be able to lay some of his issues to rest. Tom had been sceptical, but he did feel it was time to re-enter the world, and given the paucity of his social network the meal offered a good opportunity. He made a deal with the doctor that he wouldn't drink and duly accepted the invitation, the cover of which for some unfathomable reason had a picture of Jeff Stone alongside one of Prince Charles, with the caption 'Never seen together in the same room'.

As it turned out, the dinner resulted in a fresh start in more ways than one. On arriving, Tom's initial response was that the turnout was patchy, and when he started asking questions he was reunited with Ray Meadows, who, pint in one hand and panatela in the other, had instantly suggested Tom might want to become a kind of secretary to the project; a keeper of the flame, as it were.

To Tom this made perfect sense, given his status as their head boy and, more importantly, the practical advantage he offered of being on the ground, just as others were beginning to disperse geographically. He saw the administration and general paperwork that came with the new role as a small repayment for the uncharacteristic sensitivity he'd been shown by everyone (they must all have known what had happened to him), especially by Ray. Of course, there was also an opportunity to make the whole thing more professional, track down the missing bodies, make it all more complete. His pleasure may have been diluted if he'd been able to tune into the thoughts of those urging him to take the role on; namely that he was the perfect candidate, mainly because no one else wanted to do it.

Maybe if his doctor had been able to foresee this development he may have advised against attendance, but Tom seemed to embrace and enjoy the duties his new role conferred, imposing order where it wouldn't have occurred spontaneously, and enjoying the sense of being genuinely recognized by his peers, probably for the first time.

As often happens in life, one piece of good fortune was followed shortly by another, as Tom received a call from Clive Porter, the DHM from school, wondering if he might be interested in a teaching role as a physics assistant until the exams, with the possibility of a full-time position further down the line. A collector of responsibilities, as well as DHM and head of sixth form, Clive Porter was also head of sciences. It was largely a co-ordinating role: Clive Porter's qualifications (or rather lack of them) disqualified him from heading any of the actual subjects encompassed by 'Sciences', but his ability as an organizer of timetables and manager of resources was second to none, allowing the teachers under his umbrella to spend their time actually teaching.

For Tom, this came as manna from heaven. Three years spent learning on the job would be much more valuable than a degree and enable him to brush up his knowledge at the same time. As head boy, he'd occasionally been summoned to the staff room – the knocked-through downstairs of one of the old houses on the quad – but never beyond the porch, which acted as a sort of airlock between teachers and pupils. It had therefore felt peculiar to cross that threshold as a teacher, albeit a trainee, but with time it gained a sense of being natural, so Tom felt his equilibrium returning; a process aided by the DHM, or Clive as he now got to call him, taking Tom under his wing until he was ready to fly on his own.

As his confidence returned, Tom took it upon himself to introduce a note of greater formality into the meals, including a suggestion that lounge suits would be appropriate garb. At the same time, he formalized the convention of having the meal between Christmas and New Year, when most people were back with their parents for the festivities. Another innovation was a short speech between the dessert and liqueurs; something Tom found himself spending increasing amounts of time preparing in the same way a vicar might compose a sermon, although a better analogy might have been parish notices, as Tom confined himself to relaying news about fellow members, often gathered from letters and phone calls from those unable to make the meal. This he saw as an important service, keeping the spirit of the year going, even if not everyone could come to the meals. As his rehabilitation grew in strength, Tom found himself looking forward to October, when he could begin to plan the next supper.

His first year in charge had been declared a resounding success, so Tom wasn't too surprised when he was confronted with a test of his growing confidence the following year. It had started as a casual remark in the staff room which, when he followed it up, turned out to be true. Now it was his self-ordained responsibility to relay to his classmates what he'd found out. It had been bound to happen sometime, of course, but he had never, ever contemplated it happening so soon; after all, it was only seven years since they'd all been at school.

Deciding it was best to get it over with, Tom cleared his throat and tapped the side of his water glass with a knife to gain everyone's attention. Thinking about it beforehand, Tom had concluded that he'd get the usual stuff out of the way first, a sort of warm-up, before dropping his bombshell. As he stood up he felt a sudden stab of pain in his guts, as if someone had taken two ends of his entrails and pulled them together to tie a knot. Taking a deep breath, he composed himself and began, perhaps slightly too loudly, before going through his notes and finally reaching the moment he couldn't avoid.

'Finally, gentlemen, I'm afraid I have some *really* sad news to pass on.' He put a strong accent on the *really*, as if the word was italicized, which seemed to get the room's attention. 'I have received word that our classmate and good friend Jake Peterson has been a casualty of the recent war in the Falklands.' These few words caused a blanket of silence to fall suddenly on the room.

Although death was a concept most were familiar with, it wasn't one many of the diners had much direct experience of. Some had lost a grandparent, and one or two a parent, but they were the minority. Death was something abstract, something in the realm of old people, of no direct concern to fit and healthy young men like themselves. The thought that someone had been born, gone all the way through school and then simply disappeared forever, like a burst bubble, was impossible to get their heads around; especially when the heads involved had each consumed the best part of a bottle of wine, and probably a pint or two of real ale before that.

What happened next may have been an overreaction, a way of containing and dealing with what they'd just been told through action. A grief mechanism. Equally, it could have been a genuine response made by compassionate human beings. All that can be said with certainty was that it was a response, and one that was to reverberate across all their lives.

Jake Peterson, the year's conscience, its most vocal rebel, had shockingly become its first victim. Jake Peterson, the most unlikely of soldiers, dead. Departed. Passed on. No more. While this terrible truth sank in, Tom delivered the facts, scant though they were, the army having been conservative with details. Jake had been found with a fatal bullet wound in his head, at his Dorset barracks. Not strictly a victim of the war itself, of course – he hadn't been blown up by an Exocet or fallen victim to a sniper on Goose Green – but although everyone in the room knew what these cold facts implied, none wanted to voice it.

Instead, most were thinking the same thoughts: how Jake would have been facing an irresolvable dilemma. The prospect of a full-scale modern colonial war; one with an aircraft carrier, fighter jets and bombs, maybe even nuclear weapons, ranged against a second-rate power on the other side of the world. Starved of any sense of justice or moral authority, and powerless to do anything, he'd taken the ultimate course of action.

Sensing the mood of the room, Tom sensibly decided to pocket the short tribute he'd jotted down in note form on a set of index cards, and surprised himself by simply raising his glass of sparkling water and proposing a spontaneous toast.

'Gentlemen, to Jake Peterson. Our local hero.'

As everyone around the table stood, the noise made by their collective chairs scraping against the hard wooden flooring of the hotel's function suite echoed down the corridor outside, and after a brief reflective silence, everyone followed Tom in raising their glasses and repeating: 'Jake Peterson. Our local hero.' Although, unlike Tom, those around the table had made sure they had something worth drinking in their glass.

A fresh stillness fell on the room following this salute, a contemplative silence broken only by the ticking of an old grandfather clock on the other side of the door, and more scraping of wood against wood as the assembled young men began to sit down. Holding the silence triggered memories among many of them of the annual Remembrance Day ceremony at the school's war memorial, and was held for at least the minute required of them on those occasions. During this period, a reflection, unshared in order not to speak ill of the dead, was that perhaps the world had never been good enough for poor old Jake, who'd found his own way out. Most of those present had their chins nestled firmly at the tops of their chests as they spent time with their inner thoughts, their eyes fixed on the sometimes swaying edge of the table, so in the end no one was quite sure who it was who broke the silence with a question.

'Is this what it's all about then?' The question came from sharply dressed Andy Thompson, whose hands were gripping the sides of the table as if he was about to start a séance. Staring straight ahead, as if deep in thought, he continued, 'I mean, at the end of the day, what's life all about?'

'Work?' Adrian Smart, still known to many around the table as Emcee, suggested, although his voice seemed to betray some uncertainty.

'Marriage?' chipped in Les Andrew.

'God! Kids?' asked 'Fingers' Dalgliesh, with one part incredulity at the very thought of children and how, well, adult that notion seemed, and the other part panic at the mess children could cause.

'Not you, obviously, Chas.' Eddie Perks chipped in to lighten the mood and was rewarded with a flicked V-sign in response. Charlie Young was well known as being camper than a scout jamboree although, curiously, where he preferred to lay his hat had never been explicitly discussed.

'Rotary Club?' Jeff 'Dumbo' Stone suggested, only half-jokingly, the light from the lamp behind him illuminating the veins in his ears.

'Policemen looking younger than us?' chirped someone from the back of the room.

'Holidays on the bloody Costa Brava,' muttered Terry Mungus.

'Incontinence pads,' came a voice, also from the back, the speaker's voice lost in a smattering of nervous laughter that momentarily broke the mood.

All of a sudden, the atmosphere was broken by a loud, animal-like howl, so dissonant from the attempts at humour to lighten the mood that it couldn't be ignored. Eyes scanned the room and alighted on Ben Bradshaw, who seemed to have lost all control. A general air of embarrassment ensued, not least from Derek 'Stalin' Henderson sitting next to him. Alone among the young men, Stalin had eschewed a suit in favour of a simple white T-shirt and a jacket with long tapered lapels. The one on the right sported a collection of badges bearing slogans such as 'Coal Not Dole', 'Support the Miners' and 'Stop Trident Now', while the one on the left had a similar set with messages stating 'Don't Blame Me, I Voted Labour' and 'Maggie Out', as well as a smaller one with a red star and the single word 'Militant'. Faced with the sobbing grown man next to him, 'Stalin' felt slightly ridiculous.

Adopting a stiff-upper-lip attitude to this interruption, Paul Briton decided to restart the flow of conversation, although he chose to dial it down a little more into serious territory.

'Fewer and fewer of us turning up to these meals every year, probably.'

This led to an immediate flurry of cigarettes being hurriedly stubbed out. Paul was that rare thing: a personable mathematician, whose gifts in the cerebral department were counterbalanced by unfortunate puffy hamster-like cheeks, which seemed to bulge out as if he was a jazz trumpeter in permanent full flow. How he'd avoided a nickname at school remained one of life's mysteries. His one saving grace was his smile, which transformed his face and stretched an impressive width when he chose to deploy it, which fortunately was often.

'Imagine it,' Paul continued, warming to his theme: 'one by one we pop our clogs until there's only a handful of us left, each year turning up wondering if it's the last time we'll ever meet, falling one by one like leaves off a tree until there's only one of us left.'

'The last man standing,' suggested Les Andrew.

'Or, more likely, sitting, probably in a wheelchair,' Paul suggested, 'sipping his liquidized meal through a straw, dribbling half of it down his chin and dropping horrendous farts without a care in the world, with no one left to share them with.'

'Wearing incontinence pads,' the persistent joker to the side repeated, this time to silence, before adding, 'pushed around by a nurse with tits to die for, which we probably would be prepared to do, just for one last …'

'All on his tod, more like,' Terry Mungus suggested.

'And then what'll be left of us?' asked Les, placing emphasis on the final word.

'How do you mean?' Addy asked, his face suggesting his imagination was still stuck with the image of the old man in his wheelchair.

'Well, us. All we've been through,' Les replied. 'Once the last one of us goes, the spirit of '77 will go with him. It'll be as if we, as a group, a year, never even existed.' He added a click of the fingers and 'Poof!' for extra effect.

After a moment of shocked silence, this thought seemed to erupt into a tornado of conversation, moving the assembly on from its previously maudlin path towards something more positive. Frustrated, and unused to self-pity, the collected young minds seemed relieved to have something constructive to apply themselves to: a way of making sure the spirit they were all there to celebrate could endure forever. A means of keeping the flame of youthful rebellion alive, something to rally around as the combined forces of adulthood that they all knew were heading their way squeezed them into conformity. What had started as a dinner and was briefly in danger of becoming a wake, now became a meeting; a feeling reinforced by the formal clothing and the unspoken selection of Tom as chairman, through whom suggestions and remarks were channelled.

A single thought dominated the discussion: how to convert the common experience they'd all shared into something permanent, something tangible. To create something palpable out of the indefinable sense of common cause they'd shared, both at school and, to a lesser extent, since. The focus was on the need to create something they could get their arms around, to touch, smell and see. This then morphed into practicalities and the need to create a pool of money in order to do something; even if they were still struggling with what that 'something' was.

None of them could offer any proper money, the sort their parents might have, but the realization soon dawned that this was irrelevant as they didn't need money now, but would at some distant point in the future: fifty, sixty, maybe seventy years hence. So long as at least some and eventually one of them – the last man standing – was around, then there would still be someone left to deliver the will of them all, however they eventually decided this should be achieved.

Tom fished out the index cards with Jake's eulogy from his pocket and started writing on the back of them some of the ideas erupting from the volcano of debate taking place around him. They started by attempting to come up with a name, as it was thought this would be the easy bit. The idea of the Peterson Memorial Prize was dismissed as sounding too much like a sports day trophy, something Jake would have abhorred, and anyway, it – whatever 'it' turned out to be – could hardly be described as a prize. Other ideas included the Policy, but this sounded like some kind of iffy insurance product, while the Pact sounded like a truce and the Terminal Bonus, something that might be used to reward a hitman.

Eventually Les Andrew, draining his glass as he did so, took to his feet – an act that included taking half of his chair with him before it fell from his backside like an overripe fruit. The sight reminded many of his infamous 'Last Supper' speech at their first gathering, prompting some to speculate whether he was about to offer a suggestion based on the resurrection of Jesus. Les had never quite got over the response to his 'bonds of friendship' idea when he first suggested they make the meal an annual event, and sensed an opportunity. Waiting for the room to settle down, he stood, holding his silence, and then spoke.

'Gentlemen, I give you … the Bond.' And with that simple gift bestowed, he marched towards the gents as if the matter was settled which, curiously, it was – by general acclamation.

As more drinks were sunk the meeting moved on to details. As it turned out, this was much easier than the name – the basic idea being deceptively simple, with everyone chipping in ideas and the best ones carried by consensus, which proved remarkably easy to achieve. It was agreed that everyone would pay a small subscription into a fund administered by a set of trustees. Everyone subscribing to the Bond (and it was agreed it would be possible to pay your sub even if you couldn't actually make a meal) would be entering into a contract whereby the last one to survive, the last man standing, would take on the responsibility of creating some means of passing on the baton of the spirit of '77 to succeeding generations, the exact nature of which would be decided as time went on. As the brandies started to appear it was further agreed that anyone would be free to lob in suggestions at any meal, although Tom later phrased this slightly differently in his minutes.

With the skeleton of the idea formed, a general feeling infused the room that the Bond would provide a vehicle to hold and nurture the essence of their year, to give it an annual refreshing. Privately, Tom was also pleased that it would also give their suppers greater purpose, a raison d'être that went beyond eating too much and getting drunk; an extra dimension that he heartily approved of.

Tom was also delighted to accept the role of the idea's guardian and to prepare a formal document for people to sign, as well as to get in touch with everyone he still had contact details for so that they could also be invited to join in. After years of being on the periphery, Tom finally felt involved, part of the team, accepted; and before he went to sleep that night he offered a small prayer of thanks to his Creator.

------------------------------ ✱ ------------------------------

The seminal 1984 Seventy-Seven Society dinner was equally memorable for Sam Davidson, but not in a good way. He hadn't wanted to go at all, but, as had once been pointed out to him by one of his polytechnic mates, he clearly had what had been described as unfinished business when it came to his schooldays. Apart from his friendship with Mushtaq, Sam found it hard to come up with a single positive aspect of his time at school; it had been a place where he'd existed rather than lived. Despite this, something stopped him from moving on. Maybe his mate had it right: he needed to exorcise his demons before he could really kick on with life. It was to test this theory that he'd replied in the affirmative to Tom's very formal printed invitation.

Things hadn't started well. When he arrived at the pub the first person he met was Terry Mungus, who freely shook his hand and without a hint of embarrassment admitted he didn't have a clue who Sam was. When the party moved on to the restaurant, Sam found himself manoeuvred to the end of one of the long sides of a U-shaped table, hemmed in among a group of what could only be described as scientists. This was a problem because for Sam, all scientists looked the same – something he blamed on them all wearing glasses. As a result, not only was he surrounded by people who didn't know him, but he had no idea who they were; and as the food came and went it became clear that the people around him had the same power to engage him as an opera sung in Swahili, while the food itself offered little compensation, coming less from the school of Cordon Bleu and more from the house of Berni.

Sam vaguely recognized the face of the man sitting opposite him – maybe he'd been a prefect or some sporting whizz, but his name eluded him. While potentially awkward, it didn't really matter, as he managed to maintain Sam's attention simply through the act of eating.

He seemed to regard mastication as a competitive event, chewing so enthusiastically that Sam thought there was a serious danger he was going to dislocate his jaw. Although transfixed, Sam realized there was only so long he could sneak surreptitious glances before the subject of his fascination called the police, so in a welcome lull after puddings Sam decided to excuse himself, his request to the person on his left to budge in a little so he could pass being the extent of his conversation all evening.

One of the hotel's particular charms turned out to be its old-fashioned modesty, which included an apparent desire to avoid mentioning the whereabouts of the toilets. Sam wandered past the unmanned reception and into a poorly-lit corridor, and on coming to a door with an illuminated sign above it, leant his weight on it to open it. Once inside, the spring holding it in place thumped shut as he groped for a light switch to relieve the sudden blackness he'd walked into.

The sound of a loud metallic click filled the room before any light, and when Sam finally managed to find the switch he was surprised to find himself not in the gents, but what looked like a store cupboard, painted an insipid cream colour and smelling oddly like chlorine. Even if he'd had a cat conveniently to hand, it would have been impossible to swing it. A row of shelves, stacked from floor to ceiling, filled each of the three walls before him. The one directly in front seemed at first glance to be carrying sheets, but they turned out to be neatly ironed tablecloths, while the one to the right was loaded with cruet sets and boxes upon boxes of condiment sachets: red sauce, brown sauce, vinegar and mustard (French and English), as well as salad cream and mayonnaise, each allocated their own identifying colour.

The shelves to the right were less full, although those uppermost were stacked with boxes of what turned out to be biscuits. A grey aluminium double bucket sat on the floor, slightly dented down one edge, with one side open and the other revealing a conical gap pierced with slats. A mop propped up in the open side betrayed the bucket's role in life, something confirmed by the acrid smell of Domestos that had leached into the metal over the years.

Realizing his mistake, Sam turned to leave, and it was then that the full pitilessness of his situation hit. The loud metallic click he'd heard signalled a security device. He was locked in. No amount of fumbling with the lock managed to shift it, and matters were made worse when, after what seemed like only a minute, the light switched itself off.

And so it was, that the morning after the momentous decision had been taken on what was now known as the Bond, Sam Davidson was found by a startled young woman at six in the morning, stretched out on the floor of the store cupboard, draped with tablecloths and surrounded by discarded wrappers from packets of rich tea and digestive biscuits, as well as the overwhelming smell of stale urine emanating from the aluminium bucket she'd come into the room to retrieve.

For Sam, it just about summed up his whole relationship with the Red Coat, and while it wasn't quite the closure he'd come to the meal to find, it was enough for him to pledge never to have anything to do with the school, or his old school colleagues, ever again.

------------------------------ ✳ ------------------------------

Ray, on the other hand, saw his school network as an asset, and he was often found dropping the name of one of his Red Coat connections when he was touting for work. Usually, this was when he recognized a surname of someone from school, which allowed him to ask if the potential client had a son called Andy, Mike or whatever. Not only was this a useful conversation opener when he was cold-calling, it also seemed to offer a shortcut to credibility, whether or not the person at the other end of the line happened to be related to the ex-school colleagues in question.

Ray had joined a local financial planning agency, which turned out to be a posh name for two old guys flogging insurance, assisted by their ageing assistant, Pam. With short bobbed hair and milk bottle-end glasses, Pam ticked every cliché for a spinster secretary, but she was kind to Ray, and once it became clear she was the fulcrum around which the business revolved, Ray was kind in return. He even indulged in some playful flirtation, which Pam ignored a little too dismissively. Ray guessed she was in her mid-fifties, but by his own admission he was rubbish with older women's ages.

The business was owned by twin brothers, George and William Grey, who, strictly out of hours, Ray referred to as Statler and Waldorf from *The Muppets*, partly because they liked a good grumble, but mostly because mocking them behind their back made working with them easier. The Grey brothers seemed to belong to another era, one whose values they felt obliged to perpetuate. Occasionally they mentioned their military service in the Second World War, a period of history Ray found it difficult to comprehend, and he suspected that when they raised it in his presence, it was a way of somehow putting him down; as if he and his generation would never really be worthy of the sacrifices of their own. They had taken Ray on because they liked the idea of having a young dogsbody to carry out the grunt work they were no longer willing to do. Each had his own office leading off the central reception area where Pam worked, and where an extra desk had been squeezed, a little too tightly, into one of the corners for Ray.

The offices were reached via a set of stairs that headed straight up from a door sandwiched between a Mothercare and a local undertakers', a location that opened up so many obvious jokes it wasn't even worth the effort of trying. In a rare moment of insight, the brothers had decided thirty years before, when they'd set up their business, not to name it after themselves, choosing the company name Cretum, after the Latin for 'to expand'. The name was chosen to represent the Grey brothers' aspiration to grow their customers' wealth, while the possibilities it offered for anagram lovers had flown straight over their heads.

While his ex-school friends had been cultivating the art of squeezing people into telephone boxes, Ray had cut his teeth in the then relatively straightforward world of financial products. Most work days were pretty simple and revolved around that most basic of office tools: a diary. In Cretum's case this was the large Letts Office desk diary, a hardback A4 book with red covers which became increasingly worn as the year progressed, with each week spaced over two pages inside. The top right-hand corner of each page had a small arc of perforated paper which was ceremoniously torn as the first task every Monday morning, a duty performed by Pam to signify the start of a new week. As the year progressed, this small gap progressed from an indentation into a cliff, until the new year would begin all over again. The book's importance was emphasized by the fact that it was the deluxe edition with gilt-edged pages – something Ray had only ever seen before on Bibles, a comparison that turned out to be prescient as the diary was the office's most holy of documents.

What was unusual about this particular diary was that it ran six weeks ahead of the real date, a practice that seemed to make Christmas go on forever. The reason for this was that the diary contained details of all the contracts coming up to the firm's annual review, and six weeks gave them enough notice to get in touch with the customers concerned, to visit them if absolutely necessary, to have the required discussions with brokers, and, finally, to close the deal, before sitting back and waiting for the commission.

Over the years, Statler and Waldorf had refined the process down to a fine art, but it hadn't taken Ray long to notice that, through a combination of complacency and boredom, they were losing the plot. Ray's appointment had been a sort of implicit agreement between them that their time was probably better spent on what was euphemistically called 'entertaining' both existing and, they claimed, potential clients.

Ever since their time in the womb the two brothers had enjoyed a spirit of healthy competition, which both were convinced was the driving force of their business's success and longevity. However, while they used that tension to outdo each other in winning fresh business, once Ray was in place the competitive urge was manifested in efforts to out-schmooze each other. At first Pam had tut-tutted or gently raised her eyebrows whenever one of them arrived back in the middle of the afternoon after an elongated and largely liquid lunch; but the battle lines had been drawn, and it soon became clear that each was vying with the other to make sure they got back last.

From here it was a short step for them both to realize that the only foolproof way to win this particular contest was not to come back to the office at all, a development that was to cause Pam to turn up the volume on her disapproval to a fully rounded 'harrumph', as she and Ray were left to do all the actual work.

Like the Grey brothers in their prime, Ray and Pam soon evolved into a formidable double act. But there was one small cloud on their shared horizon. The financial world was, and is, built on trust, and no one trusts their life savings to a drunk, let alone two drunks. As competition between the two brothers hotted-up, it became increasingly clear to both Ray and Pam that the business was quite literally disappearing down the urinals of the town's more refined hotels and golf clubs. During increasingly frank conversations held in the afternoons when they were on their own, Ray and Pam agreed that the way things were going, what should have been a nice little number was in danger of becoming a zero – taking their jobs with it.

Something had to be done.

And so, they hatched a plan.

1985–86

Fifty-two had always been ridiculously young to retire, especially on a public- sector pension. Even calling it a retirement was a euphemism; the truth of it was, he hadn't really been given a choice. Eight years down the line, despite all his careful planning, Harold Mitchell was living the nightmare he'd worked so hard to avoid: unemployed and unemployable, and sitting in the only armchair in what the estate agent had labelled a bedsit, but Harold called his bedshit.

Judging by the state of decoration when he'd bought it, the previous owners had loved it almost as much as he did. Magnolia-painted woodchip covered the walls and looped up over the ceilings in what seemed like a gravity-defying act of DIY, one that had produced a slight curve at the edges where the same roll of paper had been carried over. With an empty whisky glass dangling from one hand, while the other gripped the chair's arm, once again Harold Mitchell reflected on his favourite question: how had he come to this?

Sometimes he blamed the Queen, but given that she was still alive and he'd already flirted too closely with the idea of treason, he settled for her father. If only he'd been a little less fond of the coffin nails, maybe he'd have lived a bit longer; after all, his wife seemed to have the constitution of an ox.

At the heart of it all, the problem was that the Queen couldn't have had a worse year for her Silver Jubilee, or indeed a less opportune time of year to celebrate it. Yes, of course June was when she'd had her coronation, but didn't she know that June was also when the outgoing sixth form exited, stage left? The day every staff common room in every school up and down her fawning realm dreaded. The day when a horde of, by definition, well-educated young people, primed for the outside world, were given licence to blow smoke up those who'd provided that self-same education. The day with an innocent name masking a malicious intent: Muck-up Day.

The thought of smoking ignited something in Harold's subconscious, and he reached into his pocket for the packet of B&H

he'd picked up the evening before. Lighting up, he inhaled the first deep hit of nicotine and let the smoke pour out of his nostrils like an angry dragon. Naturally, given their track record over the referendum, they'd all expected the Class of '77 to go beyond the usual antics of stink bombs, penises spray-canned on the playground, or underwear run up the school flagpole. The Class of '76 had managed to fill an entire classroom with helium-filled contraceptives, so the only way of getting rid of them, barring spearing each one individually and being left with shards of decaying Durex everywhere, had been to open a window and let them fly out over the school. That had been bad enough; a warning, perhaps, that they should have been better prepared for their successors? Harold treated himself to another sip of whisky.

The referendum debacle had only been the latest in a long line of antics when they had challenged authority. There was the time they started reallocating books in the library, putting the religious texts in the fiction section, for example, or all the school memoirs under Ancient History. Harold had decided to play it cool and not give them the satisfaction of notoriety, but that had only led them to take things to the next level. When the school librarian had come in one Monday to find every stack turned on its head and all the books upside down – except for the ones they'd reallocated, which were now the right way up – it had taken an entire Sunday to sort them out. That hadn't been the work of a couple of mavericks, it had taken planning.

Then there was the incident with the goats. Somehow, the miscreants had managed to get hold of some of the unfortunate creatures, dyed their coats red and set them loose on the grass in the middle of the quad. For most years that would have been enough; but no, the Class of '77 had painted numbers on their back, a one, a two and a four. Harold had had half the staff room out looking for number three before they'd clocked that it didn't exist. Thankfully, he'd managed to keep the lid on that one and avoided the obvious 'Red Goat' headlines.

He'd become skilled at hiding things from the press when it came to the Class of '77, but his luck ran out when it came to the Jubilee.

There were only so many street parties a journalist could cover, and the Class of '77 had given them the perfect antidote, something with a bit of extra bite. The editor of the local rag was an ORC, and therefore fairly malleable, so instead they'd alerted the TV, a cocky young reporter called Taxman, or something like that, from the BBC's *Tonight* programme.

Harold Mitchell had chewed it over endlessly, and having tapped the ash from the end of his cigarette into the dregs of his whisky glass, now balancing precariously on the shiny fabric on the arm of his solitary chair, he did so once again, trying to work out what he could have done differently. Outside, the last rays of light from a watery spring sunset were filtering through his thin net curtains, lending an ethereal air to the room.

He'd got complacent, that was the problem.

The consensus in the staff room at the time was that they'd worn the little bastards down, that the referendum stunt had been their last hurrah. Even before the sixth form had begun, there'd been that incident with Matron's girl. Then there'd been that unpleasant business with turds being left all over the place. What kind of sick mind did something like that? Okay, there was no proof it was one of them, but it had their fingerprints all over it; metaphorically speaking, anyway.

As he tilted his glass and stubbed out his cigarette on its inside surface, Harold allowed himself a smile. If he said so himself, he'd handled that particular issue rather deftly. A couple of the governors had been nagging him to 'clean things up' a bit, and he'd caught their drift. What was more, getting rid of the Asian boy had earned him a few brownie points, as it were, among elements of the CCF where there was some history, getting them onside before the referendum. It was difficult, a bit of a gamble, but one that paid off. Lucky, too, that the deposits had stopped shortly afterwards.

The thinking behind making that nonentity Tom Joules head boy had been to inject a dose of blandness into their bloodstream, but then along came that nuisance Peterson. Dead now, of course, Peterson. Maybe he'd got complacent after landing the referendum result? Harold stretched his chin upwards to relieve a growing crick in his neck as he returned once more to this familiar conclusion. Outside, a carrot-coloured blast was filling the sky as daylight signalled its last hurrah, but Harold was in no mood to enjoy it. He was never really in a mood to enjoy anything these days. Instead, he closed his eyes and relived those fateful days one more time.

The staggered A-level timetable had worked in their favour; that, and the study leave beforehand fragmented them and gave them other things to concentrate on. As the exams ended they seemed to simply scatter like pigeons released from a loft, some of them gathering in the local pubs (he knew for a fact that one or two had jobs serving behind bars), and suddenly it felt as if they'd never been; the year that had been so much trouble finally extinguished, much like the cigarette he'd just put out in his glass.

The first signs that anything was up came when small round stickers about the size of a two-penny coin started appearing on noticeboards, lamp posts and windows around the school, consisting simply of three letters, 'STJ', written in red on a white background. They weren't anyone's initials (Harold had got his secretary to check), and they didn't stand for any of the raft of new political groups that seemed to be popping up all over the place.

Then, overnight, they'd disappeared, only to be replaced by fresh stickers displaying a curious face: a perfect circle, as if drawn with a pair of compasses, with cartoon ears, three wisps of hair and a big smile. The design was once again in red, and the stickers were placed in exactly the same position as the originals, as if part of a clearly orchestrated campaign. The smile on the face was strangely condescending, as if it knew something the people looking at it didn't.

The mystery had niggled, but no more than that, until one glorious early summer's day in June. Harold arrived at school at his normal time, around eight in the morning, and walked across the lawn from his grace and favour apartment. As he approached the upper playground he could hear the sound of metal grating against metal, and his first reaction was that the ancient boiler was playing up again. The noise sounded like it might be expensive, so he headed for the heating plant between the upper toilet block and the quad.

Nothing could have prepared him for the sight of three suits of armour staggering awkwardly out of the toilets, clanging about as the bodies inside clearly struggled to cope with the simple act of walking, each wearing one of the school's red PE singlets over their chest. Harold stood transfixed, as the last of the suits nodded a polite greeting and the line progressed on to the grass.

Four more suits then emerged from the sixth form centre, the early sun catching on bright metal, and it was at that moment he'd understood what was going on. Muck-up Day. This stunt was their contribution. Having paused for a moment to regain his composure, Harold lifted a finger to call the suits of armour over, to maybe even congratulate them on their inventiveness, and to begin negotiations; but, of course, he hadn't known who was inside them. That, he realized in an instant, was the point.

While he stood still, considering his options, Harold became aware of clusters of other suits – in the far corner of the quad, coming through the school gate, one even getting off a bike. All the suits were the same, and all had the red singlets on. Slowly, they began to congregate, as if pulled to the same spot by some giant magnet. Groups of three or four became six or eight, and these in turn became dozens.

The whole process had been, through necessity, slow, as those inside the suits had to cock each leg out in turn at an unnatural angle and swing it through a swivel of the hip, for all the world as if they were trying to relieve themselves inside their suits. They were coming at him like cyborgs, unstoppable machines, and even if he'd wanted to, it was unlikely that Harold could have taken out more than one of them at a time.

He was about to march to the staff room to see what reinforcements he might be able to muster, when he spotted the TV crew. Pausing to take a fresh cigarette out of its pack as he recalled those events,

Harold remembered how he felt when he'd seen the cameraman, weighed down with a heavy shoulder-mounted camera, alongside the lanky reporter with his mike and cables. He'd felt defeated. The whole operation had clearly been planned down to the smallest detail and he was doomed to be a bystander, an extra in someone else's film. He considered ordering them all off the lawn; but he knew the press well enough to realize he'd only come across as ridiculous, especially on film. The situation had moved from the possibility of containment to an attempt to emerge with some kind of dignity.

It transpired the suits of armour represented a sort of modern republican New Model Army, and that this was a protest against the time and money being spent on the Queen's Silver Jubilee. The stickers represented Roundheads, and as the head of history told him later, the republican New Model Army had also been known at the time as Red Coats. Although the whole exercise had been surreal, he had to acknowledge it had been rather well thought through; a stunt, on grudging reflection, worthy of the year.

They'd had their own Oliver Cromwell, the son of the local MP, which went a long way to explaining why he'd been chosen: not only a parliamentarian, but also, as far as Harold, and more importantly the governors, would have been concerned, untouchable, whatever the scale of his crime. Behind him, for reasons Harold had never understood, George Rowlands stood dressed in a dinner jacket.

By that point Harold was joined by most of the teaching staff, with the more loyal sycophants by his side, others staring, confused, from the staff-room windows. It was inevitable that the press would turn to him for comment, and he had to decide on a response. Following a swift assessment of the situation, he decided to join in, describing the prank as a welcome expression of opinion from boys educated to think for themselves. Publicly, he saw the funny side of the whole thing. Privately, well, he'd think of something.

The boys hadn't finished, though. From among their huddled metallic mass had come a fresh burst of activity, and a homemade pike was slowly hauled up into the sky, a Guy Fawkes-like effigy hanging from its tip, the sharp end inserted into the back of its head. A sign dangled around its neck, daubed with three words: Stuff The Jubilee.

STJ.

It was as Harold was staring up at the focus of this macabre turn of events that he noticed that the effigy being raised into the sky was a woman in a dress. For a dreadful moment he thought it might be the Queen – the body was wearing a plastic mask that looked horribly like that woman who made a living acting as her double – and at that moment Harold had started to rapidly revise his plans: maybe they'd gone too far, giving him the opportunity to adopt a more offended and censorious approach?

As Harold approached the dummy he felt bile rise in his throat, as if his stomach was demanding the opportunity to empty his breakfast on to the pristine grass of the quad. His eyes told him that it wasn't the Queen he was seeing dangling from a pike on the enclosed lawn. No, it was much worse than that.

It was that of her sister, Princess Margaret.

The Class of '77? If he'd had his way he'd have got them all out of their suits of armour, lined them up against the wall and given them a damned good horsewhipping.

----------------------------- ✳ -----------------------------

The red Letts Office desk diary was all they needed, or rather a red Letts diary. As soon as the 1985 edition had become available in the local John Menzies, Ray nipped out and bought a copy. Through the rest of October Pam had taken responsibility for transcribing the entire book not once, but twice, initially into the 'official' diary, which had arrived by post direct from Letts themselves, and then again into their 'shadow' version. This she kept in the bag by her side, safe in the knowledge that neither of the Grey brothers would ever dare to rifle through a woman's things, largely through fear of the unspeakable things they might find.

Meanwhile, Ray had made it his responsibility to meet as many of the firm's lesser-profile clients as he could face-to-face, spending most evenings creating a list of the most lucrative in terms of commission, and separating out those he knew the Greys would try to see themselves. In the course of these meetings, Ray also made it his business to find out as much as he could about the clients' future plans, rating them on a star system of one to five as to how promising they looked for a fresh approach.

With only a few pages remaining in the 1984 diary, Pam made her shock announcement (to her employers, anyway) that she was handing in her notice. It was her mother, she explained, hinting at a sad combination of lost marbles and gynaecological problems that didn't invite deeper questioning; the fact that Pam's mother was living in Spain with a man twenty years her junior and could honestly say she'd never been happier, or indeed more supple, being irrelevant.

Ray followed suit the week before Christmas. He was sorry to leave them in the lurch, of course, but he'd been offered a new position elsewhere with better working conditions, a higher salary and a directorship. The Grey brothers may have been persuaded to start bargaining over the first two of these but the third was unimaginable, as Ray had known it would be. Ray was silently pleased with himself that all three of his reasons for leaving were true, as he and Pam became joint owners and equal shareholders in Meadows and Son Ltd (Independent Financial Planning Services). The deal was simple, sealed one night over a crème de menthe and a beer in a pub the other side of town. Using accumulated savings, Pam had put up the cash for some premises and sundry working capital. The deal was that they'd build the business together, and after a couple of years Pam would sell half her 50 per cent share to Ray, in the expectation that it would be worth enough by then for her to become a lady of leisure, with the rest following in instalments, providing her with a generous pension.

The name had been chosen to lend the new business a sense of gravitas, rather than due to any involvement from Ray's dad. Both Ray and Pam were astute enough to recognize that Ray may have come across as a little wet behind the ears to many of their client base. Now travelling the country in children's sandals, Meadows senior would have been the first to admit he couldn't tell an annuity from his anus, and his presence in the firm's name was purely spectral.

And so it was that by the time the details of the Seventy-Seven Society Bond were being put together, Ray had become a successful local businessman, while the careers of most of the others at that year's meal had yet to take off, and, as such, he'd been nominated as a trustee by general acclamation, accepting the invitation with a combination of humility and greed, although only one of these had been obvious.

Ray had never been really convinced that the Bond had much to it, and had always thought it contained a fatal flaw; but the post of trustee gave him a springboard to offer himself as a credible adviser to a group of potential new clients, most of whom were likely to need financial advice in the future. As for the Bond, Ray was sure he couldn't have been the only one to spot that even if it did follow through on its presumed conclusion, what was to stop the last man standing spending the money on anything he chose? Ray had already seen how people behaved when presented with great wads of unexpected cash, and it was rarely a sight to restore your faith in mankind. Besides, even if the Bond did play out, surely the final man would be so decrepit and senile that he'd be incapable of making a rational decision. Still, he concluded, it might be interesting to go along for the ride.

Alongside him on the list of trustees was Eddie Perks, who was generally acknowledged as a straight-up kind of a bloke who wore a semi-permanent waistcoat and a benign smile that he used to hide his personality. Eddie had gone straight from school into a stockbroking firm owned by his uncle, and had the look of a boxer about him, including scars around his eyes that he'd picked up in battle or, more accurately, on the rugby pitch. The third trustee, almost by default, was Tom Joules, thereby confirming Ray's view on the pointlessness of university, as they didn't have a degree between them.

Tom, good old reliable and unflappable Tom, the bloke who got things done and back in the day had acted as the buffer between them and the real world, was the perfect candidate as the talisman of the Bond. He even wore the red and white barber's pole OCR tie to trustee meetings.

Few present at the time had been sober enough to spot, or to later remember, the process whereby Tom had been nominated to the committee. Ray's impressive tolerance of alcohol had kept him the right side of lucid when momentum had grown behind the idea of the Bond, and it had been him who'd nominated his old comrade in arms from the sixth form centre, the same way it had been him who'd put Tom forward as secretary. During their year in office, Ray had learned a lot about how to play and influence his erstwhile colleague.

As it happened, the practicalities of putting the Bond together ended up taking more of Ray's time than he'd anticipated – not least because Meadows and Son was going through a growth spurt at the time – but Ray had been happy to take the longer view. Time spent on the Bond was an investment, one outside his little arrangement with Pam, even if he didn't know how and when it might eventually mature.

------------------------------ ✳ ------------------------------

Another of the Class of '77 to have spent the final three years of the seventies well was Ben Bradshaw. Immediately after school, his priority had been making the team for the 1980 Olympics in Moscow, up at five every morning for four hours in the pool before it opened to the public, length after remorseless length, three for stamina, one for speed. Afternoons were spent generating cash through a scheme he'd come up with involving the exciting new concept of sofa beds. The initial challenge had been to sell the idea – a sofa that could be converted into a bed for guests! Imagine that! Guests staying overnight, in the living room!

Ben had proved to be a convincing salesman, driven perhaps through direct experience of sleeping on sofas, and not just for one night. His parents had expected him to go to university after seeing him through the Red Coat, and had promised his room to his brother.

Apparently, the prospect of Ben in the Olympics, representing their country in a tiny swimsuit with a Union Jack on the side, hadn't been enough to trump this promise. Ben hadn't been surprised, no one had ever truly believed in him, but he'd show them.

He started by going door to door to get orders, and armed with these it had been a case of hiring a Bedford van every third or fourth day and dealing with fabricators down south, placing the orders and picking up the finished articles, and before you knew it Robert was your father's brother. Once he'd got over the initial cash-flow hump, there'd been sufficient margin to make a tidy living – enough to move out of his parents' and into a ground-floor flat in town.

Soon, the combination of impatience and the hassle of buying and cooking food piled up, along with cleaning and all the other responsibilities that came with living on your own, and his training suffered. Just failing to make the qualifying times for Moscow had been a disappointment, but after a few dark weeks reality kicked in and he saw it as his cue to take himself seriously and get a shop. With some clever advertising (he'd hired some scouts during bob-a-job week to do some leafleting), he soon found that punters were happy to come to him rather than him having to go to them, and the business took off. He found a local firm prepared to take on the manufacturing, and he created four different ranges of sofa to make it easier for the punters to choose.

The opening years of the eighties had been a boom time on the high street and Ben's timing had been perfect, but he was restless. Sofas weren't the most convenient things to move in and out of houses, the arms always seemed to get in the way; and besides, others had muscled in on the act, depressing his margins.

What he'd needed was something more steady; a nagging demon had been telling him sofa beds might be just a fad. He'd been mulling over the problem one morning when he realized the answer was right underneath him. Beds. Everyone needed a bed, and whereas most homes had only one, maybe two, sofas, they might have three, four, even five beds.

Back then, all the so-called experts had said that out-of-town stores were only any good for food and DIY, but Ben thought otherwise. Using all his savings and some crippling loans from the bank, he'd opened not one out-of-town superstore, but three, all over the same weekend, and only stocking beds. It was a big risk, but really it was just the same old story: Ben Bradshaw having to prove himself; swimming against the current, you might say. Not even his own parents had ever really had faith in him. He'd had to plead to take the entrance exam for the Red Coat, and even after he passed, all they'd done was moan about the cost of the uniform. He'd enjoyed it there, but he couldn't really say he'd had much of an impact. He knew what they called him: Tadpole, small and inconsequential, almost certainly doomed to failure, just one of thousands of insignificant spermatozoa racing towards the egg. Well, he'd found the egg, and it was going to be golden. They'd notice him ... oh yes, they'd notice him.

---------------------------- ✻ ----------------------------

It was the cry of 'Wotcha, Freddie' from the grinning hamster Paul Briton that had eventually driven Mike McQueen into the gents toilet for what he called a 'little refresher'.

For Mike, his erstwhile school colleague was the archetypal '77 dude, all Rotaract and cufflinks. The last album he'd bought had almost certainly been *Abba's Greatest Hits*, probably *Vol. 2*. Mike McQueen felt nothing in common with him at all. With the door closed behind him in the gents, the small orange pill he tapped out on to his palm from a used film container looked more like a Haliborange vitamin C supplement than a pastel-coloured fizzy sweet. It was, of course, neither. Mike couldn't remember precisely why he'd come to the school reunion meal; he'd only been once before and that was a pretty freaky experience, with a heavy death vibe and all that talk of money. Mike had returned the paperwork that followed but he hadn't really understood it: a subscription in order to keep in touch, which was ironic as he didn't really give a stuff about that.

The period between Christmas and New Year could go either way for Mike – sometimes out on the road, sometimes kicking his heels. He usually did something on New Year's Eve itself, and he felt obliged to make the effort to call in on his folks, although that summer they'd retired down to the West Country and he hadn't really been on for more travelling after months on the road. He could have gone back to the pad in Marrakesh, but he simply couldn't face Heathrow again; not after the previous week when the crowds had been simply crazy, like sheep on acid.

He'd told himself going to the supper would involve hooking up with some of the old crowd and getting out of his tree on one thing or another, probably the other. Generally chilling. What he hadn't counted on was how much so many of them had changed. Reggie Richardson, for one, was almost unrecognizable: he looked like he'd had a fat transplant that had gone wrong, looking closer to fifty than going on thirty. Most were even wearing ties, and all they seemed to want to talk about was their jobs, as if it was some kind of competitive sport – how much they were earning; how busy their bosses kept them, yanking their chains. Pathetic really, a pack of breadheads and deadheads. They probably saw him as a cop-out, when the truth was they'd all done exactly what was expected of them by the system, and when you stopped to think about it, wasn't that the biggest cop-out of them all?

Mike McQueen preferred to go with the flow, surf the vibe. In the early days one gig led to another, and every now and then he'd got a tour as a sound man, all expenses paid and a wad of cash at the end. Live Aid had been his big break, bad news for the starving in Ethiopia, but the making of old Mikey-baby. While everyone had been losing their cool at Wembley, he'd discovered his inner organizer, marking himself out as a fixer of problems, a rare beast in the chaos otherwise known as the music business. He became in such demand that he got himself the pad in Marrakesh to escape when he needed to get his shit back together.

He shared this with Stevie Sanders. Mike liked the thought that everyone else in the room probably guessed he'd 'done a Stonehouse' and simply disappeared, missing presumed dead. His dash out of the classroom during A-level revision hadn't really come as a surprise to anyone; he'd always been one of those people who was either going to discover a cure for cancer or burn up from the intensity of trying.

A couple of years back, Mike spotted him at Kings Cross station with a can of Red Stripe in one hand and his trousers halfway down his thighs, all the commuters rushing around him like rats after the lights came on. Mike gathered him up and put his head back on straight, or as straight as it would go, and he guessed he'd sort of adopted him. Their arrangement was smooth. Stevie managed all his post, meetings, scheduling and crap, and generally looked after the joint, making sure the local cats were kept in line – both the two- and four-legged varieties (Stevie loved adopting stray cats).

As Mike re-entered the room, the pill he'd popped began to kick in, taking the edge off the general babble that greeted him. A mellowness hummed in his head and filtered down to most of the joints in his body. His hearing wasn't all it used to be, and he felt as if he was swimming in thick water as he drifted through the room back to his seat. Experience told him that if he kept his face forward, walking like a horse with blinkers, he'd be able to find his way back without too much trouble, and once sat down he could chill out and enjoy.

Maybe it was the whole school thing that made him feel like he was back in a classroom when he got there. An expectant silence had descended and people were adopting their best behaviour, doing up buttons on their threads and straightening ties, as if a teacher was about to enter the room. Everywhere he looked fingers were surreptitiously straightening cutlery, in the same way their hands, as schoolboys, had ordered pens and pencils on the tops of their desks ten years before.

Up at the front he could see Tom Joules getting to his feet, extending himself to his full, not inconsiderable, height, and just at that moment Mike felt himself beginning to trip: a hazy, floaty kind of trip, nothing too heavy. He started to slip back in time, to a few minutes before, when some dude had mentioned the party they'd had the summer after lower sixth. He scanned the room, an owl trying to echolocate a mouse, but the only voice in the room now was Tom's.

George Rowlands ... it was George, Mike suddenly remembered, who'd mentioned the party. Back then, pretty cool, Mike remembered, but now just like all the rest in his suit with broad stripes and white shirt and a pair of crimson red braces. Ben Bradshaw had been staring hard at George as he started boasting about some chick he reckoned he'd had at the party, Mike recalled, almost as if he'd been lip-reading. It was George's favourite subject, all the chicks he'd had at school, nothing he loved more than banging on about how the shapes of their tits varied so much, as if this was common knowledge, when he knew perfectly well it wasn't. Most of their collective knowledge on the subject had been gained from the glossy pages of *Mayfair*. Rowlands had, of course, been notorious for his Rowlands Scale, a sort of Beaufort Scale for breasts; although feigned modesty meant he never claimed responsibility for giving it that name himself. This had focused on size and used a seven-point scale, using fruit as its benchmark, starting at tangerines and escalating towards the pinnacle of watermelons – a level that had existed more in imagination than reality; although Matron's chick had come pretty close.

As the sounds around the room began to echo, Mike became aware that reality was slipping away from him. The room had dissolved into a photographic negative and he found himself slipping into a vortex, back to the day of the party. Although it had hardly seemed credible at the time, that summer had been even hotter than its predecessor. Terry Mungus had tried to reignite the whole swimming pool vibe, until he was reminded the pool had been filled in. When a spell of blue skies was forecast a couple of weekends after the end of term, someone else had floated the idea of a party, and hey, parties were never a bad idea.

The nominated pad had been one of the old terraced houses where Matron lived. She was away and her crazy daughter had said it would be okay. Wow, she'd changed a lot in a year, completely different from the prick-tease of the year before; she'd turned into some freaked-out badass fox who didn't seem to care about anything. Kinda cool, but wacky.

The refresher had begun to really kick in, sending spirals spinning round his brain. Where had he been? Yeah, Matron's daughter, some days as high as a kite, other days so low you'd need a forklift to pick her up. Still on the edge of the crowd, looking in, but not joining in; or more accurately, perhaps, staring out vacantly. Fragile, distant. Luckily, the day of the party had turned out to be an 'up' day.

A party on school premises had seemed a cool, edgy kinda thing to do. The girls had got the food together, the blokes the juice; although judging by the stash in the kitchen, which included party kegs of Double Diamond and Ind Coope, and even a couple of bottles of home-brewed wine, access to funds was tight. He, naturally, had sorted the music. It had all been groovy. The dudes were mainly in T-shirts and shorts, although Mike had opted for a pair of baggy Nepalese harem pants and a vest. The chicks, meanwhile, were either in bikini tops and cropped denim jeans, or skirts and peasant blouses: it seemed to be an either/or for them. A barbecue was going on in the quad and someone had managed to make a copy of the key for the sixth form centre, so there was an overspill going on there around a pool table. It hadn't been a copping-off-together sort of party; it had been more, well, chilled.

Mike had generally floated through the party and at one point found himself by the bottom of the stairs inside the house. A group of guys, led by that smug arse Les Andrew and his sidekick, Philip Christopher – Bonnie and Clyde without the charisma – were crowded around the TV watching some test match highlights, and they'd been, like, totally immersed in the action, if that was a word that could ever really be used to describe cricket. The music was under control: two large Wharfedales, one-fifty watts per channel, had been led out on to the small patio out the back of the house where the sound echoed off the science block into the quad, and rigged up to a tape deck and amp run out on an extension cable. He remembered someone had replaced his tape with Supertramp when he went for a slash; hardly the crime of the century, they said, when he stared them down later, but at least it hadn't been Wings or some other crap like that.

Mike now remembered walking up the stairs of Matron's house with an exaggerated step, like he'd been on the point of scaring some children, and then finding himself on the landing at the top. There, he'd clocked two bedrooms. The main one to the right looked out on the street and had been decorated with clean, bare wood furniture and plain forest-green curtains – a medium-sized room, neither a double nor a single but somewhere in between, neat and tidy, with an underlying scent of freshly laundered linen. Bold patterned wallpaper had been barely visible in between numerous photos exclusively of Matron's daughter at different ages. A Bible rested on a bedside table by one side of the bed: an implausibly thick edition with the words *Holy Bible* embossed in gold on the front to avoid any possible confusion; words that glowed with the fading blush of orange from the setting sun outside, as if in warning.

A mirrored cupboard on the landing separated the two bedrooms, the second of which was much smaller and altogether more psychedelic, with posters covering much of the walls. It looked out on to the quad, where Ray Meadows and some his rugger acolytes were waving their hands around the smoke rising from their oil drum-based cooking. Clothes spilled out of drawers as if they were trying to escape, and Mike pulled back on to his heels to avoid being seen as he retreated across the threshold of what he safely assumed was Matron's room.

As he did so, a puff of wind from an open window started to close the door behind him, revealing as it did so another door hidden behind which had been papered over and painted, as if there'd been a deliberate attempt to disguise it, leaving only a hairline gap around its edges and an open-mouthed gap revealing a lock. Mike was intrigued, and it didn't take much time to find the key, dangling by a piece of string on a hook under a dressing gown hanging from the bedroom door.

It felt like some kind of karma demanded that he open the door, so he inserted the key in the lock and turned it. It yielded easily and with a quarter-turn he pulled the door open using the key itself, only to be confronted by darkness. Reaching a hand out he found a heavy velvet curtain. Confident from the silence that there was no one there, he lifted it to one side.

A muffled cheer came up from the stairwell at that precise moment, making Mike jump, but muted applause suggested it was simply celebration of a six from an English batsman. The brief pause gave his eyes the few seconds they needed to get used to the semi-darkness in the new room, and as the shapes began to form so did the realization that he'd found an alternative way into the Head's study, the inner sanctum: *un-be-fucking-lievable*.

There was a lot of wood, mainly in the form of wainscoting up to waist height around each wall, one of which had been lined entirely with storm-cloud grey filing cabinets, four drawers high, with small business card-sized pieces of paper indicating different sections of the alphabet. A large white board dominated another wall. It had been wiped completely clean, presumably with the J-cloth hanging like a drying tea towel from a hook screwed into the board's wooden frame. There'd been a small sofa and coffee table, Mike remembered, a lockable cabinet and, to the right, the main door, which presumably led out to the corridor. Under the heightened senses from his refresher, Mike recalled the musty, antique shop smell of the room.

The room had been dominated by a large oak desk, and Mike remembered thinking it probably had some kind of name – an admiral's desk or a gamekeeper's desk or something – as it had the odd feature of small brass eyelets, about an inch in diameter, in each of the four corners: the sort of feature whose purpose has been lost to history, like the extra buttons on the end of a jacket sleeve, but is retained to make the ignorant feel just that: ignorant.

A look around the back of the desk revealed a slim drawer across the middle, which yielded when Mike tugged at it. Inside were three rattan canes of varying thicknesses and lengths, building up to one nearly half an inch thick and close to three feet long. Mike picked up the heaviest and weighed it in his hand. It had felt cool to the touch, and remarkably light. Two quick flicks in the air delivered such a loud swishing sound that he put it back hurriedly and stood still to see if anyone had heard, as he waited for the shivers gripping his spine to subside.

A quick check confirmed that the filing cabinets were locked, which came as a disappointment, a vague hope at the time being that he could perhaps find some dirt on the referendum result – although he doubted the HM would be stupid enough to have kept anything incriminating. The room had an almost Dickensian vibe about it, with odd curios such as a broken oar, old bits of rope and even some sections of chain scattered among sporting trophies and certificates, like a modern pub done up to give a nautical vibe.

His curiosity satisfied, Mike started to make his way back through the heavy curtain. In this velvety no man's land, he reached for the door and heard a heavy clonk, the muffled sound of metal hitting wood. Clutching around in the dark, he expected to find another key, so it was a surprise when his groping fingers found a pair of regular police-issue handcuffs, the two circles looped around each other and over a door hook.

At that moment, everything clicked into place. The rope, the chains, even the broken oar, plus these handcuffs. It didn't require a massive leap of imagination to picture the scenes that were apparently played out in the hallowed sanctuary of the Head's study. On the other hand, a triple jump might have been necessary to guess the effect imagining these scenes had on Mike, which mainly involved stirrings in the crotch area of his harems.

Back in the present, Mike suddenly fell into a fit of uncontrollable giggles, which was unfortunate as Tom Joules had just finished leading the room in grace and was following this up with the equally sombre ritual of passing round pieces of paper, which were apparently something to do with the mysterious money thing. Mike pulled himself together and made a mental note to get Stevie to explain what the scam was when he got back to Morocco, even though as he did so he knew he'd forget. On receiving his copy, Mike folded it into eight and dug it into one of the pockets of his purple satin waistcoat without even giving it a glance.

-------------------------------- ✳ --------------------------------

The Red Coat board of governors wasn't what you'd call a dynamic group, as Harold Mitchell had once found; it was probably easier to dislodge a high court judge than one of their number. Being invited on to the board had come to be seen as some kind of honour, and one for life at that. As such, they tended to have long memories, and whenever they allowed

themselves to remember the events of 1977, the thin crimson arteries on their uniformly puffy cheeks tended to become more pronounced.

The initial reaction among the powers within the school when they learned that the spirit of the Class of '77 lived on in a tangible form was one of denial. When, in time, that form proved more durable, and they heard that it had crystallized into the Bond, the veins in their foreheads rose in sympathy with the blood in their cheeks.

It was with no small relief, therefore, that they finally made the connection that Tom Joules, now one of their own, was such a leading light in the whole enterprise.

They had insurance against the Bond.

Making Up the Numbers

1987

The Class of '77 was hitting its stride now. While some of their number had hit the ground running after school or university, and others had taken a year or two to sort themselves out, after ten years one thing was irrefutable: they'd all learned to stand on their own two feet. The next few years were going to be critical in shaking out who among their number were going to be successful, and who were going to be doomed to perpetual frustration.

In parallel, the process of forming responsible young men, defined by influences beyond work, was now well underway, with the class discovering various ways of defining themselves: not just as employees, but also as husbands, and even, in a handful of cases, fathers. Against this backdrop, the annual Seventy-Seven Society meal offered many of them a chance to toss those responsibilities aside for one night, to turn the clock back and be what they once were: young, free, and defined by hope and potential rather than the reality of the slog of realizing that potential. They were individuals, but individuals sharing common ties which, although they might become slightly stretched and flabbier with time, felt strong when viewed through the distorting lens of memory provided by this one night together.

This freedom, the opportunity to experience time travel, however briefly, was something many observers on the edge of the whole Seventy-Seven scene envied; in particular, the new grouping of wives and significant others. This envy – for some, bordering on almost hostile jealousy – was particularly powerful among those who felt they'd had a walk-on part in some of the times remembered so vividly, and increasingly inaccurately, by their menfolk each year between Christmas and New Year.

These were the girls, now women, who'd first come on to the scene at the swimming pool in 1975, and then become woven into the growing social scene enjoyed by all as they discovered pubs, parties and other, more one-to-one activities. Eventually one of these walk-on players had enough. For her, the meal wasn't a single night of indulgence, an

113

evening when she was left alone with the Christmas double issue of the *Radio Times* and a box of chocolates, but more like the beginning of weeks of purgatory. Her husband seemed to possess a staggering ability to remember every conversation from these nights, and while the stories seemed so dramatically alive and important to him, she found it an increasing struggle to put names to faces. Even the names were difficult as her husband oscillated between real names and nicknames, using some kind of private code she didn't really understand. For her, school had been simply a period of her life, a phase; for her husband, it seemed to be the sun his life orbited around.

It wasn't just the incessant recollections afterwards. He hadn't missed a single meal and, although she couldn't prove it, she even suspected that he prepared himself beforehand, crafting and polishing anecdotes and accomplishments to make sure he came across in the most dazzling light. She'd never understood this constant need to prove himself, especially to that lot. He was doing pretty well, yet still seemed to crave affirmation, recognition, call it whatever you like, from his old school buddies.

As had become predictable pretty much since puberty, Susie Hamilton had fulfilled her destiny and ended up marrying the Tadpole, Ben Bradshaw. Predictable to everyone else, that was; less so to Susie. The two had hung out together, shared their first kiss, and quite a bit more, together during their teenage years; but to Susie this had just been fun, nothing serious. Perhaps she'd just been naïve? It was true that looking back, Ben had always seemed to be there by her side, although for the life of her she'd never really worked out why.

Getting married seemed the obvious next step, but for some reason it never seemed to find itself on the agenda. They just were. Boyfriend and girlfriend, hanging out, but nothing more. Slightly shorter than most of her friends at five feet three, Susie had an almost gamine look about her as she was growing up: thin and fragile-looking, with cocktail-stick arms and legs and a shambling, almost balletic, walk. In reality, she was actually quite robust and could pick up quite a speed if she needed to. Maybe it had been this apparent delicate quality that attracted Ben: a need to protect her?

His attention to her had felt quite claustrophobic at the time, but comforting, too; a sort of shield against the vagaries of growing up. They socialized with some of the other couples in their set, but her identity seemed to merge with Ben's. She'd sometimes felt that anyone wanting to get to know her better needed to complete an application form for Ben's consideration beforehand. Very few passed the test, and certainly no other boys.

Things hadn't been helped by the fact that her parents seemed to approve so wholeheartedly. Ben had come across as a sensible lad, always polite whenever he came round for his tea, and clearly dedicated to his swimming. Dedication was a form of loyalty and trustworthiness, and they'd liked that. He'd said the right things, given her regular advice on things such as what kind of hairstyle looked good on her and what clothes she wore best, and had generally just been there – her safety net in a complex world during a confusing time.

Was it love? She didn't have anything to compare it with. Affection, certainly; loyalty, too, on both sides – she stuck with him through his failure to make the Olympics, and then subsequently, as he'd got his business off the ground, and he with her as she went through her nursing training. It had come as a bit of a shock when Mary Langley and David Lu had got married, and maybe it had been that which had forced Ben to finally propose.

Dress, church, flowers, disco, and she was married. The time for meditating on what might have been had vanished. At first, they'd shared his dingy flat, but before long they gained their own Habitat-inspired perfect home, funded by Ben's hard work. Susie qualified, and Ben continued to build his business, but it didn't take her long to discover the shadow that loomed over their lives.

January was always a miserable month to get through anyway, but for Susie it was unbearable. After each Seventy-Seven meal he became a man obsessed, spouting on about who'd done what and how they'd reacted when he told them about his accomplishments. Bit by bit,

Susie had the whole evening replayed to her: who ate what, who got drunk and who wasn't doing as well as Ben.

Initially Susie listened, but she soon spotted a pattern. The sulking would continue into February, leading to a gradual thaw by the spring. By early summer, things were usually back on an even keel with all their troubles forgotten, until the dreaded day, usually around mid-November, when the invitation arrived for that year's meal, and the cycle would begin to crank into action all over again.

Susie decided to do something about it. She made a few phone calls, starting with her own ex-school friends and, turning a deaf ear to Ben's disapproval, got a group together for a night out of their own in town on the day of the meal. In total innocence, for she could have had no idea how things would turn out, she christened the group the Seventy-Seven Widows Club.

---------------------------------- ✳ ----------------------------------

Ray Meadows was determined to be one of life's winners. Their plan successfully executed, the first thing he and Pam did was to get rid of the red Letts diary, which had become the embodiment of the old way of doing things. They replaced it with an up-to-the-minute card index file, complemented by three different coloured Rolodexes: blue for current clients, red for contacts and possible clients, and white for different brokers.

The new system was something Pam had been wanting to implement for years, and it wasn't the only thing. Behind her unprepossessing exterior Pam nurtured an astute business brain, one whose potential had been unleashed by the prospect of ownership and profit. In short, Pam became a new woman. The offices they'd chosen were situated in a side road off the High Street, on a slight hill, where there was a row of terraced Georgian houses. Ray was taken by the two white stone Corinthian columns outside the impressive-looking front door, itself painted glossy black to contrast with the matt white of the columns. The property oozed class and discretion, and, more importantly, was on an initial five-year lease with a remarkably low premium.

Pam had been watching the Grey brothers for years and had become increasingly frustrated by their reliance on repeat business. She pointed out to Ray that existing clients were soft targets, not only for repeat custom but also for fresh business, specifically in some of the exciting new areas of the growing financial services market. As she succinctly put it, 'We need to sell them things they don't know they need.' On top of all this, they'd been using the same old brokers for years, mostly friends or golf pals of the Greys, and there were much more favourable commission rates to be had in what was an increasingly competitive market.

Within eighteen months, the combination of Pam's business nous and Ray's irrepressible salesmanship had created a money machine that seemed to generate its own momentum. As the wider economy picked up and financial rules were loosened, Pam and Ray seemed to find it impossible not to make money, and it wasn't too long before they'd needed help to optimize their potential.

No one knew better than Pam and Ray the need to be careful when it came to hired help. Their approach, therefore, was to only take one person on at a time, and to make sure that they were both absolutely convinced of that person's trustworthiness before giving them any proper responsibilities. They took precautions, of course, but they weren't stingy when it came to rewards, either. This combination of carrot and stick had proved to be successful, and by 1987 the business was employing seven people, all of them younger than Pam, most of them older than Ray.

Meanwhile, Ray exercised moderation. In his case, the pleasure of watching the business account grow was tempered by the knowledge that each day was one day less with Pam in the business, as well as one day closer to her big pay day, which he was going to have to finance, and the more money they made, the bigger that pay day would be. As such, Ray had restricted himself to a relatively modest lifestyle, ditching the MG in favour of a two-year-old Ford Orion, resisting the Escort Mk III he craved; a top-end suit from John Collier, not bespoke; and a basic ground-floor flat near the office with a manageable mortgage. All this self-denial allowed him to pile up cash in a series of deposit accounts with different banks and building societies spread across town.

Outside work, Ray continued to play for the Old Red Coaters, initially in their First XV but after a couple of years dropping down into the Seconds and then, suddenly, the Thirds. As the years progressed it came as a shock to find that the bruises from the previous week carried over into the next game. What with training sessions and work, he was too tired for much else, despite his mum's nagging that he should find a 'nice, clean young girl', in contrast, he supposed, to a dirty one. He was up for it, but he found that the combination of work and rugby left little space for anything else.

It had come as some surprise, therefore, when he found himself being pulled towards one of the firm's first recruits, an attractive-looking blonde whose hair seemed to tumble down the back of the charcoal-grey business jackets she seemed to favour, leaving translucent locks lying around as a constant reminder of her presence. Doe-eyed – a look she used judiciously applied make-up to accentuate – but with a steely cold gaze, Sandra O'Brien gave out few signals.

Until she spoke, that was. Sandra's most distinguishing feature, and the one she couldn't affect, was without doubt her voice. When she spoke, she sounded as if she gargled daily with gravel washed down with TCP. It was a deep, almost masculine growl, and when she was on the phone listeners tended to hear the sound she was making as much as what she was actually saying, which – given the complexity of some of their newer products – was probably an asset.

Ray knew she lived on her own, but beyond that details were sketchy. There were no sprogs, he knew that, and she'd kept her figure, even though her CV suggested she was approaching thirty. Smallish but not petite, Sandra was professionalism personified and took to the business as John Travolta had taken to dancing. She'd been an Avon lady in her time, and knew a bit about getting the customer onside and closing a deal. She was Ray's kind of woman – in more ways than one, as it turned out.

He hadn't got this far to blow everything on a fling, however. If nothing else, Sandra was a real plus to the business, and it would have been a tragedy to scare her away. Focus, Ray continually reminded himself, focus. Initially she was the archetypal icy blonde but after a while Ray sensed a thaw, and he found himself glancing up at her more and more often and finding excuses to tour the office, lingering a subtle moment longer at her desk when she was around.

He'd been contemplating his options, wondering whether to consult the oracle of Pam before making a move, when out of the blue he received a letter from one of his sleeper addresses. Meadows and Son operated a simple letter-first-then-phone-call approach to potential new business. Their contact list was one of the firm's prime assets, so one of the precautions Pam had woven into the system was a smattering of sleepers in the mailing lists given to their staff. These were fictional names at real addresses scattered among people Ray and Pam trusted. The arrival of the letter meant two things: that the system worked and, more importantly, that someone was playing away with their contact list.

The letter carried a different letterhead but otherwise the wording matched their own successful formula word for word. The only other difference was the contact number. It was the work of moments to find out that this particular sleeper had been in a list given to Sandra. Ray's first reaction was one of admiration, that the girl was cast out of the same mould as him; but Pam had rapidly introduced a note of pragmatism. The devious wheeler-dealer in Ray had briefly wondered whether this was a problem or an opportunity, and he decided to sit on his new-found knowledge for a few days while he pondered his options.

That was his mistake. She scarpered, pronto. She must have had a system that counterbalanced their system – and once again, Ray couldn't help but admire her. Pam's opinion was less generous.

'Let me put it in words you might understand,' she'd offered. 'She was after your buck, not a f…' Ray stopped her with a hand before she demeaned herself with changing-room language.

There was no way of knowing how much damage Sandra had done, so while Pam did what Pam did best, going through the records, Ray took the role of Action Man and tracked her down. Playing amateur policeman, he discovered she'd upped sticks to Ireland – a contact in the ferry business tipped him the nod that she'd left Holyhead for Dublin the day before, so he followed her.

Ray had got used to wading through council estates, and encountering the crap that people were prepared to live among, on his travels through the heart of England; but nothing had prepared him for Dublin. He thought kids wandering around in their bare feet was something you only saw in history books, not in the latter part of the twentieth century. Then there'd been the flags, Irish tricolours everywhere, hanging like flaccid members in the absent breeze. The belief that joining the EEC was going to somehow lift them all out of misery was just the latest promise that history had reneged on for the Irish.

Finally, there were the drunks. Again, God knew he was used to seeing a few blokes having one over the eight, but whole streets full of thickset, desperate-looking types in greatcoats puking up into gutters – and that was only the ones with a good aim – was enough to make him turn his hire car around and head for home. A phone call to Pam confirmed limited damage, and he'd decided to cut his losses. From that day on, he was going to get female company the same way he got his pizzas: buying them in.

------------------------------ ✳ ------------------------------

The thump on the doormat told Harold Mitchell all he needed to know. By now, he'd learned how to recognize it: too heavy for a tax demand, too light for a new *Thomson Directory*. Sometimes the postman didn't push them all the way in and they'd hang from the back of the letterbox as if they were clinging to the top of a cliff.

Yellow padded envelopes, always yellow padded envelopes, stapled and then wrapped around the top with brown packing tape, neatly cut with what were obviously sharp scissors. A customs docket on the front described the contents as 'printed material', which was fair enough, but this didn't even begin to tell the story of what was inside. The stamps hadn't been franked on this occasion, but otherwise the pattern was the same: somewhere exotic and always different postmarks, marking all corners of the world. If he'd been a stamp collector he'd have amassed a halfway-decent collection over the years. Years during which Harold Mitchell had come to hate the daily ritual of the arriving post.

It was madness. It had all happened ten years ago, yet it was with him every day: the brief few seconds that had gone on to define his life ever since. Sure, he couldn't say for certain that they'd ever been used against him, but just the hint of their existence would have been enough to kybosh any chance of a decent job; as a result, he couldn't take the risk of applying for anything. He didn't think they were the reason he'd got the push at the Red Coat, it was probably the Muck-up Day shenanigans which had done for him. The governors were a petty and vindictive lot, and the enemies he had there would have seized their chance.

The packages were only ever a beginning, and whenever he held a new one in his hand he always found himself torn between dread and curiosity. The contents were always the same: a plane ticket and a postcard with a name on the back. No ordinary postcard, but one featuring himself on the photo side, caught in the act, and never from a flattering angle. Later, when all was done, they'd leave him alone again for a while, after which the wait for the next package would begin. The only thing that was certain was that there would always be another package.

It was as if the flashes from the camera had frozen his life in time. Barely a day went by without him remembering those few seconds, and no matter how many times he rewound it in his head he could never work it out. Who was behind the camera? How many of them were there? How had they known, and how had they got in? Then there was the biggest question of all: why did they continue to persecute him after all these years?

It was the last day of summer term, an hour or so after the end of the traditional send-off. To call it a party would have been to oversell it – more of a wake – but Asti Spumante and nibbles had been involved, followed by a short speech to acknowledge those moving on and the achievements of the year. It was a tradition, and the Red Coat was nothing without traditions, and as such it was something that had to be got through despite the events of the morning, an opportunity to draw a line so they could start again with a clean slate, come September. Given those events, the tone had been understandably subdued, even sombre, and people had dispersed as soon as it was polite to do so.

With the boys long since gone, Howard made a tour of the grounds to ensure that absolutely everyone else had followed suit, even the maintenance people. He checked and double-checked that there was no one left on the premises, he was sure of that, other than the one person he now needed to see.

Nothing had been arranged, but she'd been waiting outside his study all the same. She was wearing her uniform, wisps of short cinnamon-coloured hair peeking out from underneath her starched peaked hat. Her clean white tunic had navy piping on the sleeves and a collar, while a golden clip pinned a watch to her chest, worn upside down. Harold experienced mixed feelings when he noticed her slender bare legs, with the small feet of a ballet dancer. Tights were always a nuisance in these situations, whereas stockings … he hadn't lingered on the thought; what was done, was done. It was a long time since he'd been treated to stockings.

She was sitting on the chair outside the study, her hands folded neatly in her lap, a look of feigned concern shrouding her face. Harold paused on seeing her, took a deep breath and advanced slowly towards her.

'Trouble, Matron?' he asked, nonchalantly.

'I'm afraid so, Headmaster,' she mumbled, staring down at her shoes.

'Speak up! I can't hear you!'

'I'm afraid so, Headmaster,' she'd repeated, much louder this time.

'Out with it, then.'

'I'm afraid I've been very naughty and been sent to see you, Headmaster,' she replied, directing her seductive brown eyes shyly towards the floor.

'Naughty, eh?'

The routine dictated that it was his turn to adopt repetition in what had become a well-rehearsed exchange over the years. At this point in the script, he was required to put his hands behind his back and pace up and down with a worried look.

'Well, if you've been naughty you'll have to be punished, won't you?'

'Yes, Headmaster.'

'Follow me, then,' he commanded, unlocking and opening the door to his study with great ceremony, coupled with a sham reluctance.

What followed varied, but without fail called into play many of the otherwise innocent items that lined the walls of his study, as well as the brass eyelets on his desk. These were the moments when he came closest to the bliss that a man of his persuasion could reach. These were the times he was prepared to undertake all sorts of subterfuge to achieve, to risk everything to get his due reward for all the crap he'd had to put up with.

It was at the height of this bliss that his head exploded, or so it had seemed. Suddenly the room was full of flashing lights, and for a brief second he wondered whether he was entering a new realm of delight, rather than the living hell it later turned out to be.

In that moment, he experienced what it must feel like to be a celebrity walking the red carpet. The blue flashes came from every angle, and other than the sound of rapidly closing shutters, the presence that invaded his most private space was silent: no shouts or instructions, no warnings or abuse. Harold was standing at the time, his back to the door, his trousers still round his ankles, the sweaty palms of his right hand holding a whip. He'd turned and revealed the full extent of his excitement to the cameras and, as those he'd seen since confirmed, the photos that ensued traced the moments when Matron lifted her head as high as she could, given the restraints upon her, to see what was going on. Her uniform dishevelled, her limbs spread-eagled, her wrists and ankles constrained, her eyes wide, staring out from deep sockets – it wasn't a look any woman would choose to have captured on film.

Harold momentarily froze, but Matron let loose a volley of screams that filled the room, as if the blue flashes were gas flames from hell turned up to maximum. At some point everyone in the Red Coat had heard Matron at what they'd assumed was her full volume, but it turned out they'd been wrong; there were at least another three levels on her dial.

Temporarily blinded, Harold lifted his arm to his eyes in an effort to make out the shadowy figure or figures behind the cameras. After ten or fifteen seconds – maybe more, maybe less, he didn't know – he advanced, conscious that he had to do something, however futile the gesture might turn out to be. What followed was pure seaside pier farce, as he tripped over his rolled-up trousers, lifted one foot to extricate himself, and then stumbled over a loop of his belt and fell, face first, on to the carpet. Unfortunately, the first part of his anatomy to hit the deck was probably the last organ of his body he'd have wanted to.

The pictures that followed, in their storyboard sequence, would have shown first Harold's backside level with the floor, then Harold's backside slightly arched, followed by Harold rolling on to his side clutching his groin, and finally Harold adopting the foetal position. A wide shot would have shown all this with Matron firmly secured to his desk as she awaited her 'punishment', her neck craned, her mouth open and, if the quality of the film was up to it, her epidermis, among other things, clearly visible.

Something not very deep in Harold's subconscious had told him, even while it was happening, that the nightmare he was undergoing represented the end of his career. What he couldn't have known was the timing. The first few minutes after the whole sorry episode had been all about crisis containment, calming Matron down, and considering his options. Phoning the chairman of the board of governors and offering his resignation on the spot had flitted across his mind, a course of action that had the virtue of minimizing the risk that the photos would be used; but in the end, he decided to sleep on it.

What followed was the longest weekend of his life. He spent the Saturday looking for clues and trying to avoid Marion, and most of Sunday sitting at his desk, once his most prized possession but now a crime scene. Nothing had happened, and by nine-thirty on Monday he found himself caught up in the normal routine, mainly year-end paperwork. He'd dared to hope it wasn't as bad as he'd feared.

Then the phone went. A soft melodic 'brrr' from his dun-coloured Trimphone, like the sound of someone shivering, only speeded up. The chairman of the board of governors. There was to be no last-minute reprieve. It seemed there'd been a call from 'the Palace' – the palace in question not needing to be named – and, in the light of this, the governors, who'd met in an emergency session, had reluctantly come to the conclusion that he wasn't the man to take the Red Coat into its next phase.

No mention was made of the photos, and in a strange way, despite the news he'd just received, Harold felt as if he'd been let off the hook.

----------------------------- ✳ -----------------------------

Pam left Meadows and Son early in 1987, laden with a good proportion of Ray's cash, and joined her mother in Spain. There, she bought a villa overlooking Fuengirola, where she put her feet up and started to work her way through the entire Jackie Collins canon.

There was no doubt about it, the deal Pam had struck with Ray was a good one; for her, anyway. It came as a bit of a shock when they had the business professionally valued; enough of a shock for Ray to demand a second opinion, but when this came in twenty-five grand higher than the first one he closed the deal, draining all the secret accounts and taking out loans for the rest. A cool hundred grand. He could have bought half his parents' street for that. He was going to have to bust his knackers to keep up the payments, and that was just the lump sum. On top of that, there was the standing order to pay off the rest, in order to keep Pam in the style to which she was now becoming accustomed.

He was still young, that's what he kept telling himself, not yet even thirty: time was on his side. What he needed was someone cutting him a break. Instead, between agreeing the price and the loan kicking in, interest rates had risen from 9 to 14 per cent, and the bastard bank demanded four points above base for a business with so few tangible assets. The best solution to Ray's problem would have been to get another business partner in, preferably one with a wallet so thick he had trouble sitting down, but this was easier said than done. Life had taught him to be suspicious of other human beings, and his business was all about trust and perceptions; putting his name about might make him look desperate. Besides, there may be some issues with full disclosure.

In the meantime, all Ray could do was maximize the business's income, and juggle like fury while waiting for a miracle regarding interest rates. The business itself had still been performing well: the funds he had under management, either directly or indirectly, ran into the millions, but it wasn't real money. What he needed was access to cash, folding stuff. The problem was, Meadows and Son was set up to develop long-term relationships that grew the business steadily over time; not instant big wins.

The answer came with something called escrow. Some uppity well-educated arsehole had told Ray it came from the French word *escroue*, apparently, a scrap of paper that acted as a deed until a deal was completed. For Ray, it meant a new type of account: one laden with cash. He'd got in with a company of house conveyancers, a new sort of business that had started to take on the stuffy lawyers, offering a fixed price to do a decent job for a fair fee. This allowed Ray to get into mortgages, just as the housing market was booming.

The way things worked, there was often money sloshing around between sale and completion, deposits especially, and these were put into these escrow accounts. Pure cash lying around with nothing to do, which he could put to work. When it was needed again by its rightful owner it didn't matter because there was always some fresh cash coming in from the next deal. The more deals they had on the go, the more the escrow account expanded, providing a nice little pot that could be dipped into as and when required. Nothing serious, Ray wasn't stupid, but at the very minimum it kept the bank vultures at bay.

What Ray hadn't reckoned for was 19 October 1987, the day the newspapers and commentators soon started calling 'Black Monday'. Who could have predicted a fall of 25 per cent in the stock market in just ten days? Overnight, people stopped buying houses.

------------------------------ ✳ ------------------------------

Reggie had deliberately set off early that year, keen to avoid what seemed to have become an annual meeting with Ray Meadows in the school car park. With the meals settled into a familiar format, Reggie liked to use the short walk to whatever venue had been chosen that year, to reflect on his school years: something he found useful, if for no other reason than to remind himself how far he'd come. At the early meals it was much simpler: events from school days were still fresh, and they'd enjoyed going over familiar ground. In recent years, they'd tended to home in on where they were now, although Reggie's exact position was a question he found he'd been asking himself more and more. Rapidly approaching a rut, was the answer he kept returning to.

Recently Reggie had tried going to the gym, where he'd learned two things. First, that he hated most modern music, especially when it was played too loud for him to think; and second, that it didn't matter how much he ran, rowed, pulled weights and stretched, his weight never went down. Besides, he'd never really got the hang of packing his gym bag: he always seemed to forget something, be it his towel, a spare pair of pants or his water bottle. This seemed to confirm that Reggie and exercise just weren't meant to be.

It was already dark as he pulled into the empty courtyard past the war memorial, and settled his brand new VW Golf Sport into a space halfway up from the bike sheds. Okay, it was a bit small for him, but the car was some compensation for all the hard work he'd been putting in since his last promotion – it even had a mock golf ball as a gear knob. The air outside was fresh, with an undertone of rotten leaves, and Reggie took a deep lungful in an attempt to clear his head.

Having locked the car, Reggie removed the key and put it in the pocket of his crisply ironed jeans (most people preferred to enjoy the opportunity not to wear a suit these days), before standing still and listening. Nothing. He was safe to make his escape, maybe even go for a wander around the park; it wasn't too cold, and he had time. With a determined stride, he set off for the gate, when out of nowhere a maroon Ford Orion came screeching towards him, its lights on full beam, its exhaust sounding like it needed attention. In a plume of blue smoke the brakes were jammed on and the window came down in a single smooth motion.

'Aha! Same idea, I see, get a head start, eh?' The smile below the ginger fringe was unmistakable.

'Shall I get you one in?' Reggie asked, in a tentative and at the same time desperate attempt to postpone the inevitable.

'Nah, hang on, be with you in two shakes, we can go in together.'

Reggie's languid nod was one of resignation rather than anticipation.

------------------------------ ✳ ------------------------------

It seemed everyone wanted to get married, even have kids, although the two events weren't always connected. In the previous eighteen months George Rowlands had been to no less than seven weddings involving old school friends, and that excluded the other three he hadn't been able to make because he was abroad on business. He'd got to the point where he was seriously thinking of using that excuse more often in the future when responding to the embossed cards inviting him to share someone's 'special day'. Sometimes he knew the bride, sometimes the groom, and on three occasions he'd known both. Twice he'd even been the best man. He often kicked himself for not buying a morning suit at the outset. That, or shares in Moss Bros.

Definitely and defiantly single, usually sporting an unseasonal tan and with jowls that looked like they'd never even entertained the idea of excess flesh, George struggled with the concept of marriage, especially for a bloke still only in his twenties. He knew the institution held attractions for others, it was just that he didn't share them. He enjoyed his independence too much. The world was a big place and half the people living on it were women, both of which meant there was a lot of exploring still to be done.

To George, weddings symbolized more of an ending than a beginning. What really irked him was this implicit assumption that marriage was a secret club which everyone was supposed to want to join, whether they appreciated it or not. George's pet hate was the 'plus one' attached to the invitations he received. He knew this was the etiquette, but he also half suspected it was there to flush out whether he was with anyone, to see if he was going steady, as they'd put it; in other words, whether he was close to joining their club.

George understood the whole rite of passage thing; it was just that his observation was that this particular passage tended to end with a ruddy great brick wall, ten feet high, at the end of it. He had no craving for the companionship of a life partner. In fact, he'd found over the years that he didn't really need friends much at all – that was one of the reasons he came to the Seventy-Seven bashes, to make a conscious effort to stay in touch with people; something he doubted he'd do otherwise. Besides, wasn't this year a big one, ten years? He was curious to see how people were getting on and to match them up against his own success.

George had reached the point where he could almost recite the marriage service word for word, but he always got stuck on the bit about procreation. While he took a keen personal interest in sex, he was less attracted to the end product nature had designed it for. In fact, there were times when he could make a good case for Herod being one of the good guys, not least because of the effect it seemed to have on women. Pregnancy seemed to undo the restraints on so many women's bodies, as if a zip was undone that caused them to flab out, like a blob of clay thrown on to a potter's wheel. Moulding it back into shape appeared to be something women found incredibly difficult, and after a few months of trying too many of them seemed to give up.

Then there were the psychological side-effects. If crossing the threshold from virgin to sexually active represented the start of one, largely exciting, phase, passing into motherhood seemed to represent another, often sanctimonious, time: one where sex lost its fun and became either a chore or a means to an end. That was how George had heard it, anyway, from more than one source. A couple of times he'd had a go at testing this theory out, offering the new mums an opportunity to try something different, but he'd drawn a blank. Mary Langley, as was, came to mind, as did old Stalin's missus. Both cracking to look at, but both as frigid as the Antarctic since they'd started dropping sprogs.

Then there was the effect that children had on blokes. George had seen the haggard faces on tired new fathers. That top-of-the-rollercoaster look they adopted when they realized what they'd done. They all tried to disguise it, but there was no getting away from the impression that, in George's experience at least, they looked like they felt they'd been hoodwinked, that they'd signed a contract without reading the small print. George could spot it every time, and he could see it right now on the face of Jeff Stone opposite him.

'Go on then, what's it taste like?' George asked.

'Okay, a bit gamey, and these bloody bits of lead are dead fiddly. You can keep it, as far as I'm concerned.'

'Not the pigeon, you idiot,' George sighed.

'The '83 Margaux? Too early, still a bit tannic.'

George stared into the eyes opposite as if he was attempting hypnosis. It was no wonder they called this man Dumbo at school.

Jeff Stone became conscious of a falling silence and other pairs of eyes turning towards him. This was what he hated about sitting near George Rowlands, the way he seemed to be able to draw the attention of those around him like some kind of magnet. Ben Bradshaw seemed particularly engrossed.

'What?' he asked, genuinely confused.

'Not the wine, either, you dipstick. The stuff of life, the product from your wife's magnificent orbs – breast milk.'

It was at that moment that Jeff discovered red wine wasn't supposed to be snorted, sending a roar of laughter up the table.

At the other end of that table the conversation was revolving around flab. Reggie Richardson knew the secret to losing weight, he could sum it up in just four words: eat less, do more. The problem was, his job seemed to require him to spend most lunchtimes at one of the new Michelin-starred restaurants that seemed to be constantly popping up around the City, adding another spare to his already more than adequate spare tyre.

On top of that, his wife Ellie insisted on them eating together when they got home, showing off the skills she was learning at her Cordon Bleu cookery course. By the time he got home every night, the nanny had usually got the children to bed and Ellie insisted they enjoy what she called their 'quality time' together around the dining table, when all he really wanted to do was either watch TV or sleep. It was difficult to resist her enthusiasm and, of course, her food. Eating less, therefore, wasn't really an option.

Then there was the 'do more' bit. There had been a time when he'd cycled everywhere, but that had become simply impractical with his suit and the deep briefcase full of documents he needed to carry around. The days of school and then university rugby were long behind him, and having failed with gyms, the most exercise he got was probably writing cheques.

Having shared these thoughts with those around him, Reggie announced his conclusion: an alternative four-word mantra.

'Stuff it, stuff yourself,' he announced, briefly lifting and shaking his developing bowling-ball belly. 'Life is good and is for living. I understand that in other countries an expanding waistline is something that earns you respect.' And with this, he took a sip from the brandy that had appeared in front of him from nowhere – he must have ordered it, he just couldn't remember doing so. This was one of the delights of the Seventy-Seven Society meal, the ability to share your innermost thoughts with people you knew well but saw rarely. It was like having a set of secret confessors; much like he'd heard therapy could be, only considerably cheaper and less demanding on the diary.

Terry Mungus's brain had, by then, become slightly befuddled, but he had to admit Reggie's theory sounded, well, sound, or did he mean round? God, so many of his old friends had stonked it on a bit. Was this how things were going to be from now on, a load of plump, balding, smug middle-class blokes? There was a time when they'd raced each other round the school swimming pool as if they were bees on speed.

The swimming pool days. Once the alcohol had saturated their systems, memories of the summer of '75 invariably bubbled to the surface at these dinners. The challenge that year was to try to sum it up in a single word. From his vantage point at the top of the table, Tom Joules watched the wordplay gather momentum without joining in, feeling rather pleased with himself. He'd managed to put his stamp on the suppers over the years, making them less, well, raucous and bacchanalian, with less trouser-dropping from the old rugby team. He'd made a special effort that year to celebrate their tenth anniversary, tempting in what he called his 'occasionals' as well as the regulars, and unearthing a few who were subscribers to the Bond but very rarely actually turned up. He'd secured them a function room, which made it easier to hear what each other was saying, away from all the clanking noise a busy restaurant usually generates. As such, there seemed to be a more meditative edge to attempts to come up with the perfect word.

'Magical?' Reggie suggested, getting the ball rolling while delicately cushioning a staccato episode of wind.

'Nah. That doesn't hack it,' Andy Thompson responded: 'we didn't all produce white doves from our sleeves.' A slight pause followed.

'Perfect?' 'Fingers' Dalgliesh offered, the word tinged with a faint rolling of the 'r's, but everyone ignored him, perhaps because the deep tan he always seemed to have these days caused his features to merge into the poor light in the room.

'How about "idyllic?"' Jeff Stone said at last.

Reggie Richardson pondered this alternative. 'Closer, but was it really ideal? The weather was, sure, but even then I seem to remember thunderstorms. In fact, there were times when I was actually quite bored.'

'Freedom?' came another suggestion

'It was bloody hot, I remember that,' Charlie Young added, joining in the discussion, the amber lighting in the room casting a deep shadow over his high cheekbones.

'Remember how Freddie got burned? Christ, we ended up peeling an A4 sheet of skin off his back, didn't we? Poor sod.'

'Wasn't the only one,' Fingers agreed. 'The grass turned browner than the proverbial ...'

'Toxic,' Ray Meadows, now joining late into the game, offered, prompting an awkward hush to descend.

Paul Briton broke the silence. 'Well, you're right there.'

'That pitch was never the same again,' Ray went on.

'It's true, you can't argue with ...' Mark 'The Saint' Spencer didn't get a chance to finish his contribution, as he hurriedly raised himself from his chair in a rush to get to the gents before he threw up.

---------------------------- ✳ ----------------------------

It wasn't the fact that his ex-school colleagues (he would hesitate to use the word 'friends') had without exception called him Brucie all night that riled David Lu so much, or the fact that as many as five of them had asked the waitress if they served Chinese.

No, it was the fact that not a single one of them had shown any interest in what he was doing now. This was despite the fact that to a man they used their own jobs as a way of defining themselves. What exactly was a systems analyst, anyway, and what was so remarkable about being in town planning? The attraction of a career in procurement was completely beyond him, and weren't pharmacists just doctors who hadn't made the grade?

When he first entered the room, David was struck by the fact that everyone seemed to have a thick leather-bound book placed ostentatiously by their side, some of them monogrammed either with their own initials or the name of their employer. It turned out these were a form of glorified diary, with a name that sounded like a type of delicate pastry. The thicker the book and the more ragged the pages, they seemed to say, the busier and more important their owners were.

It was fair to say that David had endured rather than enjoyed school. He'd suffered all the clichés – the last to be picked for the football team, the last raised hand to be answered, the constant forgetting of his first name – but he hadn't let it get to him. For him, school was just a stepping stone towards the greater ambition of qualifications and a good job. He'd seen most of his peers as morons who didn't realize how privileged they were. People whose breadth of imagination could be measured by the fact that the most prominent person of Chinese origin they could think of was Bruce Lee, hence the nickname. It could have been worse, of course; leaving aside the potential offered by his surname, they could have called him Ho Chi Minh, or Mao, and he'd always taken great care to avoid going around in groups with three others for fear of being labelled one of the Gang of Four.

As such, David had avoided the Seventy-Seven Society meals, and now he remembered why. He'd come partly because Mary thought it would do him good to get out, and partly because Tom Joules had asked him. He'd always had time for Tom. Mary seemed to think he needed to make more of an effort to keep up with his old chums, as she called them, although he suspected the real reason was that she wanted to justify meeting up with her own chums in the group Susie Bradshaw had got going. A man needs friends, his wife had told him, but seeing as they'd largely ignored him at school, why should they start taking an interest in him now? He'd gone partly to get some peace and quiet at home, and partly to see what they were doing with the money he gave them every year, which he suspected was actually financing a giant drinks kitty.

He'd soon discovered that it certainly wasn't being spent on the food, which looked decidedly unpalatable. The fish was so grey and soggy it wouldn't even have been served in an old people's home, and he'd never really understood the calorific disaster that was a British Christmas meal, with all the so-called trimmings, which was what most people ordered. Instead, he'd opted for the vegetarian dish of the day, December Delight, which seemed to consist mainly of lentils and cheese; a decision that, it turned out, probably saved his life. He made his excuses at around ten and went home.

The phone call from work came through at two in the morning. David was needed at the hospital. They'd just had a mass influx of patients with severe diarrhoea and vomiting, a suspected case of institutional food poisoning. They were taking up an entire ward and causing chaos, with a fair few also showing signs of mild alcoholic poisoning. It was a case of all hands on deck, and once dressed, he'd grabbed his white coat, starched so stiff he could have practised origami with it, and made his way to the hospital. A recently appointed registrar on the general medical ward, living near to the hospital, David was an obvious candidate to provide two of the required hands.

The scene on the ward wasn't pleasant. The nurses were working double-quick during a part of the night when they'd normally be catching up on their magazines, and the sluice room was operating at a rate that probably required a warning call to the local water board, if anyone had had the time. The patients, although victims may have been a more accurate description, were writhing masses of flesh, some still noisy with drink, and it was only after ten minutes of rushing around that he recognized Andy Thompson from the Seventy-Seven meal.

Further investigation revealed that everyone was from the group he'd been dining with only four or five hours before, their pallors as grey as the fish he'd seen earlier in the evening: a coincidence that David soon realized might be not be down to chance. A psychosomatic sweat broke out briefly on his brow before he remembered he'd had the vegetarian mush.

The professional in him quickly kicked in and he approached the consultant in charge, a man whose routine grumpiness was magnified by the fact that he too had been summoned from his bed. Amazingly, it turned out that the source of the contamination had been isolated to the turkey dinner, not the fish, and, having declared his position, David was given the all-clear to pitch in. As he approached the nearest unattended bed, he could see the leaden face of another of his old school colleagues staring across the room, his back propped up by a pillow and his hands cradling a reinforced cardboard kidney dish.

'Brucie, old chap. What are you doing …'

His eyelids now performing an Irish jig, David stopped him going any further, and with some satisfaction told him, 'My name is David, David Lu. But you can call me Doctor.'

As the days went on it became clear that something more than mass food poisoning had occurred. No one in the ward seemed to get any better and the whole wing was put into quarantine. After a couple of days, other symptoms appeared: temperatures, fevers, aching muscles and severe headaches. The consensus was they'd all contracted a flu bug going around just when they were at their weakest, and the usual treatments of rest and plenty of fluids were applied.

That they'd all been struck when they were at a low ebb was a correct diagnosis; the flu, however, was not. Eventually, a link was made to a similar outbreak earlier in the year in Stoke, and a name was finally put to what was going on: Legionnaires' disease.

Of the thirty admitted to the ward, twelve didn't make it.

1988

There was something about having kids that made you do things you wouldn't normally do, like watching cartoons and singing nursery rhymes. Or visiting tourist spots you'd normally avoid as if they were harbouring the Bubonic plague – and, horror of horrors, even climbing up them.

Not only did Jeff 'Dumbo' Stone hate heights, his low centre of gravity also meant he had difficulty climbing steep steps. On top of all that, he also suffered from asthma, and a combination of fear and rapid temperature changes, along with sudden exertion, had a tendency to trigger an attack. He knew this, his wife knew this, his kids in particular knew this; so why did no one take him seriously? Like a younger royal, Jeff sometimes felt as if the arrival of each new child had shunted him one place further back in the family pecking order.

His otherwise anonymous grey metered-dose inhaler, his 'poorly pipe', as the kids called it, was an especially important piece of kit when he was away with the family. This particular year, having vetoed Jeff's suggestion of Holland, they were enjoying an Easter break in northern Cyprus. This precipitated some debate, as following the Turkish invasion over ten years before, the destination wasn't on the regular tourist map, and it was said that having a Turkish Cyprus stamp in your passport made it impossible to enter Greece. Jeff saw this as a positive: all those white-painted villages perching precariously on mountainsides. As it happened, their passports needed renewing soon anyway, so it wasn't an issue.

Jeff would be sorry to see his battered old blue passport replaced by the distinctly less impressive and somehow much blander European burgundy variety. They told the story of his twenties – backpacking pre-kids, work trips, family holidays, all battle scars tracing the story of his adult life so far. Thirty seemed ancient, but the proof of his adult life and responsibilities was irrefutable, like the four-year-old already scampering out ahead of him.

What Jeff hadn't bargained for when they'd booked this holiday was the island's historical link with the Knights of St John and, especially, their tendency to build castles on hillsides miles from anywhere, certainly miles from any hospital. One in particular, St Hilarion, just outside the northern port of Kyrenia, was listed on a leaflet as being Walt Disney's inspiration for Snow White's castle. Jeff regarded this as marketing bollocks, but the magic word Disney meant ignoring it wasn't an option.

The drive there had been enough to trigger the need for a quick gasp on his inhaler: hairpin bends and a passage through a threatening-looking military post, all in a car from a hire firm which seemed to regard brakes as an optional accessory. All the way up, his son insisted on pointing out sights far below, but this had been an old trick which Jeff knew to ignore. Having parked the car at the base of the castle, they'd paused for Cokes, coffees or corticosteroid according to taste, and Jane, showing a classic lack of support, had announced that she would stay in the café at the base and look after their two-year-old daughter.

There was no doubt that viewed from its base, the castle was impressive; it was the climbing bit that worried Jeff. A solid-looking square tower, crenellated in the usual way, followed by a series of winding paths, it bore about as much resemblance to Walt's castle as Joe Bugner did to Snow White, Jeff thought.

The tower was deceiving, however; a blind for what was to follow, leading to a series of ever steeper steps which led to a further set of buildings and a point that seemed, to Jeff at least, to be not only beyond the tree line but also into cloud territory. He had no choice, though: his son was already bouncing on ahead of him and he had to follow. A light mist had descended, and his son was refusing to obey entreaties to wait, knowing, quite rightly, that his father would only suggest it was time to turn around and head back to the hotel.

With his legs and heart both crystallizing into lead, he kept going, his head already full of thoughts about the inevitable journey back down. As usual, he was fantasizing whether a helicopter might be an option, but given the poor visibility he judged the chances as less than zero. It had also suddenly become terribly cold, and he was beginning to wonder what madness had led him to wear shorts for this excursion.

As tended to be typical at these sorts of places, the steps were uneven and worn, with a liberal sprinkling of loose stones to make things a little more interesting. At one point Jeff slipped, causing him to windmill his arms to regain his balance. Why had they started out on this crazy quest? Even if they got to the top they wouldn't be able to see anything, but he had little choice other than to press on, his paternal responsibilities clear.

A little boy's brief scream from up above pierced the air like aural lightning and caused him to pause, but it was followed shortly afterwards by giggles. The scream had a primeval impact, pulling Jeff up a little faster against all his other instincts, causing him to stumble again; this time, scraping his hand as he put it out for balance. He'd started to shiver in the cold and he knew another shot of chemical help was required.

Things might have turned out better if he'd just taken the time to sit down and rest, but the sound of his son's voice seemed to have become increasingly distant, despite continued, ignored admonitions to him to slow down and wait. Keeping his eyes fixed on the steps ahead, Jeff reached into his rucksack pocket and fished out the small grey container that fitted so snugly into his palm, and shook it impatiently. With a practised action he swept his arm up and covered his face with his right hand and, supporting the base of the device with his thumb, embraced the extended mouthpiece with his lips as, with a simultaneous action, he depressed the button on the top and inhaled deeply.

Any relief he might have felt was soon tempered by the realization that something wasn't right. There was an unfamiliar taste in his mouth, something sour and unwelcome, like a yogurt that had gone past its sell-by date, leaving a slight fizzing sensation on his tongue. Jeff felt a wave of nausea, and, being British, cast around for somewhere discreet to throw up. The dilemma soon became immaterial as a cloud of blackness began to infiltrate his brain. Just before he blacked out completely, Jeff noticed that the contraption he was holding was a slightly different colour from his regular inhaler: a darker grey. Just before the sun of his existence slipped behind the cloud of his consciousness, he thought he heard someone come up behind him and whisper something.

'Fly, Dumbo, fly, flap those ears,' it said, before he felt a gentle push in the small of his back.

There was no sound initially as he fell, and it took the rescue people most of the next day to find his body, even though it had fallen to a point no more than a hundred yards from the car park. A terrible accident, everyone agreed, and one to be handled sensitively if the fledgling tourist industry in this ostracized portion of an otherwise beautiful island was to avoid a fatal blow of its own. Anyway, the body was too mangled for an autopsy, and surely there was little doubt about the cause of death? In the rush to sort things out, no explanation was ever found, or indeed sought, by the authorities in charge of the castle, and no one ever had cause to look for an inhaler.

------------------------------ ✳ ------------------------------

It was no surprise that Tom Joules had vetoed any suggestion of a traditional Christmas dinner for that year's reunion. Instead, he settled for Gino's, a new Italian bistro in town, and it was only when he went to leave a cheque for the deposit that he realized it was where they'd eaten when they'd come up with the idea of the Bond. That meal had been overshadowed by death also, but it seemed inconsequential compared to what they'd been through the previous year.

The Bond had been intended to give their class a way of making their mark. Well, they'd done that all right, but not in a way any of them could have imagined. Initially, Tom had arranged for twelve extra chairs to be put round the table, plus another for Jeff Stone, of course, Dumbo; but he'd abandoned this idea when he realized the empty chairs would outnumber the full ones. He'd contemplated cancelling the whole thing as a mark of respect. On top of everything else, he couldn't help but feel a bit guilty; after all, he was the one who'd cajoled many of the eventual victims to attend. By his reckoning, at least half of them hadn't been regulars, and wouldn't have been there if he hadn't persuaded them.

It wasn't only the events of the previous year impacting on attendance. Tom understood from the papers that things hadn't been going too well in the world of business, either. First, there'd been the financial crisis, then the insurance industry had taken a hit after the Great Storm. He suspected there might have been some redundancies among his ex-colleagues, not something they'd feel like celebrating, or sharing come to that.

As seemed to always be the way, George Rowlands had managed to locate himself in the middle of the single table the small gathering were occupying. Opposite him was the sinuous frame of 'Fingers' Dalgliesh, wearing a cheesecloth shirt and some old brown corduroys. George could even see some soil lodged beneath his fingernails; at least, he hoped it was soil. He couldn't help noticing how his strange erstwhile colleague was busy separating the food on his plate into four sections, with clear spaces between them occupied only by gravy. George knew what it reminded him of: a CND symbol. He decided it was time for a little fun.

'Advocating world peace then, Fingers?' he asked, raising his voice just the notch required to ensure he attracted an audience.

'Um?' came the uncertain reply. Such was Fingers' concentration on his task in hand that his hearing had gone AWOL. 'Peas? Yes, they were lovely, thanks. Perhaps a little too much *Salvia officinalis.*'

A few drunken giggles escaped from the small band of acolytes gathered around George, most of them skilfully disguised by raised wine glasses. George merely raised his eyebrows in query.

'*Salvia officinalis,*' Fingers repeated. 'It's the Latin designation for sage.'

'*Saliva offensivealis,* more like, tastes like spit,' George retorted, generating further appreciation from the crowd around him, although he hadn't considered it one of his better quips. 'Fingers' Dalgliesh was easy sport, in most people's eyes one sandwich short of a picnic, and he knew he should have done better. As such, he was pleased to see that Tom was sorting through his pockets, preparing himself to give his usual speech.

Having taken soundings, Tom had come to the conclusion that he should go ahead with his usual report on the Bond, the early tragic demise of so many of their number, if anything, a vindication of the whole idea behind the scheme. The Bond would still allow the last man standing to keep their memory alive; it was just that the time frame may now have been condensed a bit.

With due gravity, Tom, one of the few who still insisted on wearing a suit to the meal (some said it was the same suit), mustered his emotions and needed only a small cough to get the room's attention. This achieved, he read through a list of the names of those they'd lost to the Legionnaires', at the last minute adding Jeff Stone, who he'd almost forgotten: a recitation heard in respectful silence.

Raising his previously bent head and taking the following silence as permission to go on, Tom pulled himself up to his full height and continued.

'Gentlemen, if I may, I'd now like to bring you up to date with the progress of the Bond'. A murmur went around the table, a tangible manifestation of the discomfort they were all feeling. Single sheets of A4 were passed around, and the silence as everyone picked their copy up was reminiscent of that moment in exams when the invigilator said they could now turn over their papers. As discreetly as he could, George Rowlands extracted some reading glasses from his inside pocket. They were a new addition to his wardrobe, and not one he particularly wanted to shout about.

Seventy people had originally signed up to the Bond, falling a disappointing seven short of the ideal number. Each had committed to pay in ten pounds a year by direct debit, a sum that kept them in the scheme, whether or not they made the meal. Tom had handled the administration and set up a building society deposit account offering a respectable rate of interest, and on reporting that the total was already well on the way to four thousand pounds, burbled approval rumbled around the room, until it was broken by an indignant voice.

'Four grand? Is that all?'

Andy Thompson hadn't immediately realized that what had been going through his head had escaped from his mouth. It was an affliction that had got him into trouble before, notably at a party to announce his best friend's engagement a few months previously. All at once, Andy became the centre of attention in the room, unwittingly igniting a sense of unfinished business, a feeling that not enough was being done, without really being able to express what 'enough' might look like.

Those in the room who'd been at the previous year's meal were well aware it had only been the inability to face another plate of grey meat, breadcrumb-infested stuffing and chipolatas twelve months previously that had stood between them and possible eternity. Their own mortality had stared them in the face, and while it may have decided to let them off this time, perhaps it had been a sign? The levels of chatter began to build, murmurs of frustration, of lost potential and chances missed rolled up into one. Comments began to ricochet around the room like pinballs unable to find a way between the flippers.

'Such a waste.'

'We were going to change things, change the world.'

'Not even thirty.'

'We'll never see a fly half like him again,' Ray slurred, loud enough for everyone to hear, although no one quite knew who he was talking about.

'When did we lose our sense of idealism?'

'There's still time,' someone suggested.

'Try telling that to Woody,' came the riposte, resulting in half those round the table trying to remember who Woody was, before a lone voice at the other end of the table piped up, 'I had his sister once, you know,' which precipitated a fresh silence, falling suddenly like snow.

Whenever there was silence at one of their suppers, the accepted fallback was to recall the days of more than a dozen summers before, when they'd shared the perfection of hot lazy days by the swimming pool.

'Our whole lives before us,' Charlie Young mused, in an attempt to sway the conversation. As always, he was dressed simply but stylishly in a slim-fit jacket over a white T-shirt. 'Fit, tanned, full of plans.' Deep bass voices mumbled in agreement, a Welsh male voice choir warming up.

'Oh, not that again.'

Faces turned to David Lu, a heretic lone dissenter daring to upset the respectful mood. He was leaning a little bit forward, his small hands on the table, his fingers intertwined, his pupils showing signs of rapid eye movement, even though he was clearly awake. He was wearing a thin blue and grey striped shirt with a white collar and a black tie, along with a furious look on his face. The events of the previous year had raised David's profile among the Society's members, emboldening him, and despite previous vows to himself, and encouraged by Mary, he'd eventually decided it was his duty to attend that year's supper.

'Well, let's be honest, not everyone was allowed membership to the inner circle,' he went on.

'Meaning?' challenged George Rowlands, the man who had undoubtedly been the leader of the inner circle in question. In the time it had taken him to utter this single word, George managed to straighten his back and puff out his impressive chest, as if he was some kind of exotic bespectacled bird. Opposite him, Ben Bradshaw was throwing a look down the table at David Lu which, if it could have manifested along the way, would have morphed into a pair of hands prepared to throttle any further comment.

Just as the doctor was taking a fresh lungful of air to expound upon his thesis, he was interrupted by Andy Thompson, for whom the four thousand pounds still clearly represented unfinished business. Neatly attired, Andy Thompson sported a fresh haircut and a pair of tartan braces. Even if you hadn't known, you would have guessed he was 'something in the City', with the 'something', in his case, being an investment banker. He was a man who saw spreadsheets rather than numbers, the sort of person who could anticipate ten moves ahead on a chessboard while at the same time being able to appreciate the detailing in the pieces.

On listening to Tom's report, what Andy had heard wasn't so much the numbers but alarm bells mingling with the sound of cash registers; in short, an opportunity. Building societies were for kids saving to get a mortgage deposit and old dears diversifying out of mattresses. Surely their departed colleagues deserved better than that? He usually worked on annual rates of return nearer 30 per cent, with the occasional killing on top of that. And what was all this tenner-a-year nonsense? A tenner didn't even cover the cost of a round at his local wine bar.

Before the evening was out, Andy had not only gained agreement to raise their annual subscription to £25 (he'd started by arguing for £50; you never got anywhere by aiming low), but also to the formation of what was called the 77B Group, a small committee given the mandate to make investment decisions on behalf of the Bond. Although the 'B' stood for 'Bond', almost inevitably perhaps, members of this group became known almost immediately as the Big Tits.

Andy was elected by acclamation into the newly formed group, and he would have counted the evening an unmitigated success but for a slight hiccup towards the end, when two other names had put themselves forward and were agreed on the nod. Ray Meadows he was confident he could keep in his box, but old Stalin was less predictable.

Derek Henderson used to enjoy the Stalin tag, but more recently he'd tried to consign it to oblivion. His fundamental beliefs were still alive; just buried a bit deeper below the surface. On leaving school he'd decided that the best way to undermine capitalism was from within, that he would be a more effective agent for the revolution inside the machine, understanding how it worked, than outside throwing spanners at it. He, too, had therefore entered the world of banking, although compared to Andy Thompson's big shark he was probably more of a small haddock.

Having gained a place in the system, however, undermining it had been less straightforward. One of the perks of the job had been access to cheap mortgages, and he'd used this not only to get himself a place of his own but to buy a couple of flats in London's Docklands, where prices were going through the roof. He planned to use the money he expected to make to keep the red flag flying, possibly by funding a political career, but at the moment he had too much at stake to rock the boat.

Andy's proposals had got Derek thinking. His reputation in the City was awesome – he doubted very few in the room knew how lucky they were; he was one of the new big beasts taking the place over. With Andy running things, as well as the new subscriptions and the decades they hopefully still had before them, the fund behind the Bond might become something substantial. Enough, perhaps, Derek reflected in his more ambitious moments, to even buy the school. What a memorial that would be to the Class of '77, as well as a delicious irony. He'd even thought of a name for it: the Jake Peterson Memorial School. But he kept that bit to himself.

------------------------------ ✳ ------------------------------

Should George Rowlands have still been concerned about the figures of post-partum women, a visit to a gathering of the Seventy-Seven Widows Club might have put his mind at rest. While it was true that Susie Bradshaw, the instigator of the group, had kept a little of the cumulative weight she'd put on through her pregnancies, it seemed to suit her, rounding her out. She seemed less fragile, somehow; a sense that was reinforced by her greater self-confidence, as if she'd grown into her twenties, both physically and personality-wise. She seemed to carry more of a life force about her, as if she was her own person these days rather than her husband's chattel. She wore her hair in a bun, held in place with a bamboo stick with a leather piece in the middle, which added to a general air of no-nonsense professionalism.

Shirley Tweedie, who'd been married to Eddie Perks for nearly ten years, could have been twins with Ellie Richardson when it came to dress sense. They clearly shopped in the same sort of boutiques and both favoured single-toned jackets with matching modest skirts, as if they'd rushed to the gatherings from work, even if in reality they'd both spent hours deciding before eventually leaving in the first outfit they'd tried on. Padded shoulders seemed to be out this year, the focus now on discreet, and probably quite expensive, earrings, which in each case had been gifts from their husbands after the birth of their first child. Both were wearing tights that made their legs look like they were in an advanced stage of the pox, and both had also quite clearly hit the gym.

Fiona Henderson tended to dress more casually, in a 'this old thing?' sort of way. Her favoured retailer was Next, although she steered clear of the Working Wardrobe section. Derek had suggested it was better for her to take a career break while the children were young, and after too many years working at the union offices where she'd met up again with Derek, she'd agreed. She'd come to find all the heavy rhetoric and sloganizing tiresome, so stuck in the past, and hadn't been sorry to leave. Derek's career had also taken a dramatic turn but he still retained some of his idealism, and Fiona admired him for it. She hadn't told him yet, but she'd recently come to the conclusion that she didn't want to pick up her career once the youngest started school as they'd planned; she found she preferred the freedom of being at home, and had been investigating different ways of filling her time. Of all the women, she seemed the most comfortable in her own skin: skin which was still flawless, a feature some in the group were jealous of. If she wore make-up at all, it tended to be to add a final note to her look, rather than to define it.

Together, being the most local, these four formed the nucleus of the Seventy-Seven Widows Club, and were also known to meet up now and then for a coffee or glass of wine at one of their houses, typically one of Ellie's or Shirley's grander homes, if a husband was away on business. Mary Lu also attended when her veterinary work allowed, along with Vicky Briton.

Susie had formed the group, but the first time they'd got together it had all felt a bit awkward. Perhaps she'd spent too long with her own company, or maybe the orbits she and her friends now occupied were simply different. Or perhaps she'd just been too indoctrinated by Ben. In those early days, Susie had found herself having to justify herself, and in doing so had discovered an unusual talent for crafting 'alternative pasts', as she liked to call them, although a more accurate description might be the biggest stock of whoppers outside Burger King. As the years went on, she'd become more and more skilled in the art of lying, and found she enjoyed it. In fact, she enjoyed it to the extent that she found it quite a release, with the stories becoming more fantastical; as if she was actively testing others' credulity, which, as it turned out, was a fairly elastic commodity.

It was as if none of them had much in the way of benchmarks, and craved some measures they could assess their own lives against. The secret, Susie had discovered, was to strike just the right balance between the believable and the outrageous. A good lie needed a bedrock of fact, its strength lying in what happened to it as it evolved. The tipping point at which it faded from a provable truth to something that was merely believable was a subtle one, and needed the correct mix of invention and credibility. If enough people believed it could be true, a lie gained a life of its own as it was passed on and embellished, until before long it became accepted as fact.

The audience had to want to believe the essence of the lie to be true, something made easier if it was rooted in something they already suspected might be true. She'd start with some bait, and, if it was taken, test how far it could go; the real art lay in being able to sense whether you were taking an audience with you. The whole thing also had to be delivered with a certain air of insouciance rather than pride, as if the teller didn't really have to share their story, and was doing so only because the listeners were egging them on.

As the years advanced and the numbers coming to the annual gatherings grew, the whoppers became garnished with extra bacon, gherkins and onions, sometimes with a side order of fries. As with Ben, the annual gatherings began to assume a disproportionate importance for Susie, although unlike Ben, she most definitely never shared what was said afterwards. Also like Ben, she learned the value of preparation and spent time considering her tactics. She learned to bide her time, to wait to be invited to make her contribution or, even better, to allow someone else to open up an area where she had a story ready.

Over the years there had been many stories she was proud of, some of which had become so widely spread they'd been told back to her in terms of absolute confidence by someone outside the Widows: the ultimate sign of success for a good lie. Her greatest triumph, however, had been to provide an answer to the question that had hung over the heads of all her old school friends for years: what *really* happened to Matron's daughter that summer's night at the end of fifth form?

They all knew it was something traumatic. Afterwards, she seemed to undergo a total personality change, and eventually disappeared off the scene altogether. While there'd been plenty of whispers, there was never a definitive answer, and in the absence of absolute truth, a believable story supported by a supposed eye-witness account was the next best thing.

The version of events Susie offered the group had the double beauty of both confirming what had perhaps been the strongest strand of speculation, while at the same time delivering a sharp pinprick to the aura of perfection the Class of '77 seemed to shroud themselves in. It hadn't been Susie's most inventive lie, but, as subsequent events would prove, it was her most powerful. In fact, she'd hardly had to make much of it up at all; her audience had imagined the scenario themselves more than once, and had pictures already resident in their heads. What made it so brilliant was its simplicity.

Susie began by expressing surprise that it wasn't common knowledge already, thereby making it okay for her to share what she at least had understood to be already in the public domain. The simple facts were these: a crowd of around half a dozen of the Red Coat boys had waited in the trees behind the swimming pool that day. They'd known that Matron's daughter always held back to have a final swim on her own when the others had left. She'd been like that: part of the group, but also separate from it.

Everyone listening to Susie as she unwrapped her story instantly began to run their own movie reel of what happened next, and Susie hadn't really had to supply much of her own detail; just the odd hint that maybe it was pre-meditated, or perhaps it had been a prank that had spiralled out of control. All she needed was the final piece of the jigsaw that allowed everyone to believe that what she was saying represented the gospel truth.

'What none of them knew, of course, was that Ben was still in the pool and saw it all happen, but was too frightened to do anything about it afterwards.' Susie had continued in a tone that came over as hushed but was in fact quite authoritative, creating a sense of command that belied her otherwise diminutive stature. 'Of course, I don't blame him,' she added, 'he was only one person and there was a gang of them. He's not a coward or anything.' She thereby sowed the seed of suggestion in the minds of others that that was precisely what he had been.

Her work done, Susie left that year's gathering exhausted, but also elated. Her story had the twin benefits of introducing a fault line into the otherwise perfect world of the Seventy-Seven Society, and marking her own husband out as something of a waterlogged drip. Her dearest wish was to be a fly on the wall when some of those who'd heard her story went back to their husbands that night. They'd all deny it, of course, but perhaps more importantly from Susie's point of view, bonds of trust would be fractured.

As she drove home, Susie relaxed in the knowledge that, amazing though she'd been that night, she still remained the guardian of a real secret no one would ever believe. After all, didn't everyone think that she and Ben had the perfect marriage? Revealing the truth wouldn't have required words, just the simple act of lifting up her blouse and rolling back the sleeves to reveal the bruises on her ribs and the cigarette-burn scars on her arms.

------------------------------ ❋ ------------------------------

Perhaps one of the reasons Susie felt more comfortable pushing the boundaries of her whoppers that year, and introducing a version of the holy grail of mysteries, was that her husband had disappeared into some kind of sinkhole of depression since the spate of deaths from the Legionnaires' disease outbreak. Most of the year had been pretty much a write-off as he'd let the business simply tick over, which was so unlike him. He seemed to be sleepwalking through life, a shell of his former self.

It was true that Ben was down. The deaths the previous year had hit him really hard; it was as if chances were being taken away from him. Then there'd been that decision. Hadn't he done enough to demonstrate his business credentials? Wasn't he one of the new breed of entrepreneurs the papers and politicians loved to go on about? He understood bank managers and investors, and what was more, he was a loyal member of the Society: he'd attended every meal, been supportive of the Bond, among the first to sign up to the direct debit.

So why hadn't he even been nominated to become one of the Big Tits?

He'd walked away that night fuming, doing what he always did, packing his resentment up as tight as he could so he could carry it home.

------------------------------ ✳ ------------------------------

There was nothing like a brush with death to make you feel alive. Mark 'The Saint' Spencer had been one of the lucky ones. He'd spent most of the Christmas before throwing up in hospital, and hearing the moans of his, it turned out, dying schoolmates; but he'd pulled through.

Back in the bosom of his family there'd been all that appreciating the love of others, relishing nature and, eventually, enjoying the smell of bacon again sort of stuff, but before too long real life had reasserted itself. Mark had done quite a few things he wasn't proud of in his life. Cheating on his wife, for one, but that had been a one-off at a conference, and he'd adopted the old rugby tour mantra of 'what happened at conference stayed at conference'.

Then there was the smoking. God knew, he'd tried to kick the habit, especially when the kids came along, but he'd been on the old cancer sticks half his life and they'd become part of who he was. These days, he limited himself to smoking outdoors, and only at home during the weekend, never the evening. Then, if he was being absolutely honest, there'd been the odd dodgy deal along the way, but you had to do what you had to do, didn't you?

It was probably a good thing he was in such a reflective mood, probably a side-effect of coming back from the Seventy-Seven meal which always tended to have this effect on him, of making him re-evaluate stuff, like his life. It was one of the reasons he still attended: that, and the Bond. A smart move that made you feel part of something and an obligation to keep in the loop, just to make sure it was being kept on the rails. Luckily no one had nominated him as one of the Big Tits, but with his track record that was hardly surprising.

That he was feeling so confessional was a good thing because when his brakes failed as he was heading down Longacre Hill, it became pretty clear early on that his chips were about to be cashed in. When his Ford Escort ploughed through the railings and then flipped up in the air before smashing spectacularly into a stained-glass window, the Victorian Parish Church of St Michael was ready to receive him in probably the closest to a state of grace he was ever going to achieve, something not unrelated to the fact that he was also well over the alcohol limit.

While the three emergency services rushed to the scene, a shadowy figure on the opposite side of the road made the sign of the cross and then disappeared into the night.

1992

Late summer in Ireland had been just the tonic he'd needed. It had been his first opportunity to step off the treadmill since Black Monday, five years previously. Life had been a grind since then, but he'd just about got his finances back on some kind of track; a few months more, a year maybe, and he might be able to count himself out of the woods. After that, only another five years and he'd have paid Pam off, too. As his dad had once told him, you had to be good at coping with whatever life threw at you, even if it mostly threw shit. Despite this, he was positive: you had to create your own luck – a philosophy he intended to employ with his next challenge: sorting his life out.

Somehow, he'd managed to body-swerve his way through the escrow shambles by moving out of mortgages and into pensions. Still lots of money to look after, only a steady flow rather than lump sums, and the people who gave it to him didn't expect to see it for a good few years, which had helped. A bit like the Bond.

At the time, he'd seen getting voted on to the 77B group as a masterstroke. He'd known what a financial wizard Andy Thompson was, a real Master of the Universe in the City, even though he was only in his early thirties. Although he'd avoided getting a nickname at school, Ray had heard he was known as The Leopard in the City: something to do with his skills on the spot market. Ray had some fun at the previous meal when he started calling him The Hippo, something Andy definitely hadn't seen the funny side of. Later, when Ray proposed a toast of thanks after Andy gave his update on the Bond, he'd only got as far as 'Hip, hip ...' before Andy turned and gave him a stare that implied he'd like to rip his head off and eat the contents with a spoon, something Ray actually interpreted as a victory rather than a rebuke.

The Bond seemed to grow in value all the time, and Ray hoped to pick up some good tips to put the money he was looking after to better use. Somehow, however, he always seemed to be just behind Andy's curve, always buying slightly too late and selling after the peak. Maybe he wasn't as daring as Andy. Maybe he needed more stake money to play with. What was that phrase? You need money to make money.

Relaxed, if not necessarily tanned, on his return, Ray had popped into the office to sift through the mail before going back to his flat. The place looked much as he'd left it, and carried its familiar smell of stale tobacco smoke mingled with coffee grounds from the rarely cleaned percolator. It was early evening, everyone had gone home, so he flicked on the small portable TV he'd bought so he could keep up with the Olympics from Barcelona earlier that summer. The TV sat on top of a sideboard and, reaching into one of the shelves below, Ray extracted a tumbler before retrieving the bottle of Tullamore Dew ten-year-old single malt he'd brought back with him, before triaging his mail.

A sudden change in the glare from the picture caught Ray's eye, and he looked up. The camera had been static and the situation confused, zooming in and out, as if the cameraman was unsure of his subject. Out of nowhere the Chancellor of the Exchequer, the oddly squat and cartoonish figure of Norman Lamont, had emerged alongside two minders. They looked determined as they made their way to a standalone microphone on the street, like they had something significant to say. Ray reached over and turned the sound up.

'Today has been an extremely difficult and turbulent day,' he began, before brushing away a stray hair and adopting a grim expression. It wasn't a promising beginning. Looking quite calm considering his opening remarks, the Chancellor went on to announce that the country was pulling out of the Exchange Rate Mechanism and that the second of that day's interest rate hikes wasn't going to happen after all, keeping levels at 12 per cent. Ray had been travelling, and hadn't realized it had even gone up to a crippling 12 per cent.

The statement had been brief, around a minute, and the newsroom had then cut to a commentator who described what had just been said as 'the most dramatic U-turn in government economic strategy for twenty-five years'. It seemed that the pound was going to be allowed to float free, and at that moment Ray knew how it felt. It also emerged that the second of the rate rises had been to a cloud-touching 15 per cent, which given Ray's liabilities would probably have been enough to finish him for good.

It was as if all the ropes he'd only recently flung out to the shore of financial stability had simply slipped off their mooring rings and dropped back into the sea. It looked like 16 September 1992 was going to go down in Ray's personal history, as well as that of the country. The newsman had already started to call it Black Wednesday.

Ray wondered how many more days of the week the politicians were thinking of blackening before they ruined him.

1993

Marion Whittle had married for love, although more for her God than for her husband. She'd first become aware of the man she eventually married in the staff room, but they'd then kept seeing each other at church, after which it had seemed a natural step for them to get together for Sunday lunch, seeing as they were both on their own. Over time a certain affection developed, followed by a deeper sense of caring, and given that this might be her last chance, Marion had said yes when Tom Joules had finally got around to proposing.

He was, of course, much younger than her, twenty years or so, but even if she said it herself, she didn't really look her age, and neither did he – although in his case he looked and dressed older than he actually was. In her quieter moments Marion had started to wonder if the thin lines on her face might be merging, and after weighing up the pros and cons of sharing her house with someone else, and the increasing sense of loneliness since her daughter had left, on balance marriage hadn't seemed such a bad idea. Besides, Tom's age had offered its advantages: he'd be malleable.

Tom, too, had been uncertain whether or not he was in love with Marion. He thought he was, but had no way of being certain, regarding love as something more suited to adolescents. He'd seen their marriage more as a communion, a word that had given him some reassurance.

The church had become a great comfort to both Tom and Marion over the years. From the start, Tom had appreciated the certainty a belief in God had offered, the availability of a rock on which he could secure other parts of his life. He'd also enjoyed the order, the ritual, the sheer act of worship itself, along with the sense of relief he invariably felt each week when he repented of his sins and received absolution.

Marion had started going when she first found herself on her own, deprived of both her daughter and her strange association with the headmaster, in quick succession, some fifteen years before. She liked to think she'd always had some faith; she was just glad that no one had ever asked her to describe it. Her frequent appearances at the back of the church meant she was soon mopped up by the handful of regulars who really ran the place, and, in time, she was asked if she'd like to run the Sunday school. It seemed that her links to the Red Coat provided all the qualifications needed for this vital post, regardless of the fact that she wasn't actually a teacher.

Ever diligent, Marion had found that teaching the young pre-school children Bible stories had reignited a dormant interest in something bigger than the daily grind. Starting with a blank page, she'd cultivated her own brand of Christianity and found her own level. She and Tom had got married in their church by the school chaplain who, in a break from tradition, had stayed on at the school, dividing his time between his duties at the Red Coat and taking services and pastoral work at the local parish church. There had been a moment ten years or so before when Marion had got the sense that the chaplain was interested in her, but she had not encouraged him and the moment had passed.

Their wedding had seen the biggest crowd either of them had ever commanded, or were ever likely to again. The regular churchgoers and a good contingent from the school had all swelled the congregation, and the school choir was also enlisted to bolster the meagre numbers from their respective families. The new headmaster had been kind enough to give her away, and all would have been perfect, except that Marion's daughter hadn't been there. No one knew where she lived any more, and Marion just hoped that one day the lost sheep would find its way back to the flock.

----------------------------- ✳ -----------------------------

Ben Bradshaw liked lists. Lists and charts. Some years before, he'd found an art supplies shop off a side road in the centre of town, and it had turned out to be an Aladdin's cave of paper: ruled, graph and plain, in sizes ranging from A1 to A5. It also had wonderful Faber coloured pencil sets (his favourite was their sixty-pencil set, which had shades of every colour of the rainbow and most of everything in between), stickers and labels. He liked rolling the pencils in his short fingers, marvelling at their smooth painted lengths and perfectly flat hexagonal sides.

He kept these materials in his study, which had been designated as a play room on the estate agents' particulars when they'd bought the house a few years before. The house had been a complete tip back then, and during the renovation work Ben had diverted one of the workmen to install an underfloor safe: a secret only he and the workman shared. This was kept hidden under a triple layer of floorboards, thick foamy underlay, and a plain jade carpet to match the walls.

Susie would never have dared to come into his study without knocking, but being a cautious man, Ben still locked the door when he was working on certain documents, as he was now, sitting at an old bureau he'd had brought over from his offices – a legacy from the previous tenant. He'd liked the look of it, with its shiny black leather studded to the sides, and its slightly pitted top. He sometimes enjoyed speculating about all the business that must have been conducted over it through the years, imagining it had once belonged to an old Captain Mainwaring-type bank manager, even though the people who'd had the offices before them dealt in garden supplies.

Susie was out and, as had increasingly become the case, Ben didn't have a clue where she was or when she'd be back. She was her own woman these days. The carpet and underlay had been pulled back and the safe was open, two lifted floorboards placed carefully next to the skirting board, one on top of the other. Ben was sitting in a leather armchair he'd picked up second-hand, which complemented the desk perfectly. He was still in his work suit, his tie draped over the slight belly he was sporting these days, the result of too little exercise.

In his hands he held his Seventy-Seven file, a loose-leaf compendium separated by tabbed dividers, with a page for everyone he'd been at school with, including, for the sake of completeness, some who hadn't even made it to sixth form. It was here that he kept his notes, logging snippets he picked up each year from the meals, as well as a record of attendees. He was on the Ds, specifically on the entry for Paddy Donoghue. A heart attack, at his age. Poor sod.

Donoghue had been a decent enough type, not what you'd call a mover and shaker, but that was irrelevant now. Ben had him tabbed under amber, although in truth he'd probably been more borderline green. Under the traffic light system in Ben's book, main targets were marked in red, with amber for possibles and green for odds and sods. Ben reached for a permanent marker. Black. Black was for 'out of the picture'. He waited a minute for the ink to dry before returning the book to the safe and retrieving the first of the floorboards.

---------------------------------- ❋ ----------------------------------

It was said that the secret to good comedy was timing, but Andy Thompson reckoned you could say the same about careers. He couldn't have chosen a better time to go into banking if he'd tried. The first few years had been tough, it was true, but it rapidly became clear that the tectonic plates were moving. The bowler-hatted brigade were still around, but they had increasingly become dinosaurs: still thinking they were still powerful, but doomed to extinction, leaving the forests clear for the young guns like him to get on with the important task of making some decent money. The grip the old established public schools had on the City was slowly being prised off, and having somewhere like the Red Coat on your CV was a real benefit – not top-drawer, but hardly an oik; someone who could probably be trusted, and in time assimilated – or so the thinking went.

By the middle of the decade, Andy had got himself a team and a reputation as a first-rate investor. In truth, he didn't know how he did it; he just seemed to have the knack. In his more exuberant moods he genuinely wondered if he had some kind of Midas touch, but in more sober moments he reasoned he was just a naturally lucky guy – luck, that was, combined with innate skill. At the same time, he knew that the more hours he put in, the luckier he got. First into the office and last out: that was Andy's mantra, and it had served him well. Not only did he meet his targets, but he got noticed too.

The back end of the decade had been big for him, both professionally and personally. Not only had the City had its Big Bang, but he'd also taken on responsibility for the Seventy-Seven Society's bond. Although the latter wasn't really much of an obligation, more a case of applying knowledge he'd picked up at work, he saw it as a personal challenge. His life wasn't exactly divided into neat compartments labelled work and play, anyway; they merged into one, with work more a state of being. He managed the Bond in his stride, a work-related hobby, something that would hopefully do some good; although exactly what shape that good would eventually take he'd never know. He certainly had no expectation of being the last man standing, not with his lifestyle. After the dreadful events of '87 he regarded managing the Bond as a privilege, an obligation to those who wouldn't be coming on the journey.

One of the big American banks had come in for him back in '85 and he'd helped them set up their trading desks prior to the big changes. The amount they'd been prepared to spend had been phenomenal, matching their ambition to succeed – something Andy shared. The trading desks had been like Mission Control Houston, screens with fluorescent green numbers and banks of flashing lights, so big that the traders had to stand up and shout over them to get attention. Andy had his own compartment on the open-plan floor, at the top of the room by a wall, slightly raised, looking out on his boys, his troops, in the daily war for deals and profit.

In Andy's experience nothing, absolutely nothing, could beat the thrill of trading. They'd had practice sessions before going live, of course, but nothing could have prepared them for the reality. The phones went crazy from the off, with people talking into two mouthpieces at once, putting deals together while a third sat waiting on a cradle on their shoulder. The energy, the testosterone, buzzed across the floor like an electric charge. It was irresistible, addictive.

The international financier and investor George Soros had been one of Andy's heroes from the first time he'd heard him speak at a conference early on in his career. Ever since he'd made it his business to know Soros's business. That was how he'd avoided falling into the trap so many others had plunged into on Black Wednesday. Sure, he'd sweated it a bit, having bet half the bank on black, but it had paid off. After that, he was untouchable; one of the stellar boys, pay rises every other month and smacking big bonuses every time he had an offer to jump ship, take his team elsewhere and make money for someone else.

He'd taken the same approach with the Bond, which was, after all, the very definition of a long-term investment, with plenty of time to bounce back from any setbacks. Despite the fact the amounts involved were miniscule compared to what he was used to, the hand of responsibility had at first sat uneasily on his shoulder, as if he was dealing with his kids' pocket money, but he soon shrugged it off. Before long, he was treating the Bond like any other long-term client. He was helped, of course, by a legacy from one of the unfortunate victims of the Legionnaires' incident. It turned out he had a life assurance policy but died with no one but his parents to benefit from it. In their grief they'd given all fifty grand to the Bond, which had made the whole thing slightly more lumpy.

When people saw the figures they tended to forget to factor this in, looking instead just at the headlines and assuming Andy was some kind of genius, and who was he to disabuse them? With time, Andy put up some glass between him and the team at work; he was still there in spirit but they didn't need him nannying them all the time. This gave him a little more thinking time, and more chances to fire up the small square floppy disc he kept with the Bond's spreadsheet on his new IBM computer.

Every year he put together a report for the meal, and twice a year he had to liaise with the other members of the 77B committee. This forced him to bank gains, maybe buy some bonds, pretty the numbers up a bit and make them seem simpler; but it was only timing again. He treated the Bond as a relaxation at the end of the day, time to have some fun, take a few punts, back his guts. Who was anyone kidding? This wasn't 'real' money, it wasn't 'for' anything anyone could describe. No one was going to be thrown out on to the streets if it all went nipples up.

Having said all that, when the new decade got into its stride Andy regarded the fact that he'd turned a measly four grand into a pot of well over a hundred grand in only five years as one of his finest achievements, even if it never seemed to occur to anyone to come up to him and thank him for it.

------------------------------ ✳ ------------------------------

Another yellow padded envelope had arrived for Harold Mitchell, its stamps showing it had come from Egypt. Inside, it contained the usual: plane tickets and a postcard. The plane tickets were for a week's time and the destination this time was Calcutta. Harold's heart solidified into an iron lump: he hated the long hauls; his knees were getting too stiff. How he wished it could all be over, but he'd given up believing that would ever happen, and at least it gave his life some purpose, however deranged.

It was only recently he'd realized the significance of the use of a postcard. It was a kind of reverse psychology; clever, really. A postcard normally meant travel, only this time it was the receiver about to jet off, not the sender. On the back of the postcard were his instructions, such as they were: a name and an address, along with a date and a time, almost as if it was a party he was being asked to attend, only conspicuously lacking an RSVP.

The picture part of this particular postcard, an especially interesting angle, one he hadn't seen before, meant, of course, that Harold either had to commit the instructions to memory or write them down for himself. The one thing the sender could be sure of was that he'd destroy the postcard, and with it any evidence. Also clever.

------------------------------ ✳ ------------------------------

George Rowlands didn't resent the many trips abroad that came with his role as an IT consultant. He'd come to regard them as part of his life rather than an interruption: a bit of colour. He actually quite liked the rhythm of checking in, the lounge, and being greeted by some slightly over-made-up dolly bird on the plane. He took some pride in the fact that they always smiled sweetly at him when they looked at his boarding pass stub and directed him to the left, confirming their suspicions that he didn't look like one of the herd. Once in the sanctuary of business class, he also appreciated it when he was swept up by another girl, who took his suit jacket off him and puffed up the cushions on the back of his chair before inviting him to sit down.

Perhaps one of the best things about going abroad was that it was exactly that: abroad, not home, a place he'd found increasingly constricting in recent years. Going abroad was like time travel, going back to a place where rules were still being put together. Back home, he'd found his room for manoeuvre being constantly constrained; the list of what he couldn't do had become longer than the one saying what he could do. Friends and family, bosses, members of his team, all had expectations of him, making him lose sight of who he really was.

This was especially true when it came to the ladies. Women had always been an important part of George's life; it was only when he was around women that he truly felt himself, but these days he had an increasing sense that the women he went to bed with were assessing him less as a lover and more as a potential father of their children. Even if they weren't, others clearly were. The sighs, the signals, the casual conversations around the water cooler, all seemed to be urging him to find someone, to settle down; as if by pinning him down they could rationalize their own life choices. So long as he was a free spirit he represented danger, a symbol of what life could be and a hint that maybe, just maybe, he'd been right all along.

When George went abroad, therefore, it was, quite literally, a whole new world. When he was away he could be himself, not the person on his business card, defined by his title and company, and the expectations of others. For George, Heathrow, Gatwick or London City Airport (he never used Luton or Stansted) always generated a little buzz in the pit of his stomach. The beginning of a new adventure back in George-land. He also liked being seen as an expert, swooping in and fixing other people's problems, so long as those problems had something to do with the architecture of their mainframe computer.

Everything seemed to change when the plane's undercarriage hit foreign soil. George wondered if he gave off different pheromones when he was away – rare was the trip abroad when he didn't attract some female company. This latest encounter had thrown him, though. Lying in his bed gone midnight, in a Scandinavian city the name of which he couldn't be bothered to remember, let alone try to pronounce, he was flummoxed. Sleep was impossible, but concentration was hard too: partly because of the alcohol still circulating round his arteries, and partly because of the icy blast being sent out by the air conditioning unit. He'd never mastered the thermostats in hotel rooms. A single sheet lay between him and the cold, but he didn't want to get out of bed to find a blanket, even assuming one was available, mainly due to the quite glorious stiffy that was holding the sheet up like the pole in a boy scout's tent.

It was extraordinary. A basalt obelisk standing rigid and proud, a magnificent monument to manhood, like nothing he'd experienced for years. It reminded him of being a randy adolescent again, although even back then he wasn't sure he'd ever had anything quite like this. He decided to lie back and revel in its magnificence: it seemed to have a life of its own. Even if his mind wandered to other things – politics, work, politics at work, even the different stages involved in assembling a piece of flat-pack furniture – it remained as solid and upright as ever.

He'd been woken up by it, the sheer physicality of the sensation disrupting him from a deep, dreamless sleep. Maybe this was the dream? He was having difficulty separating the two. He'd been in a bar with some woman, that much he could remember. They'd chatted. Not chatted-up, just chatted, about anything and everything. She wasn't what he'd call a stunner, although the light was poor. Cocktails had featured, he recalled, something exotic, and then they'd eaten together. The dessert course had been the moment when everything clicked. He didn't usually bother with puddings, but she'd ordered this amazing pie stuffed with some kind of local berries, light navy in colour, and when he finished his more boring choice of crème brûlée he ordered one for himself, breaking his own rule about never eating or drinking anything blue. George recollected a sour taste – not altogether unpleasant, just unfamiliar – but somehow that hadn't mattered.

A connection had taken place at that moment. He felt stupid even thinking it now, but it was as if their auras had suddenly linked together, perfect fits in an emotional jigsaw, as if they were different versions of each other.

Then it struck him.

Could this be what others called love? Had he, George Rowlands, finally succumbed? The feelings washing through him were certainly like something he'd never experienced before. They disarmed him, made him lose control of himself, but not in an unpleasant way; in fact, if he let the feelings engulf him, they were strangely comforting. It was as if he was finally being let into everyone else's secret, and on top of everything there was the added bonus of this boner to end all boners.

George remained on the bed, letting this thought sink in, but after a while the painful truth encroached. However wonderful he felt, however confused, the pole standing proud below his stomach was refusing to go down. He was now in a state where all he really wanted to do was get back to sleep and hope everything would be all right in the morning, back to normal, but his physical state made that impossible. Besides, he had begun to feel woozy, as if his brain was beginning to suffer from the diversion of blood to other parts of his anatomy.

Maybe it was his bladder playing tricks on him. He knew strange things happened in that department as you got older, it was just that he hadn't expected it so soon. Perhaps he should try walking it off? With not a little reluctance, George threw back the single sheet and lowered his legs to the floor, rotating on his backside as he did so. He always slept naked, and fortunately at that moment the air conditioner was in one of its down moments, so he wasn't assailed by an icy Nordic blast. Fumbling for the light switch, he remembered that it hung by a cord from the ceiling, and he flapped his hand in the dark trying to find it.

The room filled with a mean amber glow, and George began pulling his lanky frame upright from the waist up. The protuberance was still there, sticking out incongruously like a salami. George stood up and immediately felt a tingling sensation in his legs, a cross between pins and needles and cramp. He really did need to get walking. Cautiously, almost instinctively, he made a step towards the short corridor to the bathroom. The pain in his legs became, if anything, worse, and seemed to be spreading above the throbbing beacon in his groin. His stomach and then his chest started to tingle, and he felt his fingers go numb.

Not just his John Thomas, but his whole body began stiffening up. He found it difficult to walk and his vision became distinctly hazy. Signals were passing across his brain in moments of time too short to be measured, and soon one overriding message was received by that most vital of organs, his heart. His chest sent out a jolt, projecting George backwards with unexpected force, as that message was processed into action.

It was a case of 'time up' for George Rowlands, still only in his mid-thirties and with so much yet to do. No time left to run a marathon, to achieve the much-desired directorship: his body had given up on him. As he fell to the floor, no more life left inside him, his member finally deflated, like an airbed with a sudden puncture.

In time, the chemically induced stiffness in his now lifeless body would be replaced by the more natural process of rigor mortis. George lay alone in his anonymous hotel room for two more hours before a key could be heard in the door, which opened gently and sent a triangle of light into the room before it closed again.

Two bare feet walked up to George's lifeless body, where they then paused, and a pair of fingers were lowered on to his neck to check his clinical state. As his invisible medic prepared to leave, they bent down and lowered their mouth to whisper into his inert ears: 'Georgie-Porgie, pudding and pie.'

------------------------------ ✹ ------------------------------

Back when Mary Lu got married, she'd surprised not only her mother but also herself. Up until then, she always regarded herself as a fairly self-sufficient type, and although she'd never explicitly ruled marriage out, she always reckoned it would have to be someone pretty amazing to tempt her into it. Her mother had encouraged this view, which only went to multiply the general levels of amazement all round when Mary had fallen for David Lu.

For a while she told herself it was probably just a crush, but it hadn't taken her too long to realize it was proper 'I want to live the rest of my life with this man' love. What was more, being the logical type she could see certain advantages to getting married young, and if putting her mother's nose out of joint was one of them, that was an added benefit. Part of David's attraction was his, well, his different-ness. He carried an air of the exotic about him, and she also liked the idea that should they have children at some time in the future, then they would be a bit different too. Mary liked being different.

On top of this, David was attentive and thoughtful, as well as hard-working. Mary had always enjoyed a wonderful relationship with her father, a consultant cardiologist, so she understood the pressures of being a medic's wife. David was also highly supportive of her continuing her training to be a vet, and they often swapped war stories from their professions over dinner.

They had surprised themselves at how quickly their son, Stephen, had arrived, and how well they both seemed to adapt to him being part of their household. Given the fact that many babies tend to look slightly Chinese, especially when crying or filling their nappy, it took a while for it to become clear that Stephen shared features of both his parents: not that this was something either had been concerned about.

A mother's help had been engaged, Mary had continued with her job, and they'd been perfectly content in their little micro-ecosystem when Susie Bradshaw, a blast from the past, had got in touch to see if Mary wanted to come to her Seventy-Seven Widows group. Mary hadn't regarded herself as a Seventy-Seven Widow – David never attended the school reunions – but the invitation spurred her into action. Perhaps they should both make more of an effort to engage with others, break out a bit.

The invitation made her realize how much David seemed to distance himself from his school friends. When she'd tackled him on it in the past, he responded by saying he didn't have particularly fond memories of his schooldays, and the more she probed, the more she got a sense that he didn't want to discuss them, that there was something mysterious going on. This made her all the more determined that he should go to the dinner. If there was something lurking beneath the surface, she wanted to know about it.

As things turned out, it had been a strange evening for both of them. First, of course, there was that dreadful phone call after they'd both gone to bed, and David having to rush down to the hospital – only to be confronted by dozens of the people he'd just been having dinner with, and grown up with, practically fighting for their lives. Literally, for many of them, as it turned out. A dreadful, dreadful thing to happen. Mary was surprised by how David reacted: terribly coolly, dispassionately, very, well, clinically – which you could say was only another way of saying very professionally, she supposed.

Equally intriguing were some of the things that had come up in conversation with Susie and the others. The little revelation that had slipped out about Matron's daughter, especially. Mary didn't quite know what to make of that.

------------------------------ ✳ ------------------------------

'Journalism's a bit like acting. Lots of people think they can do it, and while quite a few can, only a very small handful really make a living out of it.'

If Sam Davidson had wanted to sum up his own career, after over a decade of solid slog, he couldn't have put it better. As it was, this little gem was the opening gambit of his first lecture in the Introduction to Journalism module he'd written for the course he'd been asked to teach at Mid Notts University, one of the wave of recently created new universities, formerly known as Mansfield Polytechnic. The module was compulsory, and as such, he knew not everyone in his audience would be hanging on his every word, but Sam wasn't that concerned if they were doodling in the margins of their notepads or scratching their arses. The most important thing about the course was that it had come just in time to provide him with a steady income.

Sam felt he'd been unlucky to never really find his niche in journalism. Somehow, he'd never found a specialism, that little something that would make him the go-to person when stories popped up. Sam wasn't the sort of person to accumulate contacts, but more critically, he'd never seemed to catch the breaks. As such, he never felt he was running ahead of the pack; more like running behind, struggling to keep up, the runt of the press pack.

He'd done all the right things, writing for the student newspaper at university and then becoming a stringer for the local rag, sharing a desk and an old Olivetti Lettera typewriter with an alcohol-infused old retainer. He'd even had a go at being a sports commentator on local radio on his days off, but it hadn't helped that he wasn't that interested in sport: something that had come through on his commentaries, apparently.

The paper had provided a grounding and an income for a few years, but there were only so many times you could get excited about mass outbreaks of ducks escaping from a village pond, planning applications, and problems with the local traffic lights. Like the wannabe actors Sam cited in his lecture, he'd waited patiently for the scoop that would make his name, but it had never seemed that bothered in finding him. He did occasionally go out and look for it, but he didn't really know where to start.

For one brief moment, though, he'd thought he had it, his big break, when he heard about the outbreak of Legionnaires' disease following the Seventy-Seven Society supper. To Sam it had everything: a bit of health, loads of human interest and, what was more, he had a unique in. It was *his* story. The problem was that none of the editors he approached seemed to agree. By the time Sam gave up pitching it, the story had gone as cold as the victims of the dinner themselves.

Although disappointed, part of Sam had been secretly quite relieved. He hadn't been sure he wanted to plunge back into the whole school thing. The memories of his one and only Seventy-Seven dinner had stuck with him, and to this day he still couldn't stand the smell of English mustard. Digging through his papers, he discovered he still had a direct debit outstanding to the society, which explained why he still received the annual mailing, as well as updates on the life assurance scheme they'd cooked up. In the end, even for Sam, there was something a little bit tacky about trying to build your career on the backs of dead school friends.

That had been the moment when Sam should have realized he was never going to cut it as a proper hack; instead he persevered, resigning his job at the paper and going freelance. The paper, previously part of a regional group, was bought by a big anonymous conglomerate and the whole thing had become more corporate, with a personnel department and fancy technology. The days of taking shorthand, typing your copy on to paper, and the smell of drying ink had been consigned to history. Fresh ways were found to reduce costs, and it hadn't taken much nous for Sam to realize he was one of those costs. He'd jumped before he was pushed, taking advantage of the hefty redundancy package being dangled in front of him.

The money been enough to take the sting out of the first few months, and in the meantime he found that glossy county magazines seemed happy to take a few pieces from him, although they were less inclined to pay him enough to live on. Society pieces, local celebrity gossip and interviews provided fifty pence a word, but in writing these Sam discovered that photos actually paid more than words per column inch, which seemed a damning indictment of the reading public.

A couple of years later Mid Notts had advertised for part-time lecturers, and Sam had done the only thing he knew how: he put another sheet of paper in the roller and started typing.

-------------------------------- ✳ --------------------------------

Reggie Richardson took some care in choosing his first company car. He wanted something with good performance, of course, but also something a bit different: stylish, distinctive. In the end, while most of his workmates had gone for BMWs, he'd opted for a Saab 93, a yellow convertible with light tan leather seats. He figured he owed it to himself, something for him at last after watching his salary disappear every month in various direct debits and bills. By hurrying the lease company up, he'd managed to get it in time for Christmas, allowing him to use it on the annual run to Wales to see the in-laws for New Year, which would also be a good opportunity to try out the car's trip computer.

For once, Reggie found he was subconsciously hoping to meet up with Ray Meadows in the old school playground. He even told himself he might offer Ray a quick spin in his new wheels: after all, it would be a shame not to spread the appreciation of such a fine piece of engineering.

On approaching the school gates, Reggie had taken his foot off the pedal and cruised into the playground. He was determined to get the on-board computer reading thirty-six miles per gallon. The car rolled to a stop and he pulled up the handbrake before checking everything was in order before getting out, leaving a light cloud of Old Spice, a Christmas present from his daughters, behind him. He'd booked a B&B in town, no point in taking chances, and would pick the car up in the morning, certain it would be safe overnight. Pressing the key fob, he activated the indicator lights which flashed three times in rapid succession and automatically activated the locks.

The car's interior light remained on for twenty seconds, a feature Reggie still had to get used to, but this gave enough light and time to see a figure sitting in a car two down from the Saab. He knew who it was simply by the bullet shape of his head, but it was harder to make out the car. It looked like the same old wreck Ray had been driving for a while now, and Reggie allowed himself a slight smirk of satisfaction – not least because he suspected it had been parked on purpose out of the tangerine glare of the streetlight on the other side of the playground.

As Ray got out of his car, Reggie thought he looked a little thicker round the middle, his ginger hair, short for as long as Reggie could remember, a little longer, and more dishevelled than usual. Overall, he looked more haggard, with his eyes, always deep-set, having retreated further into the lair of his skull. As he ambled closer, Reggie couldn't help but notice what looked like a small orange teasel under Ray's nose, which he realized was a moustache. If he'd been able, or wanted, to get closer to it, Reggie would have noticed small flecks of grey in between the ginger.

'Christ mate, you look knackered', Ray began, exercising the knack he seemed to have for turning Reggie's thoughts against him. 'Had a hard day at the orifice?'. When Reggie offered only a wry grin by way of acknowledgement, Ray changed tack, directing his gaze towards his companion's wrist.

'Got the time?'

Reggie glanced down at his watch and started to compose a reply when he was interrupted.

'It's beer o'clock!' Ray yelled and, giving Reggie a slight nudge in the back with his elbow, added, 'Your round, I think!' thereby claiming victory in that particular verbal joust. As they ambled to that year's venue, the Saab was never mentioned once; but then again, neither was the moustache.

It was the fifteenth anniversary of them leaving school and, as a concession to the landmark, Tom Joules had asked the hotel to provide a cracker and a party popper at each setting. Fortunately, 'Fingers' Dalgliesh put his head round the corner half an hour beforehand and straightened these offerings up, carefully placing the poppers on their flat tops and the crackers on the right, by the knives.

As was usual, Ray and Reggie entered the bar together, passing a disconsolate-looking Ben Bradshaw sitting on his own. He had a face on him like he'd ordered a double and got a single – whisky that was, not a bed – and Ray quizzically raised one of his bushy ginger eyebrows at Reggie on the way to the bar. Equally bemused, Reggie simply shrugged and replied, 'There's no rhyme nor reason to it, old chap. One of life's mysteries, like how women manage to spend so much money on make-up.'

His free drink acquired from Reggie, the two separated, and Ray noticed that people seemed to be talking about business and the MBAs they'd either just got or were in the process of getting. He wasn't quite sure what MBA stood for, so he settled for his own interpretation of Massively Big Arseholes, which made the constant mention of them more bearable. It seemed people were either doing very well in the current climate or struggling massively, with little evidence of a middle ground, and as he passed through the gathering crowd he overheard Toby 'Crackers' Connor, Eddie Perks and Simon Grant having a three-way conversation. It was something Simon had said that caused Ray to pause and tune into what they were saying. Simon Grant had a mean little money-box slit of a mouth and high cheekbones, and had mentioned something about no one ever actually making anything any more.

'What do you mean?' Toby asked. He'd never really lost the studious manner he'd had at school, the sort of look that seemed to sit comfortably on *University Challenge* team captains: arrogant when right, dismissive when wrong.

'Well, my old man built houses and yours ran a factory. Our parents' generation seemed to have the satisfaction of making real things, things you could hold, see or touch, you know what I mean?'

'Hold on,' Eddie interjected, 'not quite true. David Lu over there …' – all eyes turned to the doctor sitting at the end of the table, having a quiet conversation with Charlie Young, as he added sotto voce: 'Notice how he's stuck to the old one-child policy, by the way?' He returned to the earlier theme: 'He makes something. He makes people better!' Both Toby and Simon groaned, but Eddie continued undeterred: 'While Reggie, Andy, the bankers, well, they make money, and me,' – here he paused briefly before delivering his punchline – 'I make sweet lurrrve most nights.' And he thrust his groin up from his hips for emphasis.

'No, seriously,' Simon resumed, having left a few seconds for Eddie's contribution to dissipate. Warming to his theme, and determined not be to derailed, he elaborated: 'Making stuff, things, being creative. None of us seem to be creative.'

'Some of Paul's accountancy is pretty creative,' Reggie offered, being one of a handful who had joined in the conversation, switching to a more serious tone when this contribution fell flat. 'You're missing the point. We are being creative, we're creating wealth. Don't you remember the basic Keynes we were taught in economics? I do my job and get paid, then I buy things from other people, and this pays them, and they in turn buy things off other people, and so on; so the big wheel turns. It's called capitalism, except we now deal in services, not goods. We can leave the lathes and factories to the yellow- bellies in Korea and Taiwan; what we're good at is money. Think of the UK as a money factory, if it helps.'

At this point, Ray removed himself. He found his bladder extraordinarily sensitive to the first pint these days, and the conversation wasn't helping his already sombre mood. If only life were as simple as those idiots seemed to think, he pondered, as he stared at a sticker for an STI clinic on the white tiles of the gents. Not for them the coalface of actually selling to ordinary people face-to-face; for them money was something abstract, whereas for him it was all too real, or not real in his case, as he had so little of it. Taking a final deep breath, unexpectedly urine-scented, he finished his urination, and rejoined the melee.

Back in the bar things hadn't got any better, the conversation having turned to death. Not so much its imminence, more its inevitability.

The normally upbeat Nigel Bennett, a man whose face and job as an airline pilot positively demanded a moustache, had started it with the observation that he'd turned thirty-five that year. 'Halfway to my three score years and ten,' he announced, to no one in particular, although someone must have heard him as the remark was met with a call of 'Bloody hell, cheer up' from behind him.

Nigel continued, turning as he did so, to find the grinning face of Paul Briton in front of him. 'Well, face up to it. It's not so much the first flush of youth these days – more a case of having to watch your back to guard against the next generation coming up.' And, as if to emphasize his point, he arched his spine, although this was actually to take some pressure off his sciatic nerve, which was playing up. 'All that sitting down all day,' he explained.

'I know what you're getting at,' added Philip Christopher, returning from the bar holding three near-to-overflowing pint glasses. 'Did you know my boss is actually younger than me?'

'Incredible,' Les Andrew agreed. 'Same thing, day in day out, keeping the mortgage payments coming. It sometimes feels like I'm just making up the numbers while others get all the credit.'

'Tell me about it,' his old friend agreed.

'Still, at least we're still here, breathing, drinking,' Les concluded, lifting his glass in emphasis, studiously avoiding the topic on everyone's mind: the untimely death of George Rowlands earlier that year. As if to acknowledge the fact they were on the same wavelength, Philip picked up the thread.

'Still, he wouldn't have made a good old man, would he?'

After a brief pause involving a fair bit of nodding, Les agreed, adding: 'Maybe a good dirty old man, though?'.

The loss of George had hit everyone hard. It was as if a keystone had been knocked out of their annual gathering. George had been to every meal since the start and his little asides and mind games had been an integral part of the experience for many, both positively and negatively.

Les shifted the conversation to the Bond. 'Still, when we're all gone at least there'll always be the last man standing to act as our talisman.'

'Not much chance of it being me,' Nigel piped up, 'not with this back.'

'You can count me out, I'll go in my sleep when I'm good and ready. I'm not that interested in hanging on for its own sake,' Philip agreed.

'You're right there,' said Nigel. Another brief silence followed before he wondered: 'Who do you think it might be, then?'

'Who, the last man standing?' Les asked.

'God knows? Brucie Lu? Or don't doctors have a notoriously short lifespan? I can't remember.'

'Tadpole?' Nigel offered. 'He was always fit, wasn't he?'

'Tadpole? Blimey, have you clocked him these days? Don't think so.'

'Probably be Tom, he deserves it, and would probably know what to do with the cash,' Nigel concluded. 'Buggered if I'd have the first idea.'

It seemed a reasonable compromise, and at that moment they were called to order to progress over the road to the restaurant. Ray had followed the exchange but kept quiet, and after they were relieved of their coats by the waiting staff and shuffled down the long table, he found himself sitting opposite Andy Thompson, which didn't lift his mood. Andy seemed to have become a smug bore since he'd become so successful; not least in the miracles he'd performed with the Bond, the true extent of which Ray probably understood better than most. He'd never admit it in public, or probably even to himself, but Ray remained slightly in awe of Andy, who was at that moment taking a sip from a half pint of grapefruit juice topped up with tonic.

That year's meal was a flat affair, and as the empty dessert bowls were being taken away, Andy picked up on the earlier conversation in the bar. 'I always love that bit in our company's annual report where we say our people are our greatest asset, when in truth we all know they're our greatest cost. Last year I had to lay off a dozen of my team, but has it affected our profitability? Not one jot. I rest my case.'

'I had to hand out twenty P45s last year,' added Reggie Richardson, in what was in danger of becoming a bizarre round of bidding in a game of redundancy poker, a cycle prevented by someone's pager going off, resulting in half the room checking their inner pockets to see if theirs was the culprit.

At that moment, Ray decided he couldn't take any more, so to break the mood he reached over and grabbed a handful of party poppers, lodged them between his knuckles, and let them all off at once. As it happened, this Tom Joules was just standing up to give his traditional speech.

1996

One of the delights of his frequent visits to the Arab world was undoubtedly the hammam. Mark 'Addy' Boothroyd had gone straight into the oil business after university. He reasoned that the world would always need oil, certainly for as long as he wanted to work anyway, and he liked the travel aspect. As his career took shape he specialized in the established markets in the Middle East rather than the developing markets, which often seemed to be in the most inconvenient, as well as the coldest and bleakest, parts of the planet, and he found himself drawn to Arab ways and their general take on life. Okay, there were the obvious disadvantages, not least the sometimes strange and not always consistent attitudes towards women, and of course the whole alcohol thing; but he greatly appreciated the ethos of hospitality, which in his experience had always been genuine.

Mark's mum often expressed concern at his frequent trips to the Middle East but, as he told her, it wasn't all PLO terrorists, constipated calls to prayer and Terry Waite-style kidnappings. When she told him how brave he was, he often retorted that he felt a lot more threatened in Manchester on a Friday night than he ever did in a medina.

Mark always tried to get at least one trip in to a hammam, the Arab equivalent of a Turkish bath, usually at the end of a stay: a little treat to round off a trip. Out of politeness he usually asked his clients the best place to go, but Mark preferred the challenge of finding one himself using his basic Arabic. Usually they were hidden away down a beaten track with little more than a chair with a towel on it outside signifying their presence, and unfailingly he found a warm welcome on stepping through the arched entrance. Stripping yourself naked and allowing a stranger to manipulate your body in ways he sometimes suspected it wasn't supposed to be manipulated was the ultimate expression of trust, and Mark revelled in the thrill of it all.

No two hammams were exactly the same, and understanding the routines followed at each was part of the fun. They all started with a steam room or sauna designed to sweat all the impurities out of the skin, followed by a process of showering down, sometimes by the simple expedient of having cold water scooped out of a small stone reservoir and tossed over you.

This was followed by the massage: a bone-crunching set of contortions involving manipulation of every joint in the body, from the neck down to the little toe, to a melody of cracks and crunches it was sometimes hard to listen to, especially when you realized your body was the instrument being played. At the end of it all there was, of course, the mint tea, usually in a communal room where everyone would gather, beaten about but thoroughly refreshed, to chew the cud or just chill. He was thoroughly cleansed afterwards, both physically and mentally, and the hammam left Mark ready for the long trip home.

One constant among the hammams was segregation, with men and women taking their baths separately, in line with wider Muslim beliefs. This didn't mean that women weren't involved; in parts of North Africa he'd been massaged by women, usually covered by flimsy cotton uniforms that inevitably stuck to them in the humid atmosphere, enhancing their figure rather than hiding it. Women also tended to pass through with supplies of soap and cold water, but the whole thing was totally innocent. When you were on the massage table, the last thing on your mind was fooling around.

Steam or sauna was another variable, with the former more typical, while some massages lulled you into a sense of false security by starting by a scraping of the skin with a strigil, something that went back to Roman times. One constant was the suds, enough to make you think you'd entered a car wash, and if the massage was vigorous enough it could feel like you'd been through one, too.

On this particular occasion, Mark had found the hammam tucked away at the end of the main drag in the souk, located, as was often the case, near a mosque. The entrance had been unusually prominent, with a black and white checkerboard decoration sweeping over the top of an arched doorway and a pair of red and green striped pillars either side. He stepped through and was met by a member of staff who took his money, gave him a nod along with a towel, and led him towards a changing room as if he was just another punter. Peeking inside the towel, Mark was relieved to see a black swimming costume, and as he entered the changing room his nostrils were tickled by the scent of exotic essential oils competing with disinfectant.

Although his trip had gone well, his client had other commitments when Mark asked him along, and while he made it clear that it distressed him not to extend the hand of hospitality – which actually caused him to use his outstretched hand to cover his heart with his palm, and pull a sad face – he was sure that Mark would understand the demands of family.

In fact, Mark hadn't been altogether unhappy with this turn of events. While the North Sea had given Britain some credibility in the oil game, a sense of inferiority was never far away. Also, for all their poker-faced charm and outward innocence, many of those he did business with had been educated at some of the very best private schools Britain could offer, and when clients enquired where he'd been educated, the answer rarely impressed. Besides, on this trip Mark's client had been an unusually fat man, even by Arab standards, and the prospect of seeing his blubber unfold and then extrude sweat was one he was glad to have been spared.

His arrival in the steam room was greeted by a discrete fizzing sound, as if some unseen person was taking the anonymity provided by the steam to vent themselves in a prolonged and, it appeared, particularly satisfying way. It was in fact just an injection of fresh steam, something controlled by a thermostat and designed to top up the humidity lost when Mark entered the room. The steam entered through a flexible plastic hose, at the apex of which was a small pressure tap designed to allow guests to top the levels up according to individual preference, performing the same task as the ladle and bucket of water in a sauna.

Mark duly sat down and assumed a comfortable position, one where not too much movement was required, so the steam could do its work. Surrounded by a cloud of hot water vapour he could be anyone and everyone; no more pretending to anyone about anything, a time just to be himself. Slowly, the sweat poured out and fell through the light down that covered his slight chest, mingling with the occasional burning drip that tumbled from the invisible ceiling like drops of acid.

Content with his thoughts he sat for fifteen or twenty minutes, his feet tucked up behind his thighs to keep them off the burning heat of the hard stone floor. There was no way of telling the passing of time but the hammam was one place where time didn't matter; there were no numbered tickets or timetables, you emerged when you emerged. Eventually, out of a sense of ritual as much as anything, Mark rose to make his way into the next room.

As he opened the door he was followed by his own cloud of steam, and it was difficult to make out whether the masseuse in the almost surgical-looking off-white uniform was male or female. Mark was in the mood for a good workout, so he hoped it was the former. The ghostly figure led him to a black marble slab, one of two lying parallel to each other in a recess, and gestured to him to lie face-down.

Mark obeyed and was experienced enough not to be too shocked when a bucketful of barely tepid water was tipped over him, followed shortly after by another. This process was repeated two more times before there was a short pause, as something happened behind him and the person responsible for the process seemed to be scrubbing up. Seconds later Mark could feel the lather of unscented carbolic soap being massaged into his back. Bones clicked and crunched as the unseen hands worked their magic, and Mark fell into a strange state poised somewhere between relaxation and torture. Achieving this state, it turned out, had been the masseuse's purpose, for they chose that moment to apply maximum pressure on a point at the top of his spine.

A sharp crack filled the air of the humid chamber, enough to make anyone who might have been listening look up and wince. But Mark was alone with the anonymous masseuse, and in seconds even they were gone, having hurriedly exited the room. Indeed, in any real sense there was no Mark either, for that crack had severed his spinal cord from his brain and, in an appropriate state of grace, he had already left this world for the next.

So when another pair of hands were placed under his shoulders, and his lifeless body was dragged back to the steam room, Mark couldn't complain. Here, he was placed gently on the floor, the back of his neck deliberately on the corner of the seating. In a world where health and safety was summed up in the single phrase *Insha'Allah,* 'If Allah wills it', Mark's death would be marked down as an unfortunate mishap. Before the killer left, one of their hands scraped a little soap under Mark's left foot before sliding the small white bar, no bigger than a matchbox, across to the other side of the room.

Standing up, the white-coated figure performed a final check and decided to bend Mark's other foot backwards to produce an altogether more convincing tableau. A muffled voice uttered two final words over the body, 'Adieu Addy', after which there was the sound of a door closing as the unseen officiant departed.

----------------------------- ✳ -----------------------------

The beatings eventually stopped. It took years of countless promises that it would never happen again, years of threatening to leave him; but where could she go? The police had been useless: they insisted they couldn't get involved in 'a domestic' – until it was too late, of course, but by then it would have been, well, too late.

If his temper had been a firework it would have had a quarter-inch fuse. For a small man he didn't half pack a punch, even if his problem was often actually landing it. Underneath his shirt he had the torso and arm muscles of a weightlifter, but over time their fights, if you could call them that, had acquired a pantomime element. If she saw him coming in time, all she had to do was grip his hair, plant her feet and lean back. In this position he could swing all he liked but he couldn't reach her – the miserable little dwarf, buzzing his arms around like an out-of-control windmill, yelling and screaming all sorts of abuse.

It hadn't taken much for Susie to spot that the match that lit his fuse usually concerned his old school buddies. They seemed to have the capacity to wind the insecure little prick up like a clockwork toy until the spring broke, and it was then that the fists usually began to flail about.

A casually dropped remark, something written in his school magazine, or even a newspaper, or perhaps one of her 'alternative truths', mentioned over the breakfast table: all had the capacity to set him off. Watching him squirm developed into a secret pleasure. She'd learned how to get him on a hook when he hadn't even realized she was fishing, and she could play him like a marlin, exhausting the fight out of him. As time went on he became confused, unable in his fog of anxiety to work out what was going on.

The year after the Legionnaires' tragedy had been the worst. If pugnaciousness had been his trademark before, after the deaths he descended into the persona of a punch-drunk boxer who'd had all the sense knocked out of him: still thrashing around but without purpose, as if he didn't know where he was, or what he was doing any more. For months, he'd undergone a period of very visible grieving.

Susie enjoyed the sense of power her realization brought her, and keeping the Widows going was a good way of restocking on ammunition, whether this was real, or whether it was something that gave her an idea to spin another story. There were always little titbits of knowledge to be sucked up, like stubborn dust stuck in a corner. She also found the meetings useful to gauge how other people lived their lives, and to gain some appreciation of what 'normal' might look like. The answer turned out to be complicated.

Some of the Widows had clearly decided to stop fighting the unwinnable fight against the flab, although personally Susie believed there should be a rule decreeing that after a certain size it was no longer acceptable to wear jeans, ideally some time before the two-pumpkins-in-a-denim-sack stage. Others, like Vicky Briton, had only just set about starting a family. The classic example of a late mother, Vicky spoke as if she was the first person to experience motherhood, whereas to Susie it all seemed like another lifetime ago.

Others had started to show signs of going completely bonkers. A good example was Mary Lu, who was clearly in the initial stages of chronic paranoia. She seemed to be making a conscious effort to look more mannish, including a short pixie cut to her hair. She only had the one child, and her marriage was clearly an odd one. She was constantly making all sorts of insinuations about her husband, the insipid doctor David, dropping comments such as 'It'll all come out one day', without ever explaining exactly what 'it' might be.

Shirley Perks, or more accurately Tweedie, as she preferred to be called once again, having divorced Eddie three years before, also came along, even though no one felt able to point out that, strictly speaking, under the unwritten laws of their gatherings, membership of the Widows was restricted to those whose husbands were at the Seventy-Seven Society supper. If some of the Widows had taken the decision that weight management was optional, Shirley had clearly become addicted to the Cindy Crawford workout. Always a lanky thing, if Shirley had stood still long enough the previous summer she may well have found runner beans growing up around her legs. It didn't seem to be doing her any harm, though, storming through her career in publishing and clearly being taken seriously by the men she was surrounded by.

Through time, a sort of unspoken truce seemed to break out between her and Ben, during which Susie resolved to branch out, to find her own way in life. If he left her alone she turned down the chatter about his school friends, allowing him to channel his frustrations elsewhere and giving her the space to think. If he started up again ... well, she knew how to put him back in his box.

For Ben, 'elsewhere' turned out to be the business, which seemed to go through a gear change once he got out of his slump, and started making serious money. Susie, on the other hand, saw this as an opportunity to engage a nanny and apply for a job. British Airways had been going through a phase of taking on more mature women as cabin attendants, which is what they'd started to call air hostesses. Apparently, the marketing people wanted to portray a more professional image, moving away from the idea of trolley dollies, and as she'd been thirty-four years and ten months old when she'd applied, she'd just made it under the threshold that apparently constituted 'too mature'.

Susie had always dreamed of travel when she was growing up, and this had been her chance. The stewards she travelled with, nancy boys to a man, looked after her, keeping the pilots at bay; although she'd enjoyed the thought, at least, that other men still found her desirable. Just another step on the ladder towards discovering the real Susie Bradshaw; in fact, for professional purposes she followed Shirley Tweedie's example and reverted to her maiden name of Hamilton.

--------------------------- ✳ ---------------------------

Yellow. Padded. Envelope. How many more?

Harold Mitchell was losing patience at having his life controlled by some unseen hand. He was getting too old for this, but he had no choice. He'd tried moving, to Wales, even changed his name by deed poll, only to change it back when the ruddy envelopes kept on following him. Like a dog you can't shake off on a long country walk, they refused to go away.

It was Amman last time, Jordan. His first reaction had been that he'd have to pack some earplugs: all that caterwauling five times a day, it made getting a decent night's sleep nigh on impossible.

The picture side of the postcard had showed off Matron's qualities in a way that stirred a sense of nostalgia for better times, and it would almost have been worth keeping if the overall effect hadn't been ruined by the focus on his naked hairy buttocks, much firmer then, slightly off-centre to the left. He turned the card over and read the instructions. This had become his life: waiting, and then acting – if you could really call it a life, perpetually being at someone else's beck and call. Resigned to his fate, he reached under his bed for his holdall.

--------------------------- ✳ ---------------------------

David Lu had his job and he had his son, but somehow he'd always thought there might be more to life. Stephen, now a clever teenager and a worthy chess opponent, had been their own little emperor, the cliché lone Chinese child, although this hadn't been through any lack of desire on David's part for more. Mary, on the other hand, seemed to regard the idea as preposterous.

There had been a sea-change in their relationship shortly after Stephen was born, and while David of course knew that such post-natal withdrawals of affection were a common response, he didn't buy this as an explanation. Mary hadn't shown symptoms of depression so much as allowed all signs of love to evaporate, leaving an empty shell. They continued to communicate perfectly reasonably, but in an arms-length, semi-formal way, almost as if Mary was frightened of, or disgusted by, him. Sometimes when they were watching television he'd catch her looking at him as if he was a specimen in a jar, an object of curiosity, her mind wandering and wondering – about what, he couldn't guess.

He didn't confront her with his worries or try to discuss what had happened between them. He knew the ties that bound them had become fragile and he chose to avoid the risk of snapping them altogether. Every time he thought he might initiate a discussion, some crisis or another cropped up at work and the moment passed. The truth was, he'd rather have the Mary he had than no Mary at all. Furthermore, the thought of divorce, and of only seeing Stephen every other weekend and for school holidays, was unthinkable.

Over the years they'd settled into a kind of accommodation and David had reasoned that, in this regard, they were probably like many other couples. They still functioned as a pair at family and other social events, but not as a couple. They even shared a marital bed, although that was all. Mary didn't seem to want to challenge the status quo either, which suited him, so they remained as they were. He still loved her and wasn't at all tempted to stray, and he was fairly convinced she wasn't seeing anyone else; although he wouldn't have liked to risk asking her outright if she still loved him.

But still there were those looks, that underlying something David just couldn't put his finger on. It was as if he permanently gave off a bad odour, so noxious and unpleasant that not even his own wife could bring herself to tell him.

------------------------------ ✳ ------------------------------

Living in Berlin in the mid-nineties was a bit like living with a diagnosed schizophrenic who'd been told to pull themselves together. Half the city acted on the basis of optimism, that things were on the up, while the other half seemed to lack self-belief, with the two halves not necessarily defined by geography. The combined sense was one of nervousness mingled with self-deprecation, as if they hadn't yet earned the right to walk back on to the world stage. It seemed as if the events of 1989 had demolished a physical barrier but left a mental one.

Adrian Smart had lived through those events and regarded himself as a true Berliner; not the jelly doughnut that Kennedy had apocryphally declared himself, but a citizen, not only of the new united German capital but also of Europe. Back home, his family had taken this badly. His parents were both rabidly anti-Europe, the sort of people who regarded the *Daily Telegraph* as only one step up from *Pravda* and the Channel Tunnel as a national disaster. They'd have preferred a giant drawbridge they could raise up when they wanted, and blow metaphorical raspberries to the soap-dodging foreigners on the other side. His mum still sent him what she regarded as Red Cross parcels of English food: a poor man's picnic of Kellogg's Variety packs, Marmite and chocolate bars.

Adrian had studied modern languages at university, majoring in German, and after discovering the jobs desert on graduation he decided to take a gap year to give the economy a chance to pick up. Armed with a EuroRail pass, he drifted through seven different countries, practising his languages, sampling life and love, earning cash through bar work, picking grapes, and offering a few language lessons on the side. Every now and then he settled somewhere for a while and caught up on developments back home, which as far as he could see weren't good, certainly on the job side of things, so he decided to stretch his gap year to two, then three.

More through a sense of obligation than actual desire, he went back home in '82 and even attended one of the old school reunions: something he still did from time to time. It was then that he realized he'd probably blown his best chance of what might be called a regular career. When he graduated there'd only been his year looking for jobs, but now there was a whole army of desperate graduates, all chasing the same infinitesimally small number of posts. What was more, the younger ones seemed to be keener, less worn down by the world, with bright shiny new CVs, as against his, which to an outsider's eyes would have looked like the diary of an extended holiday.

Adrian shrugged his shoulders and went back to Helga, the girl he'd met in Berlin. They lived in a variety of places, ranging from squats to abandoned US forces flats, and became two of the oldest inhabitants helping to run a commune in a tower block in the old eastern part of the city, overlooking the Fernsehturm, the spiky TV tower landmark with a giant golf ball near its top that acted as a sentinel over the city.

When Adrian had first approached Berlin back in the eighties, his image of the place was coloured by his teenage obsession with the film *Cabaret*. They'd even called him Emcee at school, he remembered, and were prone to lifting their arm when he walked into a room, although the gesture was usually modified at the last moment into a stretch, to scratch their backs or reach for something on a high shelf. It seemed to Adrian that Berlin in the nineties had a lot in common with the version he'd revered while growing up – a sort of 'anything goes' decadence beneath a veneer of seriousness that he found exciting; a liberating contrast with home.

After over ten years in the city, Adrian had risen to be junior professor at his college: although the term 'professor' meant something different there. When he'd arrived in Berlin it was with the idea of exploiting the one asset his travels had told him everyone wanted: his facility with languages. The irony that he'd spent three years learning other languages, only to find that the one he'd spoken all his life was the only one people were really interested in, had not gone unnoticed. His college taught English as a foreign language, and young people from behind the old Iron Curtain flocked to attend their courses. Business was good, even if the money wasn't, but unlike back home, getting rich wasn't what Berlin was all about.

The only thing he missed from home was English chocolate, and it was because of this that he continued to encourage and thank his mum for sending the food parcels through, resisting the temptation to tell her the airlift was over. Adrian's guilty pleasure was to wander along a backwater of the Berlin–Spandau ship canal where it joined the River Spree near the Hauptbahnhof, that cathedral to the efficiency of the Deutsche Bahn. Unlike the canals Adrian remembered from home, the Berlin–Spandau was like a wide river, except it was channelled between thick concrete banks, whose walkways were spotless. The canal was a feature of the city, not something hidden away, and Adrian loved to wander along it at any time of the day, enjoying the different ways the light fell on the water and the sound of birdlife.

Adrian had always felt very safe in Berlin, so he didn't bother to look around him – even though it was gone midnight and he was on his own – as he wandered across the short Invalidenstrasse road bridge over the canal, just before the waterway turned into the Humboldt port. In fact, he wasn't even conscious of the footsteps behind him, as he was plugged into his CD player and enjoying the best of a Rowntree's selection pack that had come from home the day before. He therefore had no time to react when he suddenly felt his feet go from under him and his body toppled awkwardly over the thin metal guardrail, all that separated him from the water below.

Adrian never actually felt the sensation of hitting the water. Part of the manoeuvre that toppled him over involved an arm round his neck which had subsequently been twisted, like that of a chicken destined for the pot, his own weight turning sideways doing most of the damage. The sound of the splash as he entered the canal echoed against the top of the bridge, but then dissolved, as if it had never happened. On the pavement he'd been walking on just seconds before, two half-eaten fingers of wafer-covered chocolate now lay, along with a red and white wrapper with the word 'KitKat' emblazoned on it.

Adrian's unseen assailant scrunched the wrapper up and tossed it into the water along with the uneaten bar. As they leant over the railing to check with a torch that everything was as it should be, they found themselves humming and then singing, ever so quietly, 'Auf weidersehn,' followed by a short pause, 'À bientôt' – another pause – then, 'Goodbye.'

------------------------------ ✳ ------------------------------

The Saab hadn't lasted long – unsuitable, Ellie had called it – so Reggie decided to lay off the booze for that year's supper. He couldn't contemplate the five hours to Wales in the new Renault Espace people carrier with three young kids and a hangover.

He didn't attend the meals for the boozing, although it was true the drink did help lubricate proceedings. It was more the banter he enjoyed, the opportunity to regress a little, even if just for one night. He loved his family; even so, it was good to get away from them for a solitary evening and revert to looser, less pressurized times.

He left the house early, with the kids engrossed in their Ty Beanie Babies, Teletubbies and Tamagotchis, although for the life of him he couldn't see the point of the latter: an electronic pet, for God's sake, another product of the strange Japanese mind. Maybe they should have just got him a tortoise; it was marginally more exciting and at least it hibernated over winter.

He used the extra time he'd created to go on a short tour of old haunts: the first house he'd ever lived in, where they'd moved when he was eleven, and the old school playing fields, where little Barratt boxes were now scattered over the hallowed sward where once he'd scored heroic tries. Afterwards, rather than head for the school playground, he decided to park in the multistorey, which was now open until eleven for theatregoers; although quite why the pantomime went on until eleven he was unable to fathom.

The truth was the Espace was a bit of a bus and he didn't fancy taking it through the school gates, and there'd be hell to pay if he scratched its crimson paintwork. Perhaps he'd have risked it if he'd known he was destined to meet his nemesis in the concrete maze that lay behind the Somerfield. The one bastard year he chose to park there and Ray Bloody Meadows (over the years Reggie had found it increasingly difficult not to think of him without adding a middle name) had done the same. Was he stalking him?

'Ray, fancy seeing you here,' Reggie remarked calmly, checking something in the glove compartment to avoid having to make eye contact with Meadows.

'Christ, yeah, you following me around or what?' Ray asked, in an uncanny reworking of Reggie's own thought processes a moment before, moving round to check that the boot of his Sierra was locked. As he did so Reggie noticed he was limping. What he didn't know was that Ray was suffering from an old rugby injury which caused his kneecap to dislocate every now and then, requiring him to click it back into place manually, an act that brought about paroxysms of unbelievable pain. It had happened that evening, and it was all Ray could do to manoeuvre the new, old Sierra into the multistorey before performing manual surgery on himself. The knee would give him gyp all night, requiring plenty of anaesthetic. Politely ignoring Ray's manoeuvres, Reggie set about the delicate task of extracting his not inconsiderable bulk from the high perch of the driver's seat of his Espace.

'Off to Dublin in the morning, in the green, in the green,' Ray announced, a propos of nothing, putting a brave face on things. 'Shall we start off on Guinness?' he enquired, before starting to dance a jig, something he immediately regretted as a spear of searing pain lanced its way up from the ground into his knee.

It turned out to be a workaday supper and towards the end, when Tom Joules had got up to do his traditional 'Matches and Hatches' slot, he seemed to be overcome by a certain awkwardness. He knew his little speech was known by most of the group as 'Matches, Hatches and Dispatches'. What he didn't know was that over the brandies a fourth instalment was discussed informally: 'Mismatches', covering divorces – actual, imminent, and, it seemed, advisable.

There was a solitary death for Tom to announce that year: the ex-school friend who was more 'ex' than most was Charlie Young. He'd been at the previous year's meal but hadn't looked well. In fact, in the words of someone who'd been there, he looked as if someone had inserted a vacuum cleaner up his backside and sucked all the life force out of him.

His cheeks had sunk back to the bone, which had the added effect of making his chin look more prominent, while his collar bone stuck out from under his shirt as if he was wearing an oversized necklace. His arms were stick-thin and his eyes stared out from deep black holes, as if he was auditioning for the part of Yorick. Given Charlie's history, his condition was clear for all to see; but of course, no one mentioned it.

For Tom, homosexuality was in the same category as devil worship. He understood that it went on, but equally it was something he preferred not to think about and he hoped in time it would simply disappear, while all the time knowing this wasn't very likely. As it was something too rife for him to have any influence over, his preferred tactic was just to ignore it; something he was about to find difficult. Tom had thought deeply about how he would handle the announcement beforehand, and decided to use a straight bat.

'Finally, I have to report the loss of one of our members,' Tom began.

'Ooh! Sounds painful,' Ray Meadows suggested, pulling a face, although it was nothing to the face Tom gave him in return for spoiling his flow.

'As most of you probably know, our dear friend Charlie …'

'He certainly wasn't cheap,' someone offered from the dark in an over-camp voice; a comment that was met with another adding, 'Shut that door!' in a poor Larry Grayson impersonation.

Tom ploughed on: '… had been unwell for some time.' This was as far as he got before yet another interruption broke his stride.

'Really, what was wrong with him?' asked Ray Meadows.

'He, er, had problems with his immune system.' At this point Tom noticed one or two people taking notes, as if they wanted to remind themselves later what he was saying, but he didn't have time to work out why.

'What sort of problems?' asked Toby Connor.

'I believe he had a disease,' Tom said, looking to one side, which prompted more note-taking from a different set of people.

'What sort of disease?'

'Alas, an incurable disease.' More notes, but only one or two this time. Tom prepared to pick up where he'd left off when he was interrupted by an inappropriately grinning Paul Briton.

'Wait a minute. Are you saying Charlie was …'

The question was left unfinished, a door invitingly left ajar for Tom to walk through. 'Yes, I believe his interests lay elsewhere.' Thankfully, very few seemed to write this down.

'Elsewhere?' enquired Andy Thompson.

'He walked on the other side of the street,' Tom suggested.

'I'm sorry, you've totally lost me here, Tom,' Les Andrew interjected. 'Are you suggesting Charlie was some kind of streetwalker?'

'No, no, no,' Tom replied hurriedly, in a state of mild, rising to severe, fluster. In a rush to correct the impression he may inadvertently have given, he continued: 'No, he was, you know, one of the others, one of those.' This prompted a flurry of further note-taking, as well as a few smirks.

'One of whose?'

'He was of the other persuasion.' More notes were hurriedly made in among the audience. 'A friend of Dorothy.' Yet more notes. 'A, shall we say, Bohemian.' Less note-taking. 'A Catamite.' Faces showing confusion; no note-taking at all. Tom was struggling to get his message through, and becoming increasingly frustrated by the way things were going. It was moments like this that made him wish he still drank.

'A queen,' he offered, inspired, which prompted a sudden flurry of note-taking, but faces still looked confused.

'A fudging homo, dammit …'

'Bingo!' came three voices at once, and it was then that Tom realized what had been going on. Everyone had been marking a similar piece of paper, a grid with boxes containing single words or short phrases: Tom Bingo.

As he sat down to a round of applause, and slaps on the back from those either side of him for being a good sport, Tom couldn't help but overhear an exchange between Ray Meadows and Nigel Bennett from across the table.

'Would you credit it?' Ray was complaining, 'I only had "poof" left: you would have thought that was a banker.'

Nigel nodded in sympathy. 'Same here, although I was miles off: still had 'bender', 'turd burglar' and 'shirtlifter'.'

Derek Henderson was less empathetic. 'I had "friend",' he revealed, as he stood, pushed his chair back, and made his way unsteadily to the gents.

1999

It was the blonde hair, always the blonde hair, that got him. Brunettes never stood a chance with Ray; the suppressed memory of getting that tar-like ink out of his own hair all those years ago still haunted him.

He often found himself looking in his car mirror to check out the features of blondies he passed in the street. He knew that Sandra O'Brien would have changed – after all, who hadn't in the last fifteen years – but he still clung to the memory of what she'd looked like back then. For all he knew she may not even be blonde any more, although surely she would have kept what had, without doubt, been her most startling feature; well, until she started to speak, anyway. Sandra O'Brien had unknowingly changed his life, sowing the seeds of distrust that had haunted every relationship he'd had ever since. In short, he had unfinished business.

His life had fallen into a pattern. Monday to Friday, plus most Saturday mornings (so long as there wasn't an away match) he devoted to the business, in turns rescuing it, building it, maintaining it, and generally coping with all the crap the fates had thrown his way over the years. Ever since school, from the end of every summer through to the following spring, Ray's life had revolved around Old Red Coaters' rugby. The passage of the years had been marked by a steady drop through the ranks all the way to the Fifths, and finally, ignominy of ignominies, to the Veterans: the cellar where the embarrassing old farts were kept and indulged.

He now spent more time in the clubhouse than on the playing field, as his knee had become about as reliable as the weather, locking out at the most inconvenient times. A couple of years ago he'd had a brief flirtation with the idea of becoming a ref, but he couldn't bring himself to cross over to the dark side. No one ever bought the ref a drink after a game.

Ray had served a spell as club secretary and filled in behind the bar on match days. He fully expected to become president one day, and while there were a few in the queue before him it remained something to look forward to. The clubhouse was his second home, offering everything his flat didn't: warmth and a welcome, with food and grub on tap. His real home was little more than an address, a modest flat in a small development near the town centre, only slightly bigger than his first place but with a garage, which had been a big plus now that yobs seemed to patrol the town centre most nights. There'd been a time when he wouldn't have let them trouble him, but he'd never be able to catch them these days; and besides, you weren't allowed to dish out random clips around the ear any more, were you?

Business tended to trail off in the summer as people went on holiday, and it was the hotter months he devoted to tracking down Sandra, for the first few years picking the ferry up at Holyhead and taking the current jalopy for a spin through Ireland's rapidly improving roads, taking in a little fishing along the way. Here, a combination of a few carefully bought pints of Guinness to loosen tongues, and some careful searching of newspaper libraries, gave him the leads he needed. These had then taken him around Europe and the Mediterranean, although the trips usually ended with as many questions as they answered. That people recognized the picture he'd kept from her old CV was both encouraging and, at the same time, disheartening; but it was the added detail about her voice that usually clinched it. He'd also learned that he was only the latest at the back of a long line of people who'd appreciate a 'little chat' with her, across various jurisdictions.

His most recent trip had taken him to Spain, where he stayed for a while with Pam, by then a living advertisement for avoiding the expat lifestyle. As she'd always been able to, she saw right through him and managed to get him to confess his mission. She advised him to forget it, but he couldn't. As it happened, she had some contacts in the police and, using his usual technique of buying a few beers, he was able to find out that someone matching Sandra's description had been a suspect in an insurance fraud a few years back. The trail had gone cold, though, and the case was closed. The word on the *calle* was she'd fled to Greece.

--------------------------- ✳ ---------------------------

Sometimes a single meeting could change your life.

Ben Bradshaw was ready to step up to the next level. He'd become tired of spending his life on the road flitting between his stores, especially when the road in question was the M1. He'd begun to hallucinate road cones and convenient places to insert them into the people who set them out. The man with a van had metamorphosed into the man with a plan. It was now time to be the man with élan.

Ben's business already had a name: Doze. What he needed was advice: on how to exploit it, and how to ratchet the thing up and go national. Ben had got this far on his own, but he'd come to the conclusion it was finally time to call in the experts. He'd already had a number of meetings with the money men, who seemed obscenely keen to finance the cash flow, and he'd sketched out a plan on how far and how fast to take the expansion. At that very moment a formal business plan, his first ever, was being put together, but he still needed input from the marketing guys. In the back of his mind, Ben was still looking for the golden 'something' that would set the whole masterplan into action; a search that had led him to the so-called creatives.

It wasn't a move he'd taken lightly. He had an inbuilt suspicion of the sharp-suited brigade, but he saw them as a necessary evil, part of the deal he'd made with himself to crack the big time. He didn't just want to become mega-successful – he needed it. He needed to be recognized – not just in the papers, but for what he'd done; and this meeting was a necessary step to helping him achieve this.

The marketing agency was called Blue Sky and their logo was just that, with a golden sun just beginning to emerge over a deep Smurf-blue horizon. They occupied the whole third floor of an otherwise nondescript modernist office building off Charing Cross Road, a glass and chrome edifice sandwiched between two Victorian blocks which had seen better days. Having signed in at reception, Ben took the lift to the third floor where he repeated the exercise and was handed a pass, which he promptly pocketed. Ben Bradshaw wasn't defined by a name badge. The décor and ambiance couldn't have been more different from the antiseptic nothingness of the ground floor: cream leather sofas (Ben recognized the manufacturer) were grouped around, with, of all things, a pond, complete with goldfish and a small fountain, in one corner. A large version of the company's logo dominated one wall and followed through on to the ceiling. The pervading scent of a lavender air freshener was losing the good fight against the raw acridity of freshly smoked Gauloises.

Ben was feeling positive. It had been a good trip down; he'd taken the train and then walked, having dismissed taking a taxi as an unnecessary extravagance. It was the unofficial first day of summer, the day when London girls had decided as one that it was time to free their legs from the spider's- web tights that were the fashion the previous winter.

The arrival of an efficient-looking woman wearing heavy glasses broke his reverie. She half-spoke, half-breathed his name and smiled, indicating that he should follow her down the labyrinthine maze of partitions that broke up the open-plan floor. A glass-walled room occupied the centre, a sort of inner sanctum, and it soon became clear that this was where Ben was being led. In his best three-piece suit and ORC tie, Ben began to feel slightly out of place among Blue Sky's workforce, who were either wearing jeans and T-shirts, or high-end designer suits with pencil-thin collars on narrow-striped shirts.

On entering the room Ben noted four others besides himself, the receptionist having withdrawn. They rose from the end of a black glass boardroom table, two each side of an overhead projector upon whose platen sat a transparency with the single word, Doze, which, through the magic of light, was replicated on a large white screen on the far wall in letters three feet high.

All four were men, and one of them, aged somewhere between thirty and forty, stepped forward: Greg Eccles-Brown. Ben had met

Greg twice before: the first time to check him out, and the second to commission him. Both meetings took place in restaurants, with Greg picking up the tab on each occasion, which was probably just as well, as on both occasions Ben thought the prices paid no relation to the ant-food portions they'd been served. Nouvelle cuisine? Nouvelle rip off more like.

Ben thought he was a bit full of himself but didn't judge him for it, having reasoned that this probably went with the territory. Compared to some he'd met over the previous weeks, whose preferred dialect seemed to be bullshit, Greg was more of a schmoozer, and the salesman in Ben half-respected this. His main distinguishing feature was his hair, or rather someone else's hair, for the thatch perched on top of Greg's head was operating on a slight time delay, moving half a second behind any turning of the head in a constant race to catch up.

Hands duly shaken over the table and with Ben now sitting down, Greg got up and wandered around the room, closing the blinds encased between what turned out to be two sheets of glass separating them from the rest of the office, leaving the quintet eventually tucked up together in their own private box. While he did this, Greg got his colleagues to introduce themselves. The lead man on the project, Steve something, looked like he was barely out of college, but he had that air of confidence that Ben had noticed in a lot of early twenty-somethings; a quality hovering somewhere between self-belief and arrogance.

Perhaps as a way of expressing sympathy with Greg, or more likely in an effort to make himself look a bit older, he'd taken to shaving his entire head; a complete Kojak. Briefly, Ben wondered whether Greg had kicked himself the first time he'd seen this guy's exposed pate. Having committed himself to a lifetime of falsies, here was someone who'd had the guts to go full egghead. As its owner probably intended, the bald head and its glossy glow acted as a beacon, drawing all eyes towards him.

He launched straight into his pitch, spending the first ten minutes telling Ben things he knew already about his own company. Conscious that he had to go with the way things were done in an unfamiliar world, Ben relieved himself of his jacket and undid a couple of buttons on his waistcoat as he contained his impatience and waited for the meat of the presentation to come out of the oven.

'Doze now needs to undergo a paradigm shift,' Steve suggested, and although everything in Ben's head was shouting 'Get on with it!', he limited himself to a polite nod, combined with some deliberate sitting forward to suggest he was impatient to see what his fifteen grand was buying him. At last the opening slide on the projector was changed, and expecting more words, Ben was genuinely surprised when confronted with the iconic image of Lord Kitchener, in full 'Your Country Needs You!' bombast, filling the screen on the back wall.

Steve registered Ben's surprise with a pleased smile; this was exactly the impact he'd been aiming for. 'Yes, Ben Bradshaw,' he announced, pointing his finger and locking eyes with Ben, 'your company needs you! You: to not only be the engine under its bonnet but also its driver, mascot and navigator.' Ben said nothing as he absorbed not only the image, but the idea this young man was putting forward. 'You will become Doze's Omar Khayyam, the face that says you love the company and believe in it so much you want everyone to hear about it.'

Ben sank back into his chair and blew out his cheeks. Picking up on this, Greg took it upon himself to jog Ben's memory, perhaps to buy time, perhaps to underline how clever the whole idea was, or possibly just in case Ben had missed the reference. 'You loved the product so much, you bought the company!'

Ben nodded. He understood what they were trying to say, but before he could offer any reaction Steve whisked a fresh slide on to the platen and the word 'Straplines' filled the room. 'But what are you going to say? What will be your catchphrase?'

'Let me paint you a picture,' Steve offered, dropping a tone and adopting a more serious persona. 'Your face on the telly. Mr Honest, Mr Average, just like the people who buy your beds. The people whose jobs and lifestyles make them feel stressed, as if they're only just coping.

You are their saviour, their messiah. You are the man who is going to give them their eight hours' uninterrupted sleep. Heaven. You've sold them the idea, you now want them to come into your stores. Here's what you say.' Steve paused for dramatic effect before whipping the slide off and placing another on the platen. The two words 'Chose Doze' filled the back wall.

Ben hadn't been able to stop himself lifting his eyebrows.

'Exactly, Ben!' Steve exclaimed, apparently pleased with himself. Ben hadn't been sure exactly when they'd moved on to first-name terms, but let it pass.

'This will be your catchphrase, your "Finger Lickin' Good" or "Vorsprung durch Technik". We'll have stickers made up for the punters to put on the back windows of their Ford Fiestas and their Vauxhall Cavaliers, badges and balloons for the kids, baseball hats for ...'

Ben decided he could take it no more and interrupted. 'Do you mean, "I Chose Doze?"'

'That's the point, Ben, it's a universal catchphrase; it won't need the "I", the "I" will be implicit.' Steve went on as if explaining something to a simpleton. 'Straightforward, honest, clean – like you,' he offered, stretching out his hands in supplication. 'We could even add a hand gesture,' he added, warming to his theme, 'like Ted Rogers on *3-2-1*; a thumbs-up, maybe? Or you could form a "D" with the fingers of one hand against the thumb on the other.' Steve offered a useful demonstration as if this was something he'd just thought of and he wanted to show he was a veritable fountain of inspiration. It wasn't the hand gesture that had been going through Ben's mind at that moment.

'Then you hit them with the killer line.' Another theatrical pause followed. Four sets of eyes focused on him as a fresh slide was prepared.

The words 'Don't sleep on it!' now filled the far wall.

Ben half expected a round of applause as the faces of all four Blue Sky representatives turned towards him for his reaction, each of their owners offering an expectant smile, as if they could clinch the deal with their body language. The pitch had, it appeared, reached its climax, and there seemed to be a sense, in one part of the room at least, that it had gone extremely well.

Ben hesitated before responding, allowing silence to work to his advantage. Where did he start? He allowed the silence to snowball until it grew so big it began to gather people up. Sweat began to form on Steve's dome, and Greg was dabbing his own forehead with a handkerchief. It was Greg who finally broke the silence with a single word.

'Thoughts?'

Ben let the silence linger still longer before finally replying.

'Thoughts? What I'm thinking is how is it possible that an agency with a reputation for being clever could possibly employ a set of people so stupefyingly moronic.' Ben let this broadside hit its target and, before it had a chance to explode, started to use hand signals of his own, extending the index finger on his right hand and beginning to count off.

'First, I may not have had the fancy classical university education you no doubt had, probably Oxford I'd guess, or somewhere equally useless, but even I know Omar Khayyam was an ancient Persian mathematician and poet.' Ben trowelled on another layer of silence like a master bricklayer. 'It was Victor Kiam who loved the product so much he bought the company.' Steve geared himself up to come back, Ben guessed with some kind of clever or pretentiously witty remark, but he wasn't given the chance. 'Second, I didn't buy the bloody company; I fucking created it.' No histrionics, just the facts, keeping calm.

'Third, there's "Don't sleep on it", what the Jesus H. Christ is that all about? That's like trying to sell Coke by telling the punters not to drink it, or selling wigs by telling people they'll look a complete prat in them.' As Ben intended, this remark caused Greg to abort an intended interjection to calm things down. If anything, it was time to ramp things up a bit.

'"Chose Doze? Chose Doze?" Or should that be "Choose Doze"?

Bleeding hell, man, you can't even spell! It's not the "I" that's silent, but an "o"!' At this point had stood up. In his experience of selling, taking people by surprise, occupying their territory, usually resulted in taking control.

'You sit here in your fancy offices and your ridiculous clothes, throwing out your vacuous phrases as if you exist in the real world.' Ben went to the nearest set of blinds and opened them, revealing to the rest of the office what was going on in the meeting room. An audience had gathered, roused by the muffled noises coming from within, but quickly turned away, like children caught sneaking downstairs to watch adult TV.

'The real world is one where most people get up in the morning and wonder how they're going to get through the week on the miserable pittance they get paid. Their kids want the latest *Star Wars* action figure but they need to be fed and clothed first. Maybe they also need a new bed because they simply can't carry on sleeping in the rusty old bunks bought second-hand by the grandparents.' Ben continued his wander around the room, opening each of the sets of blinds with a determination that went unchallenged, all the eyes in the office, along with, more surreptitiously, those from outside the glass box, homing in on him as if he was a master conjuror performing an impossible trick.

'But beds cost money. They want the best for their kids and no one really fancies a second-hand bed; other people's dust mites, bed bugs and shit, and I mean real shit – every kid occasionally follows through on a mattress, and trust me, you can never get it all out no matter how hard you scrub.' By this stage the glass room was totally exposed; he'd performed an entire circuit of the room. He picked his jacket off the back of his chair as he passed.

'I'm going to leave now. Think about what just happened here, and don't even bother to think about invoicing me. Treat it as my gift to you, a lesson you'll remember for the rest ...' At this point Ben froze, '... of ...', he added, straightening his tie, '... your ...', he went on, now opening the door, '... lives.'

With this, he marched out of the office, took the stairs rather than the lift and finally waltzed through the reception area, into the warm London air.

------------------------------- ✳ -------------------------------

David Lu was used to being watched. Watched while he did his homework as a child, watched while he played in the garden, watched while he learned at university, and watched all the time at work – at first by the consultants, more recently by junior doctors, nurses and sometimes even the suits, each and every one of them covering their own back. It was one of the reasons he enjoyed volunteering for all the conferences his colleagues seemed to hate going to. Maybe it was the foreign travel, maybe it was the time away from their families, but for David they represented opportunities to be alone, yet at the same time get lost in a crowd of like-minded people. He went to every conference, symposium, seminar and convention he could.

Perhaps it was this imperviousness to observation that meant he failed to notice he was being watched at home, too. The time between home and hospital, in theory at least, should have been time he could call his own; his wife, however, had other ideas. At first, she used other people to do her spying for her, although the traditional image of a mac-clad Raymond Chandler-type private detective had proved to be far from the mark. Most of them, Mary had discovered, were seedy little men: usually ex-policemen who'd taken early retirement, working from Ford Fiestas with mobile phones and a seemingly endless supply of crisps. They all managed to monitor her husband's movements without being noticed, and to a man they reported that David seemed to live in his own little bubble.

Their reports spoke of a man you could set your watch by, such were the precision of his movements. His lack of variation should have inspired pity as much as frustration; he even bought the same chocolate bar every day from the stall run by the Friends of the Hospital in the foyer, a Toffee Crisp, as if a casual pack of Munchies might represent an unacceptable break in his routine.

The people Mary hired would invariably come back to her looking even more bored than when she'd first met them, and it took a lot to bore a private detective. The more honourable ones would try to convince her she was wasting her money; there was simply nothing interesting to say about David Lu. No hidden secrets, no vices, women, gambling, drug-taking. Nothing. Zilch. Rien.

When she'd run out of names in the *Yellow Pages*, Mary had taken on the job herself. She just knew there was something there; she merely had to find it. She even bought a second-hand car to follow him, registering it in her son's name, and when she tired of observing her husband from a distance she took professional advice on make-up and disguises so she could get closer. At home she checked his phone for sent messages and made lists of dialled numbers, phoning some of them back when she got the chance to see who they were. They were all work-related.

As time went on she began to understand the private detectives' lack of results. He was good, all right. The problem was, she was better. She'd find something, she was sure, some kind of proof; it was just a matter of time.

------------------------------ ✱ ------------------------------

Theirs was an unconventional relationship, not what most people would regard as 'normal'; but then again, Tom and Marion Joules didn't aspire to everyone else's version of 'normal'. As the millennium drew to a close, the very notion of normal had, in their eyes, become just a little bit scary. Their relationship belonged to a period several decades before, and if it had been possible to pick them up and deposit them into that world they'd have felt considerably more relaxed: but it wasn't, and they weren't.

Tom and Marion 'got by'. There was genuine affection between them, but love, well, that was a concept they were more used to dealing with in the abstract, in relation to a supreme being without known form or substance. In the circumstances, it was hardly surprising that it wasn't a word they used when referring to themselves.

It wasn't the only area off-limits in their relationship. Tom's pre-Marion breakdown was one, and Marion's pre-Tom life was another – in other words, the past. Their marriage had been a fresh start for both of them, with the past consigned to a deep pit of oblivion. Furthermore, unlike other couples sharing the same workplace, when they got home they chose not to discuss school matters. Chatter in the staff room was just that, and stayed there.

Another area that went undiscussed was children. When they got married there might still have been an outside chance that Marion could have had children, if they'd been quick and persistent, but neither of them felt inclined to be either. Marion had assumed Tom wasn't interested in propagating his seed and Tom had assumed, well, Tom didn't really want to think about it at all. There was sex, but it was never discussed beforehand, or indeed afterwards, being something that was performed and then ignored. Of course, Marion already had a child, and of all the taboos in their marriage this was the biggest. Marion's daughter wasn't a cloud over her marriage; more like a 1930s London fog, a topic so impenetrable that it was best left to disperse of its own accord whenever it descended.

Tom was blissfully unaware of the finer details of what happened to his wife's daughter in the months and years immediately after he left school; he had other issues to cope with at the time. He'd heard the rumble of rumours at the beginning of the lower sixth, but the boys who hung around the swimming pool that previous summer hadn't really been his crowd; largely because he'd never had 'a crowd'.

Every now and then, in the early days of their marriage, Tom would hear snatches of conversations in the staff room when fellow teachers, still getting used to the fact that Tom was married to the matron, would let their guard down and offer theories on what had happened to 'poor Matron's daughter', the prefix of 'poor' being universally applied. Theories ranged from her finding her father, a figure no one had solid intelligence on, through to more sinister theories involving homelessness, drugs and prostitution, with the term 'wild child' featuring a lot, the general consensus seeming to be that it was all very sad. As time went by the gossip dwindled, as fewer and fewer teachers from that era remained in the staff room.

The only thing that was certain was Matron's only child had disappeared off the radar. There were no phone calls, no letters, no cards on Mother's Day or even at Christmas. It was as if she'd never existed. In his more emotional moments Tom considered it an odd situation for their benevolent God to allow, but he consoled himself that there must be a greater reason. Indeed, he knew the events of that time were the catalyst for Marion drawing closer to the church; so, in a way, some good had already come of it.

------------------------------ ✳ ------------------------------

Few could deny that Stuart Dalgliesh was slightly odd. Most of his acquaintances wouldn't have needed too much time to draw up a list of his eccentricities. It's unlikely, however, that any of them would have homed in on one particular quirk: that, unique among all old school friends, he quite liked his Red Coat nickname. After school he went straight into horticultural college where, unsurprisingly, everyone regarded themselves as somehow gifted in all matters botanical. He therefore quite sensibly held back from replanting his moniker in that particular medium, but after college he took to introducing himself to non-gardening folk as 'Stuart, my friends call me Fingers.' This proved to be an interesting opening gambit at parties, especially among women.

As time went on, the label put down roots and blossomed, even when he was lucky enough to move on to Kew after college: a post so junior he had to make the leaf sweepers' teas. Despite working alongside some of the most esteemed names in his profession, he managed to get everyone to start using his nickname again: something he found reassuring, having never enjoyed unnecessary change.

Kew had been a fantastic apprenticeship, and Fingers would quite happily have spent the rest of his working life climbing the Royal Parks ladder, gradually enhancing his reputation as an expert in his chosen field of herbs, had it not been for the cutbacks. It was the 1980s and times were hard, especially for a body with 'Royal' in the title. A round of redundancies was seen as politically appropriate, and in a profession where maturity and length of service carried especially high status, it was a case of 'last in, first out', and Fingers was one of the very last in.

At this point Fingers discovered there wasn't an awfully big demand for herb specialists in the midst of a global recession, but after an unsatisfying couple of seasons at a large seed supplier in East Anglia, spent mainly on the packing lines, he discovered tea. Or, to be more precise, he was discovered by tea, in the unlikely form of a stout but ever-smiling Portuguese woman with short-cropped jet-black hair which, as it turned out, also thrived on her arms and shins, where it flowed in waves thick enough to be capable of being combed.

It was hard to pinpoint her age exactly, but she was certainly well beyond her main flowering season, which made it all the more ironic that her name was Juvenilia: Juvenilia Gomes. Heavy-set, with hips that looked as if they'd been built for a bigger frame, Juvenilia lived near Fatima, almost exactly halfway up the country, a town that lived off the pilgrims who converged on its famous church of Our Lady of the Rosary, which housed the Marian shrine. The area was therefore associated with miracles, and indeed Fingers was later to consider it a miracle that Juvenilia had managed to locate him working on a conveyor belt in a small village three miles outside Norwich.

Something of a late-flowering hippy, Juvenilia's big thing was teas; not the sort picked in Sri Lanka, India or China, but teas made from the herbs and roots that went into most people's compost heaps, if they went anywhere at all. Traditional tea, produced commercially on an industrial scale from the *Camellia sinensis* plant across the world, was in Juvenilia's opinion not only an agricultural abomination, but an oppressive means of exploiting cheap labour, and responsible for millions of unnecessary miles of transport pollution. What was more, it didn't even taste of much. All in all, it was fair to say that Juvenilia wasn't a conventional tea fan.

Having established herself as a woman prepared to buck the trend, it should perhaps have come as no surprise that Juvenilia often visited Britain, where anyone rubbishing their cup of char was regarded as not right in the head, in order to promulgate her message. Giving talks to anyone who'd listen, she introduced audiences to alternative teas, starting with the unchallenging, such as mint tea, before moving on to other infusions like raspberry leaf, blackcurrant and chamomile. Once her audiences had, quite literally in most cases, warmed up, she'd bring on teas made from nettles, fennel seed and dandelion, which, she liked to point out, were all readily available right outside her audience's doors.

Like a Mormon missionary, Juvenilia made few converts, but her visits always had more than one purpose. On one occasion she visited Norfolk, seeking seeds for common British herbs with a view to cultivating them on her smallholding near Fatima. Juvenilia made a modest living from growing, drying, packing, then selling her alternative teas to the pilgrims who visited her town, unashamedly promoting their medicinal qualities to crowds with thick wallets and confused hearts, also known as the gullible.

Juvenilia and Fingers made an unlikely pairing, but unlikely or not they hit it off from their first meeting, and within six weeks Fingers had resigned his job, got a passport and taken advantage of Portugal's new status as a member of the European Community to up sticks and move. Lacking strong ties to his native country, and favouring a life outdoors rather than inside a packing shed, for him the decision was an easy one; even if at first he had to sleep in a previously disused shepherd's hut made of desiccated olive tree branches.

He didn't mind; he had few possessions and sleep came easily after a day in the sun and fresh air, especially when the day ended with one of Juvenilia's 'special' teas. Working alongside Juvenilia, he brought a sense of organization to her otherwise chaotic enterprises, and before too long her patches of ground were neatly tilled in lines so straight airline pilots could use them to navigate by. As soon as seedlings appeared they were thinned out by hand, and as only the most vigorous were allowed to grow, yields often doubled or trebled. Given Mother Nature's preference for chaos, horticulture may not have been the most obvious of career choices for someone with Fingers' obsessions, but it did offer infinite opportunities for trying to create order, and it was from this that Fingers gained most satisfaction.

As Juvenilia grew weaker and less able to make the walk into Fatima, Fingers also took on responsibility for selling the finished goods, and before long found himself taking on staff. His connections to home, which at first he only visited on an annual basis to see his parents and to attend the Seventy-Seven Society supper, proved useful; and before long he was a regular visitor on the TAP flight from Porto to London with a bag of samples in a triple-sealed bag designed to reduce the number of times he was stopped by sniffer dogs at the airport.

The early 1990s saw a boom in demand for their kind of teas, now called 'speciality' rather than the previous, less inviting, 'alternative' appellation, and Fingers secured contracts to supply both Fortnum & Mason and Neal's Yard, as well as various delicatessens. Back in Fatima, the operation developed from a few random fields to a business capable of attracting Regional Development Fund grants from a Brussels bureaucracy keen to be seen to be encouraging rural employment in one of their new members.

Juvenilia died in 1996, less than ten years after meeting Fingers, a blend of nutmeg and lemon grass in her hands; blends being one of Fingers' many innovations. Bereft of family of her own, she left everything to Fingers, who suddenly found that he was not only profoundly content, but also really quite rich. The business continued to thrive and, in a twist Juvenilia herself would have particularly enjoyed, found an additional income from its tasting house, as the business became both a tourist stop and a regular haunt of expat Brits who took advantage of the cheap property prices in the area.

As the decade drew to a close, Fingers should have been looking forward to the beckoning new century; but not everything in his garden was rosy. A simple man with a relatively narrow imagination, he found himself slipping off into flights of fancy while walking among his greenhouses before the tourists and workers arrived. Strange colours had started to infuse his consciousness: yellows and blues, which would then coalesce to form kaleidoscopic patterns in front of his eyes. These in turn would assume three dimensions and begin to swirl and dance, expanding as they did so. These episodes were occasional but troubling, although not enough for him to have them checked out; he was far too busy for that.

Then there was the increasing trouble with his guts. He was finding it increasingly difficult to retain meals, which either came back up in spectacular fountains which often required a spade to cover up, or passed right through, a problem that was easier to deal with so long as he was near sanitation facilities. This had been going on a while (he'd even had some extra Portaloos brought in, ostensibly for the tourists), and was, if anything, more troubling than the colours. Never a fleshy man, Fingers had become positively anorexic, causing the mothering instincts of some of his more established workers to come to the fore. Unfortunately their response was to bring dishes of tripe and haricot beans to his door, the smell of which alone brought about involuntary retching. His response was to take more tea, especially a ginger, peppermint and cinnamon blend he'd devised, with a pinch of anise seed, which Juvenilia had always advocated as an appetite stimulant.

Early morning had always been Fingers' favourite time of the day, but one particular day he found himself regretting having vacated his bed. His head was thumping like the local church bell had been left there for safekeeping, and his heart was racing. The symptoms reminded him of the flu, something he hadn't had for years, and he was wondering if he should have stayed in bed to shake it off.

He was a busy man, though, and a day off hadn't really been an option. Normally he was out and about by seven a.m., beginning the daily tussle with nature, so he decided to tough it out and got dressed as usual, taking a cup of green tea with cloves as a precaution. He always started the day tending the experimental beds, but once under the glass the early morning sun did nothing for his headache, so he headed outside to take a draught of the beautifully clear mountain air, and a sit-down.

The effort of putting one foot in front of the other became impossible, and at the same time the visions returned, causing him to utter an uncharacteristically coarse Portuguese swear word he'd heard one of his foremen use. The yellows were especially vivid, twisting and morphing into shapes that seemed almost human at times, making it hard for him to see. Using his hands for guidance, Fingers made his way to one of the taps dotted along the well-ordered rows, suddenly desperate for a drink, or just to douse his head; anything to stop the pain and the images.

He never made it. His body was found by one of his workers a couple of hours later, face down in a row of sorrel. One of Fingers' prized row markers had been flattened by his fall and lay randomly on its side by his left ear. He'd always insisted on using the plants' Latin names, much to the bafflement of his largely peasant workers, many of whom could barely read their native tongue, let alone one last used in their country two thousand years before. The medical staff who'd picked the body up were more educated, but they saw no significance in the long thin label, its words burned into wood.

To a suspicious mind the letters were significant, though: instead of the name *Rumex acetosella* that should have marked out the line of sorrel, they spelled the word *Digitalis*.

---------------------------------- ✽ ----------------------------------

Andy Thompson wasn't sure if the nagging uncertainty he felt in his gut was something to do with his forthcoming fortieth birthday, or linked with the imminent millennium. He was pretty sure it wasn't connected to the Y2K panic his own firm seemed to have spent a fortune on, but thought it might have something to do with what the Chairman of the Federal Reserve in Washington had called 'irrational exuberance'. In other words, things were getting a bit too frothy.

But maybe he was just having a mid-life crisis? In contrast to work, his home life seemed to have drifted into a predictable rhythm, and life there seemed flat after a day at the office. The one beam of light was managing the Bond, and it was as he was looking at the screen in front of him that he experienced a rare shiver down his spine.

Seven figures, a thousand thousands. Andy Thompson had good reason to feel quite proud of himself. He could hardly believe it, but the numbers on the light grey flickering glow of his computer screen didn't lie. He'd always suspected that no one really took much notice of the detail in his annual report on the Bond. A bit like the illustrations they got on their pension statements, they represented a theoretical figure that may or may not one day convert into real spending money, usually underscored by a sceptical belief that it never would. Others were probably in denial. But a million, a big fat million? Surely they'd notice that!

The longer he allowed himself to think about it, the more he convinced himself they probably wouldn't. In which case, a fresh thought came into his head. If he was right, did this knowledge represent something to get upset about – or an opportunity?

------------------------------ ❋ ------------------------------

Attending the annual reunion supper made Reggie Richardson feel as if they were all on some kind of Seventy-Seven Express. Everyone was heading towards the same ultimate destination but they were getting there in different ways. Some, a significant minority, were travelling first class, while the rest were back in standard; but whatever their status, they were all travelling in relative comfort, unlike the poor sods he'd heard about on the roof. The train in his metaphor wasn't some clunky old commuter wagon, more like one of the new fancy trains that had appeared since privatization. He was also sure they were all passengers on this train, or customers, as they were now known; they were the ones ordering the tea and refreshments, not the ones serving it. Equally, neither were they the drivers.

The train never stopped. It slowed down sometimes, but you couldn't get off and admire the scenery, explore around a bit; the timetable didn't allow for that. Everyone aboard was condemned to stay on board and await the inevitable.

Lately, Reggie had heard rumours that there was another carriage at the back, one whose door occasionally opened to let another person through. These people were never seen again, but for the brief moment when the door opened a rush of happy sounds came out, as if there was a party going on inside. These were the people who'd decided they'd had enough of the daily grind – a small but growing number. Going under a variety of names – portfolio workers, home workers, telecommuters – they'd managed to exchange the treadmill of office politics for the uncertain world of setting up on their own.

The chances of Reggie joining this élite was about as likely as a British tennis player winning Wimbledon. His job gave him so much: most importantly, somewhere to spend the daylight hours, as well as his new car, a Volvo, a massive upgrade on the Espace. Sure, the Volvo said vanilla, but it was safe and suited the kids, who seemed to be growing a shoe size a month. Having chosen to go back to parking in the school car park again, Reggie experienced conflicting emotions when he seemed to avoid bumping into Ray Meadows that year.

It seemed incredible that it was over two decades since they'd left school: more years than their age at the time of leaving. Reggie still felt much the same as he did when he left, in his head at least, even if his body seemed to be developing the sort of cracks, stains and wear marks usually associated with an old sofa. He'd experienced a shock earlier that year when he lost both his parents in quick succession, leaving him as nominal head of his family. It had made him think, re-evaluate, and one of the things that struck him was that he was probably more than halfway through his total number of working years. He'd not known whether to be pleased or depressed by this.

As he entered the pub he was hit by a thick wall of grey smoke, floating like an acrid miasma, causing him to flap his hands to see through it. Ray was the first to spot him, naturally.

'Reggie!' he exclaimed. 'Waving or drowning?'

Now the focus of attention, Reggie produced one last exaggerated swipe, and in doing so, in one simple gesture, swept aside the melancholy that had begun to seep into his head on the walk there.

'Who needs a drink?' he enquired, adding, 'I know I do.' Immediately, like Excaliburs held aloft by unlikely ladies of the lake, half a dozen empty pint glasses were lifted above the smoke.

While waiting at the bar, Reggie surveyed the room and watched as a few of his old school buddies did much the same: although in their case they were scanning the ranks of young women, dressed for a night out in short skirts so tight you could practically make out where they'd bought their underwear (and from what Reggie could tell, some hadn't bothered to buy any). Who were they kidding? None of these girls would look at them twice. He wondered how they looked to those girls: a bunch of boring, middle-aged, middle-class farts, he suspected.

His round of drinks and quick survey complete, Reggie tuned into the room. They seemed to be a bit thinner on the ground than he'd expected; thirty-plus at a guess. Some were clustered in a corner of the bar, their heads bowed and their hands clasped around their groins. For a moment he wondered if he'd discovered a previously unknown religious faction within their group; either that, or they were all quietly pleasuring themselves. In fact, it was neither: when Terry Mungus suddenly lifted his still-clenched hands up to his shoulder, nearly landing a punch on one of the passing bar staff as he did so, Reggie realized they were discussing their golf technique which, as he'd learned in recent years, acted as a substitute religion for many.

Among another small group the conversation centred on music, led by Toby Connor who was busy flipping beermats from the edge of the table and catching them nonchalantly in mid-air. An unexpected discovery of jazz seemed to be a theme, along with a lack of comprehension of drum and bass, or rap – where was Freddie for guidance when they needed him? Like most in the room Reggie had experienced the steady slide through the BBC radio hierarchy from Radios One to Four, body-swerving Three along the way; a steady journey from DLT, the Hairy Cornflake, to Brian Redhead, the Hairy Interrogator, God rest him.

More beers were ordered and dutifully sunk as the ensemble slowly formed into a pack and were led by Tom across the road outside to the restaurant. Tom had selected a new Greek place in the centre of town that year, and as coats were taken and seats selected, snatches of conversations flooded around the room, rising and falling as though a force of nature, breaking occasionally to give an idea of what was on people's minds.

'But wasn't it so much better in our day? When we went there you had kids from all sorts of backgrounds, that's what gave the place its richness.' The voice was unmistakably Derek Henderson's, still spouting the same arguments from twenty years before, and he was on his specialist subject.

'What are you saying, then? That our sprogs would be better off mingling with Wayne and Sharon from the Birkwick estate?' Paul Briton responded.

'Why, what's wrong with that?' the indignant Derek demanded, his arms flying up into the air, causing a small splash of wine to fall from his near-empty glass on to the wooden table below.

'Look, Stalin, I appreciate your idealism and admire it, I really do, but the world's moved on.' Paul Briton paused to draw breath and wipe some crumbs off his hand before continuing. 'No one in the Birkwick estate really wants to improve themselves, it isn't like it was in our day; they're quite happy with what they've got. Take a kid from there and put them in the Red Coat now, and they'd disintegrate.' An obstinate crumb, stuck to his hand with butter, refused to budge. 'They're happy enough wallowing in their *Sun* newspapers and Sky television; they don't have aspirations any more, not in the sense we knew it. When we were growing up, lower-class parents used to want their kids to advance so they could have the things they never had – well, now they can, but without all the trouble of getting educated in the first place.'

'Don't get me on that subject,' added Toby Connor, these days deputy headmaster of a successful comprehensive school outside Bradford, which – while an achievement – didn't exactly represent the height of ambition his tutors at Cambridge would have set for him twenty years previously. Like many teachers, he came alive when conversation fell to his specialism: 'Made-up qualifications in made-up subjects …'

Paul Briton resumed his theme, keen to avoid his rant being hijacked by someone else's. 'Everything's changed, Stalin, old chap. The Wall has come down. The Cold War's over. Capitalism won, communism lost: get over it. Wherever you go in the world, all people want is a bit of freedom and enough money to be free from starvation, own a car, and watch the footy on TV. They haven't got the imagination to know what to do with money, so I don't really see the harm in not giving it to them.'

'Christ, you're going to have to justify that,' Derek Henderson demanded, again throwing his hands up as he spoke.

'Easy. Look at the National Lottery. When some poor dolt on the car line in Dagenham wins millions, the reporters ask what he's going to do with it. Pay off the mortgage, buy a new car, take a holiday and give some to the kids. After that, they run out of steam. That's my point: none of them talk about setting up a business. Money and opportunities are wasted on the poor.'

A couple of places down the table, Terry Mungus had had enough and decided to introduce a more optimistic tone. 'Never mind, things can only get better, eh?' prompting a round of laughter as each of them remembered John Prescott tapping out the rhythm to the song of the same name against a crowd barrier, after New Labour won the election a couple of years before.

The contemplative silence that followed was broken only by Paul Briton ordering another bottle of red, flashing one of his engaging smiles to one of the passing waitresses. In a discreet gesture, Andy Thompson caught the same woman's eye and raised the empty bottle of Chateau Lafitte he'd ordered for himself. This was definitely turning out to be a two-bottle night.

'Christ, when did we all become so reactionary?' Paul pondered as they waited for the waitress.

'Become?' Derek Henderson queried, but the comment was allowed to pass.

'We've become our dads!' Paul Briton exclaimed, as if he'd just thought of it, his face breaking into a wide grin as if he'd just unexpectedly solved Fermat's last theorem.

'Oi, you leave my old man out of it,' came the previously silent voice of Ray Meadows. The subject of his father was a sensitive one. Although his travelling these days was mostly confined to strolling down to the bowls club or the newsagent, his name still graced the letterhead of Ray's firm. Ray had always hoped this acted as a source of pride, but he suspected his old man didn't have the foggiest what he got up to. Maybe it was just as well.

Reggie Richardson drained what was left in his glass in anticipation of the fresh supplies. The top of his head where his hair had thinned was almost completely red, due more to high blood pressure than any sun it may have seen. He was the only one around the table still eating, having hoovered up the leftover bits of feta and hummus others hadn't wanted. In between mouthfuls, he offered his own analysis.

'It's all just a bit, you know, relentless, I suppose, isn't it?'

'What? Life?' Paul Briton asked.

'Yes, life, but more than that. Keeping the wheels turning at work, keeping the wife and kids happy, keeping up with all the shit in the world, making sense of it all.' The waitress arrived with the wine and, seeing that he was holding the chair, Reggie helped himself.

Reggie turned to Derek Henderson and smiled. 'Sorry, Stalin, old chap, you're right.' He turned to look towards Paul Briton. 'You too, Paul. We *have* become reactionary. We're reacting to the overwhelming pressure of just getting by, and to all the horror stories we read about in the papers. The truth is, I for one am not sure how I really feel about anything, any more, I haven't the luxury of time to think about it.'

An assorted mumbling suggested general assent to this view.

'God preserve us,' Toby Connor concluded, and everyone around the table, even Tom Joules and confirmed atheist Derek Henderson, raised their glasses.

------------------------------ ✳ ------------------------------

Celebrating was the last thing on Ben Bradshaw's mind as he stared out of his study window and saw the night sky light up with early fireworks.

He could hardly believe they'd actually reached the millennium. The year 2000 had always seemed to represent some dim and distant future; a time that belonged to science fiction. Weren't robots supposed to be doing all the work by now? The previous year, he'd reached the forty mark; and although this had come as a shock, given the news from that year's Seventy-Seven dinner maybe he should see it as an achievement.

Still the impatient fireworks lit up the sky; it seemed that people did, quite literally, have money to burn. Nevertheless, Ben's mood remained dark. Both the kids were out, and although he'd received texts from them, there'd been nothing from Susie. He wasn't really surprised. They barely saw each other since she'd swapped from serving in business class to sitting in it: a perk of her new job as an inspector for an international hotel chain. Even when they did, their conversations were more like verbal jousting, with his armour taking the most knocks; just another example of the constant fight against the malevolent forces his life seemed to consist of.

As often happened during these dark moods, a composite image swamped his consciousness; this time, one based on 'Freddie' McQueen's gangly frame. The face had Ray Meadows's bushy ginger eyebrows, Eddie Perks's teeth, Jeff Stone's ears and Nigel Bennett's moustache. The legs belonged to Tom Joules and the fingers on the hands were, of course, those of 'Fingers' Dalgliesh. Another one lost. There was another feature always crowning the composite face: a bald head. Not just male-pattern baldness, but shiny, billiard-ball, Duncan-Goodhew bald.

Duncan Bloody Goodhew. All people remembered about the swimming team at the 1980 Olympics was Duncan Baldilocks Goodhew, with his winning smile and egg for a head, his hands aloft after winning his gold medal. But for the precious three hundredths of a second that kept him from Moscow, it could have been him, not Duncan Perfect Goodhew, getting the interviews, the chat with David Coleman back in the studio, the appearances on *A Question of Sport*. It couldn't have been Ben Bradshaw, could it? The boy from nowhere who'd put his teenage years on hold, grafted at school and ploughed the lanes of the local municipal pool for hour after hour before grafting some more to earn the money to keep going. What a story that would have made – but no! In his saner moments, Ben would acknowledge that the experience had taught him that the difference between success and failure was the touch of a fingertip. You couldn't leave anything to chance. So, he'd tried even harder. It had been after the Olympic qualifiers that he'd set up his first shop, the first step in his rise. He'd show them all; the name Ben Bradshaw would eclipse old Baldilocks in the end. Life was a long-distance event, not a 100-metre sprint.

Ben had heard that some bosses wouldn't employ men with beards; in his case, it was the total shavers, and, looking back, the meeting with the slaphead at Blue Sky had been pivotal – better still, it hadn't cost him a penny. He'd headed straight for the nearest Marks and Spencer to create himself a new look, in the end going for a chinos and open-neck shirt 'I'm a regular guy like you, so you can trust me' image, which he'd stuck with ever since. Then there'd been the catchphrase, the hook people remembered, the line people shouted out at him in the street, the silly bit of nonsense that had stuck.

The first advert had been the hardest, but it did the trick. Ben could replay it in his mind without needing to put a video in the machine.

'Hi, I'm Ben Bradshaw, the man who brings you quality beds at value-for-money prices.' Zoom in. 'We've gone mad this month at your local Doze Megastore. We're offering a fantastic two-for-one offer on our ten most popular beds …' Zoom out to show Ben standing, throwing his arms out wide. '… with all mattresses on a flexible buy-one-get-another-at-half-price mega- deal, all on flexible terms. You'd be dozy to miss out, so come on down to Doze Megastores …'

Pause, deep breath, slightly raised voice: '… for the rest of your life!'

2000

Mushtaq Dhillon had always tried to get away for the Christmas period, and his favourite place was always Venice. He knew the city well, and also knew its power to impress. Rare was the occasion when the offer of a week in La Serenissima had failed to turn 'just good friends' into much more, the city's allure being enough to set up seven days of romance, and an excuse for him to get away from the turgid boredom and sudden naps that characterized Christmas with his parents.

Venice in late December rarely featured in travel brochures. Perhaps it was the mist that rose up off the lagoon and shrouded the city with a fog so dense that even at midday it was impossible to see from one side of the Grand Canal to the other. It was almost as if the sea was rising, ghost-like, to reclaim the land that was its by right.

The dampness could infiltrate your clothes and even your mood. If you let it, that was. For Mushtaq, the mists were always a blessing, something to get lost in, as well as being the perfect excuse to sample a good proportion of the city's many coffee bars for a simple espresso and maybe a slice of apple and cinnamon cake, or a quick Aperol Spritz before dinner.

Mushtaq had access to a small one-bedroom flat in the San Polo district, overlooking a side canal. It belonged to the family of a colleague of his who, like many Italians, couldn't understand the attraction of the city in winter. The flat sat at the top of a tenement down a small alleyway off the Piazza San Polo itself, and if the weather wasn't too bad and you were prepared to open the windows in the late afternoon, you could hear the sound of people with small dogs gathering to talk while their animals enjoyed the unaccustomed freedom of open spaces.

The city also held another attraction in its traditional role of being a fulcrum between east and west. Mushtaq had always felt comfortable here, more at ease than he ever did at home, and he'd taken the trouble over the years to get to learn the language. The city's history meant that brown faces, while not commonplace, were unremarkable, and Mushtaq found that his complexion made it easier for the various patrons of his favoured cafés and bars to recognize him: something else that tended to impress the ladies. Ultimately, though, it was probably his ability to converse in their own language, even using elements of local dialect, that more than anything else made the Venetians particularly hospitable to him. Even though his modest salary meant he couldn't never hope to own it, Mushtaq liked to regard the small flat as his home away from home.

It was one of the dead days between Christmas and New Year. The previous evening he'd taken an empty plastic water bottle down to the *vino sfuso* bar on the corner where they dispensed wine from plastic barrels via siphons. There, he'd filled up with a litre of decent enough Pinot Grigio which, although it looked like a sample on the way to the vets, was usually pretty drinkable. He and that year's companion had ended up drinking the lot while watching a video in the flat, and a night of drunken lovemaking had followed, spoiled only by his new friend's habit of falling on to her back and snoring every time he managed to get back to sleep, drowning out even the racket made by the tourists' wheeled suitcases outside as they bounced across the city's cobbles in the morning.

Round about five he'd given up on sleep and pulled on three layers of clothes for a solo wander around the city, aiming to shock his system back into life. Padding across the still-moist paving stones, Mushtaq was in his element: hidden and alone with his thoughts, but moving, with a purpose. These were the times he liked best, away from his caseload, although, like most in his profession, it was never that far from his thoughts.

His target was the Rialto fish market, where he planned to get the pick of the catch for a seafood risotto later that day. First, though, he'd partaken of some warm chocolate-dipped croissants and not-too-hot coffee, knocking the drink back as if it was a shot of vodka, the velvety liquid lining his throat with a quick warmth that eased down his chest like a slow-moving coat of tar, before settling into the very pit of his stomach. Thus fortified, he resumed his quest. He was an old enough Venice hand to know that if you wanted to make a good *seppioline nere*, the Venetian risotto dish using baby cuttlefish, you had to get there as soon as the market opened in order to get the fish with the vital little ink sacks still intact, the essential ingredient for making the dish's distinctive black pasta.

The smell of the market hit him just before the shouts of the traders setting up their stalls, with the chill from the water striking him shortly afterwards. The flagstones beneath the ancient market were clean, a condition doomed not to last long, as he strode towards his favourite trader in the far corner under a magnificent carving of a mermaid in the roof. For a moment he hesitated, tempted by the sight of some beautiful scallops still in their light pink shells, and some live crabs climbing over each other's backs in futile attempts at escape, but in the end he resisted and stuck to his course.

The smile and abbreviated ''giorno' when he got to the stall was enough to tell him he was in luck. Two good-sized fish, one slightly bigger than the other, were brought out from underneath the counter, the trader automatically showing him their bulging sacks for reassurance, holding them out for inspection and squeezing them as if he was a doctor checking for testicular cancer. Mushtaq's reputation as a gourmet had preceded him.

He nodded, and money changed hands, the whole transaction taking less than a minute: something down to the earliness of the hour. If the same process had taken place when everyone was fully awake, it would have required a minimum of five minutes to consult on the good health of each other's families.

The fish wrapped up in plain white paper, he glanced at his watch. It was still only half past six, and Mushtaq decided freshly squeezed orange juice would be a good idea. Ten minutes later he was winding his way home, the streets all but deserted, the mist already determinedly set in like cold steam. His footsteps echoed against the towering walls all around as he stepped up his speed. The novelty of the early hour had worn off and he was keen to re-enter the warmth of his flat, his bed and his companion, in that order.

But on the way, there'd been time for another espresso. A small neon sign bearing the name of the coffee maker Lavazza, in red, acted as a beacon guiding him towards his most favoured bar. The second he walked in a tiny white cup, full of mud-like liquid, was pushed towards him by the café's owner a tall native Venetian with dark slicked-back hair, which Mushtaq suspected he used as a reserve reservoir for his cooking oil. Standing motionless for a few seconds out of respect for the coffee, Mushtaq scanned the cabinet of freshly baked brioches, wondering whether to take any back with him, before deciding, on balance, against.

He thought he was alone in the bar, so it came as a surprise when a commotion started behind him, a dropped cup smashing on the floor and someone storming out in high dudgeon. Venetians were known for their temper, but this was crossing a line, discourteous to the owner. Fights were okay in Venice, but they had to take place outside. The scene ended in seconds but shattered not just a cup, but also the previously amicable mood. Leaving some coins on the counter, Mushtaq left, the shouts from the owner at the long-departed strangers still bouncing off the narrow walls outside, followed quickly by a late 'Domani' directed towards Mushtaq. Yes, he probably would be back tomorrow, and no doubt the coffee would be on the house by way of apology, even if the scene hadn't been the owner's fault. The drink, or maybe the incident, had literally left a bitter taste, redoubling his resolve to get back to the flat. It was a coffee too far.

A single streetlamp shone an iridescent glow above his head as he negotiated the last of the many bridges that stood between the market and the flat. He cut the corner in his haste as he approached the short stretch of canal-side alleyway he could see from his kitchen window. Modern graffiti acted as a counterpoint to the ancient stone walls, small waves slapping against the ancient brickwork. No boats had moored there – the canal was too narrow – and the channel itself was only just visible in the continuing glow of the streetlamp: still, and a murky blue-green in the slowly emerging daylight. As he lengthened his stride Mushtaq was debating whether to squeeze his newly bought oranges as soon as he got in, so he could shift the taste of the coffee, which hadn't been good, or head straight to the bed for other comforts.

The silence that had previously been punctured only by his footsteps was suddenly disturbed by a flock of pigeons emerging from a side alley, rising up from the ground as if heading for Mushtaq's head. Instinctively he raised his hands, dropping the precious fish bought only minutes before. The birds kept coming, and as they did so one of Mushtaq's feet, covered only with an inadequate black brogue, these being the first shoes that had come to hand in the dark, stepped on the larger of the two cuttlefish and slid inexorably forward, with the rest of his body following the natural laws of equilibrium.

While happened next was inevitable. Mushtaq fell, his right foot moving forward as his spine tilted backwards, sending his head towards a confrontation with the edge of the canal wall from which there was only ever going to be one winner. A crack echoed against the ancient stone walls surrounding the small alley; the sort of sound a hammer might make in an unsuccessful attempt to break open a fairground coconut.

In an instant Mushtaq lost all consciousness, but his body needed a little further encouragement from the toe of a willing third party before it began to slide into the foul water below, the surface of which supported a few days' worth of detritus that the tide had been unable to carry out, giving out a reek that managed to combine the aroma of decaying vegetables with a hint of dead dog. The body completed its journey into the water almost soundlessly, its completion marked only by a gentle plop, followed by two more as a trio of oranges followed him into the water to join the organic matter already there.

The sack of one of the precious cuttlefish had burst in the fall, and a black stain spread out from the top of the pavement before dripping into the water below, where it became a barely discernible and slowly expanding nebulous black cloud.

A voice from nowhere broke the now-restored silence. It spoke as if choking slightly, laden not with emotion so much as with nausea from the smell rising up from the canal.

'Tut-tut,' the voice remonstrated. 'Stinky Inky'.

2002

What doesn't kill you makes you stronger. That's what Sandra O'Brien had always believed, and if you didn't challenge yourself every now and then how could you expect to gain the experiences that strengthened you? Anyone could just get a job and settle down, but to Sandra that wasn't living, it was existing. Besides, your time on earth was too short to have just one life. Ever since Sandra had come to this conclusion she'd been determined to fit in as many as she could.

This had pretty much coincided with the moment when she realized she had a certain effect on men. When she discovered that many of them had a thing about blonde hair, she made a point of cultivating a long tumbling mane that fell down between her shoulder blades; an effect she accentuated with dark sweaters and jackets to give a canvas for the sheen, while at the same time highlighting the stray hairs she left scattered behind around any workplace she frequented: rationed mementoes for her legion of followers.

She wasn't a dumb blonde, however: quite the opposite. In the flesh she was femininity personified, but over the phone she could come across as a man, a trick that had proved very useful over the years. She was also in a hurry. Stashing a few pounds away every week or month for an annual fortnight in the sun wasn't going to cut it for her. If she had to break some rules to get the cash needed to lubricate this, then so be it; the trick was not to overdo it, taking just enough to finance her next metamorphosis. If she was to live five lives to everyone else's one, then it stood to reason she needed to earn cash five times as quickly. Not only was this obvious, but perfectly reasonable too.

Things hadn't started well. She'd almost blown it with her very first job at a financial advisers' in England, but she got out in time. What didn't kill you made you stronger. Next time around, back in Ireland, she didn't make the same mistake and everything went to plan. She skimmed the contacts and information without a hitch, and rather than set up on her own, which would have been much too slow a process for her purposes, she sold the lot to a rival. The money paid for some surgery and eighteen months in Australia, where she managed a tidy little vineyard property scam just to keep her hand in.

Sandra took the long way home via South Africa and then up through that continent, via the surprisingly good roads of the young state of Zimbabwe, the less cushioned highways of Zambia and Tanzania, and then through Kenya and Ethiopia, thereafter following the Nile to the Mediterranean. She travelled as part of an overland group, in a large German truck with tyres so big they wouldn't have looked out of place on one of the mining trucks they passed along the way. She loved the food and the companionship, sitting out in the open part of the truck, eschewing the cramped eight-person cabin up front, even during the regular downpours. Out there she could be alone, and it was easier to brush away the unwanted attentions of some of the men seemingly attracted to her like the flies who were their other constant companions. By the time they'd reached the pyramids, the journey's symbolic end, she felt that if nothing else happened she'd already lived one full life.

But only one. Sandra had always known more were possible, and, if anything, her resolve had been strengthened to continue down the path she'd chosen. On her return to Ireland she felt restless, as if coming home was a form of defeat, so she grabbed an opportunity she'd spotted in South Wales, on the outskirts of Cardiff.

The government had been pumping money into advance factory units: great white elephants erected on a sort of *Field of Dreams* principle that if you built them, jobs would come. Sandra had been able to create a shell company and engorge her bank accounts (there were several) with public money, without doing much to actually fill the buildings with eager workers. The whole thing was a case of hope overtaking reality, with politicians desperate to be seen to be doing something, but less concerned with how effective that something was. By the time she was ready to disappear again she had enough to finance another life, again preceded by a little help from the surgeon's knife; her destination this time: the Far East.

Starting in Singapore, she'd travelled north up the western coast of Malaysia via Kuala Lumpur to George Town, on the honeymoon island of Penang. Here she rested on the beach for a while, confident that most of the men there would only have eyes for their new wives: a theory that worked, more or less. Crossing the nervous border into Thailand, she enjoyed a few months on the underdeveloped and unfortunately named island of Phuket, living in straw-roofed and reed-walled huts, watching magnificent sunsets and drinking raw Mekong whisky by the light of a single bulb powered by a generator, turned off every night at ten. It was a tropical paradise, a totally different existence from the one she'd enjoyed in Australia and Africa. Sandra was living her dream. Life – all her lives – was, and were, going to be sweet.

Ireland called again, but what she found there was something she hadn't been expecting. Love. Sandra had always avoided love, afraid of its power to tie her down; its absence from life a fair exchange for gaining a multitude of lives. On this visit she discovered the inconvenient truth that love had its own rules, and, what was more, love was an important part of life.

It started with a bunch of gypsies (although they said they preferred the term 'new-age travellers') on a patch of land outside Waterford, in the south. At the time Ireland was in the early stages of its economic miracle and land, for so long taken for granted, had suddenly become extremely valuable. Sandra spotted an opportunity for the Celtic Tiger to roar for her. The travellers had been depressing the value of the plots near their encampment, but if she bought low she might be able to sell high – assuming she could find a way of encouraging them to leave. By Sandra's standards it wasn't a significant deal, more a small diversion to keep her hand in while she contemplated her next move; it wasn't even illegal, so long as she went about it the right way.

Their vehicles were a mixture, ranging from old VW vans to traditional wooden gypsy caravans, with high wheels and a circular body, pulled by old carthorses, held on long ropes as they grazed by the side of the plot. Originally brightly painted, the caravans had been defeated by the Irish weather: where the paint had flaked, the rain got in underneath and started to rot the wood.

Sandra had inveigled her way into the group by presenting herself as one of them, something that required a lot of dressing down, failing to wash her hair for a fortnight, and generally avoiding soap for a while. She managed to get hold of the plots adjacent to their campsite for a distressed price, and the plan was to live among the travellers and, when the time was ripe, suggest that she knew somewhere better where they could go. She allowed herself a month to execute her plan: a period she regarded as generous, given their state.

One of the men looked in a particularly bad way, with drawn skin stretched tightly over a slender frame and a bad case of the coughs. It was an unlikely scenario, and really quite late for love in this life, but it struck anyway. Sandra immediately discovered a number of things about herself. She discovered she was tired, she was lonely, and she'd also found a maternal side to her she'd never dreamed existed. In the pitiable creature she'd found, she saw someone who was vulnerable; someone who needed her, and who she could help in a totally unselfish and caring way.

For the first time in her adult life Sandra O'Brien found herself not thinking about herself, but someone else.

She'd seen rescue, and perhaps she had spotted redemption.

------------------------------ ✳ ------------------------------

Turning thirty had been quiet, understated, but forty was a facer. Forty was more than half the total his pater had got to, a target which, when he stopped to think about it (which he tried not to), Andy Thompson didn't see himself beating if he carried on as he was doing. The fizz had gone out of his life. The thrill of the trading floor had been removed, and his days were taken up mainly with making sure other people did their job, rather than actually doing something useful himself. His life was now full of airports and meetings in foreign cities.

He continued to enjoy the numbers, and, to some extent, the thrill of a big kill; but the thrill was vicarious, executed by a member of his team, not him. He'd lost touch with both his own roots and those of the market. He'd become a follower, not a leader; a spotter of trends rather than someone who set them. His only contact with what he regarded as the real world, actual trading, was managing the Bond, but even there he'd started to get sloppy, making mistakes like ordinary people. He'd become an ordinary person.

He'd ducked the British Rail privatization, which turned out to be a good call for the Bond, but he dropped a bollock soon after with a tech start-up he was sure would fly, but instead ended up going down with all microchips set to zero. Typically, that was the year someone actually read the report. Perhaps it was a mistake moving to colour: the red stood out so starkly, he wished he'd stuck with using brackets to indicate a loss. Equally typically, everyone had focused on the detail; not the bigger picture, how he'd massively over-performed the stock market since he took things over.

He'd recover, he told them, and he had – in spades. The mid-nineties had been an especially good time, more than making up for the tech blip with a nice little venture into commercial property, which not only saw a 50k windfall profit but also a steady dividend flow ever since. Getting over the million mark deserved a pat on the back; but no, there was always the awkward squad. Such a sum of money demanded greater oversight, they said – that Meadows moron for one – which meant he had to play safer: more bonds and deposit accounts, more phone calls and meetings to ask permission. Ask permission! Him? Andy Thompson? He'd had enough of his style being cramped at work; he didn't need it with the Bond as well.

Still, he carried on, mostly out of a sense of duty. There'd been more successes, but they were less spectacular: he didn't have the stake money or the freedom of movement he needed to go for the big slams any more. The total valuation continued to rise year-on-year, any hiccup always precipitating a discussion about raising the dues. Idiots. As anyone with any experience could have told them, subs weren't where the growth came from. The whole thing had a life of its own; it didn't need extra gas.

The latest such debate was a turning point for Andy. The Bond arrangement was really little more than a tontine, a financial instrument with a long and not terribly distinguished past. Popular in the seventeenth century, such mechanisms had been used as a sort of life assurance back in the day, although they usually had a cut-off date for the payout, the last-man-standing approach being the exception rather than the rule. The inconvenient truth was that the mechanism they'd put in place to secure a legacy for their 'special' year wasn't so special itself. Andy had been in the money game long enough to understand that instruments like tontines were nothing more than a giant juggling act. The trick was to be out of the room when the balls were dropped.

The bottom line was that the fun had gone out of it. Not just running the Bond, but work too – everything. He felt trapped: there was no other way to describe it. Even home didn't feel like, well, a home, not any more. Instead of being the centre of his household, the sun around which all else orbited, he'd become some kind of meteorite, constantly repelled every time he tried to enter the atmosphere surrounding his family. His role was to provide the money, the oxygen that kept the whole ecosystem going; needed, but not really wanted.

That ecosystem operated from a lovely barn conversion, which they'd been able to add to in stages, with amazing views over the South Downs along with its own indoor swimming pool and gym, and all the other seemingly essential trappings of an affluent middle-class lifestyle. These days, all his wife Lucy seemed to want to talk about was the kids and the schools. That, and planning for their next holiday. They seemed to take holidays every break in the school calendar, holidays and half terms dictating the rhythm of their lives. As if he didn't see enough of airports.

Then there was the sport, especially the rugby. The boys had started in the mini-leagues and then graduated to the rougher stuff. Lucy's evenings revolved around ferrying the kids to and from practice sessions, and he was expected to watch them play school games. On Sundays, they even went to watch the local professional side; that was, if they weren't going to the hospital to have some fresh or previous injury looked at. Andy had hated rugby at school; he still wasn't sure he understood half the rules. How had the game come to dominate his free time now?

He'd created a monster, a lifestyle that sucked in all he could give to it. His salary and bonuses never seemed to satisfy the need to meet school fees, holidays, cars, entertaining, builders, clothes. He was staring down a tunnel, another fifteen years of the same old, same old. He was a wealthy man, but it didn't feel like it.

Then there'd been the run of deaths among the old school gang. Made you think. God, they'd been an unlucky bunch. Who was going to go next? It could even be him. How much time did he have left? What should he do with it?

Andy had never mentioned his plan to Lucy, she'd have laughed openly in his face. To her it would have been simply inconceivable, the ramblings of a male menopausal.

Instead, he just did it.

Andy Thompson needed to do what he had to do to become whole again, so he made sure there was enough money for the family, a reasonable lifestyle if they cut back a bit and sold the house; and he made plans. The way Andy saw it he was doing them a favour, yanking them off the treadmill. They'd thank him one day. He'd freed them from 'stuff', all the junk that weighed them down.

He bought himself a World Pass, a year-long open air ticket for one. Business class. He was going to see the world: read Tolstoy in Russia, see Picassos in Spain, eat biltong in South Africa, smoke weed in Jamaica, go to the carnival in Rio.

He was going to live life; and then, and only then, would he come home and face the music.

----------------------------- ❋ -----------------------------

Mid Notts University had turned out to be something of a revelation. It seemed there was something Sam Davidson was good at, after all. For years he'd been trying to express himself through writing, when it turned out his real métier was talking, or, more accurately, giving lectures and running seminars. In only a few years he'd risen from a humble part-time lecturer to senior tutor (media studies), a full-time, socially recognized and rather well-paid post. He'd found his niche. Also, for the first time in his life, Sam was actually quite popular, and that in turn made him feel what he'd eventually diagnosed as happiness and contentment, having never really experienced them before.

With renewed confidence, he began to start sniffing round stories again, and even contemplated a book. His problem was time. When he'd first been taken on by the university he treated himself to a second-hand Macintosh Classic, and spent his lonely evenings working up some ideas. He loved his Apple and dreamed of one day getting one of the funky new iMacs; but in the meantime, he split his time between working on the book and mastering his keyboard skills by working up the levels on Super Mario. More recently, there'd been the internet and the possibilities it offered to interact with a growing retinue of cyber friends.

The internet could have been designed for Sam. While he was aware some people his age saw it as an inconvenience, making them learn a whole new set of skills just when they were beginning to reap the rewards of mid-career slog, for Sam it acted more as a vehicle for lifting him out of the humdrum and depositing him in whole new worlds, both real and virtual. Whereas others regarded it as something that drained their power, for Sam it acted as a fresh energy source.

When the invitation came for that year's Seventy-Seven Society supper, their Silver Jubilee meal, he stopped himself from automatically throwing it in the bin, and read it. Why not go, he wondered. Maybe it was time he checked in again with his year group, to see how they were coping with the challenges of the internet age – to see if they were coping as well as he was. A lot of water had passed under the bridge since they all left school – he was Sam now; surely there'd be no more calling him by his nickname 'Period', or jibes about his religion? – so he accepted the invitation by return.

On his arrival at the nominated pub, the first thing that struck him was how thin attendance was, certainly compared to his one and only previous visit; around twenty-five men, something he supposed was down to dwindling interest, or the competing demands of family life. Even though he'd have preferred lager, bitter seemed to be compulsory. The pub was a real-ale specialist and he didn't want to show himself up, so he got himself one in. The gathering seemed to be made up of a hardcore of those who came every year, plus a few odds and sods who turned up sporadically. The dress code seemed to be jeans with T-shirts and unbuttoned shirts, designer labels, and the names of exclusive holiday resorts or golf equipment suppliers rather than political slogans on the T-shirts. Given this, Sam's three-piece suit made him stand out a little.

Some of the men Sam recognized immediately, while others had aged badly. Paul Briton, for example, was still a grown-up Humpty Dumpty with added cheeks, and Toby Connor still had that slightly smug air about him, as if he was waiting for someone to challenge him to name the capital of Turkmenistan. One of their number who he couldn't place was sporting a straggling long goatee that looked like it had been gently combed through with white paint: not a pure white, more white with a hint of beard. Sam also recognized Ben Bradshaw, but who wouldn't after all his TV adverts?

Others were obviously fighting age through exercise, the runners in particular betraying themselves with taut-skinned faces and beanpole physiques which, in many ways, made them look less healthy than those who'd clearly enjoyed a glass or two. Elsewhere, most seemed to have lost the opening skirmishes in the unwinnable fight against middle-aged spread.

Having been missing for twenty-odd years, Sam found most of his conversations began by him having to reintroduce himself and finding incidents or people they could attach him to. To his surprise, this generally required invoking Mushtaq's memory to jog people's brain cells. These stirred up mixed emotions: on the one hand, Sam found himself remembering how they'd weathered the special challenges of adolescence together at the Red Coat with affection; on the other, his sudden disappearance still lingered like a betrayal. When he mentioned the name of his ex-friend in a chat with Tom Joules, he was shocked to find that Mushtaq was more 'ex' than most. He'd been mentioned in dispatches the previous year, despite not strictly being a Seventy-Sevener, having left, or more accurately disappeared, the year previously. Still, drowning in a Venice back canal was no way to go, and for a few minutes Sam retreated into himself, remembering better times.

On the short walk over the road to the restaurant it turned out that the temperature had dropped dramatically, jerking Sam back to the present and the next stage of the evening. On entering the warmth, he scanned the seating arrangements, determined to choose carefully. He didn't want to be near Ray Meadows, a man he didn't think he'd ever be able to forgive – he might have become a more ravaged version of his previous self physically, but remained the same malicious bastard at heart – making a beeline instead for David Lu, another outcast, who still had a quiet, reserved air about him and was now director of clinical services, or something similar, for the local NHS Trust. At first, he seemed to welcome the opportunity for a one-on-one conversation, but before long it was more of a list, as David went on about medical conventions he'd attended in exotic locations Sam was never likely to visit.

'Did I hear you mention old 'Inky' Dhillon earlier in the pub?'

'Yes, that's right,' Sam confirmed. It seemed his old friendship with Mushtaq was destined to define him, but he wasn't too upset by this and was happy to engage with someone new.

It was Paul Briton asking, and as he did so he glanced down the table towards Ray Meadows and, noticing he was sharing a long and complicated joke with someone further down the table, added: 'Good stunt he pulled that time at Catterick, eh?'

'Well, nothing was ever proved ...' Sam hedged, '... but yes, whoever planned that one deserved a medal.' The two of them shared a laugh, before Paul added, 'Best not mention it though, eh? Still a bit of a touchy subject in certain quarters.'

'Mum's the word,' Sam confirmed, doubly happy now he'd been brought into a conspiracy of silence.

'But tell me,' Paul went on, 'you of all people should be able to confirm. Was it true that, you know, that he … a lot of water under the bridge now, eh? That he was, you know …'

'Was what?' Sam asked.

'You know …' Paul went on, refusing to get to the point, instead miming the unbuckling of his belt and pressing his backside deeper into his chair, at the same time feigning a strained look on his face.

'What?'

Paul leaned over and raised his hand, half whispering behind it, 'That he was the old Double S.'

Sam shrugged his broad shoulders. It was a question he'd asked himself many times. It would be convenient if it was true, and would explain so many things; but the truth was he couldn't bring himself to believe it. It just wasn't Mushtaq's style which, as the whole Catterick episode had shown, was more subtle, more intelligent; less, well, crude.

'I honestly don't know,' was the best he could offer, a look of resignation on his face that he considered to be persuasive. True or not, given the news he'd received earlier that evening from Tom, it just didn't seem appropriate to be speculating either way.

'Fairy nuff, thought I'd ask, that's all,' Paul concluded in a way that made Sam think that maybe he wasn't so convinced after all.

'Ask what?' someone asked, and Sam feared that the subject, one he wasn't particularly keen to pursue, may not be over yet. Luckily, he was rescued by the unlikely person of Ray Meadows. His questioner had been none other than Reggie Richardson, but to most around the table he was barely recognizable. The man who had spent most of his adult life on an inexorable journey towards becoming a sphere, had shed what looked like two-thirds of his body weight.

'Bloody hell! It's Reggie!' Ray exclaimed out of nowhere, genuinely shocked. Somehow, they'd missed each other in the car park and this was the first time he'd recognized his otherwise familiar sparring partner. 'He's done a Lawson!'. It was true, Reggie Richardson had lost as much weight as the ex-Chancellor of the Exchequer, if not more; the skin on his face falling in folds like fallen wallpaper as its lost elasticity struggled to cope with the speed with which the fat behind it had disappeared.

'Not the cabbage soup diet?' asked Paul Briton, a hint of fear in his voice, but one of his broad toothpaste-advert smiles on his face.

'Stand back everyone, get ready for blast-off!' Ray Meadows yelled, to the backdrop of a general scraping of chairs followed by laughter.

The whole scene had gone over Sam's head: to his eyes, Reggie looked much as he remembered him, if considerably more wrinkled. As others toasted their friend, Sam reached for his own glass. Everyone had moved on to wine for the dinner itself, although David Lu had generously offered to share a bottle of Perrier with him. As the evening wore on, so the conversations gained a veneer of introspection; less about specific memories, and more about life in general. They were all in their forties now, with some showing it more than others.

'You know you're getting old when your pubes start going grey,' came a voice from the depths of the table.

'Too late, friend, like a bloody badger down there,' came the reply from Ray Meadows, who seemed to have the ability to butt in on any conversation at will, his ears seemingly tuned to detect any decline into baser subjects.

'I haven't seen my todger for ten years,' offered Eddie Perks, giving just a little more information than was needed.

Unsurprisingly, given the high profile the Queen's Golden Jubilee had garnered earlier that year, there was also a great deal of reminiscing about the Stuff The Jubilee stunt they'd pulled as a year group.

'Reckon we did for the HM there,' Simon Grant reflected.

'No great loss really; he was a bit of a bastard,' Toby Connor added. 'Never missed a chance to wield that cane of his, sadistic sod.' A few nods around the table acknowledged the truth of that statement.

'I've just got it!' Terry Mungus piped up.

'Well, don't give it to me,' a voice came from down the table.

'No, HM – headmaster, but also Harold Mitchell.' A groan washed over the restaurant like a tidal wave.

'Christ, Hugh, you retard!' Ray Meadows knew that on this, he was speaking for the group.

Luckily, at that point Tom Joules stood up and waited for the room to slip into silence, which seemed to happen without him having to tap a glass or clear his throat, almost as if everyone was expecting it; which, of course, they were.

'Here we go: Hatches, Matches and Dispatches,' Paul whispered. Sam gave him a quizzical look. 'You'll see,' Paul assured him.

What followed was a roll call of births, marriages and, a little unexpectedly for Sam, deaths: two of them. There was a moment's silence, during which Sam noticed that he seemed to be the only one showing any hint of shock; as if the loss of two of their old friends, even if he'd never really called them friends, was something they regarded as almost commonplace. While he was still processing this thought, Tom began to pass round a small staple-bound report, splitting the pile he now had in front of him in two, and sending half in each direction round the table. Sam took his copy and passed the rest on. A quick glance at the first page revealed it was the annual update on the Bond. The hollow pop of a dozen glasses cases being closed at the same time echoed around the otherwise silent room.

'Christ, two deaths in a year,' Sam remarked to no one in particular, without a glance at the report. The aftershock of the news about Mushtaq had been compounded by this, if anything, greater surprise.

'Yes. Sad, isn't it?' Eddie offered, almost nonchalantly.

'Sad?' Sam queried, still dazed.

'Two's about average. Can't remember the last time there were none at all. Makes you feel old, doesn't it? Part of life, I suppose: normal, a bit like that section on *Sports Personality of the Year* or the *BAFTAs*, when they go through "lost friends", eh?'

Sam's reaction was that it was anything but normal. He was, in short, speechless. Then it struck him: a demolition ball out of nowhere. This was his story, the pivot around which his journalistic career could revive – a subject for his book.

Later he was to remember it as his 'Shipman moment'. The GP Harold Shipman had been murdering his patients for years, but no one ever put two and two together and saw the bigger picture – they were too close to it. Shipman had turned out to be Britain's most prolific serial killer of all time; could Sam be on to something equally sensational?

As soon as Tom sat down, he started to ask around the table for details of some of the recent deaths, and everyone seemed only too happy to help, to share what they remembered, and generally get what they knew off the greying manes of their chests.

Everyone, that was, except one.

2004

Les Andrew and Philip Christopher shared more than a surfeit of Christian names. They'd always been best friends, right through primary school and subsequently when they joined the Red Coat. Inseparable, their parents had called them, it never even occurring to them that their friendship may have been more than just that; but even if they had, they needn't have worried, for both Les's and Philip's interests were firmly in the direction of birds. Watching them, that was.

Of average height and build, Les Andrew's main distinguishing feature was his crew cut, which he knew was a cliché and marked him out as a geek at work, but it had served him well for over three decades and he didn't really see the advantages in changing it. Les's lack of any clear distinguishing features, or indeed of any clear anything, had meant he was one of the few at school to evade a nickname.

This absence was something else Les shared with his friend. If Les was dull, then Philip could be summed up simply as bland: it was the absence of a presence, along with a preference for anonymity, that defined him at school, and indeed in the life that followed. Along with Nigel Bennett, they were the only ones to attach themselves to the Air Training Corps instead of the army in the CCF. For Les and Philip, the attraction was the maps; although to be fair, Bennett seemed to have a genuine interest in flying.

Philip had worked at the Health and Safety Executive since leaving university. It was as if some greater power had designed his perfect job, and it so happened that the whole field of safety at work had become increasingly high-profile as his career had evolved, providing him with the sort of steady progression he might not have managed on his own. He saw his work as important, protecting people against themselves and their own stupidity, whether they felt they needed it or not being beside the point. He'd seen the statistics and was quite happy to quote them when required, which, as it turned out, was surprisingly often.

Les meanwhile worked for his local authority, and although his job had remained fundamentally the same since he started doing it, his actual employer had changed names four times as a result of various reorganizations. This was a detail Les often liked to trot out when people asked him where he worked, although it's probably fair to say that he saw it as more interesting than most of the people he told.

Les worked in traffic management, specializing in traffic light control. For Les, traffic flow was a solvable problem. Moving cars, buses and bikes around the roads was not dissimilar to operating the giant train set he'd had in the loft of his parents' house. It was all a matter of timing and phasing. If people ever took the trouble to understand this, they'd probably thank him; after all, the alternative was either anarchy or, horror of horrors (as far as he was concerned, at least), mini-roundabouts. To Les, mini-roundabouts were the work of the devil, allowing motorists and others to exercise discretion, which in turn produced randomness. It was largely thanks to Les that most of the county's main towns were lit up like a Christmas tree permanently, mostly in a deep crimson red.

Both men had married in their thirties, and the two couples tended to see a lot of each other. Otherwise, outside of semi-compulsory work events, the only socializing the two men did was to attend the Seventy-Seven Society suppers. Even here, they were both what Tom Joules would have labelled 'irregulars', which didn't mean a need to be force-fed All-Bran and prunes: more that they were likely to turn up to those anniversary dinners acknowledging a number of years with either a five or a nought in them.

Both their wives had produced a single child, a boy, born only three months apart: something else that had tended to pull the couples together. The boys were both in Cubs and eventually went to the Red Coat together. Every Easter break, the Cubs ran a week-long outward bound camp, and seeing that the boys both enjoyed running around, building and hitting things, as well as camping, they were allowed to go. This presented an opportunity for the men to indulge in a birdwatching holiday, leaving their wives to share the fetching and carrying.

This particular year the men had opted for Majorca, staying on the south-west coast of the island near the fashionable port of Puerto Andratx, which they amusingly called Port Anthrax when people had asked where they were headed for. Their hotel was up in the hills, away from the sound of the wire halyards of the fancy yachts in the harbour banging against their metal masts. They had chosen their base deliberately, as not only was it cheaper, but it also provided the perfect jumping-off point for the various footpaths that covered the island. They'd chosen a small family-run hotel with only a dozen bedrooms, one of which they shared, again to save costs.

Given that these holidays were for only a week, they needed to be planned, with the first three days spent exploring the local area following the well-marked footpaths, and the back end of the week using a hired scooter to scout further afield. Over the years, they had found that islands offered the perfect combination of both coastal and inland spotting, as by definition they tended to possess both cliffs and mountainous terrain, offering the maximum variety of birdwatching spots in a short space of time. Road systems also tended to be good, with the use of a scooter both effective and economical for their purposes.

One of them (Les) kept a log of what they'd spotted, while the other (Philip) was very much the photographic expert. So far, Philip had been especially pleased with the results he'd been getting from his new Nikon digital camera, the only downside being the need to build in an allowance of time each day to review the day's results on the laptop he'd brought with him. On the upside, this allowed both of them to see the pictures each evening, like the early rushes of a new movie. On balance, the loss of actual spotting time was, they both felt, worth it, as it allowed them to agree whether it was worth revisiting spots they'd already been to in order to get a better shot.

On this particular day, they had partaken of their normal breakfast of fruit and yogurt, making up ham and bread rolls wrapped up in a paper napkin which they secreted in their rucksacks to save time come lunch. The sky, as it had been all week, was a beautiful cobalt blue, and the air was fresh and perfumed, while the island itself was a mass of light green as it began the process of bursting back into life after the winter rains.

Their 50cc scooter was motoring along at a steady 30mph, falling to half that when they reached an incline, which was just fine for their purposes as both men liked to look out for likely prey, one taking the right-hand side and the other the left, out of well-ingrained habit. On this day, Les was driving and had got up a head of steam along an unpromising long, dusty stretch of metalled road. The noise of the wind, combined with the sound-deadening effect of their helmets, meant that neither was aware of the large Jeep speeding up behind them, similarly tempted, it seemed, by the unusually open portion of road.

The sound the Jeep made when it glanced against the scooter was loud but fleeting: a metallic crunch combined with the dull thud of human flesh and muscle coming up against a force it wasn't designed to resist. A sharp screeching sound followed as the scooter scraped along the black road surface, ceasing only when the scooter flew out over the edge of the cliff, after which an abrupt silence fell, followed in time by a distant series of crashes as the now-wrecked machine bounced against the rocks on its way down.

Only one person, the driver of the Jeep, who had stopped and raised a pair of binoculars to their eyes, heard the final full stop of sound, faint and very distant, as a double splash announced something landing in the sea below. That same person remained in position for a further minute, scanning the scene below through their two magnifying tunnels. Satisfied there had been no survivors, they got back into the Jeep and left silently.

------------------------------- ✳ -------------------------------

As soon as her new friend was well again she'd embarked on some real travelling, but not alone. They'd put a torch to the old caravan in a symbolic ritual designed to say they were entering a new phase of their lives – together. For her new companion, and now lover, it was the end of a long time spent being hungry, cold and dirty; of living from hand to mouth and being openly despised by everyone else. Whatever it was that had brought each other into their lives, they didn't know; they were just glad that it had. It felt fantastic to stop sprinting away from the past and to start running towards the future.

She called herself Astra, although she'd lived under a number of names over the past twenty years, reflecting her belief that names were just a label. She'd been Lou Ceet during her punk phase immediately after she left home, touring the country as a backing singer in an up-and-coming band that was on the verge of making it, just when the whole scene collapsed. She'd learned the guitar well enough to pluck out a few tunes, and made a living of sorts busking on the London Underground and in the occasional pub, when she'd been Mary Hairpin – a sort of tribute act to Mary Hopkin – which had been fine, but had limited her repertoire somewhat. There were only so many times you could reprise *Those Were the Days* and *Knock, Knock Who's There?*

She'd been an anarchist and lived in a squat, where she found it more convenient to have no name at all, referring to herself simply as Six, having been the sixth person to join; and after a spell on the streets, when her name had changed nightly so as to improve her chances of a handout from the different worthies dishing out food and comfort, she joined up with the New Age brigade, at which point she adopted the persona of Astra. She hadn't known she'd adopted the name of a car, she knew nothing about such things; the word she'd been searching for was 'Astral'. But the moniker had stuck when a new young recruit to their fold had said it was kind of appropriate, as she was an old 'un and a bit slow to start in the morning.

Life in the gypsy caravan had been okay at first; it offered shelter and got her off the streets, where there'd been the almost inevitable abuse, drugs, bad health and just general hassle. The people she'd been with had all been well-meaning: just feckless when it came to getting their hands on basic things, like food and water. Somehow there always seemed to be cider and grass, but there was a limit to the number of rabbit and hedgehog stews with a side order of dandelions a girl could eat – even though that was better than the vegetarian option, which was the same, only without the stew.

They'd toured around most of England, Wales and Scotland in the caravan, and had somehow got the money together to get to Ireland via Stranraer. She never did find out where the money had come from for the ferry, and their horse, Ginger, was always spooked whenever they got close to the sea. The collective held together more through necessity than desire, but by now they had failed to reach even that low bar.

That was when Sandra had come into her life. Astra had had a number of relationships over the years – men, women, men and women at the same time – but she'd never really known unconditional love since she'd left home. It had felt good, timely. Astra had been stuck down a hole with no obvious way out, and at nearly forty she'd lost the energy and idealism to keep looking.

Sandra had demonstrated more than enough resourcefulness to fight for both of them. After the ritual fire, they'd visited the kasbahs of North Africa, where they'd lost themselves in the pink- and orange-bricked walls of the ancient cities, immersing themselves in simpler times as they dozed to the sounds of muezzins calling the faithful to prayer from the tops of their minarets. Here Astra had recovered, looked after by Sandra's tender ministrations.

It had been during this time that they started to share each other's clothes: at first through necessity, and through time because they enjoyed this simple act of intimacy. They each had long blonde hair, which they tinted to the same shade, and it was this that tended to draw the eyes of men and women alike; not just in Africa, but wherever they went. What started as a passing resemblance to each other grew, through the judicious use of make-up and common facial expressions, until they began to morph into a single version of each other. It became easy to pass themselves off as identical twins, which had the added advantage of making sharing a room easier in less tolerant cultures.

Astra found herself drawing from the well of Sandra's confidence, while Sandra had learned to adopt Astra's more relaxed view of life. Despite this, the balance of their relationship remained clear, with Sandra the rescuer and Astra the rescued. Sandra did all the organizing and Astra was happy to be organized. Every now and then, once Astra was well enough in mind and body to be left alone, Sandra would disappear for a few weeks, sometimes months, after which she'd return, flushed with success and money, and they'd move on. It seemed the moving on part of Astra's life was the one thing that hadn't changed.

Together they travelled the world, and not in a rotting caravan. They went from coast to coast in a Winnebago across North America, and followed the Inca Trail in the South. Wars prevented them from following the traditional route to India, so they flew instead, going on to satiate themselves with temples in the Far East. They also toured Europe by rail, both the west and the newly opened east. They did all this from a base in Tangier, where no questions were asked and any snooping from outsiders would be doomed to failure. It was also from here that Sandra would execute her little sorties into the world of commerce and Astra would keep house: the perfect arrangement.

------------------------------ ✳ ------------------------------

Sam Davidson had not made as much progress on his book as he'd hoped. His enhanced position at the university had brought all sorts of extra commitments with it, not only in normal working hours but some evenings too, and then there was his other persona in cyberspace to maintain. All in all, he was busier than he'd ever been, which meant some demands had inevitably slipped out of focus.

When he didn't have a function or meeting to go to, and if there was nothing good on TV, he connected up to the internet. Here, he checked for updates on the numerous online journalism communities and forums he was a member of under various pseudonyms. Then there was his blog, which needed to be regularly refreshed to attract visitors. Sam loved his blog, which he saw as a way of bypassing the traditional publishing cartels, with their fixed ideas on how things should be written. With a blog you were your own publisher: a thought Sam found pleasing, as was the anonymity. In cyberspace, everyone could know you were there; they just didn't know who you were.

His random jottings had picked up some degree of notoriety and he was pleased when people started to respond to his posts, as the replies reassured him he wasn't just talking into a void – that he had an audience, a fan base even – although replying to them of course meant devoting more time to the keyboard. He told himself that gaining mastery of the internet would ultimately help him in his bigger quest, his master exposé, the story that would finally make his name; and occasionally he also managed to find some time to fire off emails and conduct basic research, which meant he could reassure himself that he'd opened up some lines of enquiry.

The more Sam delved, the clearer it became that he might be on to something. It seemed amazing to him that none of his old school friends had ever thought to at least challenge the relentless cycle of deaths among their number. When he asked them about it individually they were typically quite sanguine, putting it down to natural attrition: a bit worse than might be expected, it was true, but maybe they'd just been unlucky. Besides, when you looked at it, weren't the deaths just a series of unfortunate accidents or illnesses; nothing sinister? Sam was convinced there was something fishy going on; there had to be some kind of link. His task was to find it.

During the course of his discussions and email exchanges he'd drawn up his own theory as to his peers' lack of curiosity, tracing it back to the outbreak of Legionnaires' disease back in the eighties. To Sam, those who'd been at that meal had subsequently adopted a more fatalistic outlook on life: a kind of 'there but for the grace of God' mentality that pushed away logic and settled for accepting each of the subsequent deaths based simply on the bare facts that surrounded them. It had also struck Sam that the group had become habituated to expect some deaths each year. For those attending the meals, the physical act of making it each year was life-affirming; a sign that they had themselves cheated death for another year. The shifting attendance at each year's dinner also added a touch of mystery he supposed it must be difficult to resist. The gathering at the pub beforehand offered some answers as to who had made it through another year, but it wasn't until Tom made his speech that you could confirm whether those who weren't there were missing through *force majeure*, or the force of mortality.

The internet had delivered another unexpected benefit. Sam had discovered Friends Reunited and used it to build a detailed compendium of the whereabouts of much of the Red Coat's Class of '77. Not everyone had wanted to join the site, of course, but there were enough to fill in some gaps and provide some backstory.

Bit by bit, behind the scenes, he brought himself back up to speed, and what he'd discovered was intriguing.

------------------------------ ✳ ------------------------------

A familiar hush fell over the room just as Tom Joules finished off the last of his orange juice and soda and delicately wiped each side of his mouth in turn with a serviette. For regulars to the meal, this had become the equivalent to a tell in poker: an unconscious habit he'd picked up that signalled he was preparing to get on to his feet.

The atmosphere in which Tom's speech was heard had changed since he'd first introduced it all those years ago. In the early days, it had been about as welcome as a heckler at a funeral, but in more recent times his announcements were heard in an atmosphere of almost reverential silence. As a group they'd been through a lot, and Tom's speeches had, quite unexpectedly, gained the power to both inform and, at times, shock; and this particular year's was no different. Tom rose to his feet.

'Gentlemen,' he began, pausing to allow those still holding a glass to put it down and look his way. Over the years, he really had become something of a master at waiting for the silence to fall, like the curtain at the end of a powerful play.

While the purpose of his speech had remained constant over the years, communication methods had changed. While he didn't quite stretch to a PowerPoint presentation, there was no longer a need to pass round a report on the progress of the Bond, for example, when all the details were uploaded to a password-protected website. While Tom always paused to ask if there were any questions, this usually had the same reaction as a vicar asking if anyone knew of any lawful impediment as to why two people should not be wed. In many ways, the actual numbers behind the Bond had become irrelevant; its very existence was what mattered. In this respect, Sam's assessment of what brought the members of the society together each year was correct: it went beyond money, and was more to do with creating some kind of collective strength or spirit.

'Thank you. Gentlemen, I have just a few things to say this year. Firstly, we offer our congratulations to Tom Janner on his recent marriage to Chang Su.'

'Bloody hell, is he trying to marry the entire Chinese netball team? That's his third, isn't it?' Nigel Bennett asked in a hushed whisper from under his moustache, halfway down the table. Tom looked up and responded with the information that the no doubt lovely Chang Su was in fact originally from Thailand, although he had to concede that it was his third new wife in recent years, all of them from the same part of the world.

'World wide web, more like, randy sod,' Reggie Richardson suggested.

Tom let this comment go, largely because he suspected it was true: on both counts.

'Finally, our prayers also go out to Geoff Harkness, in his brave battle with illness, which I'm sure most of you are aware of.'

Ray Meadows turned to his companion to his right. 'Christ, what's all that about? I had no idea.'

'Testicular cancer. There's going to be a whip-round later on,' came the half-whispered reply.

'Well, I'm happy to contribute,' Ray offered in full voice, 'but he can't have me knackers.'

In the laughter that followed, Tom omitted to mention the sad loss of Les Andrew and Philip Christopher before he sat down.

--------------------------------- ✳ ---------------------------------

Ben Bradshaw was aware of the deaths of Andrew and Christopher, and he'd duly scored through their names in his file with his black marker pen, before closing the folder and putting it back in its usual place under the floorboards. He'd resisted the option to computerize his file; he liked extracting it, updating it and putting it back every year, even though doubts as to its effectiveness had been creeping in more and more lately. Maybe it was time to take a different approach?

No outside observer could doubt that Ben Bradshaw was a success. Doze had gone from strength to strength and now had stores nationwide. He'd continued to base his marketing on his own personality, or, rather, one he adopted for the purpose, and even though he'd come to hate doing the TV adverts, there was no doubting their effectiveness.

To that same outside observer he had money, a degree of fame and a successful marriage. Ah, if only people knew the truth! Money and fame, yes; but as for the marriage bit, well, they had what could best be described as an accommodation. Furthermore, like the Seventy-Seven file, running the business had become a bit of a chore. The days of bombing around the country drumming up custom and suppliers or checking out potential new sites were long gone. These days, he seemed to spend most of his time putting out fires caused by other idiots. Why was it so difficult recruiting decent managers these days? Too many of the ones running his business could barely do up their own shoelaces without falling over.

Ben was tired. Maybe he should just accept that he was the one who always had to make things happen. Others never came to him with opportunities; he had to make them. Take the decision to replace Andy Thompson as chair of the 77B committee with that nonentity, the grinning weeble Paul Briton. Paul Briton? Give me a break. Compared to Ben, what did he know about being a successful businessman?

Once again, he'd been passed over. It didn't really matter in the great scheme of things – except it did, it mattered a lot.

Maybe it was time to take things to a new level, ramps things up a bit?

Going Out With a Bang

2008

Fifty was the new forty, or so the papers kept saying; but they were wrong. Reaching, and passing, forty had gone by in a blur of activity of either building on the platform they'd created so far, or defending the position they'd built against the generation coming up behind them. Approaching, or reaching, fifty, on the other hand, was more a time for reflection. The time for striving had passed, replaced by a period of struggle or survival, or even a second spring. If any of them was ever going to metaphorically play for England, to reach the top of the game they might be in, they'd have known by now. It was time for reassessment.

For some, this might mean committing to at least another ten years' solid graft at the coalface, a decision with little real choice for those who still found themselves with young families. For others, whose children had become more independent or were already at university (although when did university became compulsory rather than an option, stretching the time when kids were a financial burden rather than lessening it?) there was more slack, more opportunity to think about other ways to fill their final few productive years. The distant horizon of no kids, no mortgage, a place that had assumed an almost mythical existence over the years, was finally homing into view.

Equally, relationships were being rebrokered, both with ageing parents, who were becoming more like children in their levels of dependency, and with wives and partners. Suddenly, it seemed less important to shave every day, to wear a suit, a tie, or even to go into an office at all. Cumbersome suitcase-sized briefcases had been exchanged for neat backpacks. New ways were being found to remain relevant. For some, this impulse translated into a big gesture (climbing Mount Kilimanjaro was a favourite; for charity, of course), for others it was more prosaic, typically buying a sports car or a Harley.

They weren't approaching the end, just the beginning of the start of the end. As they did so, some were in better shape than others, some had their heads up and were waving to the crowds; others were exhausted, looking for help, like that marathon runner who needed help across the line in those black and white photos from an Olympics years ago. Some actually enjoyed their work and found it difficult to contemplate a life without it, while others were counting the days.

There was a growing sense that the world was changing faster than their capacity to keep up with it. As a generation, they'd had to learn how to harness the power of computers and then the internet, and generally speaking they'd done pretty well, but who knew what was next, and whether they had both the energy and the wherewithal to cope with it?

It was a feeling they recognized: a combination of fear and anticipation last felt in those lazy days by the school swimming pool all of thirty-plus years ago. Some would react well, others would simply cope, and maybe a minority would fail completely. The next few years were going to be crucial in determining whether they finished with a whimper, or a bang.

------------------------------ ❋ ------------------------------

He didn't know how he'd managed it, but he had. For once, Ray Meadows had body-swerved a major financial crisis. It was just the sort of classic bugger's muddle that would once have blindsided him, but by a stroke of luck it had happened at a time when his assets were fairly liquid, so he got away pretty much unscathed from the so-called credit crunch, with all its sub-prime mortgages and hocus-pocus.

Any other kind of body-swerving had been consigned to his dreams long ago. His knees were completely shot and he even used a walking stick to get around, although he tried to avoid using it in front of clients. These days, these were mainly people he'd been advising for years. He'd started to run the business down, and once the lease was up on the office he planned to let that go and work from home, but that was a little way off yet. He was basically a glorified independent adviser these days, with an office, a secretary and a young wannabee to do all the grunt work and exams. In many ways, it felt like he'd gone full circle, back to the days when it had just been him and Pam. His current secretary was even called Pam, although she was Polish and had told him he could call her that, her true name being much more of a tongue-twister. Polish Pam, he called her to himself, and yes, she had blonde hair, although Ray was pretty sure hers was out of a bottle.

What was more, for the first time since those Pam days, he was on an even keel financially. He'd cleared his debts and 'tidied up' the loan book. It felt good not to have all that hanging over him. It had taken a lot of graft – but like his old man, he'd never been afraid of that – as well as soaking up all his spare cash.

Was he a success? Probably not in the conventional sense – not like his fellow Seventy-Seveners, with their four-by-fours, widescreen TVs, and, indeed, TV adverts – but he had survived: both the vicissitudes of the economic weather and, of course, in a literal sense, in that he was still above ground and walking – well, limping anyway. Ray could contemplate the prospect of retirement calmly: the long-term pension plan was coming along nicely.

He loved it when a plan came together.

*

Nigel Bennett collected luggage labels. It was a hobby: not one he was particularly proud of, but a hobby nevertheless. Besides, he was sure he wasn't the only person in the world who collected them: not because he'd ever met anyone who shared his little diversion, but because in his job he'd seen the whole spectrum of human life, and this had told him that on any scale of weirdness, collecting luggage labels counted as almost normal.

Of course, being an airline pilot made it a lot easier to indulge his hobby. He'd gone into training straight from university, but flying had always been his passion, ever since he'd been one of the handful in the Air Training Corps at school. Slipping off the bounds of gravity was the only time he felt master of his own destiny, his true self.

But back to those luggage labels. In a world of acronyms, the simple three-letter designation given to international airports always seemed to Nigel to be a thing of beauty, condensing an extremely complex system into something very simple. Everyone was familiar with the old favourites: LHR for Heathrow and JFK for New York Kennedy; but others, such as KRP for Karup in Denmark, STI for Santiago in the Dominican Republic, SIN for Singapore, of course, and then his all-time favourite, COK for Cochin in India, had always amused the schoolboy still lying dormant within him. Soon, though, he was about to collect his own: RTD for Retired.

At least, that was the plan. After over thirty years' service with various premium flag carriers, he'd waited patiently for the inevitable next round of redundancies and a tap on the shoulder from the higher-ups suggesting that maybe he'd like to make way for the next generation. He knew this wouldn't be so much a suggestion as an instruction, and if Nigel's job had prepared him for anything, it was for obeying instructions. They'd made the usual offer of some part-time work with trainees on the simulators, but no matter how good the computers got they were still just that: simulators – a bit like going to bed with a whore. He couldn't bring himself to do it.

The prospect of being anchored to the ground had been suffocating, so it came with considerable relief when he was approached by one of the budget airlines offering short-haul work. It wasn't the same clientele, of course, and destinations such as PFO for Paphos in Cyprus didn't carry the same cachet; although it did sometimes act as useful shorthand among the crew when it came to awkward passengers, with the 'P' standing for 'Please' and the 'O' for 'Off'.

He'd surprised himself, finding it really rather jolly to be taking people to where the beer was cheap, the women were loose or the sun was hot, or usually all three. Okay, air travel had become less of an experience and more of an opportunity to sell to people while sandwiches were eaten, duty-free acquired and safety demonstrations ignored. He made it a point to inject some humour into his usual half-time talk, enjoying it when he made his audience laugh. Sure, it was different, but it was certainly better than the alternative.

----------------------------- ✱ -----------------------------

Andy Thompson had been having the time of his life. He'd driven the Pacific Coast Highway and Route 66, he'd swum with dolphins in the Caribbean and seen their pink river relatives in the Amazon. He'd climbed to the base camp of Mount Everest, toured the Prado in Madrid and the Hermitage in St Petersburg, and he'd see the oceans meet off the Cape of Good Hope.

He'd driven around the Nürburgring, snorkelled off the Great Barrier Reef, flown a balloon over the pyramids, trekked the Great Wall and bungee-jumped off Sydney Harbour Bridge. He'd eaten fried locusts in Cambodia, crows' feet in China, a Madras curry in Madras and tapas in Barcelona.

He hadn't started with a list, but instead had created one as he went along. He'd eschewed photographs, living in the moment rather than through a viewfinder. For the first few weeks, he wondered if he should feel guilty about his family, and, well, just generally. The feeling had soon faded. He'd left his family extremely well-provisioned and, to be honest, his marriage had become a bit of a sham. As for any wider guilt, the way Andy saw it he was one of the 0.001 per cent of the world's population in a position to do what he was doing, and it would have been a crime not to take advantage of his opportunities. It was almost as if it was his duty to enjoy himself.

He was currently back in Africa, a continent he'd fallen in love with, but despite having been six or seven times, he'd never quite got around to doing the whole tented safari experience, so he went to Kenya. Although he kept to his no-camera rule, he was tempted by some amazing binoculars he'd spotted in the duty-free. They were designed for birdwatchers and unlike the sort he was used to, with two eyepieces and a pair of lenses you wrapped your hands round. This piece of precision engineering, known as a scope, sat on a tripod and had a single eyepiece which you bent over to look through. He'd gone for a 100mm lens which offered ninety times magnification without any loss of sharpness or colour definition, and it was an all-round awesome piece of kit.

Like all good safari rangers, the guide leading Andy and his three fellow travellers were focused on leading his charges to the Big Five: the African elephant, the Cape buffalo, the African lion, the black rhinoceros and, Andy's particular target, the African leopard. Over the previous three days, they'd managed to see the lion and elephant – in fact more elephants than you could shake a stick at; not that stick-shaking was advised. A hardened traveller, Andy suspected that the tour guides tracked the animals on a GPS, and when he was promised the buffalo and rhino towards the end of the trip, he believed them. That day, though, they were looking for leopard.

Andy's travelling companions knew leopards were his thing, so they'd been happy to give him the best position in the Landcruiser for the day. Their guide, Ayodele, a light-skinned and extremely lithe young man in his mid thirties, who carried a rifle as if born with it, had warned them that the leopard had been shy in recent weeks. Andy wasn't sure if this was expectation management or tension-building so that if they did see the hoped-for animal their joy would be reflected in the size of their eventual tip.

Eventually, Ayodele suggested they go off-track, and the group were advised to keep their eyes peeled on low branches in the trees for sleeping or resting cats. It was at this point that Andy appreciated the frustrating limitations of his scope, which really needed to be static to be effective, and he envied his companions with their penis extension-long camera lenses. Even though they assured him they'd tell him as soon as they spotted a leopard, it wouldn't be quite the same as spotting one himself.

They stopped for water and a snack in a spot popular with other tour groups, although everyone kept a respectful distance from each other, pretending the others weren't there. The hottest part of the day had passed, but everyone was still perspiring liberally, and their backsides were numb from sitting down all day on seats whose suspension had surrendered to all Kenya could throw at them some years before. Conversation was slight – safari etiquette seemed to demand silence – but they were all tired to the point of being shattered, anyway.

It was as he was munching his way through a particularly dry energy bar and rubbing the seat of his trousers at the same time, that Andy thought he detected movement in a distant tree. By keeping still and opening his eyes wide, he confirmed to himself that there was definitely something out there. Excusing himself on the pretext of a call of nature (no one seemed to question why this required a tripod), Andy trod delicately through the undergrowth to get closer.

After walking about seventy yards, he stopped and set up his scope. Scanning the trees was frustrating at first, as one looked much like the next, and naturally the leopard's camouflage was designed to blend in with the surroundings. Then he saw it. Andy adjusted the scope gently, bringing it into focus. Leaning in, he moved his eye over the sight, and then, all of a sudden, he made out the distinctive spotted coat, breathing gently in and out, as if in a deep sleep. The cat's head was over one of its forearms and it seemed absolutely content. If Andy needed any further justification for his extended sabbatical (which he didn't), then this sublime moment would have been it.

He stood, transfixed over the scope, just watching the animal sleep, and for a couple of minutes it was as if they were the only two living things in the bush. They weren't, of course, and his concentration was broken by the sound of a horn, possibly from the Landcruiser, but he couldn't be certain. Human voices followed, slightly raised in alarm, but the leopard was too special to lift his eye from.

Bent over the scope, the seat of his grey zip-off trousers could conceivably have constituted a threat if you had got out of your mud pool the wrong side that morning. Maybe it was just bored or offended by this strange five-legged creature in its territory. Whatever its motive, one creature in the vicinity proved to be surprisingly nippy once it got going. Andy could hear the Landcruiser's horns, now more of a plaintive orchestra than a single note, but he didn't feel the need to respond to them, and it's possible that they drowned out some of the more immediate sounds he should have been playing attention to.

Back at the temporary camp, Andy's companions had been joined by two other Landcruisers and everyone in them had some form of optical instrument trained on Andy's bent backside as it was butted from behind by a large and very determined-looking hippopotamus who, determined to finish the job, promptly turned around and trampled on Andy's rag-like body. Those who were recording the scene on movie cameras picked up the ear-deafening scream Andy let out before collapsing to the ground, but the incident happened too quickly to record the small speck of blood on the hippo's own backside, where a dart had upset its afternoon peace. The leopard, meanwhile, simply opened its eyes, leapt down from its branch and ambled away. The resulting footage found its way on to YouTube, and, as such, was the first of the deaths among Red Coat's Class of '77 to be recorded for posterity.

When they'd got over their initial shock, a brief conference among Ayodele and his colleagues, conducted in Swahili over crackling walkie-talkies, quickly got their collective story straight for the inevitable inquest that would follow. It was while this was going on that a tourist on one of the other Landcruisers continued to keep their eyes stuck to their more traditional binoculars, tracking the progress of the killer now sauntering back into the bush.

'Hip, hip, hooray,' they mumbled to themselves as the bored hippo slunk into the anonymous jungle.

--------------------------------- ✻ ---------------------------------

The DHM finally retired from teaching in 2008. He'd seen off two headmasters after Harold Mitchell, and the third had used all his diplomacy to get him to go, with Clive enjoying playing the reluctant bride, or was it divorcee? After all, what did retirement hold for him? The school had been his life since the army, and while there'd once been a woman he thought he could settle down with, in the end she opted for a younger model. Couldn't blame her, really: who'd want a damaged git like him? It wasn't the rejection that hurt; more the fact that she'd carried on with the new chap right under his nose.

He was realistic: all the constant walking around between classes, and all the damned steps in the ancient science block, had done for his knees. On top of that (although he'd never mentioned it to anyone), there had been moments when he'd struggled to catch his breath. How he'd never managed to make the case for knocking the whole block down and building a new one was a niggling regret, but as the school had grown, or rather developed (the number of boys stayed pretty much the same after it went private), there were other priorities.

A new sixth form centre attached to the new sports hall, for one; a new IT and modern languages block; and then, of course, the Centre for the Performing Arts (or performing monkeys as he preferred to call them), all three winners of regional architecture prizes. In the meantime, he had to continue ensuring the school continued to deliver excellent science results from facilities not that different from when he'd arrived. On reflection, maybe it was just as well he'd never won the argument for a new block, as the Head used the new sixth form centre as a pretext for removing that part of his remit. If he'd lost the head of sciences post as well, he wouldn't have had much of a job left.

Still, Clive preferred to dwell on the positives. His results had remained consistently good, and probably helped explain his longevity. Call him old- school if you like, but the traditional methods delivered results when it came to the sciences. Get the basics right and you can't go far wrong. Then there were his CCF responsibilities, which he also chalked up as a success. Again, traditional values of discipline and respect never went out of fashion when it came to the army. Sure, there was the occasional need to play lip service to the latest fad, but Clive Porter knew how to play the long game, and that in the long run, nothing really changes.

His instinct was against admitting girls to the sixth form, but he'd been politically astute enough to recognize that it was the new headmaster's pet project, with the extra income from an enlarged sixth form helping to finance the sports centre – which in itself helped fuel a gradual inflation in fees, creating a virtuous cycle. Clive's support provided a stamp of approval from the old guard, creating a debt that probably added the thick end of ten years to his career. Some of the girls even turned out to be quite good at science, which was a bonus.

Eventually, Clive had to accept the inevitable and succumb to the cringe-making speeches that, while reflecting the worth of his contribution to the school over the years, made his retirement party something of an ordeal. He'd had a good innings; time to slink back to the pavilion, or in his case, the alms house he'd moved into a few years ago. This was something the school had secured in a none-too-subtle attempt to dislodge both him and the chaplain (Clive was probably the only one to call him by his proper title), another old retainer, who'd been at the Red Coat since the late seventies. The school's management team had been 50 per cent successful, with the chaplain grabbing the first opportunity to retire, along with a small extra sinecure to act as what was called Clive's carer. Who ended up caring for who had become a moot point, as the chaplain rapidly regressed into banality, using the TV as some kind of life-support mechanism – although in his case such sustenance took the form of celebrity-driven nonsense TV and, of all things, football. Football! Clive shuddered.

The chaplain's screen-based diet did nothing for his waistline, making him resemble a black town crier, only without the bell. All in all, watching the chaplain regress served as a warning sign to Clive of the perils of leaving the activity and stimulation offered by employment. Other than things he'd seen on TV, his living companion seemed to have only one other topic of conversation: the past – constant reminiscing about past years, providing a constant background noise for their domestic life. To Clive, they were just boys. He found it difficult to differentiate between them. When one greeted him in the street, as inevitably happened, he employed his universal coping strategy of asking general questions, such as how the job was going or whether they'd managed to watch the rugger.

Over the decades there'd been very few years whose cohort stood out as a group, especially as the total number of those years accumulated. As the human body constantly renews itself with the division of the cells, so the school was a completely different organism now, with its buildings, personnel, and even the names of the houses all changed. Clive had always subscribed to the '3-2-1-Gone' way of thinking, 321 days being roughly the length of a school year, after which it was best consigned to history.

There was the exception, of course. The Class of '77. But only he, the chaplain and Mr Joules of maths remained who could claim to have had direct experience of those turbulent times. They'd proved to be a watershed. The combination of some of the personalities involved, like Jake Peterson (a promising, if confused, boy; long dead now, of course) with that fool Harold Mitchell, had been toxic. The irony was that by spurring the governors into action, the silly games of Peterson and his ilk had, if anything, speeded up the implementation of Mitchell's plans, while Mitchell himself disappeared into a well-deserved obscurity.

The Class of '77 aside, given Clive's collective amnesia around those who had come and gone over the years, it was perhaps quietly amusing that one of the sweeteners he'd been offered to step down was to assume the mantle of a new post of alumni co-ordinator, or, as his official title had it, Director of Red Coat Forever. What particularly appealed to Clive about the post was the cast-iron excuse it gave him to call in on the old place whenever he wanted, and in so doing get out of the house and away from the chaplain's incessant TV.

------------------------------ ✻ ------------------------------

Most of the upper playground where they usually parked had been given over to yet more building during the summer, and the asphalt they used to touch with their noses during press-ups was now history. Reggie wondered where they paraded now – if indeed they paraded at all, with parents probably arguing that too much marching up and down was bad for little Johnny's feet.

Instead, Reggie left the Prius charging at the local budget hotel where he'd booked himself a room. He wasn't worried about bumping into Ray any more; he was pretty sure he'd seen him paying off a taxi outside the pub the previous year. Poor old sod looked a right mess these days: a prematurely old man with his bent back and dodgy knee, his trademark carrot-coloured fringe replaced with thin gossamer wisps. Reggie remembered how initially he'd thought the shadowy figure was a down-and-out begging from the taxi driver before he'd seen money change hands the other way. Oh, how the once-mighty were fallen.

Still, it wouldn't be the Seventy-Seven bash without Ray, and sure enough he was at the bar getting a round in. On spotting Reggie he lifted a finger in recognition before shouting 'One more!' to the young barman coping with his order. The scene offered a taste of familiarity for Reggie, tainted perhaps by a sense of time slipping away. Were they middle-aged now, or even late middle-aged? Did it matter? The distinction was probably a bit like the difference between being middle class or upper middle class, although he suspected that one was less malleable.

The usual crowd was there, plus one or two irregulars: a decent turnout, close to, but not quite, twenty. If the society had been run as a loyalty scheme, it would probably have gold membership for those who turned up to every meal barring bad weather or family bereavement; silver for those who made it every second or third meal; and bronze for those who turned up occasionally. There'd be a fourth category, too: yellow, for those whose simple cowardice prevented their attendance, but who were prepared to keep paying their dues out of some kind of ghoulish interest in the Bond. That was the thing about the Seventy-Seven Society: whatever your category of membership, the rules were the same for everyone. If you paid your dues you were in: you got your invitation and involvement in the Bond.

Simon Grant would probably have been a silver member; at least, until 2005 when he suddenly stopped showing up. Such were the unwritten rules of the society that no one chased him up to see if anything had happened, and before long he became a memory, a face on a fading photograph; albeit a face about to change.

Another unwritten, but no less observed, rule was that the meal was for members only, which was a roundabout way of saying no wives, girlfriends, sisters, mothers or, heaven forfend, mothers-in-law were allowed. If there was a role for wives or girlfriends at all it was to act as a totally non-judgemental taxi service, although in reality very few members still lived in the area. Most either booked a local hotel or B&B, or wandered back through the town to stay at their parents, if they were still alive.

It might, just might, have been conceivable, therefore, for a woman to join the gathering at the pub for a quick orange juice or Coke if she knew some of the other members; although the number of times Tom Joules could recall this happening he could probably have counted on the skeletal fingers of one hand. Given this, he wasn't totally bemused to see someone in a dress sitting in the Red Lion before the 2008 meal, and he even sensed a glint of recognition reciprocated across the room as he waved a greeting: a gesture feeble enough to be dismissed as a nervous tick, but which nevertheless ended up precipitating an unintended round-up of empty pint glasses that needed refilling.

After Tom had given his usual hurry-up ten minutes before they were due at the restaurant, he noticed the woman, who until then had been chatting away with a group near the door, reach for her coat, so naturally he assumed she was on her way home, or to the gathering of wives he knew sometimes took place. It came as a surprise therefore when she turned up at the restaurant, and even more of a surprise when she chose to sit down next to him at the top of the long table they'd been allocated in the restaurant's private dining area.

Given some of the tricks he'd had to put up with in previous years, Tom's first reaction was that he was probably on the end of an elaborate practical joke – a strippergram, or something childish like that – so he resisted the temptation to pass comment or engage the woman in conversation. After five awkward minutes, however, he was given no choice when she swivelled in her chair, looked him in the eye and said,

'You don't remember me, do you? Don't worry, it's been a while.'

Tom barely had time to shake his head when she extended her hand and announced, 'Susan Grant. You may remember me as Simon.'

Given this surreal start to the evening, it shouldn't have come as much of a surprise that the conversation through the rest of it should oscillate between mundane bemoaning of the passage of time, and details of Simon/Susan's 'journey', which she seemed determined to share. Tom tried to appear interested out of politeness, but the conversation to his right, in which Toby Connor was explaining how his youngest boy had been put on a warning for supposed bullying, was of more interest; although he was relieved to find the boy wasn't at the Red Coat.

'Upstanding member, according to his head of year,' Toby explained, getting redder in the face the longer he spent on his story, his eyebrows knitting closer together to form a long monobrow. 'The kid was being taunted by some other boys two years older than him, so he let the tyres down on their bikes. Christ, in our day we'd have got a gang together and sorted them out. For that he's on notice; one more incident and he's out, expelled, suspended, whatever they call it these days.' To Tom's left, Simon/Susan was explaining the counselling she'd had to go through, to anyone who'd listen.

'Sounds like they dropped a bollock there,' Toby's companion had agreed. 'Amazing, when you think of what we used to get up to.'

'Gender reassignment,' Simon/Susan expounded. 'Then, of course, there's the problem of which loo to go into.'

'Sneaky Shitter,' Toby's companion piped up.

'All sorts of tests before the operation, at one stage I had to …'

'Show some spunk!' Toby responded, 'That's what I tell the boy. The younger generation these days seem to lack imagination. Where's the challenge, the rebellion, the pushing of the boundaries?'

'No balls,' his companion agreed.

'Absolutely!' Toby exclaimed. 'Not cocky enough.'

It was just before these final exchanges that the rest of the room fell silent, with the result that all eyes suddenly reverted to Simon/

Susan who, with an indication that he/she was more of a Susan than a Simon, responded in a deep flush of red that spread right across her silicon-enhanced décolletage.

If the sense of awkwardness that infused the room at this point was palpable, it was nothing compared to the unease felt by Paul Briton. The 77B group in charge of the Bond had fallen into the habit of letting the funds carry on as before after Andy Thompson left, on the basis of 'why spoil a winning formula?' The mid-year meetings seemed to have stopped as there was nothing much to discuss that couldn't be done by email. A bad case of flu just before Christmas had knocked him out, and seeing that things were flat at the office he'd decided to take an extended break to recover and catch up on all the little jobs he'd never got around to doing.

One of those had been to check up on the Bond. The one thing he'd learned was that Andy hadn't done simple. The money was tucked away in all sorts of pots with varying degrees of risk. Add them together and you got the whole story, and that story was amazing. They were sitting on a goldmine (indeed, they had shares in one) and if he, as one of the Big Tits, hadn't appreciated it, you could be sure no one else had.

It was good news, of course, but also potentially a problem. In his legal practice Paul often came across cases that required resolving the fallout from dividing up very large estates; and if these cases had taught him anything, it was that when money was involved it was easy to poison the well of goodwill. The sorts of sums they were now talking about had the potential to blow everything apart. Tact and diplomacy would be needed. It was self-defeating if the very thing they'd established to keep hold of the flame of their year became the instrument of their eventual destruction. As a result, for now at least, he decided to keep quiet.

2010–12

The Seventy-Seven Widows group still met, and if it had lost much of its original purpose (it didn't even meet on the same evening as the supper these days, the men tending to make other arrangements), it had found another. Or rather, a number of other purposes according to who you spoke to. For some it was a good networking opportunity, while for others it was a purely social gathering: an opportunity to catch up, share family photos on their phones and swap inside information on where to eat, buy clothes or have your hair done. For others it provided a forum for letting off steam, and much to the chagrin of the rest, who were mostly content with their lot, it was this group who tended to occupy most of the airtime.

Whatever their motives, they still came, often in numbers greater than the Seventy-Seven Society dinners. Their core members had remained the same over the years: Susie Bradshaw, who still organized things, Ellie Richardson and Shirley Tweedie, still looking like two peas in a pod, and Fiona Henderson. Mary Lu was also a fairly regular attender, although she didn't turn up every year: a fact that few mourned, given her tendency towards high-level neuroticism.

Like their husbands, the wives had weathered the years with varying degrees of success, not simply in terms of outward appearance, but spiritually and mentally. Annoyingly to some, Fiona Henderson continued to wear life well, apparently with minimal effort. Despite the fact that she was probably the only woman of her own age Susie knew who could look good in Doc Martens, deep down she rather envied Fiona. She'd kept life simple, running a small garden design business from home, while her husband had built up quite the little empire of student lets, including a small block of flats he'd created by converting one of the old bank branches on the edge of town. He'd even given it a grand name: the Jake Peterson Building.

Others, including Shirley Tweedie and Ellie Richardson, had fought the good fight in leotards and jumpsuits, attending a succession of jump, Jazzercise and jive classes over the years, according to whatever was most on-trend. Their efforts had had a positive effect, but never quite delivered the return they quite reasonably expected from the amount of effort involved. About the only thing the women had in common was that they all took dietary supplements of one form or another.

Others had decided that *au naturel* was the way to go, with assorted results. For example, the neck and upper chest of Paul Briton's new other half Jennie was layered with wrinkles only really desirable if covering the top of a bowl of custard; the overall effect of which was not helped by a songbird's flecking of deep brown moles, visible despite a determined Mediterranean-sourced tan. Jennie's very presence as a second wife at the gatherings was symptomatic of how the Widows had changed over the years. This was a phenomenon those who were now celebrating over thirty years of marriage (a club within a club, which in turn had its own further sub-élite of those who'd been at the swimming pool all those aeons ago). They were individually described disparagingly as bints; or bytes, if they'd been found via the internet.

These had to be vetted first, though, a few of them over the years having been, to Susie's mind, rather 'obvious'. She rarely ruled anyone out of the group, however, regarding fresh members who might even add some extra spice to the group as additional raw material for any mischief-making she might want to initiate. She also made a point of continuing to invite the growing number of genuine widows among the group. Susan Grant, however, was not invited. There had been some discussion around eligibility, but Susie had stopped that in its tracks. There were limits; and besides, she might be in a position to challenge some of the alternative truths Susie had unleashed over the years.

A constant of all the Widows' sessions was the state of their marriages, with some of the wives remarkably frank in their assessments. While most of the women would have described themselves as still in love with their husbands, theirs were not the voices that were heard. That year, the topic was cut short when Ellie Richardson admitted that she and Reggie had taken to only making love with the light out, not least given Reggie's diet, since which he'd resembled a roll of corrugated cardboard when naked. This arrangement suited them both, it seemed, allowing them to each get on with their fantasies without disturbing the peace. In an effort to leaven the mood, another of the women suggested that her marriage was like a glass of champagne left out overnight: the bubbles had gone, but some sweetness remained.

'You're lucky,' Ellie had snapped back, 'mine's definitely corked. Sometimes I just wish he'd do the decent thing like Andy Thompson and piss off, leaving us with the house and a decent little annuity.' Silence fell like a sudden snow. It fell to Susie to break it.

'You haven't heard, I take it?' For once, the truth was enough; no alternative truths were necessary. Ellie rushed three fingers up to her mouth. Given the group's history, she knew in an instant what must have happened.

If asked, a proportion of those attending would have described themselves as neither happy nor unhappy. They had fulfilled the role nature had given them in producing children and it was these, along with grandchildren in a handful of cases, who tended to provide a greater focus for their life than their husbands. Others, having fledged their offspring, had found their free time taken up dealing with ageing parents. Most had worked, and many had enjoyed satisfying careers, counting their blessings that they had been able to catch the wave that made it acceptable for women to aspire to being more than a secretary or, if they were bright, a teacher.

Some, having announced that they were sure their husbands talked about them at their dinners (they rarely did), were happy to discuss their sex lives; although more recently, discussion was more likely to steer towards the trials of the menopause, a topic which tended to act as a cue for one of the original widows, Shirley Tweedie (who had never remarried), to unfurl a hand fan from her handbag and wave it extravagantly in front of her face, smiling and looking up to the sky in a martyred way as she did so.

That year, mindfulness was a popular topic, with its adherents evangelical about its power. 'You must try these books,' Mary Lu confided to Susie as they queued at the buffet, as if she had discovered the elixir of life. Susie responded with a benign smile. Her coping strategy for life was to keep busy, to have a plan and to stick to it – she was too busy for colouring books. How old was she, five?

Mary let the implicit rebuff go. 'Of course, you're so lucky,' she continued, her tone one of genuine awe and congratulation, with perhaps just a pinch of bitterness, 'you have such a strong marriage. Ben has been so supportive to you in your career.'

Susie smiled a second beatific smile, accepting the compliment without an ounce of irony. 'Well, thank you, nice of you to say so,' she responded in a heartbeat. If only she knew, she thought, if only they all knew; but, of course, that would have spoiled the fun.

Susie's motives for keeping the Widows going were the same as when she'd set the group up – she was never afraid of the long game. It was true Ben had become disconcertedly 'centred', making it increasingly difficult to touch those nerves that always used to be so raw, to keep him in his box. He seemed to have become inured to her little provocations. Perhaps she needed to raise her game, ramp things up a bit, she pondered, as she reached purposefully for a generous slice of the large pork pie in the middle of the spread. That was her idea of being centred.

------------------------------ ✳ ------------------------------

There had been approaches for the business before, but Ben was never interested. The thought of letting go of Doze was about as conceivable as functioning without sleep itself. Ben knew how these things worked. First, potential suitors smothered you in flattery, then they tempted you with a mountain of money and finally, ever so subtly, and maybe after giving you as much as a year after you'd agreed terms, they applied their size elevens to your backside.

Ben had always hoped that one of his boys might be interested in taking over the business, but as time went on he'd come to realize that wasn't very likely. The eldest, Francis, had about as much spark as a clapped-out disposable cigarette lighter, while the only affinity the younger one, Harry, seemed to have with beds was lying on one playing with his Hexbox, or whatever he called it. Ben couldn't understand how someone could plug themselves into a system that sucked all the vitality out of them; why would anyone choose to do that to themselves?

Francis, at least, had shown willing, working a couple of summers on the shop floor when he was a student, but he'd been a nervous horse, frightening people both with his indecisiveness and with the implicit power his surname bestowed on him. Ben had transferred him to the office, but he'd spent most of his time shut away in the dark of the photocopy room. True, he'd been happy there, tuning in to the steady rhythm of the moving trays and the sliding platen, as if it was a portal for communicating with alien intelligence, but he seemed to be the only one who didn't see it as a bit weird.

Francis's real passion, it turned out, was hedges – cutting them, sweeping up the clippings, having bonfires – so Ben set him up with an ex-employee who ran a small landscape gardening business. Francis did the physical stuff with a couple of underlings, while the ex-employee did the money side and got the work. He'd even provided the company with a name: Hedge Fun. He was quite proud of that.

Over fifty now, Ben was successful, recognized on the street, and rather rich. The problems were that his success seemed to be taken for granted by everyone, almost a kind of joke, as if he'd been lucky or something. He couldn't even go to a park to inspect some of Francis's topiary without some wit yelling, 'Looking forward to the rest of your life, Ben?' Why didn't they ever understand that the accent had to be on 'rest'? While he might be rich on paper, though, it was just that: theoretical, tied up in the business. One good thing was that he didn't really regard his relationship with Susie as one of his problems any more: they'd become what they'd become, he'd learned to deal with it.

He never actually articulated any of these thoughts to himself, they were always just bubbling away beneath the surface, unable to find space in Ben's constantly busy head to be processed. Talking it over with Susie wasn't an option either: if she wasn't away on one of her hotel-inspecting jaunts, she was out with friends; and anyway, theirs wasn't a sharing marriage. In the end, it took a force from outside to get the wheels inside his head moving.

The first approach came from a public relations firm. Their client was looking to attach their name to a national scheme to encourage young kids to learn to swim, and had made the connection between Ben's more recent success and his distant past. They wanted to use him as a role model, they said, an example of how hard work succeeds whatever field you apply it to. He was an inspiration, they added, a one-off. No one had ever talked about him like that before.

Some months later, he was introduced to the marketing director of the PR firm's client, a high-street department store, at the Chelsea Flower Show, where they'd shared a highly convivial picnic lunch. As the day went on, in between examining hydrangeas, water features and hedge-cutting equipment suppliers, he'd been introduced to various other high-ups in the business. Conversation was light, but Ben enjoyed himself and was now ready to agree to the invitation to meet their chairman, an ex-politician, now a peer, who, it so happened, Ben had always admired from afar. At some point it was suggested that one of his skills was whispering into the right ears when the time came, and for some reason Ben had left with a feeling that the subject of knighthoods had been raised, without ever being openly mentioned.

After a polite interval, the invitation to meet Lord Access, as it seemed he was affectionately known, duly arrived; although in order to fit into his busy schedule the venue had to be the dining room of the House of Lords – if that was all right? Ben replied that it was, and a courier was sent to deliver a pass and a formal invitation, as both were required to get past security.

This lunch was another convivial affair. Again, no business had been discussed, conversation being light but somehow subtly probing, as if it would have breached parliamentary etiquette to get into detail. Instead, they confined themselves to broader topics of conversation, and Ben gained the impression that the friendly peer was genuinely interested in his thoughts on areas ranging from family to the forthcoming London Olympics. By the end of the meal Ben felt thoroughly at home, as if he'd been introduced to a world where he belonged and was comfortable. To top things off, as they'd been walking to the car waiting for him, the gracious lord suggested Francis might want to come over and cast a look at his hedges some time, and Ben was pretty certain he wasn't talking about a short run of privet.

The third meeting was the first at the company's head office, an old Georgian mansion in the heart of Oxfordshire. Once owned by Jesuits, the mansion was made of honey-coloured sandstone with an ancient clematis occupying most of its left-hand side, a series of colour-coordinated rose beds in the front and an immaculate croquet lawn at the back. The house was approached by a sweeping gravel drive where a flunky opened the door to Ben's Range Rover and took the keys for parking. He was then ushered past a reception area, where he wasn't asked to sign in, and into a long rectangular room, the walls of which were filled with glass cabinets full of crystal. Ben assumed this was a priceless collection, and he wasn't far wrong in this estimation.

Once a salon, the room now operated as a boardroom, its centre taken up with a large oval table, complete with only three settings comprised of ink blotters, a pad and a pen, as if they were going to eat their words. Ben wondered whether to use this joke when the others joined him, but discretion got the better of him. That and nerves. He was left to wallow in his surroundings for about ten minutes before a concealed door opened in the wainscoting at the far end and two men entered, each beaming thirty-teeth smiles. One was the company's chief executive; the other the finance director, both of whom Ben had been introduced to at Chelsea, although they'd each been holding a glass of champagne and a bowl of strawberries at the time, so no handshakes had been exchanged.

With this anomaly remedied, they immediately began talking about the swimming project, much to Ben's relief. They hadn't lingered on the subject for long, however, as it seemed Ben had made something of a hit among everyone he'd met in the company. He really seemed to fit in, they told him, he felt like 'one of their sort of people', and Ben realized that being 'one of their sort of people' was something he liked being. It seemed this had got them thinking: maybe the swimming thing should only be a start, maybe there was something more they could do together.

Ben had been intrigued, and asked them what they had in mind. He hadn't expected what came next. An offer to buy him out, lock, stock and barrel; an opportunity, the finance man said, to realize the product of all his hard work. It seemed the finance director knew how he must be feeling: he himself had built a successful business of his own, proven to himself he could do it, but found himself just going through the motions. He'd even had a similar experience with his children, as it turned out.

They could see some wonderful synergies with their own business. They'd been thinking about more out-of-town sites, and in extending their furniture offering who else would it be better to get into bed with than Ben? They all had a good chuckle at this. Ben could stay as involved as he liked; but wouldn't it be wonderful to start handing some of the daily grind over to a team of experienced operators? His baby, they'd assured him, would rest soundly.

Besides, they suggested, wouldn't it also be exciting to have a new challenge to fill your time with, to get back into the swimming world? They knew for a fact that Lord Access knew people who knew the guys preparing the Olympic team, and who knew where that might lead? Again, the word 'honour' was never explicitly stated, but an awful lot of the people they mentioned seemed to have Sir at the beginning of their name, including the chief executive sitting over the table from him, and he seemed an ordinary enough bloke – much like Ben, in fact.

The deal had been done in weeks. The bankers involved all agreed they'd never seen anything like it: truly a marriage made in business heaven. True, there had been a moment when everyone involved with the deal felt like bungee jumpers standing at the top of a very high cliff, wondering whether to jump, but it came and went. Overnight,

Ben moved from being merely wealthy to being really very rich indeed. Seriously rich. EuroMillions jackpot winner-rich.

Ben feared seller's remorse, waking up the next day wondering what the hell he'd done, but instead he felt ecstatic. His shoulders visibly rose as the load was lifted off them, and at the same time his self-esteem scaled new heights. He was successful, in the news. Newspapers and TV were on to him with offers to profile him, even suggesting he might join the *Dragon's Den* panel. He became a man reborn.

What was the point of flogging your guts out, only to find yourself miserable? Look at his peer group: how many of them were truly happy? Old Brucie Lu, he thought to himself, a classic example, blinking away like a demented adolescent. There'd always been a suspicion among his peers that he had the Grim Reaper's number on speed dial and one day was going to place an order for himself – to go.

Or Toby O'Connor, to take another, who'd come to hate his job as a chiropractor so much that the only way he could get through the day was by manipulating his clients in ways that made them want to fart. His record was nine in one day apparently, four from one woman, although according to him the real fun lay in watching them trying to hold it in before he delivered the *coup de grâce*. Ben had also overheard one of his ex-school friends at the last dinner, a property lawyer, boast of his ability to discover arcane obstacles capable of delaying house moves at the last minute, revealing that it was a sort of unstated game in their profession to see who could find the most obscure last-minute problem.

Then there was marriage. As the years had gone on, Ben found it increasingly difficult to comprehend the whole idea that you stayed together for your whole life with someone you'd fancied when you were barely an adult. He'd thought about straying over the years, but he didn't need that sort of lift to his vanity; besides, he was a traditionalist, so he hadn't acted on this thought, but it was strange when you stopped to think about it.

Ben found that in his case old habits didn't die hard; instead they ran out on to the fast lane of the motorway and spreadeagled themselves on the tarmac in their rush to expire. Going to the office at seven every morning stopped overnight. Patrolling the sales floors and making surprise visits to stores ceased forthwith. Worrying about the kids became a thing of the past.

About the only thing that remained unchanged was the compendium of Seventy-Seven Society members. There was still unfinished business there.

------------------------------ ✳ ------------------------------

Did he think she was stupid? You didn't live under the same roof with someone for over thirty years without getting to know all their little tricks: the conniving, the little lies like 'Oh, I'll just check my emails before bed, you go on up,' which actually meant half an hour surfing the internet.

It wasn't difficult to find out what he'd been doing: his security was awful. He seemed to favour Facebook, where he had a small but exclusive set of so-called friends, and he seemed to get emails from an awfully high number of Russian women boasting of the quality of their video cameras. Most intriguing of all was the number of so-called chats he's had with one woman in particular, who pretended to be a fellow doctor. You didn't have to be Sherlock Holmes to see what was going on. If she'd been young and pretty, with a pneumatic chest, then maybe Mary could have understood, but judging by the small picture of her on the screen this woman was much the same age as herself: certainly no better looking, and definitely chubbier.

As if this wasn't enough, there'd been all the jokes about getting old, taking aspirins every day. She'd seen right through it. He was as fit as a butcher's dog; only a few years before he'd run the London Marathon for his hospital's charity. No, he was building up to something, and she thought she knew what it was. He was going to do an Andy Thompson, but go one step further: fake his own death, go away to one of his conferences and never come back. He had to know a bent doctor among his crowd – there always was one. Get him to sign a death certificate, run off with this floozy.

She needed to be one step ahead, so she'd been to her GP with anxiety problems which she said were driven by concerns for her husband's health, just enough for there to be an official record. Then she got the necessary equipment off eBay under an assumed name, and waited. Her chance came one early summer's morning, when the sun was at last showing some signs of warmth after a long and desperate winter.

He was out in the garden, lopping back an apple tree that had got out of control, removing some errant branches which offended his eye for neatness. The dog was getting excited, picking up the fallen branches and running off with them. He was halfway up some steps operating a long-handled gadget with a blade at the end, along with a small claw, when the dog ran into one of the legs of the ladder and sent it clattering with a metallic clanking.

The dog barked, David screamed, and as she looked out the window she saw him lying on the ground, one hand clutching his head, the other raised in greeting, presumably saying he was all right. Well, that was a matter of opinion. In a single fluid moment, she dashed into the dining room and ran a hand under the sideboard, pulling out a small container about the size of a shoebox, extracting what looked like a pair of broken old-fashioned headphones with cushioned sides, linked together with a curly wire. With a practised movement, she yanked out the small lead connecting it to the mains. Green diodes were shining, indicating a full charge. Raising herself up from her haunches she straightened her back, her long toned legs poised to run into the garden.

'Don't worry, my love,' she called as she emerged into the daylight; not quite a shout, but more than just an observation. 'I'm on my way.' He should have known that something was up when he heard the term of endearment. She hadn't called him 'my love' for years.

He was on the ground, breathing with a pathetically feeble and shallow pant, but with half an eye on the commotion elsewhere. That half an eye hadn't quite known what to make of the unaccustomed sight of his usually indifferent wife running towards him, but he'd taken it as a good sign that at least something was happening. He was confused. He'd hit his head badly on the grass and the fall had knocked the stuffing out of him. Why she was holding a set of headphones? Had she been catching up on her *Archers* podcast? Even in this state it occurred to him that she still looked great, even after all these years; still his wonderful Mary despite everything that had passed between them, or more accurately had failed to pass. She looked stunning in her sports shirt and baseball hat, her white Nike trainers flashing in the low sun as she ran towards him.

In seconds she was on him, straddling his waist with her hips, her weight on his body vaguely reminiscent of better times in their relationship, as she applied one of each of the headphones either side of his ribcage. Too late, David realized what was going on.

'Don't worry', she mumbled, trying to catch her breath, the very use of these two words having exactly the opposite effect. 'I've got the answer.' Then, a little ominously, and with a distinct lack of sincerity, she reassured him: 'You're not going to die'.

During the run from the house she'd been praising herself for her foresight; how her doctor had suggested she keep a machine to hand, 'just in case'. She'd thought of everything: this was the final act in a carefully scripted play.

Maybe it was the way she said it that made David wonder if her most recent statement had been completely honest. For the first time, it hit him that he might never see the branches, currently swaying over him and resplendent with pink blossom, bear fruit that summer, or any other summer if it came to that. Like him, they held the promise of life, of many more years of productive output, but he was about to become more like the dead wood he'd just cut – already lying on the grass, like him.

Perhaps cruelly, the blossom was going to be the last thing he'd ever see. But as he realized this he felt a sense not of resentment, but resignation.

He'd seen a lot of deaths in his time and he knew that fighting was pointless: far better to melt away peacefully into the long goodnight, to close his eyes and allow the musty smell of the soil beneath to permeate his nostrils. When it was your time, there wasn't much you could do about it. With his eyes shut, his other senses became more acute, and in the distance he could hear a woodpecker in the woods beyond the garden dementedly tapping its way into the bark of a tree, like some kind of stuttering avian hand-drill. He could feel the still ever-so-slightly damp grass between his fingers, where morning dew still hid in the shade. A small piece of burned toast trapped in a back tooth gave off a carboniferous tang, as if from an old barbecue.

He could have struggled. He could have lifted his neck and seen the triumphant smile he now suspected would be blooming across his wife's face, but he knew he was a defeated man. If he resisted her, there was only going to be another time. He was going to die never knowing why she seemed to hate him so, more so even than his mother-in-law. For years it had been a question that had tortured him, and he'd come to the conclusion that she was unable to express a frustration with herself for choosing him when she could have had her pick. Perhaps they should have had more children; he'd have liked more. In withdrawing her affections she had, of course, removed that option. He'd had a reasonable life: it could have been better, it could have been longer, but it could have been a lot worse. As least he was going to be spared the extended agony of dementia, unlike his father.

David Lu wondered whether to close his eyes forever, but the rate at which they were blinking made the question largely academic, and the light was fading from them anyway. He heard a click, followed by another, and he knew what the sounds presaged.

As the charge from the defibrillator surged across his chest, set at maximum of course, he felt a moment's pain, but then nothing. The branches from the apple tree merged into the whitening sky and his chest leapt into the air like a march hare lamenting the passing spring.

Another surge followed but it was purely precautionary. The first had done its work. It was over.

------------------------------ ✱ ------------------------------

They'd generally been lucky with the weather, but that year a counterpane of snow had fallen. All along the walk to the venue, Tom's phone had been pinging with texts from people crying off. By the time he reached the pub his shoes were caked in crunchy off-white snow, and the streets were littered with abandoned cars. The glow from the streetlamps gave the town a slightly jaundiced look. Tom was making the journey to the pub just in case, although he didn't expect anyone to be there. His was always the shortest journey: a short stroll up the hill from the house he shared with Marion, and then along the high street.

Inside, the pub was eerily quiet. Just one back turned to him at the bar, and a barmaid, her hand pulling down on the pump dispensing what he suspected was not the first, or indeed third, pint to her sole patron. Her eyes lifted as Tom approached, perhaps in gratitude for someone new to talk to. The gesture caused the man to turn around. Ray Meadows. Of course. Whether it was connected to the snow or not Tom couldn't tell, but Ray seemed to have selected a look probably best described as 'contrived distressed': an unshaven appearance wavering somewhere between Ronnie Wood and the late Oliver Reed. Oblivious to the impact he was creating, Ray looked at his watch.

'Bloody hell!' he cried. 'What time do you call this?' Without waiting for an explanation, for Tom was right – Ray had indeed been in the pub since it opened, well before the sudden snowfall – he went on: 'Where is everyone? Hasn't been a bloody massacre this year, has there? Just you and me left, head boy and his deputy, last men standing?' He nudged Tom in the ribs. When he was finally given the chance, Tom explained, steadily creating a small puddle of meltwater on the wooden floor below as he did so.

The following year they were luckier, not just with the weather but with attendance, as if there was a sense that there was some catching up to do. Reggie was on a client visit and only just made the drinks beforehand. Foolishly, he'd relied on Google Maps to get him out of an unfamiliar town centre, whereas if he'd just used a real map he'd have got there two pints earlier.

Ray sympathized as Reggie explained why he was late, their annual bumping into each other beforehand pretty much an integral tradition of the meals. Ray hated all this digital stuff. He'd made his living talking to people, convincing them to part with their cash or at least sign up to a direct debit. The problem was, no one talked to each other any more; everything was at arm's length: texts, emails, web links. He'd become a dinosaur.

It was a fitting start. Each year's Seventy-Seven dinner seemed to adopt a mood, and that year's mood had been one of introspection. Intimations of mortality were not so much creeping up on them as jumping out from behind a corner and yelling 'Boo!'

Toby Connor in particular was on maudlin form. Toby tried to make as many of the dinners as he could, although if asked, Tom would have had him down as an irregular. He missed the year they'd started the Bond and went along with it afterwards because he thought the money was to pay for postage and envelopes for invitations. It was only when Andy Thompson put the subs up that he'd had it explained to him. Even then, he didn't really get it: the basic premise seemed flawed. If they couldn't really explain what it was that had supposedly made their year so special in the first place, why go to all the trouble of trying to preserve it? Maybe he should finally raise his doubts.

As the evening went on, Toby's qualms were fed by a realization that many of his ex-school friends had reached a pivotal point in their lives. Some had undergone complete career changes. Eddie Perks, for example, had given up his job as a stockbroker to become a full-time stand-up comedian, reverting to his school nickname of Bugs, and taken to wearing brightly coloured waistcoats again as part of his stage look; while Paul Briton had taken a package and was now working part-time delivering GCSE lessons in business studies at the Red Coat. He reported back, somewhat disconsolately, that no one had raised an eyebrow when he said he was from the Class of '77. Their reputation dissolved like an Alka Seltzer once the school went private, the school's history restarting again from that moment. They had become, quite literally, the forgotten generation, the lost boys, wiped clean from the electronic whiteboard of memory.

By the time they reached the dessert course, Toby had resolved to raise the suggestion of cashing in the Bond and moving on. Maybe they needed their own clean sheet. Meanwhile, Paul's comments had provoked another short exchange among those occupying a corner of the table, and Toby just caught the beginning as the main course dishes were taken away.

'Back then life seemed to be in Technicolor, now it just seems …', the voice trailed off, as if their observation didn't really need a conclusion.

One was offered anyway, from further down the table.

'…. fifty shades of grey?'

Polite chuckles followed. 'No, seriously, I wonder what the others would think if they could see us now.'

'Others?'

'Oh, Jake Peterson, George Rowlands, Jeff Stone, all of them.'

'Good question,' a further voice responded, although a slight pause beforehand suggested he had to stop to remember who some of these people were.

In due course Tom Joules got to his feet and cleared his throat. In his various parish notices the news that that Dr David Lu had had a massive and, as it happened, fatal, heart attack received a mixed reaction. Although they didn't want to speak ill of the dead, there were many in the room who'd seen old Brucie as some kind of angel of death ever since the Legionnaires' incident. Toby had seen his chance, and seizing it, he raised a hand to request the floor.

The second he finished his question the silence that followed could only have been sufficiently replicated if someone had lobbed in a stun grenade. Predictably, perhaps, and with barely a nod to the fact that he didn't exactly look like an advert for longevity himself, it was Ray Meadows who broke it.

'One blouse, woman's variety, size extra large, over here please!' Dutiful laughter followed. 'Worried about not making it past the finishing post? Looking to cash in, eh?' Ray continued, lapsing into an impersonation of Corporal Jones from *Dad's Army* as he added, 'Don't Panic! Don't Panic!'

'No, it's just that I ...'

Toby wasn't given the chance to explain the thinking behind his proposition, as he was interrupted by a particularly indignant Ben Bradshaw.

'We can't give up on the Bond now,' he exclaimed, as if the room was being asked to vote in favour of republicanism (a motion, in fact, that may have attracted more support). 'It would be a ...' He struggled for a moment to come up with the right word, and then found it: '... a betrayal!' Pleased with this success, he went on: 'A betrayal not just of all we did at school, but all we've done since, and all those who haven't gone the distance.' To a chorus of *hear hears*, Ben sat down, although not too many in the room appreciated he'd actually been standing up in the first place.

At that moment, Toby was reminded of why they'd all taken the piss out of Ben Bradshaw at school. He was a nobody who wanted to be a somebody, hence his ridiculous little TV adverts which everyone was too embarrassed to comment on. Even more annoyingly, his pathetic imploring seemed to have cut all discussion short.

For Tom, the exchange had exposed a raw fault line he'd often pondered over: was the scheme about a shared bond, or was it about being the last man standing? It was a question best left unasked, so in an unprecedented act, he called for a show of hands to maintain the status quo, and once this proved all but one in favour of proceeding as before, he called an end to formal proceedings. Everyone around the table seemed to get up at once, issuing a collective 'ooouffff' of effort as they did so, the more agile among them winning the race to the urinals.

2014

Tom Joules had always admired musicians, and although he always sensed a degree of affinity between them and mathematicians (they each shared a sense of being practitioners of a dark art open only to a select few), he'd never been able to master music himself. The best he'd ever achieved was breathing in and out on a mouth organ to imitate a police siren when he was a child.

Tom bowed his head and prayed silently to himself. He'd got a little too used to attending funerals over the years. In the same way that New York mayor Rudi Giuliani had attended as many of the firefighters' funerals as he could after 9/11, so Tom felt a certain duty to go to those of fallen school colleagues whenever he was able.

Church funerals had become all too rare; instead he usually found himself struggling to locate crematoria on the edge of unknown towns, which once you got there were depressingly similar: the towns, and the crematoria. Like the others, this one had anodyne decoration, an electric organ in one corner, and a functional conveyor belt in another, partially hidden by a curtain; and, of course, the smell of lilies: the overwhelming and cloying smell of lilies, hanging like a cloud over the proceedings, always threatening to rain thick flour-like pollen on unsuspecting mourners.

His moment of silent contemplation over, Tom turned his attention to the order of service, only to find that the familiar cross or photo on the cover had been replaced by a short statement. It quickly became clear that this was not to be a conventional service. It seemed that the departed had always been a fan of *Desert Island Discs*. As Tom read on it seemed that Mike McQueen had spent a lot of time planning his own funeral, which was odd because, as far as Tom knew, Mike hadn't been suffering any kind of terminal illness.

Tom hadn't realized quite how successful McQueen had been: famous even, something big in the music business apparently. He'd certainly done well for himself since school, despite not appearing to be very promising material: too … well, he believed the phrase was

287

'laid-back'. The room had seemed ridiculously big when he arrived, but it filled quickly, and a slight echo from the antechamber outside suggested that the service was being relayed to an overflow room. Tom was glad he'd got there early.

There were a lot of black faces in the room, many of them wide-set men, but some wiry white women too, their physical negatives. There was also a lot of conspicuous jewellery: chains, padlocks, that sort of thing. One or two of the throng were wearing sunglasses indoors: bodyguards, Tom supposed, making him wonder if he was in fact in a room full of celebrities. He looked around: one or two faces looked vaguely familiar, but no one he could put a name to.

Tom had known McQueen as Freddie, but he was pretty sure no one else in the room had. They'd known him in his post-school persona, in a totally different life, now sadly shortened. This thought momentarily made Tom feel a little superior, more important than the rest, before he chastised himself for the sins of pride and vanity.

In the order of service, Freddie had commented how being on *Desert Island Discs* had always represented both a dream and a nightmare for him, the latter due to being restricted to only eight records. Tom hadn't known it was eight; he knew the format of the programme but for some reason had always assumed it was ten. The room was by now buzzing with sound, needing the presence of a minister to calm it down, to inject some gravitas, although Tom couldn't see one, and turning to the second page of the booklet he found out why. It seemed that McQueen wanted the congregation to listen to his chosen records and then read why he had chosen them: a sort of one-way interview.

Tom prepared himself for what looked like being a long and possibly uncomfortable memorial, and surprised himself when he recognized the sound of the first song, even though he hadn't recognized the name in the booklet. It was called *The Great Gig in the Sky*, from Pink Floyd's *The Dark Side of the Moon*. A voice speaking over the music transported Tom back to another age, one when he'd sat in his lonely office in the sixth form centre, wishing his status as head boy hadn't excluded him from the wider throng. It was as if the voice was speaking to him direct, hovering over a rather poignant lilting piano, and what Tom thought was some kind of guitar. The voice told the assembled mourners how he wasn't afraid of dying; indeed, questioning why he might be, claiming there was no reason to be afraid of death. His final words were perhaps the most pragmatic, when he commented fatalistically that everyone had to go some time.

To his surprise, Tom found himself getting lost in the music and the piercing voice of the half-screaming, half-singing woman at the centre of it, whose voice seemed to represent both lament and fear at the same time. Slowly, she wound down, as if she'd reconciled herself to her fate, taking the room with her.

As an opening to a funeral it would have been a good choice, if only the technician operating the music at the back of the room, perhaps lost in the beauty of the moment, had remembered to hit the pause button in time. As it happened, the room was suddenly filled with the sound of old-fashioned cash registers ringing and some deep bass notes, followed by a bellow of 'Money!' from the loudspeakers before the right button was found. A ripple of amusement echoed briefly round the room, before people remembered where they were.

Tom was less familiar with the rest of the music that followed, which seemed to alternate between the contemplative and the simply loud and thumpy, but he did recognize the eighth and final song. It was, perhaps inevitably, Queen, with Freddie's namesake belting out *Another One Bites the Dust*, a truth so undeniable that Tom found it hard to hold back a tear. For the second time that day, Tom heard laughter at a funeral service. He liked to think that when Freddie had chosen this one, his tongue was planted firmly in his cheek, and he realized that it was this, not the earlier tune, that he'd chosen in remembrance of his schooldays.

The final lines in the order of service, as Tom still preferred to see it, stated simply that Freddie had chosen a limitless solar-powered iPod as his luxury, and *Juliette*, by the Marquis de Sade, as his book. Tom assumed this was almost certainly a reference to Sade, who'd been big in the eighties, he surprised himself by remembering, rather than the pornographer from the French Revolution.

The funeral reached that moment Tom had never got used to, when either the curtains closed around the coffin or electric motors started to whirr silently and the coffin itself started its last journey, either down into a hole in the ground, or back into a gap in the wall. This was one of the down-into-a- hole crematoria, and as the coffin began to descend, Tom spotted for the first time a black leather whip hidden among the flowers on top.

------------------------------ ✳ ------------------------------

The yellow padded envelope had seemed lighter, cheaper even, when it fell on to the mat. Harold Mitchell's finely tuned ear could tell the difference, but the contents were the same; well, similar. This time there wasn't a plane ticket: something that had come as a pleasant surprise. The mysterious blackmailer had taken to using low-cost airlines in recent years and the flights had been closer to cattle trucks, full of young girls dressed up in matching T-shirts on their way to hen weekends, sprinting across the tarmac to make sure they all sat together. Quite why they did so was beyond him, as all they seemed to do was shriek at each other when they reached their seats.

The postcard was still in there, but the picture was different: an English scene, somewhere in Wiltshire. With a bit of luck, he'd be there and back in a day; get it over and done with.

------------------------------ ✳ ------------------------------

Mary Lu had trouble sleeping. For weeks she'd been expecting to see a police car outside her house whenever she returned from an outing or shopping. She'd even started to restrict the number of times she went out, in a sort of irrational belief that she could avoid the inevitable, but she just found herself staring at the phone, waiting for it ring.

Night times were the worst. That was when the demons really

started to have fun with her head. Thoughts she couldn't suppress spun round like dervishes, driven by something greater than the physical. She'd tried exercising herself to exhaustion, but all that did was give her cramp. She also tried walking around, but found herself wandering into the garden, to where it had all happened.

To where she'd murdered her husband.

It was his face that kept coming back to her. Not the shut eyes, clenched jaw and the hint of a smile when she'd laid the defibrillator across his chest, but the one she'd seen across the table at her twenty-first birthday party. The innocent, slightly bemused face that struggled to retain a semblance of decorum as he slowly descended into the soft lawn of her parents' home. It was the face she also saw in her son, a young man now, but still innocent; unlike her. She was a murderer, and she deserved to be punished.

The only problem was, she didn't want to go to court, and she wanted to go to jail even less. Her relationship with her mother had never really recovered from her marriage to David, and a conviction for murder (the victim notwithstanding) was hardly going to fix things between them. What she really wanted was forgiveness. She wanted to be told that so long as she was sorry, very sorry indeed, and that she promised never to do anything like it again, then yes, she could get on with her life.

But who could she tell? Who would understand? Only one name came to mind. One person who would listen, who might understand why she had done it.

The person who had planted the original seed of doubt.

2015

Confession, it seemed, was good for the soul; and furthermore, it seemed to be catching. In Mary Lu's case it was triggered by a violent death; for Marion Joules it was driven more by the prospect of her own demise. Marion had been for her routine smear and been passed clear, as usual, so she'd been surprised to be called back three weeks later and hear that she'd got the results of a Mrs Jones, not Mrs Joules. The doctor was very keen to impress upon her that this wasn't their fault, and while Marion was wondering who else's fault it could possibly have been, she'd been hit with the bombshell that they had detected some abnormal cells.

Talking about health issues, especially women's health issues, came under the heading of taboos in Marion's marriage, so she'd persevered with the roundabout of further tests on her own, waiting for the moment when another, more competent, medic might say that the whole thing had been a horrible mistake and she was okay. In the end, she'd given up waiting. The simple truth was that she had cancer, and her research on the internet told her she had a pretty reasonable chance of dying from it.

Marion's initial inclination had been to keep this to herself to relieve Tom of the burden of getting in touch with his emotional side. She was convinced he wouldn't have had a clue how to react, and this would only prolong the period of awkwardness that was inevitably going to descend over them at some point. It came as a considerable surprise to them both, therefore, when over breakfast one day Tom raised the fact that she wasn't looking her usual perky self, and she burst into tears.

Years of hiding their true feelings for each other in a cupboard protected with a double lock and a chair jammed under the handle were at that moment exposed as a sham. Tom took her in his arms, hugged her and waited for her to tell him what was going on. Once she started to speak, wiping away her tears as she did so, he lowered his face and stared into her deep hazel eyes, locking his gaze into her soul as if he was possessed of a kind of truth-glare.

She told him everything, starting with the diagnosis, and with that off her chest she worked backwards through the years telling him how she felt, what she worried about, all her secrets, until she got to the late 1970s. Here she paused, but resistance was useless as Tom held his gaze and his encouraging silence urged her on. She started at the point when she'd found a note propped up against the toaster saying her only child was leaving and telling Marion not to try to find her. Out of this had come details of the dreadful night when her daughter had come back from the school swimming pool in such a state that Marion had wept for her lost innocence, admitting to Tom, and to herself, that something inside both of them had died that night.

Then, somehow, something else came out. The most guilty secret of them all, the one she'd kept in a safe hidden inside the cupboard with the double lock and the chair against the handle. A safe with a combination, inside which was a strongbox whose key Marion always kept about her person. All were opened, in sequence and slowly, as Tom waited patiently.

The secret of secrets, of her relationship with the headmaster. The moment she finished she felt a sense of total relief, as if she was a sinner who'd confessed and was ready for absolution. The years of living a lie were over.

Tom, meanwhile, having absorbed his new-found knowledge, decided to let it settle like the sediment it was, choosing instead to focus on what was really important right then. All sorts of thoughts buzzed round his head, but three intentions dominated. First, he had to find a way to help Marion through her dreadful dilemma: together they would make her better again. Second, he had to track down her girl and help them to be reconciled, just in case he failed with the first aim. Third, he realized at this point that he loved his wife with an intensity he simply didn't have the words to describe.

------------------------------ ✳ ------------------------------

His occasional investigations had been generating some titbits but nothing really tangible, and as a result Sam had steadily lost motivation in his quest to crack his big story. Besides, wasn't time running out? Sure, there seemed to be a fashion for cold case dramas on TV, but there was cold and there was sub-arctic. The arrival of an email offering a possible lead therefore came with a mix of interest and irritation. Sam was going to have to make a decision: just how serious was he?

His initial reaction had been to treat the email as spam, but whoever was behind it knew too much about the Red Coat, and specifically about their year, and indeed about Sam, for it not to be credible. He then tried to see if he could trace the source of the email, but he soon stumbled aimlessly into the Dark Web. In the end, he decided he had no choice but to plunge into uncharted territory – better known as Tibshelf services on the M1.

Sam drove in silence on his way to the rendezvous in order to get his thoughts in order. The truth was, he had remarkably little to go on beyond the bare facts. The most obvious lead was the Bond, but looking through the information on the society's website, this looked pretty healthy: very healthy, in fact, well into six figures, but enough to instigate a massacre? He doubted it. Sam had been given a time and place to meet, and had half expected to be greeted by an accountant or lawyer. What he hadn't expected was an ex-policeman.

To describe the man he met as pug-ugly would have been an insult to pugs. Not only did he have a squashed-in face, but also a raised mole: black and wrinkled, a withered raisin stuck to the left-hand side of his face where the cheek met the jawbone. A centre parting didn't help, adding years to his age, which Sam estimated could be anything between fifty and seventy. He greeted Sam with a firm handshake outside the main entrance to the services and then led him across the road to a suite of conference rooms available for hire by the hour.

The room contained a single desk, two chairs, a conference telephone (beside which, taped to the table, was a laminated A4 sheet laying out the price schedule) and, on the wall behind Sam, a clock. The walls were painted in a neutral light peach; the ceiling in white, where a plastic guard containing dead flies protected a strip light.

The room had an unloved, antiseptic air that went with its general functionality. By Sam's estimation it was, as near as he could tell, a perfect cube, around three metres along each axis.

Once they'd sat down, the man Sam had travelled to meet introduced himself as Gerald Balmer, and although no credentials were provided to prove this was his real name, he was prepared to reveal his former profession. Was this really Sam's anonymous source? Following introductions, Balmer made it clear that anything covered in their meeting was strictly off the record: something Sam, in his confused state, had acknowledged without thinking, with a clear 'Understood'. He was left with the distinct impression that he was helping someone with their enquiries.

It was a hot day, and although there was a small window to the top of one of the walls, Balmer hadn't opened it. It felt as if they were two chess players squaring up before a match, and Sam didn't have to wait long before the man sitting across the desk made his opening move. Reaching into a plain brown envelope, Balmer extracted a wad of 10 x 8 black and white photographs. Saying nothing at first (he seemed to be a man of few words), he then squared the pile and spun it round to face Sam and then, as if he was deploying a King's Indian Attack, he took the first one off the pile and placed it directly in front of Sam. A shaft of sunshine illuminated half the desk, further emphasizing the drama of the moment, motes dancing like mini-mosquitoes in the light. As the ex-policeman lifted the next photo off the top of the pile and slid it towards the first one, Sam made out the façade of a shop in what was clearly a rundown part of anytown.

The shop's fascia was painted in olive green and showed signs of peeling, and the pavement in front was cracked. The next picture was of a man looking over his shoulder, aiming for the door of the shop with a determined stride. He was wearing a peaked hat, a Rupert Bear scarf and an old Barbour jacket, suggesting the photo had been taken at least some months before. The heat in the room was building, films of sweat congregating across each man's brow. The third photo was a close-up of the man in the second.

'Just let me have any thoughts you might have as you look at these,' Balmer said, his deep voice speaking softly, suggesting a request rather than a demand: albeit a request Sam was expected to comply with. Something in the third photo scratched at Sam's memory and, without asking if it was okay, his curiosity led him to pick it up and hold it closer to his face. The light, combined with some recent trouble he'd been having with his near sight, demanded a closer inspection. Balmer paused with the fourth photo mid-air, cocking his head slightly as if to catch whatever Sam said next more clearly.

'Anything?' Balmer asked. 'Anything at all?'

Tension seemed to inhabit the room, making it smaller, more intimate. The act of staring at a photograph, rather than an image on a screen, of holding something tangible, seemed to stir deep memories inside Sam's brain.

'This is going to sound weird,' Sam began, qualifying anything that might shortly come out of his mouth. Balmer kept his silence, leaving Sam time to think. 'It's all so long ago, but ...' Balmer nodded in encouragement. '...and this is going to sound a bit crazy, but ...' A slight sideways movement of Balmer's head suggested it was okay to speculate. '... he looks awfully like the headmaster at my old school.'

DCI Balmer seemed to suppress the beginnings of a smile, before recommencing his metronomic issuing of the photos, which were now beginning to cover the desk separating the two men. The more angles he saw the man from, the more Sam was convinced he might be right.

'Where is this place?' he asked.

'It's what we call a parlour, in the business,' the ex-policeman replied, wiping the top of his head with his tie before continuing, 'an establishment where men with certain tastes go to be, shall we say, disciplined. To gain satisfaction. They're normally harmless enough, but we like to keep tabs on them.' Sam looked up, quizzically. 'The parlours, I mean; not the clients.'

All Sam could think to say was a rather lame 'Blimey' in response, as he turned his attention to the next photo. The whole set had now been laid out on the desk, two dozen in total, the storyboard for a cheap S&M movie. They told a sorry tale, a slow, almost Hogarthian descent, starting with an innocent enough arrival and ending in a violent and bloody death, the images of which caused the sweat on Sam's own brow to coalesce into a small rivulet.

'Any chance of some water, or maybe the window?' Sam asked, at which the large man placed a hand on each arm of his chair and extricated himself, reaching up to find the catch holding the window shut. The sound of rumbling traffic and the mechanical voice warning that an HGV was reversing entered the room. The final photos in the series weren't pretty, and if the ex-policeman had started with them Sam doubted he'd ever have been able to recognize the victim. Blood was everywhere, over the Head's face, chest and the rest of his naked body.

'What ... what happened?' Sam asked, still needing some water to lubricate his suddenly dry mouth.

'We don't know,' Balmer replied unhelpfully. 'What we do know is, the parlour wasn't on our radar; in fact, we suspect it wasn't a live one at all.'

'Meaning?'

'Meaning it was a dummy operation, just set up for the day. A sort of pop-up parlour. Some of these pictures were taken by local CCTV, others from the crime scene. The gentleman in question had been lured there somehow, and what you see before you was the result.' He paused. 'We'd appreciate any observations you may have, possible motives, anything we might be able to go on.'

'God, it was so long ago,' Sam replied, 'it's difficult to think.'

'Take your time.'

The sound of an automated voice yelling, 'warning, turning left, warning, turning left,' came from outside the window, impeding Sam's thought.

'He was all right, bit of a menacing figure: an egotist, I suppose, but it wasn't as if we met up for a drink or anything; he was our headmaster, a distant character, someone we were in awe of, tried to avoid if we could.' Sam licked his lips. Something gave him the impression that he wasn't adding much to what Balmer already knew, and he suddenly felt under a compulsion to give the man something, anything. It was irrational, he knew, but he felt almost under suspicion. 'We all pretended to despise him, but I don't think any of us did really; he was just a figure of authority when we were all challenging authority.'

The DCI nodded, as if he understood and was playing a long game with Sam. 'Anything else?' he asked. 'I know it's not easy, but take a closer look at the photos.'

Sam picked up a particularly gruesome shot of the Head lying on his back, his lifeless eyes staring up at the ceiling. Closer inspection suggested that the blood had been the result of a single wound. To keep himself occupied while he thought, and to take his eyes off the gore, Sam picked up one of the earlier photos and studied it again. Something in it was bothering him, but he couldn't put his finger on it. Hoping desperately for inspiration, if for no other reason than to get this sweatbox ordeal over with, he shuttled his attention between the two photographs, bringing them both closer to his eyes, hiding his face from the man over the table.

'Hold on,' he mumbled, half to himself, 'what's that?' He handed the photo in his right hand back to the policeman opposite and pointed at a small dark mark about six inches above the more obvious wound. 'Isn't that a second puncture hole?'

In a moment of almost perfect cliché, DCI Balmer retrieved a small magnifying glass, about two inches' diameter, from an inside pocket in his jacket, and held it and the photo to his eye, as if he'd never noticed it before. 'Any ideas what it could be?' he asked.

Sam did have an idea, but it was buried deep in the furthest recesses of his brain. It wanted to climb to the front of his consciousness, but it was a slow-motion crawl through mud. Suddenly, it surfaced. He *had* seen it before: over thirty years before. Images of sand trickling on to the asphalt of the upper playground began to enjoy the daylight of consciousness, and the face of the DHM, a demented look in his eyes, holding the ivory handle of his curved *khanjar* knife.

But he wasn't done yet. Sam put the photo he'd been holding in his left hand on top of the others covering the table and put a finger on a spectral, easy-to-miss figure dressed all in black.

'Him.' Sam announced. 'I recognize him, too.'

Checkmate.

------------------------------ ✻ ------------------------------

It began when he sold the business; a bolt from the blue, and a shock. The first she heard of it was when she'd been away with work, on a tour of new executive hotels – all white paint and incomprehensible electronics with restaurants totally devoid of any kind of atmosphere – when she'd seen the news in the European edition of the *Financial Times*. She'd returned home to something she was unfamiliar with: a smiling, even confident, Ben.

Swimming was suddenly back into his life. He was even talking about getting their own pool built, or maybe buying a house that had one. He'd become a man possessed, full of plans; dare she say it: happy? He had plans. He was going to set up a charitable foundation; he was going to front an initiative from the Department of Culture, Media and Sport; he was going to pay for the Seventy-Seveners to go to the Oktoberfest in Munich to celebrate their fortieth anniversary the year after next.

The last one had caught Susie's attention. Apparently swilling beer among buxom waitresses in leather dungarees had been something that had often come up at the dinners, but that's all it had been: talk. It turned out they even had a pilot among their number who Ben had been in touch with, and he reckoned he could get a plane: maybe even fly the plane himself, make it his final flight.

Susie's conundrum was how best to respond. The acid test was going to be the next Seventy-Seven Society supper: how they responded to his idea and critically, how he, in turn, responded to them. Her guess was he'd revert to type; she'd heard that his type of depressive often had a relapse into happiness, but it never lasted: the deep shit was too far down.

For the moment, she would have to cope with this new Ben. The positive Ben, the forward-looking, excited Ben. It wasn't going to be easy, adjusting to this new equilibrium between them, but she was sure she'd come up with something: she always did.

2016

Sam was half-expecting, half-dreading a follow-up from his anonymous cyber-tipster following the meeting at Tibshelf; although when it came it seemed straightforward enough. Did he still have any contacts within the school, it wondered? The way the email was phrased, it was almost as if the emailer was describing Tom, so having replied 'Leave it with me,' he tapped out another email using the contact link on the Seventy-Seven Society website.

Sam's plan was to have a gentle chat; see what Tom knew about the DHM and if he had any inside track on Harold Mitchell. He'd suggested a newly opened pub in the town centre owned by one of the big chains, located in a building which Sam remembered as a museum. Historical photos lining the walls looked disturbingly familiar from Sam's time in the town nearly forty years before.

The pub occupied two levels, the upper level consisting of a series of alcoves populated with deep leather sofas and low tables. Where people had once gazed at Roman ruins, they now sampled bottles of house white, an unoaked Chardonnay, and, on Prosecco Fridays, glasses of the fizzy stuff.

Sam reached the bar first and chose a position on the upper level which looked down over the front door so he could see Tom arrive.

To save time he got a bottle of their second cheapest, a New Zealand Sauvignon Blanc, and waited as it rested in its metal cooler bucket. As Sam had initiated the meeting, and he was the one after information, it seemed only fair that he got the booze in: well, the first bottle anyway. The place was reasonably quiet, although some people had set up laptops on the taller tables below and were enjoying a drink while still working, which seemed to Sam to be an extremely civilized way to live, and indeed work.

It was towards the end of Lent term, and Sam hoped this might make Tom more forthcoming, although he wasn't really sure why. He was feeling nervous: he'd never really spoken at any length with Tom before, seeing him as a little stand-offish, and, if he was being really honest, his position at the school and as head boy all those years ago still stirred up some prejudices within him. He had therefore prepared some opening lines of small talk and tried to put on a professional head – this was work, not fun.

The moment Tom came in through the door Sam realized he'd made a fundamental faux pas. Although Tom never really looked comfortable, he looked decidedly awkward as he entered the pub, pausing as he crossed the threshold, his face slightly grey. In an instant, Sam had a vision of the orange juice Tom drank at the Seventy-Seven Society suppers. The man was teetotal. Sam also knew he was a bit of a God-botherer; maybe he didn't approve of booze, or maybe he didn't want to be seen by his pupils entering a den of iniquity. In summary, Tom had all the appearance of a man in a gabardine raincoat entering a mucky flicks cinema.

Putting his best face on, Sam gave a wave and pointed at the stairs. There was still time to remedy the situation before Tom made it to his booth, and noticing the two full glasses he'd poured, Sam wrestled with the temptation to immediately down one of them and hide the glass, before realizing that one glass and a whole bottle would make him look like an absolute dipsomaniac: not exactly the impression he wanted to convey. While he was still wrestling with his best course of action, Tom sank into the armchair without so much as a handshake, emitting a deep sigh as he did so.

'Blimey,' Sam responded. 'Bad day?'

'Is there another type?' Tom asked, and in a single movement picked up the glass of light honey-coloured liquid and drained it in one, his fingers slipping briefly on the cool sweat on the outside of the glass. For a man who didn't drink, Sam noted, he hadn't lost the knack.

Sam reached over to top up the glass when Tom suddenly froze, like a child playing Sleeping Monsters, as if in horror at what he'd just done.

'I haven't had a drink for over thirty years,' he announced, seemingly to the entire bar, perhaps in a bid for absolution, although in the general hubbub, no one took any notice.

'It's all right,' Sam reassured him, 'I won't tell anyone,' and proceeded to top up the glass anyway.

Before Sam had taken more than an inch off the top of his glass, Tom's was empty again. 'Quite nice, this,' he remarked: 'very dry.'

Sam nodded his agreement. Perhaps he should edit the small talk and get things moving.

'What's up?'

Rarely, in Sam's experience, had two words produced so much. The drink had clearly gone to Tom's head, and from that moment on Sam became an engineer monitoring lubrication levels in a particularly delicate apparatus, making constant calculations to keep the drink levels right so that the words kept flowing, but not so much that they started to slur or, worse still, caused the machinery to seize up.

After a cascade of end-of-term minutiae, from out of nowhere Tom suddenly bellowed, 'Marion might die!' It was an ejaculation of remorse, as if he was the cause of this development. Having paused momentarily to remember who Marion was, Sam was dumbstruck. Before he had time to ask what may lie behind this dramatic news, Tom told him. Not only did Sam hear about the cancer, but also how Tom and Marion regarded it as some form of damnation, a retribution from an otherwise all-loving God for past misdemeanours. Naturally enough, this piqued Sam's interest as to what these misdemeanours might be. Fortunately, Tom had worked his way close to the bottom of the bottle by that time and was ready to tell him.

The fate of Matron's daughter, both during the summer of '75 and subsequently, had always been a subject of speculation at school and the years immediately afterwards, and the fact that it was still raw to Tom came as no surprise; although Sam didn't quite understand the relevance now. He decided to allow Tom to tell him in his own time: the problem was that by then nature had taken its inevitable course and Tom had to make a visit to the gents, breaking his stream of consciousness and substituting it with a stream of another kind. As Tom was rapidly approaching the 'best mate in the whole wide world' stage Sam decided to bring the conversation back to where he wanted it as soon as he reappeared.

This took a good five minutes, after Tom had headed in the wrong direction out of the gents, having failed to do up his fly, which in turn resulted in Sam having to leap up and steer him back into the privacy of their alcove, having decided to leave the issue of the fly for later. Tom slumped back down into the armchair and momentarily closed his eyes. It was time, the machinery was in danger of seizing up. He opted for the two-word trick again.

'Harold Mitchell?'

'Buggering arsehole fucker,' Tom replied. Such was Tom's state by then that Sam wasn't sure quite who this invective was aimed at, and he looked around to make sure the manager wasn't heading their way. The words had been used in a way that suggested they were foreign to the tongue that had issued them: the tone too formal, too respectful, missing the point of swearing altogether.

'Harold "Bastard is my middle name" Mitchell, the devil incarnate,' Tom continued. Over the next few minutes everything Sam had suspected about Harold Mitchell, their ex- (in more ways than one) headmaster's secret life was confirmed. What he hadn't expected to learn was the identity of his partner in his various sordid games. Somehow, Sam hadn't expected it to be a woman, and he certainly hadn't expected it to be Matron.

Eschewing sympathy for the sake of speed, Sam threw another name into the conversation. 'Clive Porter? The DHM?'

Tom's face jerked awake, as if he'd just heard the sound of an intruder in the middle of the night. 'Clive?' he asked, clearly surprised at having his name associated with all the filth they'd covered. 'Clive? Sound man. Runs Red Coat Forever', and with that he slumped down into the armchair and nodded off.

Once he'd got both Tom and himself home, Sam reflected that he'd learned a lot that afternoon, but his investigations were growing wider rather than narrower and he needed to re-engage with his collaborator. As dusk folded into dark he drank a couple of pints of water and sat down at his desk. He flipped open the lid of his new MacBook Pro and tapped out a message to his virtual companion. It was a long message detailing all he'd learned from Tom. The reply came back in less than the time it took to compose the original message, and was succinct.

'Interesting. What about the Bond?'

Sam typed back that he'd look into it, but added that he had a favour of his own to ask: some help in tracking down a missing person.

------------------------------ ✳ ------------------------------

Mary Lu had become a ticking bomb. Not only had she taken to coming round to Susie's house all the time for mini-therapy sessions, something Ben was bound to pick up on sooner rather than later and start asking questions, but she was constantly threatening to confess to the police. Susie doubted she was serious, but the threat was constantly there, and as much as anything, she just didn't have time for all that right now. Why couldn't she just be content with lying, even if it was to herself?

She was clearly suffering from a combination of guilt and grief, so Susie had pointed her back towards her GP, not knowing his involvement in the saga. It was the best Susie could come up with at the time (she had a flight at four and it was one when Mary turned up on her doorstep), but it seemed to work. Luckily, the GP had prescribed an anti-depressant and it took the edge off things: for now, anyway. The Mary problem was under control, but by no means solved.

------------------------------ ✳ ------------------------------

Clive Porter really relished his new role as alumni co-ordinator. He'd been allocated a room in one of the old houses, and he even had his own staff: a young woman often augmented with an intern, usually a freshly minted ORC in his gap year, who were useful for bringing him cups of tea and doing all the clever things with computers. He'd had the room filled with old furniture others in the school wanted rid of, and by decorating the walls with the wide letterbox pictures of previous years he'd given himself a ready-made aide memoire.

It was like having his own personal common room and asylum: not only a base in the heart of the school, but a sanctuary where he seemed to be genuinely revered, not simply tolerated. Although it had diminished every year when he'd been on the staff, the power and respect of his previous position seemed to live on among the interns, while his permanent co-ordination assistant, Karen, seemed to regard him as a wise grandfather, knowledgeable in all things Red Coat, which wasn't far from the truth.

Clive spent time in the office most days, inducing a sort of Dorian Gray situation at home where the chaplain, hidden away in front of the TV, aged rapidly, while Clive seemed to feel the years falling off him. Like an ex-US president, his title seemed to have become honorary, and Clive would wander around the school's site, with masters whose names he now made a point of remembering acknowledging him as deputy head; something made easier by the fact that the new head, Jack Thomas, had replaced him with three 'assistant heads'. Clive liked the fact it had taken three people to replace him. Overnight, he seemed to have seemed acquired the status of the school's equivalent of a national treasure.

Given the constant presence of the past, it was perhaps inevitable that Clive took stock of his time at the school, and given daily sightings of Mr Joules, unsurprisingly the Class of '77 came up more than perhaps they deserved: something reinforced by the wittering from the chaplain at home, whose first, and still most memorable, year it had been. Theirs had been the first First XV to ever go through the entire season unbeaten, it was true – something only the Class of '89 had ever come close to since – but they had drawn a couple of games. There was some residual grudging respect for the stunt they'd pulled on their Muck-up Day; not least because it had speeded up the departure of that idiot Harold Mitchell, and while there'd been some extraordinary events during his tenure as head of sixth form, none had surpassed the infamous Sneaky Shitter (he knew what they'd called him, like he knew all the nicknames, including his own).

Clive still felt that the Asian lad had been badly done by there. His instincts sensed the boy hadn't been the culprit, and it had been high-risk to get him to leave without proof. To this day Clive resented being the one delegated to speak to the parents. They'd been simple folk, unaware of their rights, and they'd been so mortified by the accusation that they'd pulled the boy from school voluntarily, as well as swiftly, even moving away; such was their shame. A bad business all round.

That said, there was little doubt in the staff room that the lad had been behind that tin bath incident at Catterick, with that thug, whatever his name was, the captain of the First XV; but again, alpha-plus for ingenuity and further evidence for the defence, surely. That had been a subtle, well-planned stunt, far removed from the blatant crudeness of the excrement episode.

In summary, the role of alumni co-ordinator, the so-called Head of Red Coat Forever, had allowed a different side of Clive to prosper, giving him time to clear some mental cupboards and prepare himself for the end – he was getting on for ninety, after all. Plenty of ghosts had been laid to rest. He was at peace.

------------------------------ ✱ ------------------------------

Ray felt confident everything was coming together at last, but maybe he'd mistaken confidence for complacency. It was time to cash up and let go, maybe buy a small place in Ireland and catch up on the fishing. He'd just about be able to afford an old crofter's cottage by a lake somewhere. But no, fate had one more kick in the balls lined up for him: of course it did.

The business had been slowing down for a while. First, he had to let the young lad go; then, a couple of years later, Polish Pam. Finally, as planned, he'd run the business from home: mostly old clients who trusted him, but one by one they began to crystallize their pensions or fall off their perch. The business itself had no residual value – very few outfits used his model any more and his client list was, to all intents, worthless – so he figured one day he'd just send out a few letters saying he was closing down. He should probably have done it a couple of years before, but timing had never been his strong point. The date he'd set to cash in all his investments was 24 June, and he notified the various investment houses holding what he'd managed to put by.

He'd voted 'Out' in the referendum: he hadn't bought all that Project Fear stuff. There was a principle at stake: a sovereign nation should – had to – have control over its own borders, surely? On top of that, he didn't trust all those fat cat Eurocrats with their straight bananas and regulations. Thank goodness they'd given a thumbs-down to the Euro: look at the dog's breakfast that was. Yes, there might be some pain, but it would be worth it to get the country back.

He never thought in a million years the vote would go their way; he just wanted those Eton posh boys in Downing Street to have some sleepless nights. When the result was announced Ray went into a genuine state of shock, and it took him a while to realize what it meant for his personal finances. The boys in the City had done what they'd been instructed to do, only they'd cashed in all his investments after the precipitous drop in the FTSE, leaving him far short of what he'd banked on getting. He wasn't broke, but he didn't have enough left to carry on until his state pension kicked in, that was for sure.

Desperate times meant desperate measures; he was going to have to push the big red button and activate his backup plan.

------------------------------ ✳ ------------------------------

It was the husband who got them together. 'Contacts,' he said, when she asked him how, but she didn't believe him for a moment. Tom Joules didn't come across as a man with friends in high places. She'd seen a notice on an expat website she occasionally looked at, the sort of thing she'd normally have just ignored, and after a number of enquiries using different email addresses she'd been sent his. When she sent a message asking what was so important, he replied that Astra's mum was seriously ill and he wanted to check out the chances of a reconciliation between the pair of them 'before it was too late', as he indelicately put it.

After flying out alone for a face-to-face, she believed him. Her instincts were usually pretty good; he hadn't looked the kind who could make something up, especially something like that. In truth, he hadn't been at all what she'd expected. When she learned that Astra's mum had married someone much younger, for some reason Sandra automatically imagined some kind of bronzed toy boy in budgie-smugglers. The reality was about as far away from that image as it was possible to get. Tall, straight-laced and proper, the guy didn't even drink. They'd met up in a wine bar, but it turned out this was more for her benefit than his. He resolutely refused to have anything other than orange juice with a splash of tonic, as if the splash had somehow added an 'oh, go on then' bit of daring.

It hadn't taken Sandra long to come to the conclusion that she would pass the information on to Astra and let her make her own decision. Whatever that decision was, Sandra would support her. Naturally she was going to have to digest it herself first, though, and decide how best to spin it so the right decision was made: Astra didn't like making decisions. Back home, after stewing on it for a couple of days she decided to load it in favour of a visit. The way Sandra saw it, making things cool between Astra and her mum might help prevent further shit in the future if she didn't and the worst happened. On a broader level, Sandra had been thinking for some time that Astra was ready to re-engage with the world.

It was eventually agreed that Astra and Sandra would come over just after Christmas. To play happy families over a table groaning with food and wearing silly hats might be a step too far, too fast, after such a long time. Christmas was usually a fallow time for them anyway, with half the world on holiday, so they flew in a couple of days before and spent the day itself having room service in their hotel room and watching old films on satellite TV. The day appointed for the reconciliation was a bank holiday and the husband, Tom, decided it would be better to leave mother and daughter alone for some of it; and although Sandra agreed it would be best if his looming presence was taken out of the equation, she felt the need to stay close by, just in case. Besides, she had her own agenda.

In the end, the great reunion had gone pretty well. There were the expected tears and general howling, a feature of her gender Sandra had never really related to, but Astra impressed with her general resilience. After a while Sandra excused herself for a pee, feeling it was okay to leave the two of them together, and leaving her to get on with a bit of snooping.

The house wasn't exactly what you'd call large – a reasonably strong tortoise could probably have carried it on its back – but neither was it cluttered. Sandra couldn't stand clutter. It stood on a new estate at the edge of town, rented after Matron had left her school job. Having left mother and daughter to it, Sandra drifted into the smaller of three bedrooms upstairs for a little peek around, as was her habit. The room smelt musty, of old books or newspapers, and she had to put a light on to find her way around. There was a desk with a computer, whose hard drive sat on the floor below the desk to conserve space, and a printer. Shelves crammed with red box files lined the walls, like too many sardines in a tin, causing one or two to buckle outwards. They were all neatly labelled and looked as if they'd only ever been used once. Sandra guessed they were bought afresh annually, as each one had a designated year, and there were a lot of years.

Sandra's natural curiosity led her to open one up: the most recent. With her grasp of speed-reading, within ten minutes she'd learned all she needed to know about the Seventy-Seven Society and the bond they'd all entered into. Guessing the computer would be password-protected, Sandra's practised eyes ran over the numbers in the most recent reports and she filed away the salient details in her reliable memory.

It was a simple picture, really, once you managed to cut your way through the undergrowth of bull. It didn't take her long to start planning the sting – a big one, maybe even her last if they got it right.

Go out with a bang. What made it so perfect was that executing the idea involved not just her, but Astra too. They'd secure their future together by working together.

------------------------------ ✳ ------------------------------

What about the Bond? That was the question, but Sam had struggled to come up with anything fresh beyond what he'd already told his mystery interlocutor. Besides, he was busy again, the curriculum having needed a total overhaul following a year when recruitment numbers had plummeted. He'd had a go at unpicking the spreadsheets on the society's website, but he couldn't make head nor tail of them. He thought about providing a link and the password to his mystery helper, but this contravened so many basic security protocols he just couldn't bring himself to do it.

Perhaps it was something else about the Bond: the way it was structured? It was hard finding an answer when he didn't even know what the question was; just like being back in German lessons at school. He was stumped.

------------------------------ ✳ ------------------------------

If they'd known the 2016 Seventy-Seven Society dinner was going to be their last they might have behaved differently, and the ugly scenes in the pub beforehand might have been avoided. As it happened, their familiarity with each other, lubricated with the best the new local microbrewery could offer, led to some heated exchanges over the subject that had riven the nation: Brexit. Like the country, the Seventy-Seveners were split into two ideological camps, with strong opinions unlikely to be swayed by the others' arguments; but unlike the country, the Remainers were in the majority; although the Leavers remained the more vocal and passionate.

Raised voices from the group managed to elevate above the general hubbub in the crowded pub, drawing disapproving looks from both the bar staff and most of the other patrons, none of whom looked older than thirty, including the manager. This unfamiliar anger, rather than bonhomie, was what greeted Reggie Richardson as he joined the throng, delayed through an argument over the car with Ellie, who wanted it in case she needed to visit her mother in hospital the next day. They'd downsized into a town house earlier that year, although in a different town, and part of the deal had been the halving of their family fleet to one, much to his son's, and Reggie's, discontent. He and Ellie had been going through a rough patch recently, and he didn't want to add any fuel to the fire of her moods, something Reggie put down to hormones and hoped would settle in time. In the end, he agreed to take an Uber, but given the time of year and the remoteness of where they lived, it took a while to turn up.

From the outside, his classmates looked a ragtail bunch, some wearing jackets with open-neck shirts, others in T-shirts too small for them and jeans. Whatever type of shirt they wore, they tended to avoid tucking it in, the looser arrangement being more effective in disguising their unmistakable late middle-aged spread. Reggie had managed to keep his weight under control since his diet, but it was a constant struggle. He was looking forward to a decent pint, but it was with a heavy twinge of guilt. Still, there was always dry January to look forward to, he sighed.

Ray, who Reggie correctly had down as a Eurosceptic, had uncharacteristically distanced himself from the debate and looked decidedly down in the dumps on his own – perched, rather than sat, on a bar stool; so Reggie resolved to do his best and go over and cheer him up.

'Tell you what,' he offered, raising his voice to make himself heard, 'I won't talk Brexit if you won't.'

'Deal,' Ray agreed, adding 'I'll take a half – no, make that a pint,' as he drained his glass and offered the empty to Reggie.

Their drinks ordered, Reggie and Ray looked on as most of their colleagues continued their fruitless arguing. Although he'd agreed to avoid the subject, some communication didn't need words. The bar staff, for example, were looking on with stares of contempt at the generation who, as they saw it, had stolen their future. Burdened with debt and with no hope of getting on the housing ladder, they were probably looking at the Seventy-Seveners as over-paid, over-pensioned and over-privileged; and by Reggie's reckoning, it probably wasn't an unreasonable assessment.

Reggie couldn't resist looking at the young girl who'd served him, a pretty twenty-odd-year-old (Reggie found it hard to guess these days) with an indistinguishable tattoo on the top of her chest, a nose stud and streaks of blue in her hair. How wonderful it was, he thought to himself, that she felt so free to express herself in that way. He had no problem with it, but, at the same time, couldn't help thinking how different things had been in their day. Remarking to no one in particular, but probably to Ray, he reflected: 'I suppose we're the establishment now.'

'How do you mean?'

'Well, look at them,' he replied, indicating the barmaid, who'd now moved on to serving another customer, 'they have a future, but we only have a past.'

'Cheery,' Ray observed, but without disagreeing.

'We've got something to protect, so it's no wonder we're so defensive, whereas they haven't even got going yet and can only deal in dreams.'

'Like in the election,' Ray offered.

'Exactly.' Reggie took a sip from his beer. 'Can't blame them, really. They're wrong, of course, we both know socialism doesn't work, but why should they trust what we say any more?'

Ray took a draught from his own glass, taking the top inch and a half off it. 'I suppose we were like that once.'

'My point exactly,' Reggie concurred. 'Once, but a long, long time ago.'

At that moment, Tom took advantage of a lull in the arguing to suggest they repair to the hotel over the road, no doubt hoping that a few lungfuls of cold air would calm tempers down a bit.

Against his expectations, they did, and by the time the eighteen people he had on his list had sat down, the atmosphere had undergone a 180-degree transformation. As Tom had often observed in the past, one of the advantages of knowing each other so well was the ability the group had to absorb to both strife and insult without recrimination, as well as the capacity to spin their collective mood in the blink of an eye.

Luckily he had an ace up his sleeve he could use to keep the atmosphere bubbling and introduce a fresh topic of conversation before things could revert to the negative. Ben Bradshaw had a word with him beforehand to float the idea of taking the whole group to the Oktoberfest in Munich the following autumn as a way of celebrating their fortieth year together, and when they were crossing the road he suggested to Ben that he might want to put his idea forward before they got started on the meal.

In a breach with convention, therefore, Ben happily stood up before the starter course and outlined his plans to a round of cheering and table-thumping worthy of the House of Commons. The general acclaim was something he'd never experienced before, and he felt a glow of satisfaction surge through him. 'This is only the start,' he told himself, and sat down to much back-slapping. A sense that celebrating their fortieth was an excellent plan was woven through the frenzied discussions that followed, with an unspoken undercurrent that their numbers might be much depleted if they delayed celebrations until their fiftieth. One or two had raised the idea of bringing wives, an idea that received all the support of a worn-out jockstrap, but otherwise harmony had well and truly been restored, and Tom sat back and took a deep breath. Everything was going to be okay.

Meanwhile, Sandra and Astra were upstairs in a room they'd taken in the hotel. After the successful bank holiday tea, they'd agreed they needed to gather more information, and Sandra suggested they could double their chances of getting it by passing themselves off as waitresses at the Seventy-Seven dinner: not as two different waitresses, but one. Presenting as a single person would mean one could look busy, giving the other more time to linger among the diners. Sandra was also keen to dry-run the whole two-as-one idea as it was a key component of the plan she was beginning to devise. Assuming they succeeded, they'd be able to disappear back to their bolthole for good, but after much discussion they agreed there was some unfinished business before they could finally rest: the small matter of seeing justice done to the beast who'd attacked Astra over four decades previously, ideally by dispensing said justice themselves. First, however, there was the small matter of identifying him.

They'd used their two days in the hotel to observe how it operated: its routines, quirks, timings, where the waiters and waitresses went to pick up food and where the dirty dishes went, and they'd learned that the hotel tended to use agency staff for larger functions, making it easier for them to blend in unnoticed. Just to be sure, they only made contact with the breakfast staff, who they knew wouldn't be around in the evening, further lessening their chances of being recognized.

Astra always liked it when they shared a single identity, drawing on her partner's confidence and presence as much as her looks. Being someone else was something she appreciated, as she didn't really like the person she was very much. On the night of the supper, they spent a couple of hours perfecting their joint look, merging each other's identities into one: make-up, hair, walk, mannerisms. Normally, Astra hated looking at herself in the mirror: her teeth had never got over her wilderness years, while her breasts looked like two half-deflated balloons. She started sweating again, although this time due to fear rather than the usual hormonal nonsense. Once they were ready, Sandra went downstairs first to get things rolling, leaving instructions for Astra to follow exactly ten minutes later, when they'd swap over. It came as a surprise, therefore, when she returned almost immediately, the face beneath her make-up drained of blood.

Down in the restaurant, Ray Meadows's haggard face was similarly pale. He'd seen the blonde hair; but then again, he always found it difficult to get beyond blonde hair – over the years he'd trained himself to stop staring at blonde hair for fear of a slew of restraining orders. This time he was sure it was her; but he'd been sure before. It was just a glance, but that was enough. Older, different somehow, but her: certainly, probably. Then, as quickly as she'd appeared, she was gone, and he was left totally bamboozled. He had to find her. She was here, close enough to touch, to smell, to talk to. He just had to find her.

'He's here,' Sandra panted, sitting on the edge of their bed back in the room, her long locks framing her face.

'How do you know?' Astra asked: surely she was the only one capable of identifying her assailant.

'No, not him. Ray Meadows, my first ever mark. He's a Red Coater.'

'Meadows? The name rings a bell but ...'

The initial shock over, Sandra grabbed the initiative. 'You'll have to go down. Take the service lift and blend in,' she commanded, and as was her way, when Sandra commanded, Astra obeyed. Feeling positive and self-assured, if still a little confused, she entered the function room holding two glasses of wine she'd picked up on the way, a glass in each hand. What she saw was a room of strangers, with one or two vaguely familiar faces. But before she got a chance to look properly, a big man with a thick neck and a stick began to accelerate towards her, tapping out a monosyllabic distress call in Morse on the polished floor, his face full of intent.

'Hey! You!' the man shouted, continuing his rocking passage towards her, a pointed finger raised slightly in the air. As he tottered towards her, the muscles in his face seemed to relax and his eyes narrowed slightly, as if in confusion.

Inside Ray's brain two sets of instructions were beginning to conflict. One set told him to keep going, to reach his prey; the other, that maybe he'd been mistaken after all. Was he making a fool of himself? She had blonde hair, sure, and she certainly looked remarkably like Sandra, but something niggling away in his visual cortex was raising doubts. Just at that moment he received two glasses of wine thrown into his eyes in quick succession.

Immediately following the shock, he tried to yell 'Stop!' to buy some time, but the wine was stinging his eyes and instead there were voices yelling at him. 'Sit down, you old lech,' one advised, and 'Quit fiddling with the waitresses, Ray' another, so he limped blindly back to his chair to wipe his eyes with his napkin and lick his wounds.

Back in the room, Sandra and Astra decided to let matters calm down a bit. Things weren't going according to plan, and Sandra didn't like it when her plans didn't work out. There had to be another way. A full hour later they were both back downstairs, although Astra had changed out of the waitress uniform and pinned back her long golden hair.

Back in the function room, the two women were studying developments from a hidden vantage point behind a stack of chairs at the back of the room. The husband, or father-in-law, whatever, was on his feet and the rest of the room was silent, the occupants of the chairs around the table all looking up at him. From where they were standing, the two women could see down one side of the table and, in a large mirror on the wall opposite, the other side too. Sandra followed her partner's eyes as she scanned the two rows of middle-aged men.

'That's him,' she suddenly squeaked, pointing her finger. 'That's the one who …' but she didn't finish, her knees going from under her as she began to collapse.

She didn't have to finish her sentence, as in an instant Sandra grabbed her and pulled her close, stroking her tightly compact golden hair. 'Shh, shh,' she whispered, 'it's all right, Sandra's here,' adding to herself silently, 'and Sandra's going to sort everything out.'

2017

It took Ben longer than he hoped to get all the ducks in line for the Oktoberfest trip. His new commitments had kept him busier than ever, and when it was suggested that he might want to become non-executive chairman of Doze on two-thirds of the money but only around 10 per cent of the time, it was an offer he couldn't refuse. Then, at the turn of the year, there'd been the small matter of the New Year's Honours list.

Recognition at last.

He didn't want to put too much of a burden on Tom Joules: the man had been through the wringer lately, but he was Mr Seventy-Seven and he couldn't cut him out. The good news was that his wife seemed to be pulling through, and Ben had organized a big bouquet of flowers to be sent to keep her onside. Nigel Bennett had also delivered, and secured the promise of a plane, one of the new Dreamliners, subject to the usual rules and regulations, which Ben left to him. There wouldn't be enough of them for their own charter, but sharing a scheduled flight was fine. The plan was to zip over to Munich on the Thursday night and be back in time for the headmaster's feast at the school on the Sunday – although in reality this was less of a feast and more of a light finger buffet accompanied by glasses of indifferent wine, an event that always marked the end of Benefactor's Day at the Red Coat. At this point, wives and partners would join them. An all-round perfect little jaunt, all thanks to the beneficent Sir Benjamin Bradshaw.

Ben had also taken it upon himself to reconcile the school and their year group through the good offices of Red Coat Forever, where he'd even run into the old DHM who he hadn't appreciated was even alive, let alone active. Ben was surprised to discover no raised eyebrows, no 'you must be kidding', when he'd introduced the idea of working together to track down the Class of '77. They were ancient history, it seemed: just another picture on the walls.

--------------------------------- ✷ ---------------------------------

Paul Briton wasn't proud of how things had gone with the Bond, and when Ray approached him in the role of co-steward of the 77B he allowed himself a wry smile.

Ray was in the shitter. He was having to restart his business as an online-only offering, but he needed a little start-up money for the website and publicity. Surely, this was the sort of investment the Bond had been set up to help with? In reality, what Ray really needed was a Get Out of Jail Free card, both figuratively, and possibly legally too; and finding some way to unlock the Bond was his best hope.

It hadn't taken five minutes for Paul to spark up his trademark Brilliantine grin and inform him that the Bond wasn't just in the shitter too, but that the chain was about to be pulled. Three years before maybe it might have been possible; five years ago they'd been really minted; but now, well, it was a different story.

The smile hadn't lasted long as Paul related his pathetic tale. He simply didn't have the Thompson touch, it seemed. There was still some money scattered around, but it was tied up. The rest had simply vanished, disappeared, vamoosed. Shares in banks that no longer existed, savings in banks that probably wished they no longer existed, and money in property you couldn't give away to squatters, all added up to a disaster. The only thing Paul Briton still had going for him was that no one had noticed. Not yet, anyway. He'd managed to obfuscate the annual reports enough with forward projections based on wild assumptions to avoid any light spilling on to the figures, but he doubted he could do it again for the next report. He'd run out of hiding places.

Ray empathized; it sounded a familiar tale. He'd just been about to suggest that they both went out and got completely bladdered when Paul extracted an envelope from his inside jacket pocket.

'What's that?' Ray asked.

'Possibly, just possibly, our salvation, old boy.'

Ray sat down again. 'Go on.'

'A VIP pass to the top tables at Monte Carlo, all hotel expenses paid.'

Ray laughed out loud, but Paul remained completely, and

uncharacteristically, serious. The debate that followed between them combined a mixture of hope and farce. Both were desperate, both had no alternative, and within minutes, both had booked flights to Nice on the internet. If you were going to go down, they reasoned, you may as well go down in style; and when the day came, they polished off a bottle of Krug in the airport lounge before getting on the plane.

Later that evening, safely settled into their hotel facing the Mediterranean, both could be forgiven for thinking their luck might be about to turn. The pass, some kind of client hospitality thing from Paul's work, which both of them were healthily sceptical about, had proved to be the real deal. Given the fall of the pound, they'd got good exchange rates at the currency cage, which was more like a kiosk in a private bank, and both were carrying handfuls of chips of varying sizes and colours.

Initially they'd satisfied themselves with mingling among the games and tables, soaking up the atmosphere and the miasma of champagne and decadence that seemed to hover over the room, as if they were two footmen who'd been invited to share lunch with royalty. The rooms in the casino quite literally smelt of privilege and wealth: aromas which emanated from the women who wandered their corridors and also lingered by the tables, and in the way that everyone seemed to waft through proceedings, as if the whole exercise was simply a prelude to the next diversion.

It was like wandering about in a dream. At one point Ray even thought he saw his mysterious blonde, but he put that down to the excitement of the occasion. He didn't think he'd ever be able to trust his eyes again, and he made a mental note to have them checked as soon as he got back. Meanwhile, the chips he'd bought with borrowed money were burning a hole in his pockets, but something stopped him from playing them, as if by doing so he would cross a line from which there was no return. Paul, on the other hand, appeared to be buzzing: flitting between blackjack and the wheel, tossing chips on to velvet as if distributing bread to ducks, like a man who wanted to get the whole sordid exercise over with. They split up for a while, and when they met up again Ray was surprised to see Paul's smile had returned, his mood changed.

'I'm thirty grand up,' he whispered, his eyes revealing his delight, 'and we haven't even been here an hour.' Ray had yet to place a bet. To steady his nerves he helped himself to some more of the complimentary sparkling stuff. Past experience told him his most relaxed state was just past the drink-drive limit.

'Go on, break your duck, old boy,' Paul urged, nudging him in the ribs with an elbow. 'No point in being here otherwise.' Ray returned his own version of a smile, a gesture that didn't require showing any teeth, and dipped a nervous set of fingers into his chip-laden pocket.

'Soon,' he replied, before repeating 'soon', as if by saying it often enough he'd start to believe himself.

The resemblance to the blonde was uncanny, and if it hadn't been for the diamonds round her neck, and the gold knuckleduster rings on the fingers of the big tuxedoed man with her, he may even have approached her. A clock somewhere, almost certainly an antique, struck midnight.

'Okay, let's do it,' Ray announced, shaken into action, and he slid off his leather-padded bar stool. In an attempted fluid motion, marred by the awkwardness of his limp, Ray marched towards the next room, dominated by a single roulette table sited in the centre, with a crowd of elegantly dressed adults all transfixed by the progress of a small ball, no larger than a marble, whirling round a spinning wheel lined with numbers.

'Right-oh,' Paul agreed, coming up from behind. 'Time for The Big One.'

Ray kept his gaze halfway between the table and the floor, not daring to look anyone in the eye, and still not quite believing he was about to do what he was about to do. They hovered over the table with silence between them. Paul was fidgeting awkwardly in his jacket pockets as if trying to find a handkerchief.

A sweat broke out on Ray's high forehead and he began to wish it was a handkerchief Paul had been looking for: he could have done with one at that precise moment. Instead it was a small mountain of chips, some of them still in their wrappers, as if they were giant tubes of Smarties. Without being actively conscious of doing so, Ray dug deep into his own pockets and extracted an even bigger tube of similarly coloured discs.

'Well? What's it to be?' Paul enquired, as they muscled their way ever so politely to the front of the table.

'Eh?' he asked, incomprehensibly.

'Red or black?' Paul asked, a touch of impatience creeping into his voice. Ray realized at that moment that they were both going to place everything they had on a single bet.

'Red for me. Has to be, doesn't it?'

'Red?' Ray enquired.

'Red for Red Coat,' Paul replied. 'Stands to reason.' And with that he leaned forward and put all his chips on the red rectangle on the baize, opening out his thumbs and closing his fingers to make a U-shaped shovel to do so. A small but polite gasp went around the table and heads turned towards the two Englishmen. At that moment, Ray felt obliged to act; he'd never ducked a challenge in his life. He followed suit, although his damaged legs didn't allow him to lean forward as far as Paul had done, pushing his chips out into the centre of the table.

'Here, let me help,' Paul offered. 'Where do you want it?'

'Er, I'm not sure,' Ray fumbled. If he was perfectly honest with himself he wasn't sure he wanted it on anything. He was confused. The champagne. The lights. The atmosphere. The blondie. Is this what his life had come to? Is this what everything amounted to? Time was ticking on, so Paul laid the bet for him. The croupier, a girl with a sonorous French accent, summarized the various stakes and declared the end of betting.

Something about her gravel-chewing voice made Ray look up and take in the whole scene, one he'd been avoiding up until then, as if actually seeing it was an acknowledgement that it was real.

It was her. Sandra. Not the one in the diamonds, but the croupier.

She must have changed. But how could she? Ray's mind began to do cartwheels as he locked eyes with her.

The grin that spread all over her face as he did so removed any doubt. As the three-quarter-inch diameter ball, made from ordinary nylon, began to jump as if it had St Vitus's Dance, he knew that he'd had found the girl he'd been looking for all his adult life, and at the same time he'd probably just lost all his money.

----------------------------- ✱ -----------------------------

'Did you pack this suitcase yourself, sir?'

A reflex action kicked in and Reggie replied, 'Yes,' without pausing to consider whether he, in fact, had. Did he look like the sort of man who packed his own suitcase, he wondered? After receiving his boarding pass he headed for security and reminded himself that when it came to airports, resistance was futile: you just had to slip into neutral and roll with it.

Reggie was broken from his reverie by a tap on the shoulder from Ray Meadows. It seemed to be his fate in life to bump into Ray Meadows before any Seventy-Seven Society function, something else life had taught him to just accept. Ray looked a lot older than his years, even since the last dinner a little under a year before. His eyes were in danger of sinking completely into his head, and his near-bald pate was covered in brown freckles. Although Reggie regarded himself as having weathered the years reasonably well, he had recently developed some trouble with his hearing – especially in crowded environments with echoing acoustics, where the constant grumbling of background noise seemed to cancel out specific words, causing him to rely on a mixture of lip-reading and guesswork, as Ray mumbled small talk.

Tom Joules was waiting for them on the other side of security, adjacent to the duty-free as agreed. Paul Briton and Toby O'Connor soon followed, each clutching the small carry-on bag Tom had advised them to bring to save time in Munich. For some reason Paul was wearing a tropical shirt, as if he'd not actually understood where

Munich was, while Toby was doused in an aftershave so pungent it repelled even the customs' sniffer dogs. When he'd first arrived, Toby had thought he was in the wrong place, surrounded as he was by old people, as if he was at a cruise terminal rather than an airport, before he realized he was one of those old people. Tom, meanwhile, busied himself constantly counting and recounting how many had arrived. The clipboard in front of him suggested he had a schedule for them, but then again Tom always had schedules for the Seventy-Seven; and although they weren't always adhered to, that never stopped him from making them.

Tom had adopted a position by the Estée Lauder stand and was ticking each member off a list as they arrived: a list much longer than usual, given Ben's efforts with the school and an extra push from Tom. Before long, their group was generating its own tornado of noise and Reggie was forced to press his lip-reading skills into hyperdrive. Eddie Perks, meanwhile, dressed in a smart suit and wearing the name badge Tom had provided in the post, something he'd yet to realize everyone else had dispensed with, was being kept busy with people asking him where Paco Rabanne was; and as he couldn't remember anyone called Paco in their year, he assumed the approaches were part of some elaborate joke and played along, directing his enquirers to all parts of the hall.

Despite being the trip's paymaster, Ben Bradshaw, or Sir Ben as they might have to call him – at least initially (there was a concerted effort going on to find an alternative) – was the last to arrive, looking slightly flustered but pleased to be there. He was a little more rotund these days, something he put down to all the lunches he went to; in the past, he'd never really considered lunch a serious meal.

'Bugger of a journey,' he proclaimed to anyone who'd listen. 'Alarm didn't go off, car wouldn't start, traffic on the motorway, didn't think I was going to make it.' He beamed, clearly genuinely pleased that everyone was there, and privately quite gratified to be last and make an entrance. 'Coffee, anyone?' he enquired, keen to set the ball of his generosity rolling.

'Balls to that!' Ray yelled back at him. 'Time you bought us all a real drink, mate!' and Ben raised one of his small mitt-like hands in instant acquiescence. Meanwhile Toby Connor, who had his back turned to the crowd and just caught the end of the last word, began to walk away from the gathering. Thinking Ray had just said 'gate', he raised his eyes to the TV screen showing departures, and missed the crowd drifting off towards the Scottish bar in the corner of the hall. A few seconds later, he caught a reflection of himself in the glass front of a Gucci concession. He didn't look too bad, he thought, guessing that most people would estimate his age as 'fifties' rather than 'late fifties'. There were bags under his eyes, it was true, but they came with the profession, as did the awkward posture, the result of too much standing up in front of a classroom. Too late, he realized he was staring at a solitary figure. Where had everyone gone?

The answer was that they were all in the bar, drinking, confident that Tom Joules would let them know when they had to get moving, his towering presence acting as a sort of watchtower above them. A carnival atmosphere was developing, almost as if this was to be the group's final hurrah: a sentiment that was uncomfortably close to the truth, as things turned out. Clutching his usual orange juice and tonic, Tom positioned himself opposite a screen near the entrance to the bar, which was how Toby Connor was eventually able to spot, and rejoin, the party.

As soon as the departure gate was displayed on the screen, Tom downed his juice and put a hand to the side of his mouth. 'Gentlemen!' he shouted in order to be heard, his announcement reminiscent of all the times he'd gathered his flock in pubs scattered across their home town.

'Ah! Think that's last orders, lads,' Ray responded, much to Tom's annoyance. 'Who wants another?'

'Gentlemen!' Tom repeated, 'I really think ...'

Ray was gesticulating to a barman with his stick. Reggie caught himself wondering if he might get away with ordering a shandy for this round – he only had to look at a beer these days to put on two pounds – but ultimately he decided that the opprobrium this would receive wasn't worth it. 'So, that's five John Smiths, two lagers …' At the use of this word, Ray pulled a mock look of disgust, 'and six G and Ts.' Ben, meanwhile, was extracting a credit card from his wallet. Tom gave up and resigned himself to waiting for the final call, his foot tapping on the floor as if to a long-forgotten tune, his eyebrows twitching.

A quarter of an hour later, Ben Bradshaw raised one of his pudgy hands in the air and within seconds everyone drowned their drinks and began to follow him out of the bar as if he was the Pied Piper. Toby Connor started to follow and then checked himself. He'd forgotten his bag and had to return to where he'd been drinking to pick it up. A rather attractive youngish brunette woman had already lifted it up to give to him, and as he took it Toby kissed her hand by way of thanks: something he didn't think he'd ever done before in his life. As a result, he found himself having to run to catch up with the others as they made their way towards the departure gate, a deep red bloom infusing the top of his cheeks.

As his little legs caught up with the stragglers, Toby found himself beginning to wheeze like an asthmatic with a cold, forcing him to pause for a moment and bend down, his hands resting on the tops of his knees, as he struggled to regain equilibrium. In the corner of his eye he saw a young woman, about the same age as the brunette whose hand he'd just kissed. She looked at him as if he was a dog that would probably benefit from a lethal dose of whatever they used to put dogs down. Was this how others saw him, he wondered? As a rather pathetic middle-aged man struggling to keep up, not just with his friends, but with life in general? It must be like seeing a favourite old band performing when the wrinkles and sagging chins were shouting that they should stop, act their age and preserve some dignity. What had he been thinking, back then at the bar? The woman was young enough to be his daughter; younger, probably. The smile she gave him had more likely been one of pity rather than anything else. This epiphany did nothing to hasten his speed of recovery.

In the end they were the last to join the lengthy queue that had formed in the departure lounge, much to Tom's annoyance. 'Bags of time,' Ray said reassuringly. 'No point in rushing, they ain't going to take off without us.' At that moment Tom realized he actively hated Ray Meadows, and probably had done for as long as he could remember.

Within seconds the hostess by the door flicked a switch and began speaking into a microphone. 'Good morning to passengers travelling on Flight GH404 to Munich this morning. For the safety and comfort of everyone flying with us today we invite passengers with seats in rows zero through twenty to proceed to boarding.'

'That's us!' Ben yelled, and again, as he raised his arm, everyone followed, filing past the two guard-like airline representatives by the door like the schoolboys on their first day of school they'd once been, all those aeons ago. Through Nigel, he'd managed to do a deal to get them all upgraded to business class. Once inside the metal tube that linked them to the aircraft they slowed to a post-office-queue crawl as they approached the door. With difficulty Ray craned his neck to catch a sight of Nigel at the controls, who at that very moment appeared at the window clutching a key, pulling a face and mouthing something they couldn't hear. Toby Connor at the front of the procession interpreted.

'He says they've got the wrong key, they can't get it started.' As soon as he said the words, a look of dread passed across Reggie Richardson's cadaverous face. Reggie was not a good flyer and had been anticipating problems all morning, as well as the night before.

'He's pulling your leg, you daft sod,' Paul Briton said, breaking into a laugh. He was standing near the front and witnessed the whole exchange. 'Here, have a boiled sweet.' He extracted a couple from his pocket, but Reggie declined. No eating between meals. Paul stood to one side and gently pulled Reggie in to join him.

'Ladies first,' he gestured, sweeping a half-drunk hand and arm into the doorway and allowing Susan Grant, elegantly dressed in a skirt and top with gold earrings matching her necklace, to enter before them.

She smiled, before murmuring 'Beauty before balls' under her breath as she passed, though this style of speech brought out a deeper register in her voice. Paul nodded in acknowledgement and pinched her on the backside as she went through.

Inside the plane, the men and solitary woman of the Seventy-Seven Society party waited patiently as their fellow passengers suddenly realized they were supposed to have readied themselves to sit down and, in a state of sudden revelation, began to rummage in their bags for books, e-readers, spectacles and smartphones, apologizing as they did so yet still continuing to clog the aisle, preventing any further passage.

Eventually, most people had sat down. Some were hoping to sleep, while others were flicking through the magazines in the seat backs in front of them.

'Any films?' Ray Meadows enquired.

'*The Hunt for Red October?*' Derek Henderson volunteered, to groans from a couple of his peers, and then a couple more, as they got the double reference.

'*The Munich Disaster?*' Toby chipped in, taking the seat next to Ray.

'No such film,' Ray responded, settling into his chair, wriggling his bum to ensure maximum comfort.

'Not a film; a prediction,' replied Reggie.

'Cheer up, you miserable prat.' Sam Davidson, the final member to sit down, was making his first contribution since they'd left the bar.

Toby noticed that his companion to his left had sunk quite low into his seat, causing his seatbelt to ride up over his considerable midriff, and whispered 'Sit up, Ray' through the side of his mouth.

'Eh? What?' Ray grabbed the tops of his chair's arms and hoisted himself up with a 'humph' of effort, before sitting down again. 'Damned chair,' he muttered, before dropping the whole of his not inconsiderable bulk down again.

The moment his backside hit the recently vacuumed fabric beneath, an extraordinarily loud, and oddly visceral, thump echoed through the plane, as if someone was testing a tuba's lowest notes. The reverberation itself lasted for less than two seconds – although, as it turned out, the reverberation from the reverberation lasted considerably longer.

'Ray!' half a dozen voices shouted at once.

'Can it, will you?' complained one.

'Christ, man,' echoed another.

Ray issued no denial, and in so doing, according to the ancient code of wind-droppers, proclaimed his guilt. His silence wasn't an act of self-incrimination, however; there was something odd with his seat, and the restraining effect of the seat belt was making it impossible for him to get comfortable. In another effort to do so, he hoisted himself up in a way that appeared, to any outsider who knew him, to suggest preparation for a follow-up, but the belt pulled him back, dragging him into the seat with all his weight behind him.

As his backside hit the springs, the seat collapsed and he carried on falling. At precisely that moment a loud, eardrum-splitting explosion, too terrifying to be of human origin, dominated the narrow space they were sitting in, filling it with a dark grey cloud which floated instantly to the ceiling creating its own micro-climate, sending small droplets of liquid to fall on the stunned heads below. A small shaft of daylight could be seen through the smoke, but not enough to provide air to those at the front of the aircraft, who were, by then, slowly suffocating.

A hostess, who'd only joined the plane seconds before, peeked in and then ran back down the corridor connecting the plane to the departure gate. This offered little reassurance to those in the rows nearest the explosion, who remained stunned by what had just happened. Meanwhile, those who'd joined more recently, most of whom were still standing, immediately pirouetted on their ankles and began a stampede for the entrance. Those who'd already sat down automatically reached for their seatbelt buckles and were preparing to evacuate by any means possible. In less time than it would take a hostess to smile, people were up and shoving through the wall of stunned and panicking humanity in front of them, the more materially-minded pausing to grab hand luggage from the overhead lockers in a scene that resembled the end of a normal flight, only at fast-forward speed. Towards the front of the plane, where the Seventy-Seveners were sitting, all was still.

Within an implausibly short period of time, the interior of the plane filled with men wearing body armour and carrying guns with red lights at the end, shouting at everyone to get out, while at the same time demanding room for paramedics to come through and rescue those who'd succumbed to the storm blast of gas. The result, predictably, was more panic, solved only when one of the airline's crew made it to the back of the plane to open the rear doors and summoned someone to bring some stairs.

As the smoke rushed out of the back of the plane only one person remained strapped to his seat: Ray Meadows, his damaged knees bent double, his feet resting in his lap, his head fallen forward on his chest, revealing the full extent of his male-pattern baldness. As the smoke cleared, Toby turned to his companion to see if he needed any help, but rapidly came to the conclusion there was nothing he could do: a deduction formed largely on the basis that a hole about the size and shape of a rugby ball had been blown out of Ray's groin and lower stomach and he was, quite clearly, dead.

------------------------------ ✱ ------------------------------

The Benefactor's Day service in the local cathedral had finished; although for some, it was unclear whether they'd attended a thanksgiving or a memorial. Either way, the choir had performed to their usual excellent standard, and the current Rev had spoken clearly and with compassion. Some of the congregation were now beginning to file up the central nave towards the medieval wooden doors at the front. Most of the Class of '77 and their partners remained in their seats in silent contemplation for a moment, trying to catch all the thoughts buzzing in their heads and bring them to ground. In a well-practised routine, the boys were filing out of the aisles in row order. They were generally smart and patient in a way few of the older members of the congregation remembered themselves being at that age, especially considering it wasn't even a school day.

They seemed clean-cut, obedient and just generally well mannered, and much more ethnically diverse than in the Seventy-Seveners' day:

a regular United Nations. This led more than one of those still sitting to contemplate not only the fate of their own two non-white school friends but also how they'd treated them, and maybe even regret some of the things they'd said forty years – a generation – ago.

Psychedelic particles of dust hung suspended in the air, illuminated by the fading light shining down from the stained-glass windows above, as the guests eventually filed out of the ancient building. Outside it was cold, the first blasts of autumn having finally arrived, bringing with them dilemmas over what to wear. It was just warm enough inside to not need a coat, but chilly enough outside to make you wish you'd brought one. A weak sun was on the point of sinking, and tiny tornados of wind were scattering russet-coloured leaves.

During the service, many of those now shuffling their way towards the doors had caught themselves praying for the first time since they'd been at school, when they'd been prepared to try anything to achieve their required grades. They had mouthed their way through the hymns, joining in on the chorus, and most Old Red Coaters had remembered the gist of the school hymn without having to consult their orders of service, all in all, making a genuine contribution to the combination of sound and piety that had just taken place.

The dean who led the service had alluded obliquely to those in the congregation with more to be thankful for than most; although everyone there knew who he was referring to. Understandably, he'd refrained from using the shorthand headline that the world had adopted for the experience the surviving members of the Class of '77 had been through. Thanks to the power of the internet, news of an incident at a major British airport had spread around the world almost before the last people were out of the plane, and certainly before the black body bag provided for the very last putative passenger had been zipped up and labelled.

The trauma the surviving members had been through just three days previously had shaken them all. None had ever been through anything like it before, and all now realized the perpetrator's intention was that they'd never go through anything ever again. Unlike so many others of their peer group over the years, they had survived their brush with mortality. They, it seemed, were actually the lucky ones.

Unravelling the complex emotions they were feeling was going to be a problem on a par with the annual challenge of untangling the Christmas tree fairy lights, only it was going to take much longer. Instant analysis had shown that the seat Ray had been sitting in, 7J – which, the first time he'd seen it, he'd mistaken for 77 – had been loaded with a highly volatile explosive, injected into the seat minutes before and designed to detonate when the plane was at high altitude. Enough to blow a big enough hole in the fuselage to send the plane crashing to earth. Ray's wriggling had disturbed the wiring to the detonator, causing it to go off, and only his sheer bulk had saved them all from instant death by absorbing the worst of the blast.

The press, however, didn't deal with complex emotions. Instead, in a move that gave evidence to the theory that journalists worldwide tended to operate on the same wavelength, the shock and general distress that those on the flight had been through was reduced to a short, easily digestible phrase. In Russia it was known as the воняйте бомба Заговор, and in Greece, readers came to know of the Βρωμούσες βομβιστική συνωμοσία. For a short while the French played with the snappy appellation *Pet Vol*, or Fart Flight, before succumbing to international pressure and adopting the less idiomatic *Boule Puante Complot*, or Stinkbomb Conspiracy. It was as if the world had had enough of dreadful terrorist attacks, and the press was grateful to have an incident they could make relative light of; while paying due respect to the single unlucky victim, naturally.

Outside, the chill air caused Paul Briton's round cheeks to redden. Looking around, he noticed how most of his classmates' ears seemed to have swelled over the years, with one or two evolving into the sort of appendages normally seen gracing the side of a pig's head in the butchers. He also couldn't help but notice that Reggie and Ellie Richardson were holding hands as they walked solemnly down the drive, which was odd because for years they'd been everyone's favourites for membership of the dispatches club of divorcees. It was strange the effect shock could have. As he progressed down the asphalt to the main school buildings, Paul also noticed a large white marquee on the headmaster's usually immaculate striped lawn, a stretch of sward more suited to croquet than high heels, which he supposed had been erected for the traditional feast. His arm was in a sling: a sprained wrist, sustained not in the plane, but by stupidly tripping over a discarded item of hand luggage when he'd reached the terminal, his vision still blurred from the smoke. Much of the right-hand side of his torso was still painful under the bandages protecting his burns, hidden by the crisp brand-new white shirt his wife had brought for him, still showing its crease marks.

As he walked gingerly down the drive, Paul, along with many others now emerging into the late afternoon coolness, also clocked the ranks of blue-uniformed policemen lining the route back into the school. Paul wondered whether the authorities had managed to secure its long-hoped-for royal patron and this was a protection squad, albeit a rather big one.

Paul was right about the policemen: it was a protection squad, but not for any royals. The Stinkbomb Conspiracy still represented unfinished business, and the British authorities were not in any mood for further embarrassment. As the file of guests and dignitaries reached the brick and flint exterior of the Grand Hall, activity levels among the police seemed to increase, with some checking mugshot photos on iPads and others whispering into radios.

Small clouds of smoke identified the location of a cabal of the socially ostracized, taking the opportunity to reacquaint themselves with their e-cigarettes. Most people, however, were walking on; some with their eyes to the ground in contemplation, others looking up, taking in the changes that had taken place since they'd last been there, or pointing out old classrooms and other ex-haunts to their partners.

The school seemed much more contained than in their day, with skilled architects having made clever use of the space available; although the price of efficiency seemed to be the loss of the sense of space and freedom most of the older ex-pupils recalled – at the same time, recognizing that this may have been their memories playing tricks on them. Meanwhile, anyone making a study of what the policemen were doing would have noticed they were selectively taking out certain guests and inviting them to follow a different route, marked out by hastily erected ropes borrowed from the gym, threaded through the gaps in the back of standard-issue grey plastic chairs, more usually found in the Great Hall at exam time.

Their targets were the members of the Seventy-Seven Society and their partners, all of whom had decided, in an act of solidarity, to persevere with their plans to attend Benefactor's Day. All had been subject to questioning and some also to treatment in hospital where, although few would have noticed, they'd each had armed guards outside their doors.

It was fair to say that most were unfamiliar with this occasion and its protocols, and therefore most of the women had opted for sub-wedding outfits. Others had opted for work suits and scarves: functional, but not quite enough to arrest the development of goose bumps of a size and distribution more usually seen on coarse sandpaper. The men, other than those whose injuries prevented it, all wore their best suits.

The rope led them under an archway and into the marquee. There was little conversation, as the middle-aged men and women were generally still shell-shocked and getting used to somehow being exceptions, worthy of being singled out and protected. It made them feel both special and yet inconvenienced at the same time. Most, however, were simply resigned to the fact that their lives were, temporarily at least, out of their own control. Inside the marquee, a series of heaters had been scattered which rotated their warmth like lighthouses spreading illumination, although the heat they issued was enjoyed only sporadically by those lucky enough to be in its path.

A horseshoe had been created out of more of the chairs they'd seen outside, spread out on a wooden platform over the flawless grass beneath, the stripes of which were still visible through gaps: something 'Fingers' Dalgliesh would have no doubt appreciated if only things had worked out differently. Outside, the shadowy figures on the other side of the canvas prowled up and down, their arms clutching lightweight machine guns. A table was set up away from the slope of the tent to one side, where vacuum flasks of tea and coffee had been left. One by one, people helped themselves, dispensing the tan-coloured liquid of choice by operating a pump on top of the flasks, before finding a seat. Across the other side of the tent, facing the chairs, were three large boards sitting on trestles, each covered with a green baize cloth.

Everyone was waiting for something to happen and after about ten minutes of uncomfortable mingling, a grey-haired man about ten years younger than them bounded into the room with an energy most could only aspire to. He was wearing a school tie, although not the Old Red Coater barber's-pole version, and an immaculate dark grey suit with highly polished black shoes which clattered on the wooden floor as he marched his way into the centre of the improvised stage. In the occluded light his freshly shaved face shone out like a beacon, reflecting some of the amber glow from the heaters.

The waiting throng now knew, although they hadn't at the start of the afternoon, that this was the current headmaster, Jack Thomas. He looked like a hedge fund manager who'd made an attempt at fancy dress, with his university cloak complete with a red fur-lined hood sitting awkwardly on his shoulders. Jack's parents knew him as John but given his choice of profession he had elected to go by the alternative, which he felt gave the added advantage of sounding less formal. His arrival precipitated the taking of chairs.

'Gentlemen,' he began, as soon as everyone had settled, his air that of a man used to being listened to without having to raise his voice. He went on to add, 'and ladies', with a deferential nod to no one in particular. He'd acquired the habit of adding this suffix since the introduction of girls to the sixth form, but that wasn't the same as having got used to it.

'Let me start by offering my sincere apologies for any inconvenience you may be suffering. Let me assure you that everything is being done to ensure both your safety and your comfort.' At this point he went on to detail both the fire escape route and the way to the nearest toilets, adding that those present wouldn't have to ask for permission first. The impact of this attempt at humour was diluted, however, when he added that they would require an armed guard should they feel the need to absent themselves for any reason. With this news, most of the recently acquired cups were put down in order to forestall any possibility of an accompanied visit.

With the preliminaries over, he moved on to deliver an eloquent impromptu speech, at the outset of which he visibly shifted gear from vigilant host to concerned, yet distantly connected, observer of events, expressing his greatest sympathy both for everything they'd all been through and, of course, for the loss of one of their number. He also shared his relief that they had all come through what must have been a horrendous ordeal, something he hoped could be put down in some small way to the old Red Coat Spirit, and although none of those listening knew exactly what he meant by this, it was greeted by a general murmur of assent.

'I'm now going to hand you over to a man I'm sure you all recall with affection from your time here,' he concluded, his responsibility for introducing what was about to unfold clearly discharged: 'Clive Porter.'

Almost without exception the men in the audience expressed some form of surprise, whether through the raising of eyebrows, a small gasp or, in some cases, a nervous cough. It turned out that Clive Porter, better known to the cognoscenti as the DHM, who most of the old boys rapidly calculated must be near his nineties, hadn't left the building. In another surprise, he was accompanied by the man they'd all known simply at school as the Rev, who was half-walking, half-waddling a pace behind the DHM: a human safety bag should the man in front of him fall backwards, his vestments dragging on the ground making him less the would-be disciple in sandals, and more like an overgrown Dalek. Once so fresh-faced, the Rev carried himself as a man confused, as if he didn't really know why he was there and would much rather be somewhere else. As Clive made a slow progress towards the front, an aluminium stick banging the wooden flooring on every other step, the headmaster made one final contribution to fill the silence.

'As many of you may know,' although few, in fact, did, 'Clive has made a significant contribution over the years to building and maintaining our alumni database and tracking down as many Old Red Coaters as possible, so we can keep in touch with them.' As one, the old boys present added the single collective thought: 'and send out begging letters to them', before the headmaster concluded for a second time: 'And the school is indebted to him for his efforts.' Here he paused and began to raise his hands in a brief consideration of starting a round of applause before, in the circumstances, deciding against it. It was a slightly disappointing end to his contribution, one he wished he'd thought through more carefully beforehand.

'Gentlemen,' the DHM half-whispered, half-whistled, his teeth offering further evidence of his advanced years. He seemed to be struggling to catch his breath, and in his distressed state had forgotten to include the fairer sex in his opening. As he gathered himself, few chose to reflect that while they'd always regarded him as old, when they'd been at school he'd probably been younger than they were now. In a portent of what they might have to look forward to in the future, his skin had lost most of its elasticity and the knuckles on each hand stood out like unlanced boils.

'Welcome,' he continued, and, as if to dispel a growing belief that he was going to speak one word at a time, he added: 'I wish', slowly building up a head of steam before going for the complete sentence: 'that it could have been in happier circumstances.' He appeared visibly relieved at this point and nodded to the Rev, who hobbled over to the covered boards at the back of the marquee.

One by one, the Rev pulled back three green baize cloths in slow, deliberate movements. As he did so, it became clear that each board was covered with photographs of members of the Seventy-Seven Society, all sharing one common characteristic, in that they were dead. To make matters all the more poignant, each picture was accompanied by a smaller black and white counterpoint photo of the individual in question, taken the year they left school, each of which appeared to have been enlarged from the year photo, and therefore quite pixelated.

After a few brief seconds, the stunned silence that had descended on the tent was rent apart by a deep, almost animal, sobbing noise, the source of which was revealed to be none other than the school's most recently knighted old boy, Ben Bradshaw. It was as if with each reveal, the Rev peeled away another layer of painfully acquired skin protecting deep wounds beneath that had never properly healed. The lips on Ben's contorted face had peeled back over his gums like those of a laughing monkey, with the sound emanating between them reinforcing this impression. The calm, confident Ben from the airport was gone and his wife, sitting next to him, seemed to be offering little in the way of comfort, as if she was used to it. Some tilted their heads to locate him, while all hoped upon hope that he would clam up and spare their collective embarrassment. Eventually, all eyes returned to the boards ahead.

What struck most forcibly was the sheer number of dead. They knew the facts, of course, but having their lost generation paraded before them so starkly was a shock. Reggie Richardson's thoughts at that moment probably summed up what most people were thinking: this must have been what it felt like for people coming back after the Great War. The school deaths had come in dribs and drabs and been slowly absorbed; it was truly shocking to see the survivors together in one place. Tom Joules counted the faces, in part to confirm that the number given matched his own calculation. It did. Forty-four. This didn't account for all those they'd lost touch with, of course; some had just disappeared into the ether, and not everyone had signed up to the society (although Tom happened to know that almost to a man those in the photographs had), but in anyone's book forty-four was a lot.

Each mugshot carried a label like a convict's prisoner number, and most soon realized that this represented the death date of the individual concerned. The first board, along with part of the second, carried pictures of younger men: the victims of the Legionnaires' disease outbreak back in '85. They looked so untouched by age, bubbly almost, a lifetime away, only just setting out. Reggie wondered: What had the survivors all done with the additional years they'd been granted that these men hadn't? Had they justified being spared, when any of them could have been among the dead?

Perhaps the most poignant of all the photos was the one at the far left of the array. It showed a fresh-faced young man at the start of his adult life, in a military uniform: Jake Peterson. His face stared out into the audience, resembling a less hirsute, younger and considerably less formidable Lord Kitchener. His gaze seemed to carry a hint of accusation, as if to say that at least he had died with his principles intact; though the fact that some chose to interpret the photo that way probably said more about them than it did about Jake.

The DHM went on to explain what most of them had already worked out, so they stayed patiently with the process, using the time it was taking to unwind to come to terms with the brutal reality. At some point a string of bare light bulbs overhead came on and the shadows on the other side of the tent became more pronounced as the floodlights outside warmed up. Ben Bradshaw had eventually calmed down, but could still be heard from time to time blowing his nose into a handkerchief.

'I'd now like to introduce you to the detective leading the investigation team – Chief Inspector Dhillon.'

At this point, a number of thoughts screamed to the front of most people's minds. For one thing, no one realized that there had been an investigation. Equally, no one dreamed that there might be someone heading up a team of people snooping into them; and finally, no one, absolutely no one in their wildest of imaginings would have thought that the person in charge would be old 'Inky' Dhillon.

Not strictly a Seventy-Sevener – he had, after all, left the year before – 'Inky' Dhillon nevertheless held a unique position in the mythology of their schooldays. The incident of the ink bath with Ray Meadows was still capable of raising a smile, although to do so right then would have been in bad taste; while nothing had even been proven about the Sneaky Shitter. It came as no great surprise, therefore, that there was a visible intake of breath when he walked on to the stage.

The reason Mushtaq's face wasn't featured among the gallery now behind him was down to the efforts of a team of Venetian refuse collectors, with more experience of fishing bodies out of canals than it is reasonable for any ordinary citizen to expect. The subsequent arrival of a water ambulance had the effect of waking up many of the sleepy inhabitants of the somnolent quarter where his accident had occurred, but this was a small price for the speed they used in whisking Mushtaq off to the grand surroundings of the Ospedale SS Giovanni e Paolo, Venice's main hospital.

On arrival, Mushtaq had little opportunity to appreciate the interior architecture of the converted fifteenth-century monastery he'd ended up in, as he'd lapsed into a deep coma. It seemed that by a quirk of genetics Mushtaq had inherited a version of his father's narcolepsy, and when his body decided to rest then that was exactly what it did. During this time, a combination of Mushtaq's lack of ID, coupled with Italian bureaucracy, led to him being declared at first missing, and, in time, deceased.

The clean-shaven and angular face in front of them was a matured version of someone they'd only ever known as a boy, but still unmistakably Mushtaq. He had an almost regal bearing, upright and confident. For most, it was a shock to see him this way. They'd got used to seeing each other grow and change in annual increments, not in sudden jumps; but at the same time, it was strange how the essence of the boy lived on in the man.

The most important aspect of Mushtaq's Venetian adventure was that he'd survived, and the very act of his survival had sparked the beginning of the trail that led him to be standing up now in front of so many of his ex-school colleagues (friends was putting it too strongly), and the unravelling of the story he was about to tell, even if, as yet, it lacked an ending. If it was odd for those in the audience to see him, it was equally surreal for Mushtaq to finally see in the flesh so many of the faces he'd spent the last few years living with as images on a computer screen.

For the first minute or so, Mushtaq found it hard to focus on the group, and directed his glance instead to the back of the tent where a line of current teachers were standing in the shadows, the majority of them wearing robes with hoods in a Joseph-like array of many colours. The men in particular, with their slicked-back hair and Brilliantine skin, seemed impatient, hopping from foot to foot on the damp grass at the back like teenagers keen to leave a family Christmas gathering. The women looked professional but bored, keen to get things over with.

'Evening all,' Mushtaq opened, using the classic policeman's line in a bid to lighten the mood, moving on swiftly to thank them all for coming (not that any of them had any choice) and explaining why they were there. His investigation, it seemed, had been live for a number of years, but mostly unofficially. He hadn't garnered enough information to support a criminal prosecution, but he had been able to apply his skills and experience in his spare time. More recently his investigation had picked up momentum, and the incident on the plane had led to him to go to his superiors with the data and thoughts he'd gathered, making him the obvious person to head up the investigation. Working together, he believed, they could bring the whole affair to a conclusion. Getting to the bottom of what had happened to them on the plane was of paramount importance, as he was sure they all realized.

He went on to apologize for the subterfuge, emphasizing again the need to act quickly; although he didn't share his hope that getting everyone together straight after the service, when they were still emotionally raw, would encourage a confessional air.

Before he continued, Mushtaq surveyed the scene in front of him. The years had been kinder to some than others, but it was difficult to tell for sure who they had been kindest to when their faces were contorted in some way by either discomfort or shock. He couldn't yet detect any signs of guilt. There was a fair smattering of women,

341

including Matron, who was flanked by a pair of fair-haired women to her left, and Tom Joules to her right.

What Mushtaq wasn't sharing with the horseshoe of people, or suspects as his colleagues preferred to call them, was how this situation had been forced upon him. He'd have preferred to continue using traditional police methods to track down the serial killer he was convinced lay among them, but pressure from above for an instant result, combined with the unique opportunity to get everyone together in the same place at the same time, had given him no choice. He knew it was a high-risk strategy, but he was gambling that the mix of high emotional states and stark facts would bring his killer to the surface, or otherwise reveal them. At the very least, the calculation was that the authorities would learn enough to unfreeze the investigation.

After a decent pause, Mushtaq moved on to the meat of why he was there. He began by saying he'd long suspected the deaths of Seventy-Seven Society members were linked somehow, and he'd put together a small team to see if they could come up with anything; but all their investigations had resulted in insufficient evidence to suggest the deaths were anything but random and unrelated.

'Hold on, hold on,' Reggie Richardson interrupted at this point, visibly flustered. 'Can we rewind a step or two, please?'

'Sorry,' Mushtaq acquiesced. 'How can I help?'

'Well, that lot, for a start,' Reggie continued, pointing at the board of faces on the left: the Legionnaires' disease victims. 'Are you saying they were, were …'

'Murdered?'

'Well, yes. Is that what you're saying?'

'No. Yes, you're right. No.'

'Well, that's as clear as mud,' Reggie muttered.

'Apologies again,' Mushtaq went on, 'I jumped ahead there. No, we were immediately able to ascertain that the Legionnaires' deaths were genuine bad luck. A tragedy. A problem with the air conditioning unit in the hospital, it turned out.' He paused. 'But perhaps a catalyst for what followed.'

Reggie thanked Mushtaq for clearing that up, and signalled that he was happy for him to continue. A weight seemed to lift from the assembly, accompanied by a gust of wind from under the canvas that fluttered across the roof of the marquee, which could just possibly have been caused by the combined release of many lungs full of apprehension.

Mushtaq continued. 'What we did notice, however, was a pattern. Most, but not all, of the subsequent deaths took place abroad, out of our jurisdiction, which, despite the help provided by colleagues in other countries, made our lives extremely difficult. Different policies and procedures, combined with the inevitable panic when a foreigner dies abroad – not to mention the families' understandable wishes to have bodies repatriated as soon as possible – all combined to make it nigh-on impossible for us to conduct a consistent investigation.'

'Are you saying you suspected a foreigner, then?' the previously contemplative Nigel Bennett asked, slightly indelicately. As the Seventy-Seven member with the most international miles under his belt he was beginning to feel uncomfortable about the way this was going, and was keen to widen out the list of suspects.

'We didn't rule it out, but we were struggling on the issue of motive. There had to be a motive, and this was most likely to come from home.' This seemed to be accepted as a reasonable assumption, allowing Mushtaq to go on. 'Two other things struck us. Whoever was behind the killings – assuming, of course, it was one person – seemed to have the ability to melt into the background. In other words, they were able to keep a very low profile and go in, do what they did, and move out again without leaving a trail.'

Mushtaq paused to take a sip of water. 'Then, of course, there was the unique element that linked you all together.' A few of the faces looked around the room, confused. Mushtaq knew this was a critical moment in his explanation, and he'd primed those watching the room to assess whether what he was about to add impacted in a particular way on anyone.

'You, gentlemen, had the school, and, of course, you had the Bond.'

The Bond. For most sitting in the marquee it was an irrelevance, something for the future; not a driver of their past. Besides, whatever amount of money there was in it, was Mushtaq seriously considering it was enough to drive one of their number into becoming a multiple killer; what was more, a killer of their own friends? It seemed ridiculous, and the unlikely voice, in so many ways, of Susan Grant expressed the thought out loud.

'We thought so, too,' Mushtaq agreed, 'until we looked in detail at the numbers.' This query had clearly been anticipated and a WPC joined him with a flipchart page carrying a graph, which, showing all the panache of a magician's assistant, she revealed to the audience.

'This is a graph of the progress of the Bond, up until the most recent year we have figures available for,' she explained. 'As you can see, there was a rapid growth in the value of the Bond through the 1990s and early 2000s, with the total worth reaching in excess of one million pounds.' Genuine shock seemed to bounce around the tent like a demented snooker ball, despite the fact that the graph only showed data they already had access to. 'After that, things become a little bit murkier ...' she continued, before being interrupted by Paul Briton.

'Whoa there,' he interrupted, just a little bit too loudly, 'there were mitigating circumstances. Andy Thompson had the advantage of riding the wave, the good times. Things got a bit stickier on my watch.' Paul was suddenly conscious of umpteen pairs of eyes boring into his soul.

'If I could chip in?' Tom Joules stood up, the first person in the audience to do so. The stress of the recent past had clearly got to him, giving a growth spurt to his receding hairline, so that his forehead now arched back over three-quarters of his scalp. 'I was a member of the 77B throughout, and I will readily admit that we let things slip, governance-wise, over the years, for which I apologize. In my defence, however, I had other things on my mind.' A sympathetic murmur drifted through the tent, mingled with a sense of appreciation for Tom's honesty. Over the years, Tom had become a person it was impossible to feel rancour towards. 'I always let Paul and Ray, God rest his soul, take the lead on matters financial. I confined myself to checking the subscriptions and direct debits.'

'Thank you, Mr Joules, Tom,' nodded Mushtaq. 'Ray Meadows did in fact travel a lot: mostly within the UK, for business, but also, I understand, abroad, for pleasure. I can also reveal, for the purposes of this discussion, that he was, at the time of his death, on the point of bankruptcy.'

'Well, we're learning a lot here,' Reggie threw in, once more voicing the thoughts of many, this time aloud. In the corner of his eye he thought he could see a fresh pair of policemen enter the tent and position themselves by the emergency flap to the rear.

'Ray, however, lacked another important component linking the deaths which we were beginning to think significant. Medical knowledge.' Mushtaq wandered over to the boards. 'To take some examples: Jeff Stone' – he pointed at the relevant picture – 'died falling off a mountain in North Cyprus, but analysis following an exhumation and a subsequent post-mortem revealed he had been given a high dose of stimulant through his asthma inhaler, which would have had the effect of damaging his sense of balance.' Mushtaq took a step backwards and pointed at another picture. 'Or George Rowlands' – at which point he waited as a collective sigh went around the assembly, from both men and women, although for different reasons – 'who had a fatal dose of an early form of Viagra in his bloodstream.' The finger moved to another picture. 'Adam Smart: poison, ingested, we believe, through a chocolate bar. I could go on, but I don't want to distress you.'

Uncomfortable in his seat, Tom Joules was struggling to take in what he was hearing, while at the same time feeling a sense of something that bordered on humiliation. How could he have been so ignorant of what had been happening to the Seventy-Seven Society? For all these years, by sticking simply to the facts his anodyne annual reports had, if anything, added to the sense that the deaths had been normal. By drawing the sting of suspicion, he'd almost been complicit with the murderer; whoever he was. He'd been the society's custodian, and he'd let it down.

'Freddie,' Ben Bradshaw suggested, slightly too loudly, his eyes red but no longer weeping. 'He was abroad, travelled a lot. Drugs were involved there, weren't they?'

'Yes, yes and yes,' Mushtaq agreed, although he rocked his right hand from side to side as he did so. 'Although the drugs involved there were purely recreational. We think that was an accidental overdose. No less sad and unfortunate, of course, but an accident nevertheless, unconnected to our investigation.'

He paused dramatically, then continued. 'Although the deaths continued with sporadic but depressing frequency, there was one that made us sit up, and the link to you gentlemen was indirect.' Mushtaq had piqued their curiosity, and a slight buzz went around the tent. 'Three years ago, we learned of the death of the headmaster during your time here, Harold Mitchell, and it wasn't pretty.' Mushtaq continued against a backdrop of silence.

'Here there was no ambiguity. It was murder all right, and of a particularly vicious kind.' Mushtaq went on to describe the circumstances of Harold Mitchell's death, giving as much detail as he could without straying too far over the line into prurience. Throughout, he kept one eye scanning the room for a reaction, and he saw it in Marion Joules: a closing of her deep brown eyes, and a slight reddening of the cheeks as she kept perfectly still. Reactions came in many guises, but this was one he was familiar with. It spoke of remorse and regret, and perhaps too of fear, that her relationship with Harold Mitchell was about to be exposed in the rapidly fading daylight.

Mushtaq also detected a slight smile on the face of Sam Davidson, and gave him the slightest of raised eyebrows, and a nod. The nod was returned, which Mushtaq took as his cue to reveal Sam's unwitting help in his investigations, explaining that he hadn't wanted to blow his own cover; how he'd needed someone with knowledge of, and a way into, the Seventy-Seven Society to get the information he couldn't. The idea had worked, and from Sam's apparently pleased reaction he guessed that he hadn't minded his unwitting involvement; although a few faces around the room seemed less pleased that they'd been played in this way.

'From what we learned we were able to identify the killer of Harold Mitchell.' At this point Mushtaq turned his gaze to Clive Porter, now sitting at the edge of the gathering, flanked by two uniformed policemen. For some time, Harold Mitchell had been Mushtaq's main suspect, but his murder had changed everything. Handcuffs were regarded as unnecessary for Clive Porter on the basis that he was hardly going to make a run for it. Besides, the DHM seemed perfectly content to be unmasked.

Derek Henderson was the first to break the silence that followed the inevitable gasp, asking the obvious questions. 'Why?' he stuttered. 'I mean, what was the motive? And how, for crying out loud?' The DHM looked hardly capable of weeding a window box, let alone committing a bloody murder.

Mushtaq tilted his head as if to ask his prisoner whether he wanted to explain, but he seemed too exhausted by all the proceedings. Mushtaq decided to respond on his behalf. 'Love and hate is probably the best way to explain what he did.' The DHM twisted his mouth a little, as if to say Mushtaq was being reasonable in his assessment. 'Somehow, Mr Porter learned of Mr Mitchell's treatment of a woman he'd loved, and found it unforgivable. Furthermore,' – Mushtaq continued quickly, in an effort to avoid revealing the name of the woman involved – 'he'd always disliked Mr Mitchell's appointment to the headmastership, regarding him as too new-school: quite literally, as it happened.' Here, Mushtaq paused at his unintended pun. 'This in itself wasn't enough to justify murder, but Mr Mitchell's subsequent conduct, especially around the time of the referendum on the future status of the school which, I'm sure most of you will recall, brought the school into disrepute in Mr Porter's eyes.' Mushtaq left this sentence hanging, preferring not to go into detail on what he suspected had happened with the counting of the referendum votes. That was a detail to be sorted out later. 'To go back to love,' he continued: 'Mr Porter loved – loves – the Red Coat, and for him damage to the school's reputation was as bad as the physical and emotional damage Mr Mitchell had caused elsewhere.'

The room was stunned, with all eyes now turned to Clive Porter, who at this point put his hands up in mock surrender. Mushtaq's analysis was, it seemed, spot-on.

'To answer your question of how, I'm sure you remember Mr Porter's *khanjar* knife …'

'Christ! That thing! Yeah, yeah, stop there …' pleaded Derek Henderson, who'd always been squeamish about the DHM's little toy.

'It seemed that Mr Porter had been sent a letter giving details of where Mr Mitchell would be and his purpose there.'

'But surely …' Paul Briton began to ask, glad the conversation had strayed away from the Bond.

'Indeed,' Mushtaq interrupted. 'If you were going to say that would have required not inconsiderable strength …' – Paul Briton nodded – '… you're right.'

'May the sweet Lord forgive me.'

Tom Joules sat up and lifted his gaze. The owner of the booming voice who had uttered those words stood up and offered his wrists.

'I was the perpetrator,' he admitted, 'I, too, loved Matron.' Mushtaq raised his eyebrows in frustration, for he'd done his best to protect Marion Joules. 'I was happy to deliver justice; I would do it again. May your punishment of me recognize this.' And with this he crossed himself and, rather dramatically, fell to his knees. Few remembered just how dominating the Rev's voice could be when he wanted. Equally, this admission seemed to contradict the man's reputation for blandness and invisibility. It was always the quiet ones, they supposed.

'Let them stay for now,' Mushtaq instructed the officers closing in on the two men, instructing them instead to lift the defeated Rev up by his armpits. He wanted to ensure the chemistry set he was building in the room kept bubbling.

Mushtaq was now considering how much he needed to reveal to the gathering in order to make the breakthrough he hoped for. He was fast approaching the limit of hard fact and was close to a nodding acquaintance with speculation. He had his suspicions, but no proof. What he needed was to corner his prey and get them to reveal themselves.

He knew that Harold Mitchell's murder had been initiated remotely, he suspected by a letter from abroad, luring him to the place of his death. Clive Porter had been happy to share everything he knew when they'd questioned him, and he received a similar letter with all the information he needed. Mushtaq had then detailed two officers to see if they could track down the sender of the letter. They failed, but their investigations highlighted suspiciously frequent movements in and out of the country by a woman called Sandra O'Brien. Further investigations led them to Astra, whose real name was Jane – Jane Whittle, which Mushtaq recognized as the maiden name of the Red Coat's one-time Matron; and after that, a photograph was enough to confirm his suspicions and bring them into his investigation. He fed their whereabouts to Sam, who in turn gave them to Tom. Given the matron's connection with the headmaster, the odds were even that they had a role to play in the story he was putting together, and although he couldn't at that stage say what that role was, he'd taken the decision that writing them into the script might be useful in flushing something out.

At the very least, they had to be suspects. Both were off the conventional radar, both travelled around, and Jane, at least, may well have had a motive. It was common knowledge among the Class of '77 that something had happened to her that long, hot summer by the swimming pool; perhaps she was one of those who believed revenge was a dish best served cold and, it would seem, often. It was time for Mushtaq to play his last major card.

'It was also around this time that Dr David Lu died.'

'But surely that was a heart attack?' Ben Bradshaw pleaded, his eyes welling up again. 'Please God! No more murders, please.'

'I'm afraid so,' Mushtaq confirmed. At that moment, some of the WPCs at the back of the tent began to manoeuvre themselves into position. Mary Lu, lured to the thanksgiving by a special invitation from the current headmaster in recognition of her links to the Class of '77, heard them move; the ominous sound of the handcuffs hanging from the sides of their belts rattling like warning bells. She turned around. Luckily for Mushtaq, his tactics were on the brink of working. All he'd had on Mary until then were questions, but he was about to get a witnessed confession.

'Yes!' she screamed. 'I murdered the bastard!' The women in the tent issued a collective gasp. 'He never loved me; he never stopped loving her.' At this Mary Lu stood and slowly pointed an accusing finger at Marion Joules's daughter.

'What?' Jane Joules demanded, clearly astonished by this turn of events. 'What the hell are you talking about?'

'You. Him. At the swimming pool. You're the one who started it. You let him have his way, didn't you? No surprise that afterwards he thought he could have any woman he wanted!'

'Wow, you've really lost it,' – Jane laughed nervously 'big-time.' Her slight laughter gave permission for others to be amused; after all, David Lu wasn't anyone's image of a ladies' man.

'You're the one. You're the cause of all this mayhem,' Mary Lu continued, lunging across the bodies in front of her to deliver a coup de grâce against her nemesis, but luckily the two WPCs were able to restrain her in time.

With emotion swirling around the canvas like a genie out of the bottle, Ben Bradshaw finally cracked and let out huge sobs of unrestrained crying: screams and howls that would have been enough to attract the attention of the police, if the tent hadn't have been full of them already. As it was, some of those patrolling outside were forced to turn and look towards the light inside the marquee, hoping this was a sign that their vigil was nearing an end. It was getting bloody cold out there.

'It wasn't David, you idiot. It was him,' Jane suddenly announced, finally releasing the information she'd never shared publicly before to anyone other than Sandra, by pointing an accusing finger. 'He cried like that afterwards. It was him who went for me. He was all wet, he'd been swimming: a slippery, wrinkled little eel. I couldn't see his face, just the top of his head and those hands, those pudgy, probing hands. I tried to fight him off but he was surprisingly strong; and then, when it was all over, he started to cry – just like he is now, the pathetic little weed.'

The police officers in the room looked towards Mushtaq for instructions. Things were kicking off, and in the short interval while everyone waited for something to happen, Susie Bradshaw leapt up and began swinging her handbag repeatedly over her husband's head.

'You weak little toad, you gutless snivelling little … TADPOLE!' The last word was yelled straight into her husband's face, the first letter of the old nickname sending spittle into his eyes, causing him to shut them and turn the dial down on his crying. Nearly forty years of dormant repressed frustration erupted with a force that seemed inhuman: spectacular to observe, but very, very frightening at the same time. All other sound within the tent ceased as Susie's anger filled every available space – uncontrolled, visceral anger; a force of nature. It seemed a final pull on the thread was capable of unravelling years of dissembling; a façade built up layer upon layer exposed for what it really was.

Susie Bradshaw. Abroad a lot, an early career in nursing and friends who were still nurses, a uniform retained from her time as an air hostess that allowed her to blend in with the crowd at the airport. That was it, Mushtaq realized. The air hostess in the plane to Munich hadn't run to get help; she'd run out of the building to get away. There'd been reports of a hostess wearing a particularly tight uniform, but he'd put the description down to sexism rather than the more obvious explanation that she'd grown out of it. There were also comments about it being different from the others, out of date somehow. While this was sinking in, Susie turned her wrath upon Mary Lu.

'You stupid cow! Why did you start blabbing about what you'd done to David? If you'd told me, who else were you going to tell? Never piss on your own carpet, you idiot! Rule number one. In your own home, for Christ's sake! The police were bound to get involved; look what you've done! Everything's unravelling.'

With a jerk, she turned again and faced the assembled crowd. 'What else could I do but go for the big one? This idiot ...' – she indicated a cringing Ben – '... even set it up. It was then or never. If she'd ...' – this time her finger was turned to Mary Lu – '... decided to salve her conscience by confessing to the police, or to someone stupid enough to go to the police, then the clock was ticking.'

Ben let out a wounded dog's whelp. 'Yes, yes, I assaulted Jane ...'

'Raped, I think you'll find,' Sandra growled, slightly louder than she'd intended, and Mushtaq nodded his agreement.

'Okay, raped. But she was the prize, wasn't she? The untouchable. The girl everyone fancied, wanted. But none of you could get near, could you? I won there.'

A look of understanding washed over Mushtaq's face. 'But you couldn't tell anyone about it.'

'No,' Ben agreed. 'No one could ever know what made me better than all of them. I had to find other ways of getting their recognition, their respect, their ...'

'Oh, shut up, you ridiculous man,' Susie interrupted. 'I tried to save you, you idiot! Keep you alive to let you wallow in your grief; but no, Ben Bradshaw always bloody succeeds, doesn't he! All the traps I set for you – the alarm clock, the car, the traffic – you had to beat them, didn't you?' At this point, she turned her attention back to the crowd.

'I was going to deny myself the pleasure of picking you off one by one, of continuing to peck away at this pitiable husband of mine over time, but that idiot Meadows had to blow it.'

'Literally, as it happens,' muttered Reggie, but only his wife Ellie heard.

'But why, Susie, why?' demanded Fiona Henderson.

'Because the little shit could only love them, not me. He was an emotional wreck, flicking between extremes, either hitting me ...' – a revelation that elicited a slight gasp – '... or a pathetic puddle of tears. I couldn't live with that. I had to control him, give him regular punches to his emotional solar plexus. It worked for years, could have worked forever, but then he had to go and get happy, didn't he? Sort himself out. Where did that leave me? I needed to control him: if not by drip-dripping away, then once and for all, with a massive tidal wave of grief.'

'Do you know what he did?' she continued. Without waiting for a response, she told them. 'He kept a detailed log on all of you, noting down every little detail from the dinners, keeping a record, a file. Putting together strategies to get you to recognize him, to *like* him!' She delivered 'like' with a generous portion of sarcasm. 'He never really understood the truth: that, like me, you despised him.' A murmur of embarrassed, and rather too hurried, denials went around the room at this. Ben, meanwhile, was shocked: how had she known about the file?

Susie read his mind. 'Oh, I know everything about you,' she added, looking him straight in the eye and shaking her head at the same time. 'Look at him!' she demanded of the room, gesturing to her husband, still sitting down, his face now blank and frozen, a single tear rolling down each cheek. 'I can still get to him whenever I want: it's easy. It's all been so easy. I sometimes wonder why I even bothered.'

'I think we've heard enough,' Mushtaq concluded. 'Officers!' Two more policemen appeared out of the shadows and grabbed Susie's arms.

'Susan Bradshaw, I am arresting you for the murder of Ray Meadows and …'

The rest of Mushtaq's familiar speech was lost in a babble of voices as the DHM, the Rev and Mary Lu followed Susie out of the tent in the company of heavily body-armoured minders.

------------------------------ ✳ ------------------------------

'So, in the end it was neither about money nor love?'

Along with everyone else from the marquee, Paul Briton was now in the school's Grand Hall, with, in his case, a glass of rosé in one hand and a goat's-cheese and sun-dried-tomato canapé in the other, the best he could forage from the meagre pickings still left. Given all they'd been through, the little matter of the Bond seemed to have come and gone, and he could finally relax. The Grand Hall was grand in name only. Victorian, ugly and dark, built in an architectural style perhaps best described as 'railway terminal-lite', the building held little aesthetic value.

Despite its architectural antecedents, those remaining in the hall were amazed by the crisp, clear lines of the modernized interior, with a dining area at the back that could conceivably double as an operating theatre, such was the level of its cleanliness: so different from the army mess-type conditions they'd been subjected to. There were vending machines that took pre-loaded cards, unlike the copper coins of their day; USB charging points and routers scattered around the buildings suggesting a high-speed Wi-Fi network, something that would have been the stuff of science fiction when they'd been there, when computers were operated by rolls of paper with lines of holes punched out.

'Well, it certainly wasn't about money, but I'm not so sure about the love bit,' suggested Reggie Richardson.

'How do you mean?' enquired Shirley Tweedie, her small eyes arched by quizzical eyebrows.

'Well, love comes in all sorts of guises, doesn't it?'

'What are you getting at?' asked Toby Connor, who up until that point had been on the fringe of the small circle discussing their take on the events of the early evening. Similar conversations were taking place across the rapidly emptying hall, generally conducted in discreet groups, in low voices to prevent what they were saying echoing off the high ceiling.

'Well,' Reggie went on, 'you have to ask yourself: why did they stay together?' He involuntarily shrugged his shoulders. 'There must have been something more. Maybe it was the forces they exerted on each other that actually kept the marriage standing, but it was a delicate balancing act. The forces had to be equal and opposite, when one became stronger, or maybe weaker, then the balance was lost.'

'Very profound.'

Reggie nodded an acknowledgement to Toby, before continuing. 'Who knows what goes on inside other people's marriages? Not sure I want to know, to be honest.' With this his wife gave his hand, still in hers, a little squeeze.

'But it was mental cruelty, wasn't it?' Shirley Tweedie said. 'I mean, on both sides.'

'And your point is?' both Reggie and Toby asked at the same time.

'That was grounds for divorce, surely.'

'Sure,' Reggie went on, 'but just because there were grounds, it doesn't mean either of them wanted to act on them.' Emboldened, he continued to expand on his theory. 'The way I see it, the stresses in the relationship were its lifeblood. On a deeply subconscious level, they probably both needed it, maybe even enjoyed it; saw it as some kind of game – who knows?' Reggie scanned those gathered around him and saw that he'd provided some food for thought. 'Didn't mean she had to go around topping people left, right and centre, mind you. Bit extreme, that.' This provoked a chorus of non-verbal *hear, hears* through a full spectrum of facial gestures and body language.

'Sometimes love can be an extreme form of hate,' Shirley Tweedie offered.

'So endeth the gospel according to Tammy Wynette,' Reggie agreed, raising a glass of rosé to his mouth, before realizing what he'd been given to drink, or indeed that Shirley Tweedie had gone off in a huff at his remark.

Sitting alone on a chair he hadn't noticed was stacked on another, Sam Davidson was making some notes on the Notes App on his iPhone. He wanted to capture some of the key points revealed during their time in the marquee. It had been sensational stuff: too much to take in all at once, really.

'Penny for them?'

Sam looked up. He'd not been thinking so much of pennies as pounds, hundreds of thousands; the question being how to realize them – but the voice was so stuck in his memory that he couldn't fail to respond to it. Calm and softly-spoken, with an ever-so-slight accent, it reflected its owner's character more than any voice he'd ever known. Sam jumped up and extended both arms for a man-hug.

'Mushtaq!' The two men embraced for the first time in their lives, leaning to opposite sides and patting each other's backs.

'Sam,' Mushtaq responded, with genuine affection. To have embraced so freely when they'd known each other as teenagers would have been unthinkable, as well as being deeply awkward.

'Brilliant! Brilliant to see you, and a brilliant performance this afternoon,' Sam continued. The two men patted each other's backs again and broke free. 'It is so good to see you,' Sam went on, adding indelicately, 'quite literally, back from the dead.'

'Well, the rumours of my death had been greatly exaggerated, as you can see,' Mushtaq responded, 'although I'm lucky to be here.' Mushtaq went on to describe how he'd nearly been the victim of a modern-day death in Venice and how he'd survived, by pure luck, lodged between a red and white striped gondola mooring post and an old oil drum in a side canal, until the early-morning refuse boat spotted him. The years since hadn't been so great, field work being off-limits since his narcolepsy had been diagnosed, however mild; although at least he'd been allowed to stay with the force.

'Why did she go for you, though? You were never a Seventy-Seven member.'

'We think it was probably just opportunistic,' Mushtaq explained, a lifetime of exclusion having given him a pretty thick skin in these matters. 'She must have been there on an assignment or something, and recognized me. Good job, really.'

'Eh?' Sam asked, confused.

'Well, think about it. If she'd planned it, the odds are we wouldn't be talking now and she'd still be killing.' Sam nodded his understanding. 'Besides, that's what got me involved. Nothing like being a potential victim to get your motivation levels up, eh?'

'Amazing,' Sam agreed. 'And you of course were …'.

'Who else? It was fun communicating with you, even if it couldn't be in person. I hope you understand that I couldn't reveal who I was. I could achieve so much more staying under cover and letting you act as my eyes and ears.'

Sam nodded his agreement, but in the glow of appreciation from his old friend failed to ask why exactly he hadn't trusted him to that extent – much to Mushtaq's relief. The truth was, Mushtaq appreciated that Sam had never exactly been the brightest button in the box: a nice enough bloke and a good friend; but still, a bit thick when all was said and done. Beginning to feel tired after all the events of the day, Mushtaq decided to keep the momentum of their exchange going before Sam had time to think.

'Your help with the *khanjar* knife was particularly useful,' he added. 'Threw us a bit, that one, and sent us up a few blind alleys. Realizing the Head's death wasn't connected directly to all the others opened up whole new avenues.'

'Hey, no problems, glad to be of service and all that,' Sam replied, slightly abashed.

'Nice blog handle, by the way,' Mushtaq added, changing the subject once again.

Sam chuckled. 'Yeah: Inky. Like it?'

Mushtaq flinched inwardly but hid it. 'Love it. I'll take it as a compliment.'

The two men talked a bit more before parting, with an agreement to meet up the following week. As Mushtaq passed through the hall, Sam returned to his phone. There had to be a book in this, and he knew just the man for the job.

Meanwhile, Astra, or Jane Whittle to most, was sitting on her own, partially hidden by the grand piano and perched on its stool. She wasn't feeling so good. The hall had always been off-limits when she'd lived at home, and the combination of an unfamiliar environment, along with all these people grabbing surreptitious glances at her, was taking her to a dark place. Through occasional brief looks, she took in some of the women she'd once known. Although Ellie had acknowledged her with a tentative hug, the sort a genuine widow might receive at her husband's funeral from a distant acquaintance, she'd been shunned by these particular widows.

Looking around, Jane felt distinctly underdressed in her light grey denims and men's shirt; not that this bothered her much. One of the little black numbers had just drifted past her, two church-candle white legs showing underneath, on her way to a small grouping the other side of the hall where a woman with an arse so small it barely filled the seat of her trousers was holding court. When she turned, Jane noticed she had virtually no chest and an anorexic face, a look that suggested a triathlete in perpetual training. Others hadn't made the journey to late adulthood quite so successfully, looking more akin to delegates at a Mothers' Union convention, who it was possible to imagine being active in the kitchen, and the opposite in the bedroom. Having said that, much the same could be said for their menfolk, except the kitchen bit.

Over in the nearest group, those who had a direct interest in the evening's events were still finding plenty to chew over, along with the by-now stale food. Fiona Henderson, her hair held in place in rope-like braids, had become increasingly incensed at some of things Susie Bradshaw had told her and the other Seventy-Seven Widows over the years; which she now realized were part of the wider plot to undermine what Ben had seen as perfection among his school friends. Lies, the lot of it. Susie Bradshaw had turned out to be a master dissembler; even to the point, it seemed, where she'd started to lie to herself. A lot of the things she'd heard or assumed over the years suddenly began to make sense, but now she didn't know what was true and what was a lie. The damage Susie had inflicted on all of them, beyond making quite a few of them actual widows, was incalculable. Poor Mary Lu, her mind poisoned and now destined to spend years behind bars in some dreadful women's prison.

As she was processing this thought, a mild kerfuffle by the large oak double doors at the entrance to the hall caught her attention. She was surprised to see there were still policemen around: presumably to protect their safety, or maybe to keep prying journalists at bay.

'I have to get in, I have to.' A man was being held back by two men and a woman in blue uniforms; although restrained might have been a better word. He himself was dressed highly inappropriately, in what looked like a set of bright silk pyjamas. His hair was unkempt and he had a few days' growth of beard on him. Fiona thought he could have been a homeless person, although he didn't look like he'd been drinking, and he actually sounded quite articulate. If she'd thought longer she might also have taken into account that he'd somehow managed to get this far without being stopped, which suggested some deeper knowledge of the school and its buildings.

Mushtaq Dhillon wandered over to see what was going on.

'Inky?' the man asked, his voice surprisingly high-pitched and unsure. 'It is, isn't it? It's Inky.'

A little taken aback by hearing his detested school nickname for a second time in under an hour, Mushtaq indicated to the guards that they should relax their grip a little, at the same time scanning the face in front of him for some sign of recognition. As well as the beard, which had a salt-and-pepper fleck in it, the man looked prematurely aged, with sun-bleached hair and skin that had a hardened weather-beaten look about it. He was thin-to-emaciated and, as well as the pyjamas, was wearing sandals, which must have meant his feet were freezing.

'Been on boats, trains, hitching: anything to get here, brother. No passport, all a bit of a drag.' Mushtaq said nothing, waiting to see if the man's ramblings might give a clue as to what he wanted. Instead all he got was a deep stare, as if Mushtaq was supposed to know who he was.

'Stevie, man, Stevie Sanders.'

At that second, Mushtaq realized he wasn't the only man to have come back from the dead that night. Stevie had always been a peripheral character at school, and had been one of the handful they'd had trouble tracking down when they'd gone through the list. Interpol had no trace of him and there'd been no activity on his National Insurance number or passport for decades.

'I've come to apologize. Mea culpa and all that jazz.'

Taken away into a room normally used to store stage props, Stevie revealed under questioning that he'd seen a report on the internet about the Stinkbomb Conspiracy and had travelled non-stop for thirty-six hours from Morocco. It seemed that since the death of 'Freddie' McQueen, his friend and protector, he'd been lost. Freddie had always reassured him that what they'd been doing was right, but with him now gone he was no longer so sure.

'Right about what?' Mushtaq had asked.

'About the photos.'

Stevie revealed how Freddie had taken photos of Matron and the headmaster in compromising positions – a lot of them – when they'd still been at school. For years they'd used them to blackmail the headmaster into acting as the grand whipmaster at the select parties Freddie organized for his friends in the music business. It seemed S&M was popular in their world, and Freddie was known as The Man among the cognoscenti. He'd put on events all over the world, and earned a fair bit from them, too. The MO was that through Stevie, Freddie would post instructions on when and where to go, along with travel tickets and a little reminder from the old days.

'Blackmail,' Mushtaq concluded.

'If you like,' Stevie continued, 'but there was a sting in the tail. These weren't straight S&M, if you know what I mean. More diverse.'

'Gay?' Mushtaq asked.

'Some gay, sure: a mix. Better leave it there, I think.'

'But all these years?' Mushtaq wondered.

'Yeah, odd that. We often talked about it, but reckoned he actually quite liked it. Probably gave his life some shape, as well as another grievance on top of all the others. Never my thing really, although Mike seemed to be in tune with it. It's all about control and trust when you're at your most vulnerable, he used to say.'

Mushtaq nodded.

'Anyway,' Stevie continued, 'back in the day, Freddie set up a little insurance. If he died unexpectedly, I was to send a special final envelope to Mitchell, plus another to the old DHM.'

Another piece of the jigsaw slotted into place.

'I never knew what was in the envelopes; I just did what I was told. Part of the instructions included setting up a temporary venue in Wiltshire, I think it was; easy enough when you've got the right contacts.'

'But we investigated McQueen's death. There were no suspicious circumstances: he died of an overdose.'

'I didn't know that, did I?' Stevie responded, half-pleadingly, before changing the subject, 'Anyway,' he added, getting up. 'I came here to apologize.'

'Who to?' Mushtaq asked.

'To Matron, of course. It wasn't right.'

A little bemused by this turn of events, Mushtaq asked for Marion Joules to be brought in, and Stevie sat down again. Once inside the crowded room, Marion adopted an air of studied professionalism. Mushtaq introduced Stevie and invited him to speak. On hearing his confession and apology, the ex-school matron merely smiled.

'You poor thing,' she replied, shaking her head. 'I knew who'd taken the photos. How couldn't I? After all, I had the best view in the room.' Stevie looked confused. 'I was grateful, you daft boy. I knew as the flashbulbs were going off that was an end to it.' After a few more exchanges, Mushtaq decided he'd heard all he needed to hear and called the guards off, before moving on to the more practical details of what Stevie wanted to do next.

Contrition was clearly in the air, however, as half an hour later, enough time for the thin crowd to get used to an emaciated man in rainbow pyjamas wandering among them, Sandra drifted over to Tom Joules, passing Mushtaq on the way, who was gently slumbering despite being awkwardly draped over a school chair. Tom managed a polite smile as she approached. They'd come back over to England to see Marion again and to keep her company while Tom was supposed to be away on his jaunt. The reconciliation between them was now pretty advanced, and she suspected that the events of the past few days were going to pour some quick-setting concrete into their new-found relationship.

Sandra's final big play had failed, but somehow she felt relief rather than disappointment. Maybe fate had been telling her something: to get out while she was still winning? Instead of trying to live lots of lives, maybe it was time to settle for the one she had? Besides, she had her own confession to make. Ever since she and Astra had tried to work the Seventy-Seven dinner, she'd been convinced that Tom had been Astra's attacker all those years ago. The other man standing in the room, who she now knew to be Ben Bradshaw, had looked too small, too inconsequential, to attack anyone.

As she was delivering her apology, Sandra failed to notice Astra get up and head for a side door in the hall. Once outside, she crossed what used to be the quad and entered her mother's old house, which was conveniently empty. Without needing to turn on any lights she headed up the stairs and into what had been her mum's old room. Groping behind the door she found what she was looking for – a key – and opened the concealed entrance into the headmaster's study, pushing against something on the other side to get in.

The old place had been redecorated with citrus lemon paint above the wainscoting, but otherwise it looked much as it always had: oppressive, and yet somehow authoritative. The old desk, of course, was long gone; replaced with a lighter version that might have come from Scandinavia. Its surface was neat and clean, with a flat computer screen placed squarely on one side. The sofa had gone, replaced by three chairs sat round a circular glass-topped table.

Still in the dark, she lowered her knickers and squatted down, lifting her skirt as she did so. She had some unfinished business, in more senses than one. Just a quick one, she told herself. For old times' sake.

2019

A little over eighteen months later, Tom Joules, Sam Davidson, Reggie Richardson and Paul Briton were back at the school, standing on the grass in the middle of what was now known as the new quad, which did at last actually constitute a quadrangle, alongside Jack Thomas, the headmaster. Derek Henderson had originally intended to be there, but there'd apparently been a crisis with some new tenants. The small gathering was the result of a casual conversation between Tom and the headmaster, shortly after the Benefactor's Day that would surely go down in Red Coat history. Ever so politely, and displaying a maximum of decorum, Jack Thomas had enquired about the Bond. He had, it seemed, a proposition.

Subsequently, Tom called in Paul Briton for a more formal discussion. The headmaster's idea had been a statue; he'd thought maybe to Harold Mitchell, as the man who led the school to its current status and a man, he suggested, who, as far as he could see, had been somewhat passed over by the school since his departure. Might this not be an appropriate use of the money in the Bond, a permanent reminder of the significance of 1977 to the school? Rehabilitation for a man who ultimately, whatever his flaws (and the Head had been happy to acknowledge these), had paid the highest sacrifice for the school?

Paul Briton's first reaction was to laugh. It seemed wrong on so many levels, and yet so right, so deliciously wonderful, he'd almost been tempted to say yes. Except for one important consideration.

The money.

There wasn't any.

He'd relayed this unfortunate news to the headmaster, omitting the critical piece of information that while he'd put everything on red, the wheel had decided black.

'Not enough for a statue; not even a portrait. Thinking about it, we probably couldn't even run to a sketch. All we've got is last year's subs and a few dividends still coming in.' The headmaster hid his disappointment well.

At that point, Tom interrupted. 'Well, I'm not so sure. There is the small matter of the Meadows legacy.'

'Legacy?' Paul had enquired. 'I know he must have died a rich man; after all, it's not every day you empty your pockets and put it all on a single number, and that number comes up. Seven, I think it was. The whole place went mental afterwards, the blonde croupier even had to go under the table to make sure there wasn't any kind of device rigging the wheel. Funny thing, never saw her again after that, which was a shame; thought I might be on to something there, the way she kept looking over.'

Tom had no idea what Paul was talking about, and instead continued with his news.

'It appears he left everything to the Bond in his will. I suspect it was written years ago, as originally the Bond was just one of the beneficiaries, but all the others have since died, leaving …'

'He probably just wanted an extended drinking session in his name after he'd gone,' Paul interrupted.

Tom nodded. 'Maybe. Equally, I suppose you could say the society was the closest thing he had left you might call family.'

The headmaster could contain himself no longer and broke the cosy reverie by asking, 'But there is money?'

'Oh yes, there's money all right,' Tom confirmed.

So it was that on the last day of the academic year, a murky July day threatening rain, the entire school was gathered together in rows, along with various dignitaries very few people recognized, and four representatives of a year that had passed through the school over forty years previously, standing motionless on the grass square in the middle of the school premises. An array of solar panels ranged across the roof of what had been the sixth form centre in their day, now a drama centre: shiny, yet on this day impotent, symbols of progress and change.

Three of the Seventy-Seveners wore suits, while one was in chinos and a sports jacket. Adults now, well on their way to becoming old men, back in the centre of the place that had formed them as adolescents. It felt like a massive space back then, but now it felt more cramped, more efficient somehow; less experimental. The old quad was now fully enclosed, so pupils could walk between buildings without getting wet, and most of them were under cover at that moment, waiting impatiently. In a reversal of priorities from their day, the old boys and the official party were the only ones threatened by rain.

Reggie noticed other changes, too. The door to what had been Matron's house was now rather crudely bricked up, the mortar oozing from the joints like melted fudge, as if it had only been done in the last year or so, and a conservatory had been added to the staff room, so everyone could see what was going on inside. It was a private school all right, but perhaps that was no bad thing: at least it had survived, and would probably still be there when they were all gone. Harold Mitchell had got his way in the end, but was this what he had imagined? Probably, Reggie concluded. It was a totally different school; but then again, it was a totally different world now.

When Reggie thought back to some of the attitudes they'd shared then, he cringed. They'd had to cope with a lot of change over the past forty years: technology, the internet, women vicars, gay politicians. He wondered what a school report on their generation might look like – a beta, at best; they'd probably not done enough to earn a beta plus. The best you could say was that they'd weathered the storms thrown at them and survived (well, some of them, anyway). There'd been the odd financial crash, it was true; the usual stupid wars, climate change, and now everyone was worried about Islamists instead of the Irish causing random violence, but they'd had little control over any of that. Then again, more recently and directly, there'd been the debacle of the Brexit referendum, and Reggie shuddered when he thought about that, and wondered if the fallout from it was going to be their generation's ultimate legacy.

Looking around the new quad, Reggie remembered the referendum they'd had at the school in their day. He supposed you could argue that the vote had ended up opening a path to the future rather than preserving the past, which was kind of ironic when you stopped to think about it. On the other hand maybe both, in their own way, had been equally dodgy in how they'd been carried out; but then again, maybe democracy was messy by nature.

'You okay?' Paul Briton asked.

'Um?' Reggie was abruptly broken from his thoughts. His hearing had gone further downhill since the explosion. 'Oh … yes, fine. Just wondering how this lot will turn out, and what they think of us. Ultimately,' he added, 'I guess I was wondering whether their record will be any better than ours' – indicating the gathered ranks before them.

The pupils were getting restless. Standing in their year groups, they offered a sort of seven ages of man, arranged in height order. Smart in their uniforms, or at least as smart as was possible on the last day of term, some of them had white buds placed discreetly in their ears, lest they be deprived of life-giving music for longer than was strictly necessary. As a group, they conveyed a sense of almost absolute disinterest in the proceedings.

Paul looked from side to side and, convinced nothing was about to happen for a while yet, and that he wasn't going to be overheard, offered his own thoughts.

'I'll tell you what I think, for what it's worth.' He took Reggie's silence as agreement to continue. 'Some of them will be like most of us and just follow blindly in their parents' footsteps, but most are probably baffled by us. They don't understand how we tied ourselves so irrevocably to the corporate wheel and kept the old system going, screwing it up for them in the process.' Reggie started to interrupt, but Paul carried on regardless with his peroration. 'We were brought up by the same rule book as our parents, whereas the only book these kids believe in is the Book of Face.' Despite a snort of disgust from Reggie, Paul went on. 'Their future will be so totally different from ours that it's hard to imagine; what they do with it, and how successful they are, we probably won't be around long enough to find out. What I do know is, it's time to pass on the baton, make the best of what we can of the twenty, thirty, who knows, maybe forty years we have left for ourselves.'

'You really think they're that different?' Reggie interrupted. 'Mortgages, marriage, kids: they'll all drag them back into reality, won't they?' Although the thought really troubling him at that moment was that they might still have another forty years left in them. Enough time to go through it all again.

'Maybe,' Paul continued, 'maybe not. All I do know from talking to my kids and their friends is that they think differently from us. Blame computers, if it helps, but ...' – with this, Paul ran out of steam.

'They think there's a better way of living?' Reggie suggested.

'Something like that,' Paul agreed. 'Maybe it won't be better; who knows? But it will be different. Some of them probably look at us and even feel sorry for us; others are probably just bloody angry with us.'

What the boys, and occasional girl, in front of them were actually thinking was more along the lines of 'who are these old farts?' and 'how much longer?' Having sensed the mood, as well as acknowledging the gathering clouds above them, the headmaster made a quick decision to expunge the middle three paragraphs of his speech before passing a cord, attached to a giant sheet draped over an abstract shape on the lawn, over to Tom.

Tom felt no nerves. The last two years had been good ones for him; for the first time in his life he felt at one with his surroundings, as if the sharp edges had been sanded down. He was even in the vanguard of trends: after all, even the French president had a wife considerably older than him.

The soon-to-be revealed form he was being invited to unveil sat on precisely the spot where a dummy representing a senior member of the royal family had stood, on exactly the same date in the calendar, on their own last day all those years before. The sheet was a recent addition, as everyone had seen the statue being erected and had already had time to get used to it during the days it had sat there; a handy perch for passing pigeons, who had expressed their own opinion. It took a lot longer to approve the design and have the statue cast than any of them had expected, and the events of 2017 now seemed a long time ago – although not as long ago as the 1970s, when the events that led to this moment had all begun.

Uncharacteristically eschewing the opportunity to make a speech himself, once the headmaster had finished his, Tom tugged at the cord and, in another unexpected gesture, playfully invited his colleagues to help him drag the sheet all the way off the statue, which duly revealed itself, standing proudly on the neatly cut grass. Over twenty-five feet high and cast in bronze, making it too heavy to be the subject of possible vandalism in the future, the subject of the statue was not Harold Mitchell, but a nameless life-sized rugby player, landing a try by the side of a post.

The idea of a statue large enough to dominate the view from where Matron's spare bedroom would once have been had appealed to the Seventy-Seven representatives as something those who had originally instigated the Bond would have approved of – the permanent colonization of a key landmark of the school. Although supposed to represent a generic hairy-arsed, teeth-gritted prop forward, those in the know could make out a clear resemblance to Ray Meadows in his prime, complete with St Bernard's fringe and Ray's exaggerated musculature. For those that noticed, it seemed deliciously appropriate that it should be the spirit of Ray, captured in stone forever, which would stand as some kind of guardian over these succeeding generations; the one they could see now, and the ones who would, in time, follow them. When they were all gone, it would be Ray who was left. The last man standing.

It was true that the impact the artist had intended, signifying fortitude and endeavour, could be achieved if viewed from one angle. Observed from another, however, it looked more like the celebrated image of US troops in World War Two raising the flag at Iwo Jima. Schoolboys being schoolboys, it had already been given a nickname, conferred while it was being installed. They called it the Tosser, as from yet another angle it looked as if the subject of the statue was preparing to levitate a caber into the air. The Seventy-Seveners present at the unveiling had heard the name and approved, with one abstention.

Anxious to get off into town or, for the older boys, to discard their ties and sample the offerings at their favoured hostelry, the crowd soon dispersed, leaving the four representatives of a now-ancient and largely forgotten year group standing, looking up at the statue in a sudden silence.

'I think he would have liked it,' Reggie suggested, the fresh air having brought out a delta of thin red veins high up on his cheekbones.

'Ray?' asked Paul Briton.

'Yes, of course, the last man standing, long after we've all gone'. He paused. 'But thinking about it, maybe everyone.' Reggie didn't have to explain what he meant by 'everyone'; by common consent the word included all those they'd grown up and dined with over the years, both alive and sadly departed. They'd not all been sportsmen; not that many of them had even enjoyed rugby. If they were being honest, hardly any of them had even liked Ray Meadows – the kindest word most people would have used about him was 'tolerated' – but like all good works of art, the statue seemed to be expressing something deeper. With a little imagination it suggested an explorer planting a flag on hallowed ground; the staking of a claim to territory. Still recovering from his earlier exchange with Paul, his emotions now swamping the more rational side of his brain, Reggie considered it represented an appropriate permanent reminder of their special year, and he said as much.

Sam turned his head to look him straight in the eye. 'But don't all those kids we've just seen all think of their own year as special?'

'Ah,' Reggie retorted, 'but there's special and there's *special*, isn't there?'

'Maybe,' Sam agreed, unconvinced, 'but perhaps we were just another crop of kids who got unleashed into the world and caught up in its whirlwind.'

'Worked, lived, survived,' Paul offered.

'End of story,' Reggie added, eager to have the last word; although he was ultimately thwarted, as Sam nodded his agreement and, by way of offering his own conclusion, muttered a single word.

'Period.'

Acknowledgements and Thanks

A reader of my first novel, *Golden Daze*, wrote a review on Amazon which stated that while they'd enjoyed the book, they'd been disappointed to reach the acknowledgements section and find out that it was a work of fiction rather than an autobiography. I took that as a compliment, however unintended, and take this opportunity to apologize if, in reading this, I disappoint anyone by stating the same.

The people and story set out in this work are a product of my imagination and are, I'll state again, a work of fiction. None of the characters are intended to represent real people (living or dead), and the views expressed by some of them are most definitely not my own. As with my previous book, however, it is fair to acknowledge that there are some similarities with things that have happened in my own life. For example, I have been involved in an annual school reunion along the lines of that enjoyed by the Class of '77 in this book, although thankfully ours has proved less fatal. However, where I have drawn on my own experiences, this has been done with affection, not with the intention to offend.

I would like to thank all those who have helped get this book to the point where it can be published, not least to Robert and Nicky at Betterwrite for their professional editing and proofing advice, as well as advice on the structure of the novel. It's always invaluable to have this sort of external expertise. I'd also like to thank Richie at More Visual for the cover.

Finally, the most fulsome thanks go, of course, to my wife, Annette, for tolerating me during the times I disappear into my own head.

About the Author

Nick Corble has written in excess of twenty-five books covering a wide variety of genres and topics including both fiction and non-fiction. His non-fiction has included travelogues, a biography, guide books and walking books, and social histories on topics as diverse as the canal system to fairgrounds. He has also had over a hundred articles published in the national and regional press. *The Bond or Last Man Standing* is his second novel. Most recently, he has been involved in a project to walk across England. For more on this visit www.diagonalwalking.co.uk.

For more on Nick's writing, or to get in touch with him by email, visit www.nickcorble.co.uk.